THE

COLOR

OF

DRAGONS

THE

COLOR

OF

DRAGONS

R.A. SALVATORE &
ERIKA LEWIS

HARPER TEEN
An Imprint of HarperCollinsPublishers

HarperTeen is an imprint of HarperCollins Publishers.

The Color of Dragons
Copyright © 2021 by Temple Hill Publishing LLC
All rights reserved. Printed in the United States of America.
No part of this book may be used or reproduced in any manner
whatsoever without written permission except in the case of brief
quotations embodied in critical articles and reviews. For information
address HarperCollins Children's Books, a division of HarperCollins
Publishers, 195 Broadway, New York, NY 10007.
www.epicreads.com

Library of Congress Control Number: 2021937002
ISBN 978-0-06-291566-5

Typography by Jessie Gang
21 22 23 24 25   PC/LSCH   10 9 8 7 6 5 4 3 2 1
❖
First Edition

Here's to anyone who grabs at the stars even though they're sure they cannot reach them.—R.A.S.

To my daughter, Riley, and everyone out there like her, tearing down walls and busting through barriers to make this world a better place.—E.L.

THE

COLOR

OF

DRAGONS

A BRIEF HISTORY

The lands were divided, not by name, which was common, but by a wall. Unlike the ramparts of this time, which were mostly made of wood, this wall was made of stone. Hailed a wonder of the world, it rose forty feet into the air. Nothing could penetrate or scale it.

King Umbert ordered the building of this wall. He was once considered a valiant king, the warrior who beat back deadly monsters, known as draignochs, all to save the people. Large beasts twice the size of the tallest man, with daggers for fangs and serpent tails decorated with deadly spikes, the draignochs terrorized the four lands. It took brutal strength to stop them. It took Umbert the Conqueror, a warrior known for honor and valor.

But that was before the wall.

When the war was over, the people crowned him king, and King Umbert built a glorious castle on the highest hill, a hill so tall it could be seen from every part of the land. Around the castle a great city grew, filled with those closest to the king, and those close to those closest to the king, and so on and so forth, until the city bustled and there was room for no more. The wall came next, and it was praised by all living in the city, for it offered them safety they had never before known. But shortly thereafter, the king and those who lived within the walls changed.

They forgot where the food they ate and the water they drank came from, as if it just magically appeared behind the wall or grew from the rocks they had planted rather than trees. And yet, the food and water still came, as did the thread for their fine linen clothes, leather for their armor, steel for their swords, wool for their blankets, and on and on, because a luxurious castle in a luxurious city needed such things to keep them in comfort.

No one asked where anything came from because it was always there. And it was always there because it was stolen—in the name of taxes for the king and his walled-off city—from those living outside, in the Hinterlands, where people slaved over fields, dug deep in the mines, and wrangled cattle and sheep, only to have their just rewards taken from them.

And as much as those in the walled city had forgotten, those outside talked of nothing else, every hour of every minute of every second of every day.

Anger spread throughout the lands. King Umbert's legend was forgotten. His infamy grew.

Unrest roiled in the hearts of all who lived outside. All they needed to bring change was a spark to ignite the rebellion.

ONE

MAGGIE

"Did you feel that, lass?" The bones tied in Xavier's silver hair clacked in the wind as his haunted gaze fell on the empty road behind us.

The drumbeat of cantering horses meant only one thing in the Hinterlands.

King Umbert's soldiers.

They came down from the Walled City without warning. Always dressed in the finest smoothed leather tunics stained red for their king, always heavily armed, and always hungry. The soldiers raided, taking anything and everything in the name of the crown. Livestock and harvest bounty from the South. Steel, precious gems, silver and gold mined in the East. Timber from the West. And women from all.

"I feel it."

He thwacked our old mare, Dorn, but she was no match for them even if she wasn't pulling our wagon.

"There's no other road," I said, knowing what would come next.

Xavier grimaced. "Hide yourself until nightfall, then meet

me at the village tavern. Take the back way. Some of this lot may wind up there." At least he didn't sound nervous.

"Understood." I knew what was expected. This happened at least once a month.

I checked my dagger was in my boot.

"Whatever you do, Maggie—"

"Don't be late. Performance starts just after sundown. I know."

The road bent.

"Have I ever let you down?" I gave him my best cheeky grin.

"There's always a first time." Xavier shoved me out of the wagon.

I rolled down the short hill into a shady glen, scooting behind a thick tree with low-hanging branches I could easily climb. It had the benefit of colorful fall leaves that refused to bow to burgeoning winter, giving good cover. Once perched above sightline, I heard Xavier's singing. He did that to keep the soldiers on his trail.

Xavier was a strange old man, putting himself at risk for me. I was nothing to him. No relation at all. A barely whelped foundling who wandered out of the woods, lost. I hadn't been old enough to speak or remember how to get home.

Xavier lived a gypsy life, traveling here and there, performing magic tricks for handouts. He had no reason to take on a tiny child. To hear him tell the tale, he fed me that night, and like a stray dog, I followed him forever after. That was it. He

was stuck with me. Softhearted sucker. And I would never let him down. My job was simple, really. As soon as I was old enough to hold things without dropping them, I became his magician's assistant, helping with props and passing the collection pot. Tonight was a big night for us.

The past six months the earnings pot had barely made enough to feed Dorn. Drought devastated the southern farms. There was little food to be had, and what was to be had was expensive. We'd eaten nothing but what we could scavenge from places that had already been raked over. Berries, watercress, fish, and the occasional windfall of a squirrel.

The last four alehouses were mostly empty. But this night would be different. Ships had pulled in only last night, so the marauders' pockets would be heavy, and they would be drinking their fill at the Lazy Storm, the only tavern in the western seaside village. The sots would be drunk, happy to be on land, and lulled into a dream state with full bellies. If they didn't shill a bit of pirated silver for the performance, it would be easy to take it.

As expected, within seconds, horse hooves and wagon wheels exited the road, moving into the field on the other side of the glen. Wagon wheels rolled. I saw a team of twelve horses harnessed to an enormous mandarin-colored metal cage grind to a halt on the other side of the glen. I was too high to see what was inside.

Footsteps approached, growing louder by the second. I held my breath as a beefy soldier removed his helmet, throwing it at the cage. Blood trickled down the back of his neck. "I'm going to cut off every one of that rat's claws!"

He pulled his sword.

A sniveling skinny boy about my age limped past the tree and around the soldier, standing in his way. Fresh blood stuck his scraggly brown hair to his forehead, his gray linen clothes shredded as if he'd been attacked by a wild dog. "No. You won't. You will stay away from it, Moldark!"

Moldark slid his sword up against the boy's throat, backing him up. "Why don't you try and stop me, Perig, ya pissant?" His words whistled as though he was missing a front tooth.

The soldier shoved Perig through thorny bushes that stood between them and the metal cage, rousing squeaky helpless yelps, then followed him with determination, disappearing from view as well.

This was my chance to get away. I climbed down as silently as possible, relieved when my feet softly touched solid ground. The road looked clear. Directly across was the footpath that would lead me to the back of the village. Soldiers never used it. It took longer.

A sharp cry rang out. High-pitched, tinged with frustration and sadness more than anger. My heart seized. My feet froze. I had never heard anything like it.

Another cry. Then another.

The fourth time, a scuffle broke out.

"Get off me, Perig!"

An oomph and a cry for help left me believing that Perig was losing the battle with Moldark.

A loud thwap pinged the metal cage. "Do you see that wagon piled high with bodies killed by this wretched beast? A little punishment goes a long way to—"

"This draignoch belongs to the king!" Perig griped.

A *draignoch*? Impossible.

All had been killed or captured long ago, or so Xavier told me. Once upon a time, the beasts ravaged the lands. Xavier's home, with his family inside, was trampled by the monsters. He was the sole survivor. Hinterfolk spoke of draignochs only in whispers, as if saying the name would unleash the monsters again. I hid behind the trunk, tempted. I had never seen one before.

It cried out for a fifth time.

I should leave. As it was, I was too close to the soldiers, but I found it impossible to resist a peek.

I crawled to the hedges. Kneeling, I slid my hands into the prickly branches, parting enough space for me to glimpse Moldark stab a spear through the bars.

The draignoch let out a strangled cry.

"Hurts, doesn't it?" Moldark wasn't just beefy. He was a mountain of a man. His face pocked, his hair greasy black. He growled at the draignoch, showing off the few teeth he had left in his head.

I couldn't see the draignoch clearly in the shadows of the

cage, but I could hear it. It knocked into the side, nearly toppling it over.

"Moldark!" Perig flailed his hands at the huge man. "Be reasonable! If this falls over . . . if it escapes . . ." His fearful gasps stopped.

"It can't escape a Phantombronze cage, Perig." Moldark rattled the bars with his spear.

Another first. I'd always thought Phantombronze was made up by bards who ran out of stories to tell. They sang of it being the strongest metal ever found. Unbreakable even. They said if the deep mines under the Walled City didn't kill you, the poisonous fumes from smithing it would.

"Stop it!" Perig screeched, his pitch so high it hurt my ears. "The king will have your head cut off if he hears word of this behavior."

Moldark aimed the spear at Perig's heart. "If you mention my name to the king, ever, I'll kill you before he kills me. That's a promise."

Perig backed up. "Just get away from it. I fed it a very powerful sleep dram. If you just stop riling it, it'll take effect."

"Moldark! Perig!" another soldier cried from some distance away.

Perig patted Moldark on the shoulder, delivering a pleading grin. "Sir Raleigh calls. Cannot keep him waiting."

"Hands off," Toothless growled, then immediately spun around, storming away with Perig right behind him.

This was my chance. I had to see it. I couldn't wait to tell Xavier. Bring him back something to prove it too. Perhaps the beast would be so kind as to shed a feather or scale, or drop a turd, any unnecessary random bit that Xavier could spin into a story of magic.

A quick glance to be sure the path was clear, and I slid through the bushes. Crouching beside one of the large wheels, I laid a tentative hand on the Phantombronze. It felt smooth and frigid like river ice in winter.

The creature rumbled as if succumbing to the sleep dram.

I peeked through the bars. The cage was so layered in shadows all I could see was what the afternoon sun spotlighted, the creature's back where bloody stab wounds marred its iridescent black skin. With every breath the beast took, its body shifted across the beams, its skin casting subtle, secret colors. It was beautiful.

Above me, its steely blue eye blinked open.

I cringed, expecting it to roar and give me away, but instead, it whispered in chuffs and clicks. Its head rose a few inches but was forced to stop when it hit the ceiling. It was much too big for the cell.

A claw scraped the metal floor of the cage, sliding between the bars, clasping the edge. The draignoch chuffed again. Slightly louder this time, pumping its claw, like a beckoning finger.

This was a trap. If I got too close, that claw would skewer

me—its next meal on a spit. But the beast was right there, only inches away. It lowered its head so that I could feel its breath on my neck.

Chills.

I gave in to foolishness, brushing my fingers across the claw. It was hard as stone and cold as ice. As I drew back, an invisible force seemed to press my hand down. Holding it to the talon.

The draignoch rolled a purr, like a cat settling in for a long comfortable sleep—with my hand stuck to it.

No! I panicked, yanking my wrist. But it wouldn't move. The sounds of soldiers' footsteps padding through the tall grasses, conversations of feeding and watering horses—all of this happening on the other side of the cage. Focused on the draignoch, I had forgotten that I was standing on the edge of a lion's den.

Voices came closer. I recognized skinny Perig's. Him I could take, but Moldark would be an issue.

I twisted and turned, but the force was too strong. Then all at once, beneath my palm, I felt a pulse beating a simple rhythm.

The draignoch whimpered. My heart ached with *familiarity*, as if this creature and I had somehow happened upon each other before. But that was impossible—or was it?

I had been found wandering out of a forest. Could this beast be the reason I had no family? The reason I ended up alone?

A flash of white erupted in the middle of the red in its

visible eye. The burn grew larger and larger until it was the shape of a full moon. I couldn't take my eyes off it. It was terrifying, mesmerizing, and likely an indication it was about to kill me.

Not it. It wasn't an it. It was a *her.* I felt that with certainty.

Heat shot through me. The full moon in *her* eye spread until it consumed half the red. My forearm stung. I bit my tongue to keep from crying out.

I ripped my sleeve back. The scar from my childhood was blistering and red. Three long, deep scratches. The two on the sides tilted in opposite directions, pointing toward the center. A tiny pinprick topped each one. I had no idea what had caused it. Xavier thought maybe a wild cat of some kind. But now I wondered. Was it given to me by this creature? By *her?*

I tried to free my hand again. With each pull, fresh fire shot through my arm. It burned, and I hissed.

"What do you think you're doing?" Perig yelled, startling me.

The draignoch groaned as if annoyed, pulling her claw back inside the cage. My hand fell away, freed. I gasped with relief, but as I turned to run, panic was replaced by a sudden deep sense of loss. For some insane and possibly suicidal reason, I didn't want to leave her.

Perig made a mad grab with a three-fingered hand, missing the hood of my cloak by several important inches. I split the thorny bushes with my arms, feeling the raw burn on my mark fresh with every poke and stick.

"Get back here!" Moldark rushed at me from the other side, pulling his sword. The tip burrowed into my back before I could get away. I raised my hands. Caught.

"Back up! Slowly . . ."

The draignoch roared. She threw her head from side to side, shaking the cage so hard it threatened to fall over.

Moldark made the mistake of looking back. I dove into the bushes, coming out the other side. Toothless yelled, "Halt!"

As if . . .

I ran as fast as I could through the grove and across the road, Moldark huffing after me. I hurdled a stream, then started down a muddy hill. A hard boot kicked me in the back, sending me careening into the cool slippery muck.

Laughing, Moldark stepped on my back, holding me there. The tip of his blade pressed against my shoulder, stabbing through my cloak. Another push and it would break skin.

"When King Umbert's soldier tells you to halt, you halt, boy."

Dressed in trousers with my hair stuffed under Xavier's old cloak, I looked like a skinny young boy rather than a girl of seventeen. But the sound of my voice would give me away at the first word, so I held my tongue.

He replaced his boot with a knee. He grabbed the back of my head with his free hand, forcing it to the side so he could get a look at my face.

His matted hair fell into his eyes. "What do you have to say for yourself?"

That your breath smells like you licked a pig's ass, I thought, but I refrained. When I remained mute, he shoved my face into the mud, making it impossible for me to breathe. I thrashed, but he pushed harder.

"That'll teach you . . ."

Somehow, my hand found the dagger in my boot.

He shifted, his foot moving forward to maintain balance. Before he knew what hit him, I stabbed right through his boot, feeling the blade grind down until it broke through the hard leather sole.

"Ah! Ya little bastard!" He fell backward, dropping his sword to yank the knife out with two hands.

I scrambled to get up, but my hands and knees slipped in the muck. Then another soldier stepped on my back, pinning me again. More soldiers circled, making escape difficult. At least I could breathe.

"What is this ruckus about?" someone said from behind me. "Moldark, I gave you specific instructions. That draignoch must be taken to the Walled City. Now. You don't have time for . . . whatever this is."

Out of the corner of my eye, I saw Moldark wave my knife. "This urchin stabbed me in the foot with an illegal blade, Prince Jori."

Illegal, it was, because none in the Hinterlands were allowed to carry weapons. Otherwise, we might rise up, defend ourselves from the king's stinking soldiers. All of which I would've said, but then they would know I was a woman, and likely cut my tongue out before selling me to a brothel. Silence was certainly the preferable option.

But what was the prince doing in the Hinterlands? Prince Jori was the only child of King Umbert and heir to the throne, and the only one likely, for the king was a perpetual widower, having lost four wives to fever, with all but one of the marriages ending childless. None in the Hinterlands had ever seen the prince. He was born after the wall was put up around the city.

A draignoch, Phantombronze, and the prince all in one day? I would consider myself lucky—if I wasn't about to lose my head.

"I see," the prince said. "Tell me, why exactly did he stab you?"

"Because I caught him near the draignoch's cage. When I told him to halt, he ran. Thought he could outrun me." Moldark chuckled. Some of the men joined in. "I tossed him to the ground and stepped on him like the worthless bug he is, just like Sir Raleigh is right now."

The boot holding me down shifted. "And yet he managed to retrieve his knife and stab you through your boot," Sir Raleigh said. His accent was different from the others'. Lilting and muffled, as if speaking in a hurry. I only ever heard that kind of accent once before, from a boy I met who came down from the North. The one place Xavier and I had yet to travel.

"Deserves a pat on the back for that," Raleigh added.

The men all laughed.

"He slashed a king's soldier. Law commands his striking hand forfeit," Moldark hissed.

My heart hammered against my chest. What would Xavier do with a one-handed assistant? If I survived at all. This was what I got for being impulsive. I'd had to see the draignoch.

And yet, as I pondered my demise, there was no regret. My encounter with the beast was . . . right.

The boot relaxed. A strong pair of hands slid into my armpits and hauled me off the ground like I weighed nothing. Simultaneously, two more grabbed my arms. Keeping my head down, I struggled, twisting and turning my wrists to get loose, to no avail.

Sir Raleigh came to stand before me. Unlike the others, who wore red, Sir Raleigh's leather armor was black. Dark circles underlined his eyes, as if he hadn't slept in years. The remnant brown hair ringing his balding head was dusted with gray, while his tangled beard was snow white.

"Moldark is right, sire," Raleigh replied as if he were giving permission to feed me cake, rather than cut off my hand. "Idle hands make for mischief. Should be working rather than looking at things he shouldn't be looking at."

"Teach him to go back to the farm and stay there," another said, adding to my fate.

The prince said nothing.

"The king calls for swift justice," Raleigh pressed.

My eyes lifted to his hand that gripped the pommel of his sword.

"Is that so?" Prince Jori answered, sounding unconvinced.

Did I dare hope that he would let me go? Xavier always said I was a foolish girl. Curious beyond all measure. And it was hard not to look at the prince, but I couldn't risk it.

I stared instead at his impossibly clean fingernails resting on his sword belt.

"Before we cut off his hand, perhaps we should hear from him. Ask him what happened," Prince Jori said. "What do you say?"

I shook my head.

"Come now." His hand appeared beneath my chin, tilting my head up, forcing me to look at him. His soft brown eyes surveyed mine. His long fair hair was pulled back. Not a single scar marred his handsome face. He wore smooth red leather trousers, a red knee-length cloak outlined in silver medallions, all of which were branded with the letter *U* like the soldiers' tunics. His belt carried a scabbard that housed a sword with a polished brass five-lobed pommel. A very expensive weapon.

He leaned over to whisper in my ear. "I cannot defend you unless you tell me your side of it."

The prince's tone took me by surprise. Asking where he should be demanding. Was he unsure of himself? Afraid of his own men? Or was it compassion? I almost laughed at the ludicrous thought. No matter. I ripped my chin from his hand, shaking my head no.

A crease formed between the prince's brow as he continued to study my face for far too long. He let out a resigned sigh that Sir Raleigh took as a signal to go ahead.

"Hold him still." Sir Raleigh slid his sword out and raised it over his head.

The soldiers stretched my arms so wide it felt as if they were being ripped from the sockets.

Moldark licked his split lips. "I get to feed his hand to the beast."

Not today. My plan was simple and stupid. Kick the ankle bones of the soldiers holding me and run like hell. But I didn't have to.

The draignoch roared. She threw a fit so loud the banging could be heard a hundred yards away. The whiny tilt followed by the earth-rattling crash was unmistakable. The cage had fallen over.

"Help!" Perig screeched.

The soldiers' grips loosened. I jerked, then kicked one soldier in the back of the knee. He fell forward, landing on Moldark.

I tore my knife from his hand and slashed the soldier holding on to my other wrist.

The soldier cursed, letting go.

And then I ran, as fast as I could.

Sprinting through the trees, I glanced over my shoulder every few seconds to see if they were following, but no one came, not at first anyway. They were too busy with the draignoch. Her distraction had saved me.

I wished her a silent thanks as the sun inched downward in the western sky. The village was still miles ahead. Xavier wasn't going to be pleased that I was covered in muck, and even less pleased at me being late.

I ran and ran. The whole time the scar on my arm tingled still, a reminder of what I had left behind. I would never see the creature again. She was headed to the Walled City, a place no one could enter, not without permission from the king.

TWO

GRIFFIN

Griffin had never been so nervous in his life. He pulled on the too-tight collar of the shirt Jori insisted he wear as he padded through the short corridor he thought led to the king's private chambers. He smoothed his unruly hair, then yanked on his vest, flattening any last wrinkles.

"It's just one dinner. To greet Laird Egrid when he arrives from the North," the prince had said. "My father asked for you specifically."

An honor, to be sure, for there were many other knights he could've asked. Knights of noble birth, from families at the Top of the Walled City. Griffin was a nobody from nowhere—a boy who'd snuck past the guards and into the city through a pipe like a rat. He had no breeding. No etiquette. Slaying draignochs, that he could do. Eating a meal without spilling food down his new shirt was something else altogether. He was going to make a fool of himself and never hear the end of it.

After two wrong turns, Griffin found he was back where he'd started. Having only moved into the sprawling castle last year, getting lost had become a way of life. "Hello?"

He groaned at the lack of response. A lack of guards meant he was most definitely in the wrong place.

"Sir Griffin!"

Griffin looked back, finding Bradyn running at a frenzied pace up the hallway. "Wait! Wait for me! I'm . . . escorting you." He wheezed, catching his breath when he reached him.

Barely twelve, Bradyn only came up to Griffin's elbows. What he lacked in height he more than made up for in smarts—an attribute Griffin appreciated, especially at court. If there was one thing Griffin found intolerable, it was stupid people, and there were many of those wandering the halls of King Umbert's home.

All of Bradyn's family worked in positions in the castle. His father ran the kitchens. His cousins served the king in his personal chambers. His mother worked in the infirmary. Bradyn's job in the castle was to do whatever his father told him to do. For the past twelve months, that had included serving Griffin. He knew where every passage went, both the known and secret ones, something Griffin had used to his advantage when the palace became too confining.

Griffin swatted him on the back. "Piss-poor job of escorting you've done so far, Bradyn. I mean, you have gotten us well and truly lost."

"You're blaming me for your pitiful sense of direction?"

"I am indeed. As I will blame you if we're late to the king's chambers."

"It's your fault. Not mine. Thoma and Dres were at the guard gate, causing a stink."

Griffin rolled his eyes. Thoma and Dres were Griffin's best mates, but he rarely saw them all year, a point they brought up whenever the opportunity presented itself. Lately, they would turn up without invitation, drunk, harassing the guards. "Did you tell them I had dinner with the king?"

"I did. Dres hurled his drink at the gate." Bradyn shook his head and started walking quickly the same way Griffin had gone. "Guards didn't take very kindly to that. Thoma dragged him off before he ended up pummeled and in chains again."

"I'll talk to them."

"Oh no. You have more important things you should be worried about. Tournament starts in *three* days!"

"Really? Hadn't heard," Griffin said with sarcasm.

Bradyn shook his head. He turned left, pushed through a door to a stairwell. He climbed two steps at a time.

"I hope the king understands that you need your sleep. But if not, my cousin Halig knows to remind him. And I asked my father to bring you another supper tonight just in case you don't feel like eating. Lady Esmera is joining her father tonight. I know what she can do to a person's appetite." Bradyn shivered in disgust.

Griffin hissed a laugh, remembering Jori's betrothed's visit last year for the tournament. Esmera had no use for Griffin. And yet, there he had sat at Jori's insistence, eating from the same platter of mutton she had—as he would tonight.

Her words had a peculiar effect on Jori. After her visit, the prince had refused to go anywhere without Griffin. And after he won the championship over Esmera's brother Malcolm, Jori asked King Umbert to move Griffin into the fortress, to a room not far from Jori's. He called Griffin "his protection."

Sadly, for Jori, after the nuptials, there would be nothing to protect him from his bride again.

"As I recall, she told Jori my scarred face was painful to look at. Let's be sure she sits across from me, Bradyn, and then this whole ordeal will end, maybe before it begins."

Bradyn laughed, coming out of the stairwell, starting down another hallway. "Did you see me at your practice today? I was there, getting ready for the melee."

"I didn't. Sorry. You nervous? First time I entered, I nearly pissed myself."

"You did not. You won your first time."

Bradyn eyed him with the same heroic worship many did, a look Griffin never felt he deserved. He fought to live, nothing more.

Griffin nudged him. "You'll be fine so long as you don't let the crowd spook you."

"Thanks." The smile returned to Bradyn's face. "I'll remember that. I saw you on the field. How many barrel lifts did you do? I lost count."

"Too many." Griffin winced, rolling his sore shoulders.

"Silas says you have to be fast when fighting the draignochs. But then I see you always train hard with heavy stones? Is that something Sir Raleigh taught you?"

"When I was your age, he told me that beating a draignoch requires two things: precision and strength. Sage advice I took to heart. Get in close, and make it count." Griffin lunged at him.

Bradyn laughed. "No one ever beat a draignoch running away from them."

Griffin tapped his head.

"You will be champion again. I've bet my life savings on it. My whole family is pulling for you."

Griffin frowned. Bradyn's family weren't the only ones pulling for him. Every man, woman, and child from the Bottom, it seemed, had pinned their hopes on him. He was their stand-in. Their avatar. Proof that their lives had worth when every day they were ground down under the heel of the rich and influential.

Since Griffin won the championship last year, the people of the Walled City, especially those in the Bottom, were counting on him to repeat his performance. But as champion, he was also the one to beat. Raleigh reminded him of that every time they trained, and Raleigh would know. He had held the title since the tournaments began more than a decade ago . . . until Griffin beat him last year in a scandalous upset.

Back then he had nothing to lose.

The residents of the Upper City were incensed. He could feel the weight of their stares grow as the date of the tournament approached. His spectacular defeat was not just anticipated; it was required to restore balance and order as they knew it. His reign as champion must be proven a lark.

To the lowborn, he couldn't lose. To the highborn, he couldn't win.

Griffin could only focus on one difficult challenge at time. He just wanted to get through this night without thoroughly embarrassing himself.

Bradyn headed for a set of double doors. Griffin's stomach twisted with nervous knots.

"Any advice, Bradyn?"

Bradyn hummed. "Don't use your sleeve as a napkin."

"I was hoping for something less obvious."

The guards nodded in greeting to Griffin as they stepped aside to allow him entry.

Griffin's mouth fell open at the sight of King Umbert's famed overlook windows. The king had a bird's-eye view of everything and everyone in the Walled City, and beyond. From the fortress courtyard to the large homes with plush greens in the Top, the joined cottages on the roads that wound down through the Middle, to the very slums Griffin grew up in in the Bottom.

A fire burned in the fireplace. Lit candelabras lined the small dining table that had been set for the special occasion. Plates overflowed with roasted meats and vegetables. There were five loaves of bread, two set beside the high-back chair placed for the king.

Four chairs were placed for the laird's family, and two for

the king's. *Four* chairs—Laird Egrid's entire family was coming. Griffin groaned. The mere thought was enough to cause him to lose his appetite.

The fire popped. Beside it, Griffin saw a stone parked in the corner. Almost as tall as he was, yet not wider than his forearm, a series of short horizontal marks sectioned in clumps cut the edge of the stone. As he inched closer to get a better look at it, growling greyhounds exited the king's bedchambers, heading for him.

Griffin reached for the dagger in his boot that wasn't there. He had left it in his room, as Jori requested. No weapons allowed in the king's chambers. Griffin tossed them a piece of bread to shut them up.

"Stupid rats! Silence!" King Umbert lumbered into the room from his chambers beyond the fireplace. The dogs cowered at his sharp tone. He waved and they trotted into the other room, the doors closing behind them.

Bradyn's cousins, Halig and Capp, hurried after him. Not much older than Griffin, the brothers had spent the past two years traveling with Raleigh collecting taxes in the Hinterlands before rising to this grand assignment.

Halig pushed a crown over King Umbert's bald bulbous head, and received a slap. "Not so hard!" Much too tight; skin bulged over the sides. Capp walked backward, tying the laces on the front of the king's red linen shirt that hung like a dress over his swollen form.

The stalwart, hulking king who had led a great army, who

had stopped the draignochs' onslaught, saving the disjointed lands from demolition and the people from certain death, had grown enormously fat in the more leisurely years since.

"Sire, what is this carved into the stone?" Griffin asked.

"Remarkable thing, isn't it?"

Remarkable wasn't the word that came to mind. In fact, it looked rather *un*remarkable. The art childish . . . if it was art.

"Do you know what it says?" the king asked, adjusting his crown.

"Says? Does it speak?"

King Umbert laughed. "No. At least not for me." He sounded disappointed. He cast a narrowed eye on Halig, then at the stone. Halig draped a silky red cloth over it. "Enough of that. Come here."

Griffin padded beside him, bowing his head.

"Sir Griffin, you put on a clean shirt," the king observed with an approving grin. "And one of my royal color, I see."

"Your son's doing, Your Majesty. A futile attempt to make me a suitable stand-in for him tonight." Griffin bowed.

"You'll excel as you always do, young man. Prince Jori has found a loyal friend in you. Know that it hasn't gone unnoticed." He spied the wine and jerked his chin. Halig read his cryptic gesture, pouring two chalices, handing the first to the king and the other to Griffin, before slipping back into the shadows on the other side of the fireplace.

King Umbert cradled his cup. "Jori's going to need you by his side in the coming weeks, Sir Griffin, as am I."

"Is that why you wished to speak to me before Laird Egrid arrived?"

King Umbert nodded and swirled the wine, not spilling a single drop. "The wolves are entering our house as we speak, and *he* will be thirsty for blood."

The wolves. Laird Egrid and his family. The reason for poor Jori's wedding. The prince had explained the last time his betrothed came to the Walled City. The old man ruled the North, the last of the territories not under the king's control. Egrid's armies were many in number, and the severe terrain in the North was said to be impossible to fight on unless you intimately understood its mountains, moors, bogs, and forests. Not to mention its weather. When Prince Jori was born, King Umbert decided on a marriage to unite the lands, rather than war.

If the king was worried about a threat to Jori's throne, it wasn't from Egrid. He was ancient and feebleminded, and could no longer command his own people, let alone attempt to rule all the lands. His youngest son, Cornwall, was barely fifteen and still untested in the arena or on the battlefield. The people didn't know him and would never follow him. But then there was Malcolm, Egrid's eldest son, and Griffin's biggest rival in the last tournament. He *had* been tested, in battle—on foreign soil and in the arena. He was accustomed to victory. The sole exception being when he went against Griffin.

"By *he* you speak of Malcolm," Griffin said to the king.

"You are exceedingly bright, Sir Griffin." King Umbert

raised his glass and finally sipped. Griffin gulped his down, hoping it would help calm his nerves, but instead he felt his heart pounding harder against his chest.

The king wiped his dripping chin with his sleeve. "Yes. Even with his sister Esmera marrying Jori, I worry Malcolm won't be satisfied with a knighthood. And then there's the rest of Egrid's children to deal with. . . ."

"Her sister, Lady Sybil, is warmhearted enough. I suspect she will come along with her sister and live here in the castle?" Griffin refilled his glass.

"Mmm," the king grunted. "She might even make a good wife for you."

Griffin choked on his wine, spitting it out all over the floor.

The king's laugh filled the room. He patted Griffin on the shoulder. "Marriage isn't that bad, Sir Griffin. And to marry into the royal family . . ."

"I'm flattered, sire. Truly." His words placated the king, but not Griffin's tense stomach. The last thing he ever wanted to be was *married*. "There is also the younger brother, Cornwall," he said, deftly changing the subject. "He won the melee last year."

"He did. But he's an imbecile."

"What exactly would you like me to do, sire? Something specific or—"

"Informants tell me that northern assassins have entered the city. Malcolm plans to kill me and make a play for the throne."

Griffin remembered how he'd come to be regarded by the king. He had saved Jori's life from such an assassin. He swallowed, but anger left a bitter taste that lingered. This past year the king and Jori had become like family to him. "Shouldn't Sir Raleigh be here, sire?"

"Nah. He's gone soft. He's no longer fit to oversee my armies. He's right where he belongs, collecting taxes in the Hinterlands. And if I'm being honest, I'm not sure he ever forgave me for choosing you as champion last year." King Umbert plopped a finger into his glass, then lifted it to his mouth.

A life on the roads through the Hinterlands, collecting taxes, sounded a fate much worse than death in the arena. Raleigh had taught him everything he knew about fighting, about draignochs. Hearing the king toss him aside, and for Griffin, left his stomach riddled with guilt. "Yes, sire."

"This bothers you."

"No," Griffin lied, for it would've been seen as a weakness. "It's only that it's my first time defending my title. It feels very different than going into it with fresh eyes." It felt strange speaking to the king as if he were Jori or Sir Raleigh. They were the only two he trusted in the palace with conversations that left him feeling vulnerable.

King Umbert nodded. "It is different now. You have to want it more. Sir Griffin, there's always someone coming for your title. It's a lot like being king. When you rule, there is always someone who wants your crown, who believes they can do it better."

"What can I do for you, sire? With regards to the North-men?"

He patted Griffin's sore shoulder, leaving his heavy hand. "Keep sharp eyes and keen ears. You see or hear anything from any of them that hints of betrayal, I want to know."

"Yes, sire."

King Umbert released him and picked up his glass. "You must win this tournament, Sir Griffin. There is no room for error. Malcolm cannot be seen as superior to you at anything. Understand?"

Griffin nodded as the king repeated what he had already figured out. "Yes, sire. I understand."

"Do you?" He slammed his chalice on the table, spilling his wine on a white linen napkin, turning it bloodred. He nodded to Capp, who hustled from the shadows, pouring another glass. Griffin was startled; he had nearly forgotten Capp, Halig, and Bradyn were still in the room.

"Are you loyal to me, Sir Griffin?"

"Of course, sire. Have I given you reason to doubt me?"

"No. And I don't want there ever to be reason, so I ask . . ." King Umbert's stare on Griffin narrowed. "Swear it. An oath of loyalty to me on your life."

Griffin's heart fell into his boots. King Umbert had done so much for him. He had no reason to fear an oath. He took as much when they knighted him, but somehow this felt different. Weightier. More than he was ready for, and yet he gave the king what he wanted. "I swear it on my life." As the promise came out of his mouth, he had the nagging feeling that he was making the biggest mistake of his life.

"Good." King Umbert gave him a small relieved smile. "Good. That is good."

The guards at the entrance stomped their feet, announcing Laird Egrid and his family's arrival. Bradyn helped Egrid, who crutched into the room ahead of the others. His thighbones had been broken fighting the draignochs when they stampeded through the North. Never set properly, his legs were permanently crooked. His gray hair was smoothed with so much rosemary oil he smelled like a roasting chicken. His bones were so thin and frail, his brown tunic and trousers hung much too loosely. Death loomed, likely only a long winter away.

Malcolm was behind his father. A little older and thicker than Griffin, he wore all black, setting off his ginger hair, with a green-and-blue tartan sash—the colors of the North.

The king bid a welcome to Laird Egrid.

Griffin extended a hand to Malcolm. "Welcome back to the Walled City."

Malcolm arched a brow at him but shook it. "Where is the little prince?"

"Prince Jori is in the Hinterlands with Sir Raleigh," Griffin said.

Lady Esmera made a grand entrance, dropping into a deep curtsy in front of the king. "Your Majesty."

Her long blonde hair was curled into ringlets. She wore a

crown of white lace and purple gems, as if she were already queen.

"Seems ill-mannered for Prince Jori not to be here to receive me," Esmera commented to Laird Egrid.

"Sir Griffin is here to greet us," Lady Sybil said as she entered the room wearing a warm smile. She too curtsied for the king, then held her hand out for Griffin to kiss, which he did. A quick peck, hoping it was neither too long nor too short.

"He's a poor substitute," Esmera sniffed.

King Umbert sat down in his seat, indicating the rest to join him. Griffin held out a seat across from his for Sybil. She graciously took it. Capp motioned for Esmera to sit beside Griffin, but she yanked out the chair next to Sybil and glided into it. Griffin took it as a sign that luck was in his favor tonight. He smiled, knowing she would be forced to gaze upon his scarred face the entire meal.

Esmera and Sybil couldn't be more opposite. Esmera's hands were delicately folded in her lap. Her back was stick straight. Her blonde hair neatly swept over her shoulder. She was the picture of poise.

Sybil wore purple, like her sister, but without ornamentation. Her red hair hung in a loose, haphazard braid that looked like it had been threaded on the way to dinner. Her hands fisted on the table beside her plate as if she was ready to fight her food—or perhaps fight for it.

Her hazel eyes lingered on Griffin's face longer than

necessary, making Griffin wonder if his lip was stained red from the wine. He didn't dare lick it off if that was the case, did he? It would be lewd, wouldn't it? This was going to be a very long night. Griffin wiped his mouth with his napkin—just in case.

Sybil gave a tired sigh, raising her glass to her lips. "It is good to see you, Sir Griffin."

"You as well, Lady Sybil. You must be weary from your long journey."

"Starved, actually. I suppose we have to wait for the king?" She glanced down at Umbert and her father, who were in an animated but seemingly humorous conversation, as they were both smiling and laughing.

"Get out of my way!" Cornwall tried to enter but the guards stopped him at the door. The fool was armed with two swords.

"Weapons are not allowed in the king's chambers," a guard said. "You'll have to return them to your chambers."

"I'll do nothing of the sort." He tried to push his way in, but the guards tossed him back.

"Cornwall, give the men your sword belt now!" Egrid snapped.

Cornwall's mop of brown hair bounced with every curse word he threw at the guards as he removed his belt. He passed it off. "My sword had better be in my room when I return or—"

"Or what?" King Umbert growled.

"Cornwall, enough. Get in here and apologize," Egrid snapped.

Cornwall grumbled until he stopped beside the king. "Apologize? For what? The king's guards accosted me." In a polished brown leather tunic, draped with a green-and-blue tartan sash like his brother's, he stood with his hands behind his back, showing off his indignation. No bow, not even a head nod, a slight Griffin saw register on the king's face.

"For being an idiot, and bringing weapons into the king's private chambers," Laird Egrid explained as if he were speaking to a toddler.

"He can apologize for bringing a weapon, Egrid, but we would be remiss in asking him to apologize for who he is by nature." King Umbert chortled.

Malcolm rolled his eyes and shook his head but said nothing. He set his cup beside Griffin and slid into the seat between him and Egrid.

Cornwall's face fell into a deep scowl.

"Oh, come here, Cornwall," Sybil called, patting the seat next to her.

He skulked off, taking the seat beside Esmera instead, where he proceeded to pout and whisper in her ear all the way through the abysmal meal.

No one other than the two old men spoke, making every overzealous chew, every hard swallow, every utensil scrape magnified in volume, and Griffin's lack of manners that much more obvious. Esmera, it seemed, would rather stare than eat. If not for his training's effect on his appetite, Griffin might have been too embarrassed to finish off the platter of meat all by himself.

An hour later, Halig finally cleared the food. Capp brought a pitcher of ale and set it before the king. Bradyn's cousin looked particularly grim, casting a wary glance at Griffin before retreating.

The king, still sucking food from his teeth, poured ale into his chalice and held it out. "To new beginnings and a unified land."

"How can I toast my new beginning if Prince Jori isn't here?" Esmera thumped her glass down, spilling it. "I have no wedding date. And I have to say his absence is rather suspect. Maybe there is to be no wedding after all."

"What Esmera means to say is that maybe we have been lured into a trap," Cornwall hissed. "Malcolm was right. One of us should've remained in the North."

Malcolm spun his glass, adding nothing to explain away what Cornwall had said.

"A trap? How dare you?" It was Egrid and not King Umbert, as Griffin would've expected, who got angry over their comments. Egrid leaned hard on his crutch to stand, then pounded the table with his fist. "King Umbert is my closest friend and greatest ally. Do not think to slight him this way."

"Not to worry, Egrid," King Umbert said, laughing. "As I

recall, your wife, Admerena, was in no less a hurry to wed you. Such a shame she had to die giving birth to Cornwall." King Umbert stood up with his glass in hand. "Lady Esmera, my son will be at your side by morning. As to your wedding day . . . how does the same day as the tournament's finale sound? A celebration all around."

"A whole week?" Esmera whined.

"Why not tomorrow, if he will truly be back then?" Cornwall snipped.

"Yes. I brought the dress. Tomorrow is perfect."

Griffin laughed in horror. "Prince Jori deserves a little advance notice, doesn't he?"

"Warning, you mean." Sybil smirked at him.

Esmera kicked her under the table so hard Griffin heard her boot hit bone.

"Ow!"

"This will be the most important wedding to ever happen in the Walled City. A week is little time to prepare as it is," King Umbert said, "but I'm sure Lady Esmera has a vision of what she wants."

Egrid nodded to his daughter, who was trying to hide her aggravation over the delay with a wide smile. "You give us nothing but grace, Your Majesty."

King Umbert nodded. "It will be the grandest occasion my people have ever witnessed. They shall pass stories about it through generations."

Esmera's vanity seemed to trump her pride. She flushed at

the excitement of being at the center of such an occasion. "Yes, Your Majesty. Thank you."

"Then it's settled," King Umbert declared. He raised his cup to drink but stopped short. "Oh, but then there is the issue of the northern soldiers. I'm told near a hundred are setting up tents outside the western side of the wall. What are they doing here?"

"Protection for our journey." The lie rolled easily off Malcolm's tongue.

The king half grumbled, half chuckled. "Protection. Insurance is more like it."

Malcolm leaned forward, setting his elbows on the table, clasping his hands. "Our meager force is hardly an issue with a giant impenetrable wall standing between them and the city."

King Umbert's eyes narrowed on Malcolm. "*Your* meager force?"

"That—that is what Malcolm said," Egrid answered, sounding baffled, but Griffin knew exactly what King Umbert meant.

"They are my soldiers now that the date is set." Umbert smirked at Egrid, who looked as if he had swallowed a sour pill. "Come to think of it, having them nearby saved them another long ride. I should be thanking you, Malcolm."

"Thank me after the wedding," Malcolm volleyed. "For they belong to the North until that day, do they not, Father?"

Laird Egrid cleared his throat and coughed, avoiding an answer.

King Umbert glanced at Griffin. Griffin wasn't sure if the king was looking for counsel or not but felt strange remaining silent. "Either way, I have a feeling the men, having journeyed so far, would appreciate Your Majesty's generous hospitality. Especially if it came in the form of wine or mead barrels, running freely?"

Drunken, they would be useless to fight. A thought Griffin saw register on Malcolm's face.

King Umbert nodded. "Yes. An excellent idea. Bradyn, let that be done. Speak to your father."

"Yes, Your Majesty." Bradyn ran out of the room to see to the king's orders.

There it was, a brittle peace hanging on the affable Jori marrying the spoiled Esmera. Griffin had never admired Jori for his position, but until now, he had never felt sorry for him either. This had been the most painful meal he'd ever had to endure, and it would be Jori's every meal from his wedding day forward.

"Enough now. Let's walk, Egrid," King Umbert insisted.

His hands shaking, Egrid set his crutches under his arms and set off with the king. Esmera left, dragging Sybil with her. Cornwall followed, worrying after his swords at the guards on his way out. That left Griffin alone with Malcolm.

The pitcher of ale Capp had brought sat untouched in the middle of the table. Malcolm filled a glass to the top. "Ready for a dramatic fall from grace, Griffin?"

Griffin laughed. "Is this your game? Silent and brooding.

A cutting line when you can think one up? You brought your father's men—"

"*My* men. My father hasn't been the true laird for some time."

The king was right. Malcolm did mean to challenge Jori. "Your men. His men. They're the king's men. We all are. And intimidation is futile, Malcolm. I've already beaten you. Beaten every draignoch presented. I won't fail in the arena tomorrow. Or ever in this tournament. How on earth do you think you will cause my fall from grace?"

Malcolm sucked in a sharp breath between clenched teeth, still weighing his glass. "So long as you stand beside a man like Umbert or his disloyal, lying son, you're an easy target."

Griffin suddenly felt like he'd aged ten years. Every word had to be chosen carefully or Malcolm could twist them against him. "You speak of disloyalty, but it's obvious to all that you mean to keep your sister from becoming a queen. And I stand behind the king and his son, and I'm all the better for it."

"*You* are the better for it, because they need you. Mark my words: one slip and the wind will shift direction."

The king's greyhounds bounded through the door and leaped up on the table. The pitcher fell over. Snarling and snapping, they fought for the last bits of ale spilling out, lapping it up.

"Get down, beasts!" Bradyn ran into the room.

One yelped. The other snorted, short of breath. Froth bubbled along their gums.

Malcolm's glass wove a melancholy path toward his mouth.

"Malcolm! No!" Griffin knocked the glass out of his hand and into the fireplace. Fire burst, then immediately quelled.

Malcolm's horrified gaze fell on Griffin as guards barreled into the room.

"What the bloody hell is going on in here?" one barked.

The dogs fell off the table, limbs twitching.

Gasps rang out. Someone cried, "Do something," but what was there to do?

Their eyes rolled up into the backs of their heads.

A second later, they stopped moving altogether.

Bradyn picked up the pitcher and sniffed. "Death cap mushroom. And this . . . this is the king's ale. Someone has tried to murder the king!"

THREE

MAGGIE

My stomach ached with worry all the way to the tavern. I was late. Very late. But more than that, I was shaken. The draignoch. The soldiers. *Moldark.* I dunked my blade in the stable's trough, trying to get his infuriating blood off. After it was clean, I sheathed it into my boot, worried I would need it soon. There'd been no sign of the soldiers or the prince, but I had a bad feeling I would be seeing them again soon.

I couldn't stop thinking about *her*. The draignoch was headed to the Walled City. Not a place I could ever get into. But I had to see her again. I touched the scar that still throbbed, though a tiny bit less the more time passed. Laughter and bellowing broke the evening's silence. I was exhausted, covered in mud from head to toe. And I had to be onstage in moments. The very last thing I wanted to do was stand on a raised platform for all the world to look at me.

Before I reached the side door, Xavier stormed out, his long gray hair clacking from the animal bones he'd tied into it. I noticed he'd added yet another layer.

For some reason he believed they were a source of real

magic. He was always picking up bits, declaring them power-ful. Handing over our precious coins to charlatans in exchange for anything they could spin a magical tale about. He'd traded our last coin for a wooden cup after the farmer who possessed it said it came from the fairies. Claimed anyone who drank from it had to tell the truth. Xavier made me drink from it so many times, trying to unlock the magical mysteries the ridic-ulous thing possessed. But there was no magic. Lies rolled as freely off my tongue as they had so many times beforehand. Xavier had never found real magic, and yet, here he was, with more bones in his head than sense.

The hems of Xavier's blue robe were edged with silver beads that came from the smooth sandy beaches below the cliffs in the northernmost corner of the Hinterlands. Frigid waters he made me dive into repeatedly until he had enough to cover every inch. Strapped to the back of his hands were two red jewels, round and smoothed. His only valuable pur-chase, not for their previous owner's professed transformative gifts but rather because they were ruby gems. He could've sold them this month for more money than we'd ever seen, but he foolishly refused.

"Where have you been?" Xavier's eyes grew impossibly wide at the sight of me. "What happened to you?"

"I had a run-in with the soldiers."

The old barkeep, Porchie, poked his fat head out the door and chortled. "Ooof. I'll get the buckets."

"Clean up as much as you can." Xavier shoved me toward

the barn. "And hurry! There's a room in there filled with very heavy pockets! We can't have them spending it all on drink before we start!"

Porchie returned to the barn with water-filled buckets and a stack of rags, and left without another word. After him came his pig-nosed stock boy, delivering my costume from Xavier. He tried to linger. A threatening manure-filled shovel chased him off.

I tore off my cloak and trousers, shivering from the cold night air, but set to washing. My dress was a welcome change tonight. Made from old blankets, the simple woolen dress was worn but warm. I finished using my fingers to comb out my raven curls the best I could, letting them drape over my shoulders.

Unable to do anything about my mud-covered shoes, I left a trail of caked brown bits as I came through the tavern's side door, earning me a nasty look from the same stock boy who was now sweeping the floors.

The place smelled as all the taverns did, of stale ale and smoke and unwashed men. Round chandeliers hung low, bathing the patrons in a dim orange hue. Xavier wasn't kidding about the tavern being full. There wasn't an empty table in the place.

Rowdy, well-served patrons hopped up, blocking my path.

Porchie saved me, appearing with a full tray, stealing their attentions.

I made a mad dash for the stage.

"Oh, don't go . . . ," I heard one of them whine.

A few families with children crammed into the front of the wooden platform that served as a stage. As I reached it, a movement caught my eye, and my heart fell to my muddy shoes. Prince Jori was seated in the front row. His eyes fell on me, then on my boots, and narrowed.

I tried to look away. Conceal my face. But there was nowhere to hide. His mouth fell open, and then he smiled.

He recognized me.

I darted behind the long opaque traveler curtains, trying to keep my heart from leaping out of my chest. Had they followed me here? All to arrest me? But why? According to the prince, the whole party were in a rush to get back to the Walled City with the draignoch.

Xavier came up behind me. He peeled back the cloth enough to glimpse the audience.

"That fair-haired young man—did you see?"

"Oh, I saw."

"His drawstring pouch looked very heavy. He carries coins. Probably gold, from the looks of his clothes." His hand fell on my shoulder. "The pot will be worth something tonight for a change."

I chanced a look over Xavier's shoulders and caught the prince staring in our direction. I dipped farther behind the curtain, backing up several steps until I bumped into the wall.

"What's wrong?" Xavier asked.

Telling him that the man in his sights was the real Prince Jori would only serve to make him as nervous as I felt. Then he would flub the act, thereby reducing our take, and we needed the money. Badly.

"Nothing. You're right. Going to be a banner night."

He arched his bushy silver brow. He knew I was hiding something.

A whisper slithered by my ear. Startled, I turned, reaching for my knife. But there was no soldier. Only a round window. The thumbnail moon dipped inside one of its panes like it was trying to catch falling stars.

The noise of the crowd escalated, drowning out everything else, but then I heard it again. The faintest of whispers, a whistling breeze, but there was no wind. Was it coming from outside?

I stood on my tiptoes and stretched to push open the window, but it proved unnecessary. A moonbeam, fine as a spider's silk, shot down from the dark sky. Hitting the pane, it shattered the glass, finding its target, my hand.

I scooted back. The light came with me. A startled gasp escaped. Torn between fear and fascination, I flicked my wrist, trying to shake it off, but it did no good. The light was stuck to me.

Light could do no such thing.

This couldn't be real. I was losing my mind.

A frightening chill swept through me.

All the while the subtle whisper persisted, growing louder. It no longer sounded like it was coming from outside the window, but from inside me.

I couldn't move.

Couldn't breathe.

"Time for introductions," Xavier called to me.

I lifted onto my toes, moving away from the window. The string of light stretched all the way from the moon to me. It was the most beautiful, magical, terrifying thing I ever saw. "Xavier . . ."

"Maggie, tell me after the show!" Xavier hissed.

Ignore it, I told myself. I had a job to do, and if I didn't do it, I would go hungry tonight.

A few more steps away from the window, the moonbeam flickered off. But then, it wasn't completely gone. I could still feel the cold burn of its light dead center in the palm of my hand.

Utterly confused, I stepped out from behind the curtain, singing the refrain I had sung so many times before.

"Hear me, hear me, weary travelers!"

The tavern's drowning chatter dulled.

I walked upstage, making eye contact with several, but none near the prince. "Keep your lids from blinking, I warn! For sorry indeed will be he or she who misses a moment of the wonder of Xavier, the true Ambrosius!"

Xavier's arrival onstage was met with sporadic clapping. "Thank you for your kind welcome." He paced, as he always did, taking in the excitement level of the audience, which proved lackluster. He would have a difficult job tonight.

"I've heard tell that those in this village have never seen magic before." He drew out a silver coin from inside his sleeve and held it up for all to see. "I've even heard that some here might not believe. Indulge me with your attention, I beg, and learn the truth." He folded his hand and opened it again, the coin seemingly vanishing.

The children in front oohed in astonishment. A table of drunken men in the back grumbled.

"E-even I ca' do dat," one boasted.

Xavier would soon shut them up. He always started with simple. As I moved beside the prop table, I could feel the prince's eyes on me. I risked a glance and he caught me. Smirking, he arched an irritating brow.

I scanned the patrons for soldiers. Sir Raleigh was supposed to be traveling with Jori. Sure enough, Raleigh's sweaty, balding head emerged from the back. He had another soldier with him. They wove through the tables and sat on either side of the prince.

Raleigh's lip lifted into a snarl as his eyes fell on the stage. My heart hammered. *Run.* I would, but now it would draw attention. I would have to wait until the show was over.

Xavier folded his hands together like a collapsing clamshell. When he opened them, he showed not one but two silver coins. This impressed. Making silver multiply was worth a rousing cheer. Then Xavier tossed them to the boasting drunk man in the back, silencing him for the rest of the show.

"A simple trick, a sleight of hand. Or was it? Argue as you will, but how about something that none can refute?" A few clapped. "Oh my. You'll have to do better than that if you want the magic to work."

The few children in the tavern stood up, slapping their hands together.

"Very well then. Maggie?"

Looking unimpressed, Prince Jori got up from his table. Raleigh and the soldier followed him. Perhaps they would leave. But the prince leaned his shoulder against a post in the middle of the room and continued to watch.

I set ceramic bowls on the table in order of smallest to largest. Xavier held each up, turning them upside down. "Empty. But for how long?"

Xavier handed me the smallest bowl. Prince Jori's eyes shifted in my direction. Fear tightened its grip, numbing my hands. I felt the slick surface slip from my fingertips too late.

Xavier caught the bowl midair. "What's wrong with you?" he muttered. He lifted the lip, making sure all could see the bowl empty, then cradled it in the crook of his arm. "I will now make sand appear from nothing!"

The room fell silent in expectation.

Xavier closed his eyes, mumbling in a language I never understood, and one I always suspected was little more than improvised gibberish.

He rotated the bowl while running his fingers along the

edge so that, unseen by the audience, he could open a small compartment. And like that, sand poured into the bowl.

Still tricks. No real magic.

With deft agility, Xavier flipped the compartment closed at the same time he tilted the bowl. He showed off sand, turning in all directions to be sure everyone could see. "Yes! I, the great Xavier, the one true Ambrosius, turned air to sand, but only true magic would have me pouring mead from my fingertips." His proclamation was met with a round of applause.

"That I'd pay to see!" a man called from the back.

Prince Jori pushed off the post, curious, and moved a little closer to the stage.

I spun, putting my back to him.

"Would you, now?" Xavier nudged me. "Maggie . . ."

I passed him a larger bowl, which he placed on the stage to catch the spill. "Then I suppose that will have to be the next feat, and I will hold you to your word."

Xavier waved his free hand over the bowl, humming, repeating the mumblings. He tipped the bowl forward, allowing the sand to spill out. As it crested the lip, another unseen shaft opened beneath his well-placed hand. Mead poured through his cupped fingers and into the bowl below.

The audience stood from their seats, trying to get a good look at the magic. A mixture of laughter and applause began in the back with the table of besotted men and spread throughout the tavern.

Over the next twenty minutes, Xavier kept all engaged

with dissolving rope knots, disappearing and reappearing flowers, and more. As he prepared to end the show with his final trick, he asked, "Have I convinced you all that magic really does exist?"

A fat sweaty man whistled, stumbling toward the stage. "That's what I call a piece of magic." He aimed his finger at me. "Come sit on my lap, lass. I'll give you a lovely piece of gold for your trouble."

"Remain in your seat," Prince Jori growled.

Raleigh shoved the fat arse.

The man fell backward, into a chair.

Xavier picked up our jittery gray rabbit and lifted her out of her cage, clutching her tightly as she squirmed in protest at being held like a prop.

"A simple rabbit. But is it? Perhaps this is something else in disguise. . . ." Xavier returned her to the box, swiftly closing the lid.

Waiting to crawl out from behind the slat that divided the box into halves was a twitchy red squirrel. He started a nervous chirp. The damn squirrel hated being carted around in the box as much as I hated to have to keep him there, but if he ruined our show and I got no supper, he would be roasting over a spit tonight.

I snuck a comforting hand inside. The evil rascal bit me. I bit my lip, hiding my bleeding finger behind my back.

Xavier covered the box with a blanket. He waved his staff, jerking his head so the bones clacked, spewing an incantation.

As my bloody finger fumbled for the button to drop the slat, the drunken ass from the audience leaped up onstage.

He slurred, "Hello, lovely . . ."

The latch gave way. The squirrel exited at the same time he grabbed me, capturing my arms, lifting me off my feet. I kicked him as hard as I could. My heel collided with his knee at the perfect angle. It buckled and he fell forward, landing on top of me and the squirrel, crushing me under his immense weight.

I let out an unflattering "Ooof."

Xavier grumbled, "You are an idiot!"

Bombarded by audience laughter, I felt the idiot's hands roam my sides. Our squirrel, squished beside me, bit him hard enough for the fat slob to feel it through his drunken stupor. He bolted to all fours. To my shock and horror, and that of the children in the audience, he jammed his knee down on the squirrel. His little ribs snapped like breaking twigs.

The audience collectively gasped. The poor rodent screeched. Its tiny limbs struggling but going nowhere. A chorus of booing erupted.

The fat sot sniggered, attempting to get up and lunge again, but he never made it. The prince, Sir Raleigh, and the soldier stormed the stage. They heaved him off the edge of the platform. Xavier moved to stand over the squirrel, his staff raised, about to drive the bottom down onto the wailing rodent. I groaned at the stupidity. The Ambrosius crushing the animal to death while visible onstage would earn us less than nothing!

Moonlight shot through the broken pane, finding my hand at the same time I grabbed Xavier's staff to stop him. My veins turned ice-cold—so cold they burned. I closed my eyes, trying to shut out the pain before I screamed. In the darkness, I saw the draignoch's claw dangling in the air just before me. My free hand ached as if someone was trying to punch a nail through it—from the inside out. The cold shot through me like an arrow released from its bow.

Gasps rang out.

"Do you see that?" Porchie called out.

"Is that the moon doing that?" a woman cried.

"I think he's doing that! Xavier! Calling to the moon!" another retorted.

I opened my eyes and found the moonbeams traveling the staff, striking the blue sapphire at the top, casting the room in frenetic azure droplets. Xavier glanced at the source, moonlight streaming through the busted windowpane. He began a slow chant, as if unsure what to do other than look magical.

The squirrel wheezed. Within reach, I slid my hand down the staff, planning to yank him offstage. My hand fell on his tiny chest. Broken ribs the size of toothpicks, one stabbed into his tiny heart. All this, I *saw*. Then I saw the light fuse the bones back together, guiding the last out of his tiny failing heart. Xavier's singing reached a fevered pitch. He slammed the staff on the stage so hard I felt the jolt deep down inside.

The squirrel jumped up with a start.

There was no time to ruminate over what had happened. I

let go of the shaft to scoop him up before he could get away. As soon as I did, the blue glow went out, and the little rascal bit me again.

"Ow!"

"Did you see that?" someone called.

"Xavier the Ambrosius brought the squirrel back to life!" the little girl in the front row exclaimed. She clapped furiously.

The audience rose to their feet to get a good look at the vermin. I wanted to break the wretched thing's neck but knew the pot would be full tonight so long as we finished the show in spectacular fashion. I lifted the squirrel over my head.

"You all bore witness! Xavier the Ambrosius brought this dying animal back to life!" I declared.

Xavier's head lifted high, meeting every admiring gaze. I turned around, finding Prince Jori staring into the empty box. "I don't understand. I expected another squirrel, but is that the same squirrel? Did Xavier really heal him?"

My eyes darted to the heavy coin pouch on his belt. I smiled and held the struggling animal out to him. "Oh yes. He did. He healed him, and now, if he doesn't stop biting me, I'm going to eat him for dinner."

He gaped in obvious astonishment as I dropped the snapping squirrel into the box and slammed the lid shut.

All hailed Xavier's name, giving him the loudest round of applause I had ever heard. I couldn't fathom what had truly happened. Xavier had never touched the squirrel. I had. And the power still pulsed like a heartbeat in the center of my palm.

Xavier stepped offstage. He set the bowl on the table where the prince had been sitting. Coins clinked as patrons emptied their pockets. They touched Xavier's robe as if a god stood before them, wearing mirroring expressions of fear blended with awe. Some even kissed his robe, handing over their tokens for a blessing.

All that coin. My stomach began to grumble, anticipating the meal my share would buy. Then I turned and saw the prince, standing behind me, nod to Raleigh in the crowd. Raleigh said something to the soldier, who dashed through the throngs around Xavier. Raleigh paced toward the stage to join the prince.

Run.

I started to, jumping off the stage, making it halfway there, but Xavier caught my arm. "Where do you think you're going, lass? Get the props. Clean up the mead from the floor. I'll tend to the pot before someone makes off with it. We're not foraging for watercress tonight!"

I fully intended to ignore Xavier's demands when I saw the soldier beside the exit. There was no way past him.

Unable to think of a way out, I stepped onstage, moving behind the curtain. Sir Raleigh and Prince Jori paced toward me, forcing me to walk backward until I bumped into the rear wall of the tavern, beneath the broken window.

I was trapped.

"Maggie! What did I say?" Xavier came behind the curtain and found our company. He set the pot inside the trunk, locking it, thinking they were thieves.

"Can I help you?" Xavier said to Sir Raleigh.

"Yes, you can," Prince Jori answered. "I'm intrigued by your talents, Xavier. I've heard tale of a great Ambrosius, a truly magical being, and perhaps you really are the one we seek. You see, we've seen a great many pretenders in the Walled City."

"We? Who are you?" I asked.

"Forgive me." He passed me a knowing smile. "Let me first properly introduce myself. I am Prince Jori. By *we*, of course, I mean my father, King Umbert, and I."

Xavier's mouth fell open and he gave a stilted bow. "I—I—Well, I— Your Grace . . . I am the Ambrosius you seek. I can promise you that. What can I do for you?" He eyed his coin bag.

I gripped my skirts in my fists to keep my hands from trembling, and curtsied, pretending this was news to me.

The prince continued, "You and your lovely daughter will come to the Walled City to perform for the opening night feast of the Draignoch Festival."

It wasn't a request. It was an order.

Xavier's cheeks reddened.

The Walled City held a special place in all Hinterfolks' minds. Rumors spoke of food at the plenty. Fine linens for dresses. Hearth always burning. Music and dances around every corner. A place where happiness was not earned, but free.

I wanted to see such a place. But even more than that, I wanted to see the draignoch.

Xavier's face broke into a grin. "You honor me, sire."

I let out a breath I didn't know I was holding. The prince touched my shoulder. "How is your hand?"

I pursed my lips, confused.

"Where the animal bit you, my lady?" He picked up my hand without asking my permission to do so.

I yanked it back. "It's fine. He does it all the time. And, um, I am not a lady, sire."

He slipped his hands behind his back, half smiling. "Take it as a compliment, then."

I worried I'd offended him.

He turned back to Xavier abruptly. "I'm afraid I must leave straightaway, but rest assured Sir Raleigh will deliver you both to the city safely."

"It will be done, sire." Raleigh set his hands on his sword belt and stepped back, giving the prince room to advance.

"I shall see you both when you arrive, then." Prince Jori gave me a warm, tilting smile before jumping off the stage. He walked with determination out of the tavern, with several soldiers following after him.

And yet, there were still more. At least fifteen of King

Umbert's soldiers, by my quick count. Where had they all come from?

"Can you believe our luck?" Xavier exclaimed to me. He spoke to Sir Raleigh. "If you'll excuse us, we'll pack our things and prepare for tomorrow."

Sir Raleigh shook his head in a slow, methodical way. "We'll pack your wagon. We leave at first light, otherwise a three-day journey will take four. I've secured rooms. Food and drink will be brought up. Go now. Get some sleep."

We were escorted to our rooms, making it impossible for Xavier and me to talk about what exactly had happened.

Once in my room, I couldn't stop thinking about the draignoch.

She'd done something to me. It was the only explanation that made sense.

I had to find her. I had to figure out what power she had over me.

After a dinner of warm bread and hard cheese, I stood over a washbowl, scrubbing my muddy shoes, when someone knocked softly.

I slid the bolt and found myself staring at Prince Jori's shy smile. "Excuse the late intrusion."

"Sire." I curtsied, only to realize I was standing before him in my shift. I grabbed the blanket from my bed and tossed it around my shoulders. "I thought you left."

"Soon . . ." He twisted a flower stem between his thumb

and finger. "I saw this and thought of you. It's a wild rose."

"Yes. It is." I knew them well. Five red, delicate petals surrounding a brilliant yellow center.

"They grow near the barn," he added, explaining where it had come from. He held it out to me, but I refused to take it.

It was the king's flower. "They grow all over the Hinterlands. But, sire, it's illegal to pick them."

He grinned widely. "Not for me. Please, take it. I picked it especially for you."

I should have been flattered. I awkwardly reached out for it. "Thank you."

Our hands brushed in passing, eliciting a knowing smile from the prince. "Raleigh has assured me you will be well taken care of on the way back. You will have your own tent, away from the men. But rest knowing you will be heavily guarded too." He must have seen my expression sour. "For your safety, Maggie."

I didn't like the sound of it. "I can take care of myself."

Prince Jori pressed his lips tightly together, as if holding back a secret. "So I've seen."

Ah, so he did recognize me from our encounter in the woods. I sniffed the delicate flower, trying to hide my shock.

"Sire? The men are saddled," a soldier called.

"Very well." He turned to leave. "I look forward to seeing you soon, Maggie. Safe travels."

As soon as I heard the prince's footsteps on the stairs, the guard pulled my door shut. I hid the flower beneath the washbowl, worried someone would accuse me of picking it, and crawled into bed, exhausted but unable to fall asleep. First, I pondered whether Prince Jori would've told Sir Raleigh that it was me who stabbed Moldark. If he had, why hadn't Raleigh arrested me? Was he waiting to do that once inside the Walled City? But then, why wait? Why not lop off my hand now? I stared at my tingling palm. The power. It was still there, but what was it?

I sat up to reach the window, pulling the curtain back, and pressed my hand against the glass. A moonbeam no thicker than thread dropped from the dark sky, the end dangling like a dewdrop.

Full of wonder, I pushed open the window to catch it. Cold breeze rushed into the already chilly room. But for some mysterious reason, I wasn't cold in the slightest. The moonlight traveled from my palm up my arm until it touched my scar, tracing it.

"Ha!" Incredible. The lines and dots glowed, twinkling in the darkness of my room.

I stared at the moon. "I don't understand. What is happening to me?"

I crawled to the other side of the bed, stretching the moon's thread until it was so thin it was barely visible, waiting, but for what?

"What is this?" I yelled at the moon, thrusting my hand in its face, feeling like an idiot.

The silence was infuriating.

I slammed the window shut, pulling the curtain so the moon couldn't find me. I was immediately overwhelmed by a terrible sense of loss, my chest filling with a frigid dread. Shivering uncontrollably, I ripped the curtain back, feeling relieved, yet terrified at the relief. Whatever that draignoch did to me, I was never going to be the same.

Soldiers woke us at first light in a hurry to leave. On the chance that Prince Jori had said nothing of my identity to Sir Raleigh, I left my usual traveling clothes beneath the bed in the room and put on my costume dress. I never wore it except onstage. The old wool itched and if it got wet, I would smell like an old sheep as we entered the grand Walled City, but it was better than being recognized and losing my hand.

I slipped it on and stood far enough back to see myself in the little mirror on the night table. I was heading to the Walled City, to the festival to perform. I had to look like a lady, even if I didn't feel like one. Throwing my shoulders back, I stood taller, and combed my unruly curls with my fingers, twisting a few around my face, leaving the rest loose and hanging down my back. I smiled sweetly at my reflection, feeling like a complete idiot. Ladylike I was not, but I supposed I could pretend to be.

I rode in our wagon with Xavier while Sir Raleigh and his men fanned out, some ahead and others traipsing behind. As soon as we hit open road, Xavier spoke in hushed tones.

"Maggie, the squirrel . . . the moonlight . . . ," he started, then glanced up, perhaps looking for the moon, then around to make sure the men were out of earshot. Once satisfied, he added, "I gave this a lot of thought last night. And I need to know. Was it . . . you?"

I should have told him the truth, that I believed it was, but I hesitated. Any mention of the draignoch would draw the soldiers' attention.

"No," I said with conviction. "It wasn't." A second later I felt guilty for lying to him.

He glared at me. "I ran through every memory, every motion that led up to that event. Where my hands were, how the jewels were placed, when I touched the staff to the floor. But I never did touch the squirrel. That was you. Your hand." His expression turned angry. His hot moldy breath gusted into my face. "You've found an instrument of *real* magic, haven't you? You're keeping it from me! Where is it? Where have you hidden it?" He grabbed my shoulder and squeezed. "Give it to me! Give it to me now!"

The soldiers stared at the fuss he was making.

I'd only ever seen that look on Xavier's face once before. It was the look of a man driven insane in the pursuit of something he could never have. Worse now, because he thought I'd found it and was keeping it from him.

"I have nothing," I growled. "It wasn't me!" I tried to push him away, but Xavier didn't let go.

A few months back, Xavier had bought a serpent from a traveler who claimed it had the power to turn people invisible. Before nightfall, he spread it out on a long flat rock and sliced off its head. He drank its blood, howled at the full moon. He had then laid his arms wide and smiled at me, his teeth stained rust, with the same wild eyes.

If he thought there was even a possibility I had magic, he'd sacrifice me as willingly as he had killed the snake. Would he drink my blood?

"Is there a problem?" Sir Raleigh's cool northern lilt snuck up on us. He rode his horse beside the wagon, slowing to match Dorn's pace.

Xavier calmed, but didn't let go. He sat taller and put on a pleasing expression. "No. No problem. Maggie forgot something back at the tavern, but I told her there was no turning back now." Xavier patted my shoulder.

Fuming, I bit my lip to keep quiet.

"'Fraid not." Raleigh tossed me an apple, then kicked his horse, trotting ahead.

"Thank you," I called after him, oddly hoping he wouldn't go far.

Xavier leaned over and whispered, "We're not finished."

I shifted, trying to keep my voice low. "I do not know what happened last night any more than you do. Maybe all the baubles you have finally aligned in exactly the right way. Did you ever think of that?" It sounded good to my ears.

His glare lessened, his face contorted, mulling over the possibility. "No. I hadn't. But I suppose that would mean . . ." His anger flipped. His eyes grew wide with excitement, then narrowed with worry. "But how am I to do it again? If I don't know exactly how I did it? And I must, Maggie. We are going to the Walled City. We are to perform for the king!"

"Practice. We have three nights before the performance. We can sneak off after they set up camp."

That quieted him. He released my shoulder. I rubbed the place where his fingers had dug into my skin, leaving bruises that would stay for some time.

Within an hour of leaving the seaside village, we passed the tall stone marking the border for the South. Typically, with fall came rain, but not this year. We traversed through a river that only a year prior would have reached Dorn's neck, but she was barely inconvenienced, sloshing through it as if it were a puddle. There was no sweet smell from harvested wheat to greet us in the fields. Only dried beds and cracked ground. The drought had hit the South hard.

At the sight of the first farmhouse, Sir Raleigh jerked his chin. His men dismounted horse and wagon and stormed up to the home.

"Why have we stopped?" I asked, pulling Dorn's reins.

"King's business," Sir Raleigh said, twirling a grass stem that he had chewed on since the creek. "Collecting taxes."

"Taxes? But the fields are devastated. Does the king not

know of the drought that struck this summer? There's been little water for months. This family likely can't even feed their own!"

Xavier shushed me. "Sir Raleigh, please forgive her impudence."

Raleigh walked his horse around the wagon until he was beside me.

"The East and West have already paid a heavy share this year. It is only fair the South give their part." He stared at me as if he were trying to teach me a lesson, like an old man passing out indisputable worldly wisdom.

"I'm sure if you asked those in the East and West, they would forgo fairness this season so these southerners do not need to starve."

Raleigh gave an amused smirk. "You are clearly too young to understand the way of things."

"And you're *clearly* too old to hear the truth!"

Raleigh reeled back. A crease formed between his brows. He spat the grass blade, then kicked his horse to a trot to move away from us.

Xavier whacked me on the back of the head. "I should've left you at the tavern working for Porchie. You'll be the death of both of us. Now hold your tongue before they lop it off at my request!"

I rubbed the spot, more for show than anything else. It didn't really hurt.

Raleigh's men returned with a small basket of seed grain,

probably all the family had to plant for next season.

"We passed through here a year ago. They took us in and fed us. The old man who was missing an eye, and his daughter? Have you forgotten?" I whispered harshly to Xavier.

"Yes, I have. Today I forget everything. We are the king's guests on this journey and we must act as such." He tore the reins from me. "Not another word."

The next farm had nothing to show in produce from their fields, only two pigs in their pen. Sir Raleigh ordered both taken. When the old woman begged to keep one, a soldier struck her with an axe handle on the back of the head, leaving her unconscious and bleeding.

Xavier kept hold of my wrist, keeping me from jumping out of the wagon to help her. I wasn't surprised by the king's men. This was what they did. But Xavier's ability to turn his back shocked me to my core. I'd always thought of him as compassionate. After all, he had taken *me* in—an urchin with nothing.

There were days when I was young I wished he were my father.

Now all I could think was that I was glad he wasn't.

As the scene repeated many times over, I felt sicker with each farm we passed. I had seen soldiers pillage their way through the Hinterlands every harvest. Last year, in the East, I hid with other children in the woods, along with half their livestock, to ensure the winter shelves had enough to get through to spring. Xavier was there with me, and them.

But this was different. By all appearances I was with the soldiers. The burden of guilt weighed heavy on my chest, making it difficult to breathe. I moved into the rear of the wagon, putting my back to the seat so I wouldn't have to look at Xavier, and stared at the sky, searching for the moon. I found it too. Strange. I never noticed before how visible it was, in the day or night. A new moon, when it was invisible to the eye, yes, it would then be impossible to find, but now it was there, a thin strip, smiling down on me. A tingling on the back of my neck, my palm prickled too. A reminder of what had transpired in the tavern. A comfort too. I fisted my hand, wanting to keep that feeling forever.

Meanwhile Xavier conversed with the soldiers as if he was their newfound best friend, asking about the Walled City and after the king and the prince.

Three soldiers dismounted at the last farm before the road inclined. The sun was setting. We were told we would make camp after this, which was good because I couldn't stop shivering. The moon rose higher. A radiating warmth shot through me, relieving the chill.

I smiled. I hadn't seen Xavier glance back at me.

"What?" Xavier snapped.

"Nothing." I scooted lower in the wagon.

The farm looked deserted.

Soldiers kicked open the barn and returned empty-handed. "No horses. Only old hay in the stalls. Rats everywhere."

"I'll check the house," the largest of them called. Yellow

haired, with shoulders so square he had to turn sideways to go through the door.

Yet another returned, heaving a sigh. "Stys are empty too, Sir Raleigh. Shall we go?"

"There's nothing, I swear!" a frantic woman cried from inside the house. "No. Not that. Please . . . !"

Square Shoulders returned with a loaf of bread. "I wouldn't call this nothing." He tossed it to another, who put it underneath the cover of one of their five bursting wagons.

A small boy came out of the house. His stomach protruding from starvation, he was so thin a strong wind would blow him over. "Give it back! The king won't want it! It's stale! Please!"

"Colin, come back!" His mother stood in the doorway, crying, too afraid to come out. Her skin was so thin her bones threatened to break through if she lost another ounce of weight. She needed to eat. And yet these soldiers were stealing their only food and I was sitting in the back of our wagon, letting them.

Colin rounded on the wagon. Laughing, the soldier kicked him in his stomach. The boy bent over, gasping and coughing. Then he hit him with the butt of his dagger on his forehead, sending him crashing to the ground. His head bleeding, he curled into a ball.

"No! Please . . ." His mother pressed her fingers to her lips.

Square Shoulders stood him upright. "There's a river a mile off. Go catch yourself a fine fish."

Xavier felt me move. "Maggie . . ."

I ducked his grab and jumped out of the wagon. "A fine fish?"

"Maggie, get back here!" Xavier called.

"From the dried bed? Did you see any fish? Were they invisible? Were they some sort of magic fish who could swim in nothing more than a thimble of water?" I yelled at the frowning soldier. "The boy can barely stand. He's starving. His mother is starving. What kind of monsters are you?" I growled.

The smug soldier laughed in my face. "Better them than us. That loaf is for our supper." He shoved me. "Get back in the wagon or you can go hungry tonight too."

I stormed toward the wagon where the soldier had stashed the loaf, my intention obvious.

"I wouldn't do that," Square Shoulders said.

"There's plenty enough for us to eat in the wagons." I snatched the loaf of bread from beneath the cover, then brought it back to Colin. He sat up, holding his head, but didn't take it from me.

"If he takes it, he'll lose his hand." Sir Raleigh dismounted and pulled his sword. Colin didn't run but he turned away.

Raleigh padded close enough to speak in quieter tones. "Just as you should've yesterday when you stabbed Moldark."

"What are you saying? Stabbed who?" Xavier started to climb down but stopped when he saw Sir Raleigh shake his head.

My heart gave in to the terror that ripped through me, pounding so hard it hurt. He too had known all along. I didn't get a close look at the soldiers, but any of them could've been with the prince and Raleigh when the draignoch saved me from the same fate Raleigh was threatening to inflict on the boy. I lowered my head, but my eyes remained fixed on Raleigh's.

Sir Raleigh took the loaf of bread from me. "Take your seat before you cause the boy and his mother more trouble. Prince Jori is expecting you. I assured him you would be delivered safely to the castle, along with Xavier. It's your choice if you want to arrive bound and gagged. Makes no difference to me."

I ground my teeth. "May I please help this boy safely back to his house?"

Raleigh arched a single curious brow, but stepped aside, making room for me to help the boy stand up. His shoulders were so frail, I could feel his skeleton.

"Load up, men!" Raleigh shouted.

The gash on Colin's head was so deep I saw bone. Blood snaked down his face. Dizzy, he tripped twice on the way to his mother's waiting arms, where he collapsed.

"Colin?" She patted his cheeks, but he didn't wake up. "No!"

My hand heated. The slow hum I'd heard in the tavern returned, buzzing my ears. Although I couldn't see the moonlight touching me because it was masked by the glare of the lowering sun, I could feel it. The pit of my stomach joined my palm, warming. I still had no idea what I was doing, but if I had a chance at healing this boy's head, I had to try.

With my back to the soldiers, I closed my eyes and pressed

my hand to Colin's wound. In the darkness, I saw cracked bone smooth to whole. Skin seal. When I opened my eyes, Colin was looking up at me, smiling.

His mother gasped. "How—"

I shook my head, cutting her off.

"Maggie!" Xavier yelled.

"Go," I whispered.

Colin and his mother went into the house and shut the door.

I stared at my hands, covered in Colin's blood, transfixed in wonder, then at the moon. The same moon I'd always seen. The scar on my arm burned. I cringed, unsure what that meant.

"Maggie!" Xavier yelled again, growing impatient.

"I'm coming . . ."

Colin's frail smile appeared in the window. Then he did the strangest thing. He held up three fingers and set them against his forearm. My scar. He'd seen it. Sir Raleigh's shadow fell over me. I had completely forgotten he was there. "In the wagon, Maggie."

There was a change in his tone, in his demeanor. He seemed . . . unnerved. There was only one explanation. He had seen, and yet he said nothing about it.

As I climbed into the wagon, Raleigh squeezed the bread. "The boy was right. Fools," he snapped at his men. "The loaf is stale." He tossed it back at the house and mounted his horse.

We camped in a small grove out of the wind. The soldiers stayed away from us, taking care of the horses and standing watch over the wagons. Xavier disappeared into the woods to practice. He asked to go alone. I was happy to be rid of him for a little while. They put up a tent for me, but I always preferred sleeping under the stars. I set my bedroll near the fire, ate the apples and hard cheese Raleigh brought, and fell into a deep exhausted sleep.

The next day was more of the same, long flat roads running by blighted pastures. The soldiers continued to pillage anything that resembled a dwelling. That night, long after I'd fallen asleep, Xavier woke me in a panic. He dragged me away from the smoldering fire's delicious heat, into the dense darkness in the woods, away from the prying eyes of the soldiers.

"It's not working. Maggie, we cannot go into the Walled City if the magic is gone." The wall looked even bigger now, and we were still miles from it.

"There's no turning back, Xavier. Show me what you've been doing? Maybe there is something you've forgotten. What are you trying to do?"

He gestured to the ground.

Our rabbit lay unmoving, a bloody wooden sliver beside him. "Why would you do this?"

"I was trying to heal it." He held up his hands, which were covered in hair and blood. "It didn't work!"

"Clearly." I ground my teeth. The rabbit's side lifted. At the very least, he was alive.

"What are we going to do, Maggie?" he whispered harshly.

"Go on then. Let me see what you've been trying before our

prop bleeds to death." By the looks of him, he wasn't going to last more than a few minutes.

Xavier fumbled with the gem strapped to his head and the others on the backs of his hands. He picked up his staff. He raised his arms over his head, chanting, then touched the rabbit with the bottom of the staff, nudging. Standing still as a statue, he watched the skies while I watched our furry friend.

"You see? No moonlight and the rabbit . . ." He threw the staff on the ground.

I saw only a frantic soul standing on the precipice of failure or greatness, with a sad rabbit dying at his feet. But pretended I saw something else. "Yes." I picked up the staff. The shaft warm, it felt heavier than usual. What was I going to do? Xavier couldn't keep harming our animals. We didn't have very many, and those we kept had taken time to catch. Time we didn't have. Not to mention barbaric butchery hardly seemed like a stunt that would be a crowd-pleaser. But then I had another thought. "Hold your staff as you did at the tavern."

He took it from me, shifting his hands up and down the shaft, then posed. "Like this, wasn't I?"

I walked around him, adjusting the jewels on his hands, moving the bones in his hair, as if any of it mattered. Ridiculous; if I could, I would've laughed. I yanked a bone harder than necessary.

"Ow! Maggie!"

"Ah. Several of these have come loose. That could be the issue. Have you removed any?"

"Yes!" He pulled one from his pocket. "It fell off." He pressed it into my palm.

"Kneel down." I glanced into the dark skies.

He did, and I retied the bones, securing them. Clouds rolled over a thumbnail moon. It was waxing and would be easier to see in the coming days. Perhaps that would help in the Walled City.

"Up. Let's do this exactly as we did that night. Your back was to me. And you, uh, had your eyes closed the *whole* time."

"Ah! Yes! I did." Xavier turned, lifting the staff. He slammed his eyes shut, then began singing his mystical words.

I held my hand up. A crescent-shaped moonbeam landed on the center of my palm. An intense warmth ran through me. My breath turned frosty and visible. My ears buzzed with a monotone hum.

This was it, the way I felt in the tavern, only stronger. More powerful, and it felt good.

I stifled a laugh. "Louder, Xavier. You were much louder!"

As his voice grew in volume and pitch, I fell on my knees, setting one hand on the bottom of Xavier's cloak's train and the other over the rabbit's wound. My heart hammered a thunderous beat, terrified that any minute the soldiers would come to find us.

I closed my eyes for the briefest of seconds. The wound sliced deep but was already knitting together. When I looked, the rabbit hopped up, scooting beside my feet. I traced his fur with my fingers, the moonlight gilding his outline.

"Are you seeing this, Maggie?" Xavier's eyes were open. He stared at the brilliant light cascading over his shoulder, then at the rabbit, alive and well at our feet.

"Yes! You did it, Xavier!" I stood, moving my hand to his arm. Light shifted, skating down his arm, up the staff, hitting the gem. The facets broke the beam, as they did in the tavern. Blue droplets landed on trees bristling in the breeze. "So beautiful. This is what the audience will cheer for, Xavier. You don't need to sacrifice our animals this way. Draw the moonlight and put on a glorious show of light."

He hummed, intrigued.

Twigs cracked. Our rabbit spooked, scurrying into the woods, getting away.

"Xavier! They're coming!"

Raleigh and several other soldiers hurried into the glen, carrying torches.

"Look at that!" one cried.

Sliding farther behind Xavier, I peeked in their direction, worrying about having to find our stupid rabbit before morning. I could suddenly feel his fur beneath my fingers.

The soldiers stared at Xavier, mouths open.

"What is that?" one of them asked.

"It's a rabbit!" another said, pointing at Xavier's shoulder, where my hand happened to be.

I looked up. My breath caught. A glistening rabbit drawn in moon threads stared down at me from atop my hand on

Xavier's shoulder. Xavier's head jerked, his eyes finding the ghostly aura. He squeaked in surprise.

"I don't remember giving either of you permission to leave camp!" Raleigh barked.

I glared at him. The sparkling rabbit jumped off Xavier, following my gaze, launching in Raleigh's direction. Before it reached him, on instinct, I closed my hand, breaking the connection with the light. Darkness fell like a closing curtain. The delicious scent of fresh snow lingered in its wake.

"Was that a ghost?" one of them asked in the hushed silence.

"Nah. It was *magic*," another said. The awe in his voice unmistakable. It was there in their stares at Xavier too.

"See?" I whispered to Xavier. "This is what the king will want to see. When he meets you, he will truly believe in magic."

Wind rustled the leaves.

"Get back to camp. I'll escort them," Raleigh ordered, taking a torch from the soldier beside him. His gaze firmly on me, he padded toward us. "Don't know what sorts live in these parts, but I'm sure they're not used to whatever that was. Time for sleep. Been enough rehearsing the past two nights. If you're not ready now, Xavier the Ambrosius, you never will be."

FOUR

GRIFFIN

Griffin couldn't sleep. He went to the practice fields beside the armory before dawn, strapped on his leather breastplate, gauntlet cuffs, and shin guards, and started running. It had been three long days since the attempt on the king's life. Three long days since Jori had left. And three long days since Halig and Capp had been taken by the guards to be interrogated.

Bradyn was inconsolable.

With Jori gone, Griffin had no one to turn to for help. For the first time in his life, he felt useless, and didn't like it.

According to the physician, for the mushrooms to work that fast, a full cup, dried and ground, had to have been mixed into the ale. And Bradyn claimed that the king's food and drink were tasted in the kitchens before being brought to him.

It was brought to the table already poisoned by someone between the buttery and the chamber.

An assassin. King Umbert had been right. His life was in danger, but not from Malcolm. The Northman had willingly poured his own drink from the pitcher. If the dogs hadn't drunk the poison first, he would be dead now too. Wouldn't he? Or had he done that for show, believing the king would drink it when he returned?

Griffin had seen the surprise in Malcolm's face. He hadn't done it, but then who had?

Griffin rolled his wrist, swinging his sword downward, stabbing the ground. It was opening day of the tournament. He had to set all that aside. He needed to put on a good show, win over the crowd as the king asked, and for that he had to be focused on the task at hand only. That's what he had told Bradyn about the melee. Now he had to heed his own advice.

"Focus on what you can control."

The cold fall air stiffened his limbs. The only remedy was to put them to task so that he was ready for the monster to come. He ran harder, faster, until he could no longer feel resistance in his legs or lungs. He used a rough rock to toughen his calluses to keep his sword's grip from slipping. Then he took practice swings, thrusting upward in different angles until his arms no long protested the awkward position.

Two hours later, Griffin made his way over the bridge and into the performers' tunnel, ready for day one in the arena. The melee had started. The field was carved into small squares for matches. He stood at the end for a few minutes, staring down at the event. Bradyn was down there in the midst of the cracking wooden swords, somewhere, as was every boy from ten to sixteen who wanted to show off burgeoning skills, or reveal the lack thereof. Victors moved square to square, sparring to disarm each other until the champion was the last man standing in the center.

Griffin tried to watch to the end, but the tunnel flooded with actors for the play that followed. He was forced to back up into a horde of guards blocking the stairs that led to the dais, and the king. Griffin wondered if Jori was up there now. High time he had made it back.

Rousing applause and a horn let Griffin know a winner had taken the circle. The actors shifted, making room for the boys to exit the lift swiftly so they could enter. It would take several trips.

"Who is it?" Griffin called to Bradyn, who was sidestepping through the actors to get to him.

Bradyn shook his head. "If you're asking if it was me, it wasn't, my lord. Got walloped by Wallison in the first square, the lard ass. He took the prize. How unlucky is that? I mean, who puts me against that man-child first off?"

Wallison, the beastly son of Sir Wallis of the Top, lumbered into the tunnel, his sword resting on his shoulder as if he were going to keep it as a souvenir. At fourteen he was nearly as tall as Griffin. He raised his sword over his head in triumph, looking for a reaction from Griffin.

Griffin aimed a finger at him. "Well done, Wallison."

Bradyn hit Griffin on the arm. "He finished off Zac by farting on his head so loud His Majesty heard it on the balcony. Laughed at him heartily. Zac will never live it down."

Griffin laughed. "Serves Zac right for ending up under Wallison's arse."

"Oof!" A wooden sword swung playfully in Griffin's direction, wielded by young Master Zac himself. "One day you'll pay for that, Sir Griffin," Zac laughed, tossing his wooden sword at him. Griffin ducked, letting it hit the wall. The boys surrounded Griffin and began cheering his name. The actors joined in.

"The king's champion will triumph again!" Wallison called. "Grif-fin! Grif-fin! Grif-fin!"

Griffin's chest swelled with pride while his cheeks burned with embarrassment. He couldn't imagine anyone cheering his name when he'd first arrived in the Bottom. Kicked by soldiers more times than he could count, disrespected by every noble family. Now surrounded by admiration from the very sons of those who looked down on him.

"Foundling Son of the Bottom!" Thoma bellowed at him.

Dres trailed after him. The two gaped at Griffin as if they were meeting a celebrity-stranger and not someone they'd known since he was eight. Both shorter by a head than Griffin, Thoma was fair, with a dimple in his chin and an always-warm smile, while Dres was dark haired with caterpillars for eyebrows, and a permanent furrowed brow that made him look perpetually angry.

"You look like a gladiator," Thoma teased, shoving his shoulder.

"He looks like a Topper. Fighting with all that on," Dres

chortled. "You should go out naked, like our ancestors."

Thoma slugged Dres on the back. "Have you seen the northern girls on the balcony? I've seen him naked. He'd never have a chance with them if he did."

Griffin grimaced, mortified. This was the last thing he needed right now. The guards by the door to the king's balcony glared at them. They weren't supposed to be in here. They weren't supposed to sit in the Top sections at all, but there was no way they would make it to the Middle, let alone the Bottom before the match began. Griffin didn't need to ask their intentions to know they planned to do something they shouldn't.

"Get out!" Hugo yelled at them. "Griffin doesn't need you blathering fools wasting his time. He has a match!"

"Ah! Finally, the most important man in the Walled City!" Griffin's heart filled at the sight of his former employer.

"We'll find you after!" Thoma said.

"Not if he's dead, we won't." Dres laughed again.

Hugo hustled toward him, carting a new axe, bumping a few boys who refused to get out of his way. The blacksmith was the closest thing Griffin had to family—a hulking human, with little hair on face or head, and hands forever caked in soot. Terrifying at first, Griffin had realized the truth of him quickly. He was as bighearted as they come.

"Here you go, lad!" He handed over the axe. "Double-edged like you asked. Hickory handle. Strongest there is."

Griffin examined the edges. No one sharpened a blade as finely as Hugo. Griffin rotated the handle through his warm-up moves so as not to kill his cheering friends, finding it perfectly balanced. "Thank you. Truly. It's perfect."

"Do us proud," the smith called, leaving as the play began.

Griffin had seen it more times than was necessary, but after the melee brigade left the tunnel to find seats, he grew restless and ambled over to watch the folly. Grim-faced actors marched side by side around the arena. They played the part of a fictitious army heading into a grand reenactment. A bard told the legend of how King Umbert gained his throne and the players moved around the field in their predictable patterns. Only after the final moments of King Umbert's victory were cheered would Griffin finally find out who this year's competition would be.

Five pillaging draignochs were played by counts of six. Three were stacked on shoulders to reach the height of the head. The others were in a line filling out the body and tail. Fabric and wooden posts finished the costume. There was "the king" without his crown, "Egrid" before his legs were broken, and fifty more to represent the noble houses and their armies, who traveled with them.

Wooden spears sailed, hitting the puppet draignochs—and the beasts fell, wriggling for attention, then stilled. The throngs' cheers held until the actor-king was crowned and he had taken his oath of loyalty and protection to his people and his lands. This was the reason the people loved King Umbert, and always would. He had truly saved everyone, both in the Walled City and the Hinterlands, from the beasts that plagued the land.

"Some show," Cornwall chuckled, sounding unimpressed.

Griffin was surprised to find Lady Esmera's youngest brother in the tunnel. "Why didn't you join the melee with the other boys?"

"Because I have been chosen." Cornwall set a hand on the pommel of his sword, his grin stretching from ear to ear.

"Chosen for what?" Griffin asked.

"I wasn't finished!" Malcolm stormed into the tunnel and pushed his young brother up against the stone wall, holding him there. "You're going to refuse. You're not ready."

Griffin's jaw dropped. "Malcolm, you're not saying—"

"My name is on the list. That's right, Sir Griffin." Cornwall shoved Malcolm off him. "And I *am* ready, brother. I've heard all the reasons you can come up with. My age. My size—"

"None of that matters," Griffin said, because it was the truth.

"Out of the mouth of a champion." Cornwall nodded in appreciation to Griffin, then walked to the arena's entrance, turning his back on his brother. "You're afraid I'll overshadow you, Malcolm."

Malcolm's glare aimed at Griffin was filled with bitter disappointment.

"What do you want me to say?" Griffin asked Malcolm.

"That he is not battle-proven. That he is unready!" Malcolm growled.

Griffin shrugged. "That wouldn't have helped. Your brother is impulsive and stupid."

"Hey!" Cornwall's retort died there because he could think of nothing more to say.

Griffin nailed him with a stern glare, then looked back at his looming brother. "Would *you* drop out, once chosen? I know I wouldn't."

"No," Malcolm confessed.

The lift returned full of actors, ending the conversation.

Two more joined them as the actors rushed out. Silas and Oak. Somewhere in his twenties, Silas was a member of the elite guard who secured the castle. Silas, with sun-bleached hair and weathered skin from hours on the practice field, nodded in greeting to Griffin. His family was one of the most highly regarded in the Top. His father was Ragnas, the chieftain of the East before the realms folded under King Umbert. It took a title last year to earn that nod. Griffin graciously returned it.

Griffin chortled. "Zac did all right, then, Silas. Made it to the final match."

"My brother will never live that down." Silas wickedly laughed.

Griffin wasn't surprised that King Umbert had chosen him. Besides Malcolm, Silas was the only other who posed a risk to Griffin's title.

Oak, on the other hand, would die in his first draignoch match. Closer to Griffin's age, Oak was too fat to get out of his own way. He too was of a noble family, from the West, which was the only reason Griffin could think the king would've chosen him. Griffin thought of warning him off, telling him to wait another year, or ten, but like Cornwall, he would never heed his advice. Griffin was the enemy.

All of them wore rich linens and fur-lined tunics. Only Griffin was in armor. He would have to truly fight today.

The king must have raised his arms, for the crowd silenced. "People of the Walled City, Sir Griffin, our champion, will have four seeking to unseat him. Brave knights who will face the vicious draignochs, trying to best his performances against the beasts. And let us not forget the skills matches, favor added for each spear thrown farther than Sir Griffin's, each arrow flying truer in targeted strikes, daggers and axes, and anything else I think to add to the start of the days. Now, stand with me as I call out the chosen's names."

The stands shook. The chatter with guesses over who would be coming out of the tunnel escalated. The lift waited to be used as a balcony, holding the chosen high enough for all to see.

King Umbert silenced them again. "It gives me great joy to count both sons of Laird Egrid of the North among the four: Sir Malcolm and Sir Cornwall."

A blare of trumpets. Cornwall dashed onto the lift, not waiting for Malcolm. Sporadic applause met them. This was all the Walled City was willing to give the brothers from the North today.

Silas followed Malcolm. And finally Oak, who stumbled along the way, earning the first boos of the tournament.

Then it was Griffin's turn.

"And lastly, your champion, Sir Griffin."

Unified stamping sounded like thunder. Griffin waited a few long seconds before coming out, earning the loudest of cheers. He gave a gracious bow to the king and waved to the people. He rolled his shoulders in anticipation of his fight. But King Umbert made no move to announce it. He sat, the tankard in his hand being refilled as the throngs continued chanting Griffin's name.

King Umbert waited patiently, letting the crowd determine the pace. If they wanted to raise their champion's name to whatever gods roamed above, then His Majesty was pleased to let them.

On the dais, beside his father, Prince Jori raised a fist in his direction, which Griffin returned. The people saw and whistled their approval at Jori, heralding fists to him as well. This was what the king wanted, for the people to see that Griffin and Jori were a united front. The future of the realm safe with a strong king, a capable prince, and a champion at their side. Déjà vu struck Griffin all at once. This day last year when it was Raleigh standing in the arena, the king's champion. Since his loss to Griffin, he couldn't remember the last time he'd seen his mentor at the king's table for a meal. And here he was, so overlooked he had yet to return from his journey into the Hinterlands.

The other challengers were escorted back inside the tunnel, leaving Griffin alone with the marshal, Duncan, on the lift as it slowly descended.

Duncan ran the armory, but today, and for the rest of the tournament, he also served as referee. Dressed in a red tunic and a matching leather cap with a long white feather plume, halfway down he lifted his arms, silencing the crowd. "People of the Walled City, your champion is granted the honor of the first match."

Adrenaline coursed. Griffin stretched his neck, then put his helmet on. When the lift hit the arena's floor, Griffin pulled his sword. He picked up his axe in his other hand and jogged into the ring until he stood beside the beast's exit point. There, he dropped his axe and raised his sword, giving the signal to raise the iron door.

Griffin centered his attentions on the beast's exit point. The throngs' cries faded to fuzzy and distant hums, drowned out by the steady rhythm of his own heartbeat. His nerves buzzed like a dragonfly he could never kill, so instead he ignored the bastard.

Rusty chains slid against pulley wheels, screeching with each turn, yanking the iron gate upward. The beast roared at the crowd before running into the ring.

"A cowcodile!" one young boy yelled. That was what many called draignochs, and the name was somewhat appropriate.

The beast looked like a fatted cow crossed with the giant croc-odile, a monster brought back from a distant land that had been stuffed and exhibited in the palace hall.

Almost thirty feet long from the tip of its toothy snout to the top of its heavy tail, this particular draignoch was on the larger side, likely close to two hundred stones in weight. A scaled monster with teeth the length of swords and curved claws that could cut through flesh and bone as easily as a freshly sharpened blade slicing through cake.

The humorous name the children tagged on draignochs didn't account for a third feature that was neither cow nor crocodile: a small pair of leathery wings. A draignoch was too heavy to fly, of course, but furiously flapping those wings could lift the front half of its torso from the ground. Griffin had seen many knights crushed under the incredible weight.

Griffin summoned his anger. His mother's last cries echoed in his ears. His father's final breath, taken in his arms, flashed before his eyes. Vengeance always tasted bitter when Griffin stood against a draignoch in the arena. He spat loudly, catch-ing the draignoch's attention as he stepped out of the shadows and into the creature's full view.

The wings went to work immediately, lifting the mon-ster up on its hind legs, raising its head nearly thrice Griffin's height. The beast opened its jaws wide—displaying a maw that could bite the head off a man with ease. The draignoch landed on all fours beside him. Griffin spun out to the side. Its head craned to strike Griffin but wasn't fast enough to catch him. He leaped, swiping his blade, cutting deep across the draignoch's sensitive wing.

The creature's screeching elicited startled cries from the crowd in response that were quickly drowned by rousing cheers.

"Yes!" King Umbert's thunderous roar was the loudest of them all.

Griffin raised his sword to deliver a harder blow, but the draignoch struck first, sweeping the injured wing, using its claw like a morning star.

The first hit knocked Griffin's helmet off. The second sliced his cheek. The opened gash bled, forming rivers in the deep grooves of the U branded on his chest plate. Before Griffin could recover, the draignoch's spiked arm belted his sword out of his grip, sending the weapon flying into the middle of the ring and driving a spike through his hand. Miraculously missing bone in his palm, it tore the gauntlet right off when the draignoch ripped it out.

The throngs fell silent in shock and horror.

Burning agony spread like wildfire through Griffin's hand. He shoved it beneath his underarm and bit his lip hard to keep from screaming bloody murder.

He was losing—and losing wasn't an option. The king and Jori were counting on him. Griffin stumbled backward, leaving a trail of blood from his cheek. The tip of his boot collided with the sharp edge of his sword's pommel. Griffin touched the grip at the same time the draignoch's tail struck him across the backs of his knees, knocking him forward, gathering him in close for a killing bite. Then the bastard stepped on the blade before Griffin could pull it from the ground.

"Keep the damn sword." Griffin rolled toward his axe.

The draignoch chased after him, its mouth inches from the back of Griffin's head. Two nerve-racking passes, and Griffin's hand at last found the wooden axe handle. "There you are . . ."

He reversed, half rolling, half scrambling back the other way, beneath the snapping mouth, past the uplifted front legs and through the draignoch's back legs as the beast flopped down. Before the draignoch could crush him, Griffin snapped off a heavy backhand and felt a satisfying jerk when the blade struck hard bone.

"Lucky swing!" Cornwall called from the dais.

Griffin couldn't agree more. Taking the axe with him, he rolled out and jumped to his feet.

The draignoch stumbled sideways, leaving a trail of steaming gray blood that mixed with Griffin's own. He flung the axe end over end at the draignoch to keep it back long enough so that he could retrieve his sword.

The draignoch fell on all fours, turning to snap at the axe. In a single move, Griffin rushed forward, jumping into the air as high as he could while at the same time flipping the sword, blade down. With all the strength he had left, he buried the blade deep into the draignoch's back.

The beast reared, tossing Griffin. But the deed was done.

It tried to growl, but more groaned. Then, staring hatefully at Griffin the entire way, it fell over on its side.

With the help of his boot, Griffin yanked his sword out and stabbed it in the back again.

The crowd jumped to their feet, chanting his name.

The draignoch's chest heaved, gasping for breath. Its tongue darted in and out. A slow moan escaped its throat. Death was imminent, but not fast enough for the crowd—or for Griffin.

"Kill it!" a man yelled.

Griffin looked at King Umbert, waiting for a thumbs-up or -down, a tradition left over from the gladiator pits. A thumbs-up, and Griffin could kill the draignoch because his performance was deemed a win by the king. A thumbs-down meant Griffin would have to stop no matter how much he wanted to kill it. It would mean the king thought his performance was lacking, and he should have done better. It would also give the others confidence that he was vulnerable. Griffin had never received a thumbs-down.

And the king . . .

. . . didn't give him one now.

Griffin drove the blade in the draignoch's jaw, stabbing his sword so hard the tip of the blade cracked through the skull.

The light went out of its eyes as it expelled its last breath.

"Grif-fin! Grif-fin!" His name echoed through the arena.

Griffin stood taller and turned with his fist raised to all four sides of the field, then he bowed to the king.

The crew hurried into the arena, lugging thick ropes tied to a team of sixteen horses. Griffin retrieved his sword before they dragged it away with the carcass. He rode the lift sitting, his feet dangling off the end, waving to the crowd.

Prince Jori jogged out of the doorway to the balcony, into the tunnel to meet him. He wrinkled his nose at Griffin's bloody cheek. "It's a good thing your face is already scarred, otherwise that gash would be noticeable."

Griffin laughed, then cringed. His face stung.

His hand prickled, painfully regaining feeling, his palm slippery with blood from the spike's stab. A week was all he had for it to heal, before his next turn in the ring. His stomach tightened with stress, knowing it wouldn't be enough.

"Quite a performance." Jori gave him a brotherly pat on the shoulder. "Next time, though, I think you should use my father's dagger to finish him off. That would be a show."

Jori worshipped Griffin's Phantombronze dagger because it was meant for him. King Umbert rewarded Griffin with it when he saved Jori's life. It was the day everything changed for him.

Hugo had sent him to deliver a new weapon made for the king to the fortress. He passed it off to a servant, and afterward, cut through the Great Hall on his way out because he had never seen it before. Griffin didn't believe in fate, but he did, fully, in luck. Luck had brought Jori wandering into that same hall at that same time, swinging a hatchet around as if it were a toy, and greater luck still had placed another man in hiding behind a tapestry, armed with a sword.

The assassin jumped Jori, getting his arm over the young

prince's chest and his blade against his neck.

Jori dropped the hatchet and pissed himself.

Griffin used his dagger to pierce the assassin's kidney before the would-be murderer could slice Jori's throat.

The king gifted him the Phantombronze dagger as a reward. Jori said he understood, Griffin deserved it for his bravery; nevertheless, he brought it up whenever he had the opportunity, which Griffin found amusing. The prince had everything, and Griffin nothing, except the one object the king had gifted him.

"*My* dagger, you mean," Griffin countered. "And I would never taint a thing of such beauty with draignoch blood."

Dres and Thoma jaunted over the Toppers' bridge.

"Sir Griffin, the mighty Draignoch Slayer!" Thoma cried.

Dres tried to enter the tunnel, but the guards pushed them back. "Return to your seats . . . in the Bottom."

"It's all right. They're with me," Griffin called.

"You heard the champion. We're with him," Dres said, but the guards continued to shove.

Jori shook his head. "Griffin, we can't keep affording them special attentions."

Griffin squinted. "Why not? They were allowed here last year."

"Things have changed. After what happened *recently* . . ." Was Jori saying this had to do with the assassination attempt? If so, there was little room to argue.

"Sorry, mates. I'll see you later, yeah?" Griffin bellowed.

"What? You can't be serious," Dres spat.

"It's fine. Fine! We understand." Thoma pushed Dres away from the entrance.

"What? Suddenly he's too good to be seen with the likes of Bottom feeders? *He* is a bloody Bottom feeder! See that, Thoma, moves in the castle, and now he thinks he's too good for us!" Dres yelled for Griffin's benefit.

That was all Griffin heard. The guards pushed them away and would make sure they didn't return.

"Stop looking so ill. You are too good for them," Jori added.

"It's all good. Dres will act like a bitter ass for a while, but a few tankards of ale on me and he'll change his tune. So, fruitful journey, I hope? After forcing me to eat with your betrothed." Jori had refused to tell him where he was going or what he was doing.

"Better you than me." The prince rolled his eyes. "Yes. We returned with two prizes. One we expected and one rather unexpected. The unexpected, you will see tonight." Jori's beaming smile was enough to give away what this treasure was.

Griffin groaned. "Have you brought another lousy magician to perform?" Jori smirked in reply. Griffin rolled his eyes this time. "You're obsessed, man. Magic isn't real."

"And I'm telling you, Griff. Xavier is the Ambrosius. This man will change your mind." Jori threw a heavy arm over Griffin's sore shoulders. "And he has the most"—the prince paused to choose his words carefully—"intriguing assistant. I don't know what it is about her, but I am very glad she is soon to be within our walls."

Griffin paused at the wet linen hanging just inside the exit of the tunnel and wiped the blood off his sword. "I wouldn't let Lady Esmera hear you say that."

"Lady Esmera only cares about her wedding. Which she will have soon enough. I had been hoping you, as my friend, would have found a way to delay that a little for me?" Jori griped. "Perhaps given her the poison meant for my father?"

"If I only had known, I would have switched the glasses."

Griffin laughed, but Jori didn't.

"Sire!" Perig called, stealing the prince's attention.

"Excellent! It's here." Jori clapped his hands and jogged toward the gamekeeper.

Griffin hurried after him. "What's here?"

Jori walked backward, speaking to him. "I found a present for you in the Hinterlands."

Perig was the third gamekeeper in the last year. He and his predecessors were all called Perig, a title coined because the king only remembered the name of his first gamekeeper, who had been dead for a decade. His head bandaged, his clothing covered in dried blood, his limp more pronounced than usual, he looked as if he'd gone into battle and barely escaped with his life.

"From the looks of Perig, I'm not sure I want it. What is it?"

"A very special draignoch."

Griffin slowed. "Are you telling me this beast was caught in the wild?"

"Oh yes. First in a very long time. But this one . . ." Perig sounded almost giddy. "This one is different. Bigger. Stronger. Smarter!" He grew more animated with each boast, waving his three-fingered hand.

"Smarter," Griffin laughed. "If it's so smart, how did it end up trapped?"

"Because it stopped fighting," Perig explained.

Griffin shook his head in disbelief. "Draignochs don't stop fighting until they're dead."

"This one did," Jori added. "Bested half a regiment. And then suddenly just stopped."

"You witnessed this?" Griffin asked.

"I did," Jori affirmed.

Griffin shook his head. It was impossible to believe.

"Maybe it decided it wanted to see the Walled City." Perig laughed at his own jest in a way that made Griffin wonder if the boy had gone mad like his predecessor.

"I must go with Perig. Make sure all goes well with its transfer into its cage in the Oughtnoch," Jori said to Griffin.

"I'll come." If this creature was to be his next match, and was so changed from the typical draignoch, Griffin needed to see it.

"No, no. King's orders. He told me not thirty minutes ago that no one is to see this draignoch until its first match." His brown eyes and his grin filled with mirth. "Besides, your cheek needs attending. See the physician."

Griffin's jaw set at Jori ordering him around. "My cheek will wait. I need to see that draignoch, Jori."

Jori started walking across the bridge toward a soldier holding two saddled horses, shaking his head.

"You heard the prince, Sir Griffin!" Perig cackled. "But rest assured, we have finally found you a worthy challenge."

FIVE

MAGGIE

The next morning, the soldiers packed up quickly, in a hurry to get home. After three long days in the wagon, I considered walking, but the last part of the journey was entirely uphill.

Xavier's demeanor changed overnight. He exuded confidence instead of panic, giving me hope that we would pass through the gates of the Walled City without another incident.

"Tonight, I will perform before King Umbert. When he sees my power, do you know what that will mean for me? I will remain in the Walled City. And you with me. No more eating scraps and sleeping in the woods. We will have everything we ever wanted for the rest of our lives!"

I was conflicted. Tales of the luxurious Walled City reached far and wide. Its entertainments, its opportunities, its delights. Yet, from the outside, the Walled City looked like a prison.

The wall itself was forty feet tall. Forged with stone and steel. Impenetrable. Unclimbable, and I couldn't see a single gate in or out. The city was completely hidden behind it, except for the crown where King Umbert's fortress was perched, built on the flat rocks that sealed an ancient volcano.

People said that King Umbert wanted the Hinterlands to know he was watching them, like a god from above. Others believed he built his keep on high so that no one could attack the city without him seeing them well before they reached it. Either way, it was an imposing sight.

I could smell the place too, long before we reached it. The putrid odor wafted from a wide moat of still water swarmed by flies. Parts overflowed, running down the hill we had climbed, poisoning everything in its path. All that should have been green was lifeless and brown. Neither Raleigh nor any of the other men gave notice. Xavier pinched his nose. I gagged and coughed, trying not to vomit.

"This way," the lead rider called, changing course, following the curve of the giant wall.

We rode for another hour, circling the solid base until we came upon a field littered with northern soldiers. I'd seen them before, when Xavier and I had performed in a small village close to the moors. I recognized their green-and-blue tartan sashes worn over their heavy fur-lined cloaks. Many fires burned. Spits spun, roasting meats while men drank from large tapped kegs with plenty more to spare stacked in a pyramid. Strange. They were Northmen, and they planned to be here awhile.

A few minutes later we finally came to an entrance, a metal portcullis so heavy it felt like it took a lifetime for cranking pulleys to raise it. A foreboding wind escaped with a fierce whistle. Dorn hesitated. I didn't blame her. I thwacked her, getting her moving. Her reluctant rattling snort did not stop until we were on the other side and there was no turning back. The entrance was only large enough for a single wagon to pass through at a time. As soon as the last soldier came through, the gate fell with a loud bang, sealing us inside.

"Is that gate the only one?" I asked Sir Raleigh.

He slowed his horse to ride beside us. "Yes."

"And is it always closed?"

"Yes."

"I see. What if I wanted to leave?"

Xavier grumbled beside me. "Leave? Impertinent every step of the way! I would tell Sir Raleigh to ignore your foolish questions, but I'm sure he's learned to do just that."

"Not at all. Best to set expectations. You simply ask, Maggie." He smiled as if that was somehow a comfort.

"And if the answer is no? I'm trapped in here? All these people are trapped inside that monstrous wall?"

He laughed and changed the subject.

Raleigh explained that crags and cliffs separated the Bottom from the Middle, and the Middle from the Top. But that wasn't all I noticed separating them.

In the Bottom, tiny shacks made from scrap wood served as shelters for so many they spilled out and into the road. Many of the dwellings stood in a thick layer of filthy runoff from above. The ducts carrying refuse to the moat outside the wall overflowed here too. Children slid through mud for sport on their way to answer the call of barking masters. Most looked gaunt, but not so starved as those in the South.

A blanket of black soot hovered above a large section, the bitter air from ovens heating metal. There was clanking and banging too. It was the largest smithy I'd ever seen.

Lost in a maze of changing directions and connected buildings, I heard *her*.

The draignoch.

Her voice floated on the gentle breeze, fanning the roadside flames.

The draignoch had made it to the Walled City, and so had I. And she was close.

I smiled. I wanted to jump out, to race to her. But I knew I wouldn't get very far without knowing which way to go.

Raleigh noticed my head flipping back and forth. "The tournament opened today."

"The draignochs," I wondered aloud. "Where do they keep them?"

The corners of Sir Raleigh's mouth hinted at a smile. "You do ask a great many questions. Doesn't matter, not to you." He kicked his horse, pulling ahead, my frustration growing with every step his horse took.

It did matter. It was the only thing that mattered.

Frustrated beyond measure as I was, there was only one thing to do.

As we crossed another road, I shifted in my seat to slide out, hoping the heavy shade from the setting sun would mask my escape.

More soldiers folded in behind us, Moldark leading the pack.

Xavier grabbed my wrist. "Where do you think you're going?"

There was no possible escape route. "Nowhere. I'm just tired of sitting." I turned around quickly before Moldark could get a good look at me.

As we left the Bottom, the road leveled, smoothed by the introduction of shaved cobblestones. There were no signs of nature in the Bottom, no trees or grass, only muck and stench. But as we rose out of the depths, patches of green emerged between the cobblestones. Torches lit the road, giving the passage a romantic glow. People were on the streets here too. Children squealed, playing chase around drunk revelers, who scooted out of the way while toasting their silver mugs at our procession.

The road rose sharply, then leveled again, entering a place the likes of which I had never seen before. The Top. Manicured greens outlined in neatly trimmed bushes greeted us at each enormous dwelling we passed. Intricately carved stone sconces and bronze knockers decorated iron doors.

A vacant space gave an open view of another part of the Top, just beneath the homes, where the king's soldiers sparred and rode in sprawling fields. Spectators watched from the sidelines, cheering them on. Children wearing fine linens and fur cloaks ran into the street, waving wooden swords. I thought maybe Xavier's reputation had preceded him, but they moved past our wagon, not seeing us at all. They were here for the soldiers.

In the Walled City, King Umbert's soldiers were heroes. And why not? These children saw them as providers, carting back food and livestock, clothing and silver. They were doing their duty, serving their king, taking their share from the Hinterlands and giving it to them. These children never saw the wake of destruction their heroes left behind, but one day, they would. The day that giant wall came tumbling down.

SIX

GRIFFIN

Griffin woke to pounding on his door. He rolled toward the window and was disappointed to see darkness.

The opening day banquet.

His aching cheek would make it impossible to eat and drink without misery. The physician had cleaned and stitched the wound shut, but there was little to be done with his hand. The numbness now completely worn off, it throbbed incessantly.

Sleep was much more appealing than food.

"Start without me." He covered his head with a pillow.

The door opened so hard it slammed into the wall. "Are you still sleeping?" Jori bounded into the room as if his father had given him the keys to the kingdom.

Griffin flopped onto his back. "No. I'm thinking with my eyes closed."

"My father has called for the ceremonial entrance of the champion and challengers. You are to lead it. Or shall we give that honor to Cornwall since he's already standing in your place?" Jori ripped the soft linen sheets off him. "You do look a mess. Come! Up! Up!" he sang.

"The draignoch used me like a pincushion today, if you didn't notice." Griffin cringed. His face felt tight and the pain still raw. "And what's the matter with you? You're positively perky. After an evening spent with your betrothed, I would've expected griping, pouting, loss of appetite, severe depression." Griffin combed his hair with his fingers, then padded to the wardrobe. "Although, I suppose, why gripe. She'll be all yours in mere days. Permanently."

"Maybe. Maybe not." He winked.

Griffin stopped searching and looked back at him. "Malcolm isn't playing games, Jori. He told me at dinner and again today that he's not happy with the idea of the North being under your father's rule. He's coming for the throne."

"Maybe."

"Maybe? That's all you have to say?" Griffin grabbed the first blue linen shirt he could find and slipped it over his head.

Jori smirked, waggling his eyebrows. "The sorcerer I told you about, Xavier, arrives momentarily."

"Yes. Call them sorcerers when not a single one has ever had a lick of magic."

"Xavier is different. He has something that is real. He *is* a sorcerer." Jori's eyes darkened. "He will be what saves me from marrying Lady Esmera. With magic at my father's side, and mine, the North will come to heel without this ridiculous marriage."

"So that is why. All this time, all the searching . . ." Griffin strapped on his belt. "The magic wasn't an amusement. You've been searching for—"

"A weapon." Jori nodded. Griffin had never seen him quite so grave.

He turned to face the prince. "A bet, then. Over Xavier's *powers*."

Jori's laugh started slow and sinister. "A bet. Are you sure?"

"Are you?" Griffin challenged him.

"Your knife, then." Jori scooped it up from the table, sliding it from its holster. He held it up and examined the sharpness. The candlelight reflected off the inset rubies on the cross guard, but not so much the blade. It absorbed the light, making it stronger. Years working at a smith shop, Griffin never truly understood all the secrets of Phantombronze. Jori turned the grip, reflecting the ground, rendering the blade invisible. It was a very useful weapon, one Griffin would rather not lose. But he would not lose it—because magic wasn't real.

"My knife, against a view of the new draignoch."

"My father would kill me." Jori slid the knife back in its holster.

"Oh, he would not. You're his only heir."

His jaw shifted from side to side, mulling it over. "Very well." He held his hand out for them to shake on it.

Griffin didn't take it, not yet. "A caveat."

"Are bets with you always this complicated?" Jori held on to the blade as if he had won already.

"I have your permission and your protection from the king's wrath to put the supposed sorcerer to a sincere test," Griffin added, reaching his hand out.

"You always put them to the test. My father, the noble families, we all live for your jibes at the poor pathetic souls."

Griffin crossed his arms. "If my knife is at stake, I mean to be a right bastard." He held his hand out to Jori.

The prince laughed. "I will make sure to explain to my father if he gets upset in any way." Jori shook it and handed Griffin his knife. "Bring it with you. I'll expect payment as soon as the performance is over."

"As will I," Griffin said.

Jori threw open the doors. Six guards folded in behind them as the prince set a fast pace through a drafty corridor that led to the stairs, that then led to another hallway and another flight of stairs. Damn castle. It was a maze.

He could hear the music and chatter from the party below as they descended the stairs, and see the other competitors lined up beside the closed doors to the Great Hall. Griffin cradled his injured hand as they reached the reception area.

Jori paced toward a man who looked . . . the only word for it was *insane*. Bones tied in his silver hair, his dark eyes shaded with kohl, his robe so long it swept the floor. Standing beside him was a young woman no older than Griffin. She wore a wool dress made from an old blanket, tied with rope along the waist to give it some kind of shape on her thin frame. Her dark hair fell down her back in long delicate curls. Her eyes roamed the room, stopping first on the stuffed cheetah, then the crocodile.

As Jori and the man spoke, she padded slowly across, to the cheetah. Her delicate hand swept the stiff spotted fur on its back.

She glanced over her shoulder, catching Griffin staring. He'd never seen such beautiful eyes before. To call them simply blue would be insulting. They sparkled in the torchlight, like sapphires. Her attention returning to the animal, her brow knit.

Griffin moved next to her. "A cheetah," he said, answering her unasked question. "And that"—he nodded to the long-tailed reptile—"is a crocodile. Gifts brought to King Umbert from far-off lands. He hunted them for sport and then had them stuffed and placed here for all to admire."

Her lip curled in disgust. "I would've preferred to admire them alive." Her hands swept the back of the cheetah once more. "So graceful. I can imagine how it moves."

Her gaze fell on his scarred face. Griffin's chest tightened. He should introduce himself, but for the first time in his life he felt . . . shaken.

She smelled like the woods after a long rain. "Me too."

Jori walked over to her, claiming her elbow. "Sir Griffin, I see you've met Maggie."

Griffin glanced back at Malcolm and Cornwall, both of whom were staring at Jori's hand on Maggie. Cornwall was standing in Griffin's place in the procession. "I have now, sire.

Excuse me. I believe I'm being usurped by a sniveling moron."

"I believe you are," Jori laughed, then led Maggie toward the strange-looking old man. This was the assistant, then, and that odd man, Xavier, the supposed sorcerer.

"Jori." Griffin sighed his friend's name as he walked away.

"My sentiments exactly." Sir Raleigh appeared beside him. The old soldier's shoulders sat back, and his neck was cocked in such a way that Griffin could tell he had been riding for a long time. "Shouldn't you be over there, whelp?"

"Your favorite whelp, am I not?"

Raleigh didn't rise to the occasion as he usually did. Perhaps nostalgia for last year made him melancholy. His stern expression shifted to Xavier, Jori, and Maggie.

"Last month it was Desiree, the month before that, Duncan's daughter. What was her name? Vivien? Infatuations. He lives for them. But Lady Esmera has arrived," Griffin said. "If that worried look is for the negotiations with the North—"

"The prince has his own mind, Griffin. Nothing is ever settled until the bitter end." He laughed—why, Griffin didn't know. Why was everyone acting so strangely? Was this marriage not the plan all along?

Raleigh jerked his chin toward Cornwall. "Better take your place, champion, before the brat pisses, marking the spot."

Griffin had never seen Sir Raleigh so intense. He did as he asked, walking with determination toward Cornwall, who flinched at the sight of him and stepped back, relinquishing his place without argument.

The drums banged. The doors opened. The crowd stood.

King Umbert was at the far end of the hall. He raised his cup. "Hail our champion, and all who would try to defeat him."

Griffin led them through the Great Hall. The vast room held upward of a hundred, but with so many from the Top of the Walled City invited, it was stretched way beyond capacity. Challengers peeled off to sit with their families. Oak sat with his mother and little sister. At the table beside the king's was Silas's family, including Zac, and his father, Ragnas, and mother, Aofrea. That left Cornwall and Malcolm, who were still with Griffin, heading for the king's table. As if one meal with them wasn't punishment enough.

Two soldiers, who looked as tired as Sir Raleigh, carted in a table, trunk, and screen, setting them in the center, which had been left empty for the entertainment.

Flutes and lyres plucked lively tunes while chatter picked up where it had left off before the king's interruption. By the time Griffin reached the head table, Laird Egrid and the king were regaling the assembly with tales of the draignoch war. Egrid shoved his sleeve up and ran a crooked finger over a long scar.

"Biggest one I ever saw in the wild. I thrust my blade deep in the beast's neck; it should have died at once. But no, not this bastard. It thrashed and cut me from elbow to wrist with its eye tooth."

"Thrust your blade," King Umbert chortled. "We were taking a piss, and the thing came round the tree. You shit your britches and got your nasty slog water all over my boots." His laughter grew until he was forced to suck a sharp breath, holding his side from hysterics. "*I* stabbed the draignoch. *You* were cut by the fang when it fell."

"That's not the way I remember it." Egrid grimaced at King Umbert. Then laughed heartily too.

Behind them, on an added table, guards stood over Buffont, the bald, fat cooker, as he and several of his staff were forced to taste platters of food and swig every pitcher of ale. Bradyn was there too, frowning with worry as he watched his father from the side entrance.

Jori caught up to Griffin. "She's something, isn't she?" He didn't stop to hear Griffin's response. The prince sat down beside Lady Esmera. He lifted her hand to his lips. "You look lovely this evening."

"Why thank you, Prince Jori." The yellow dress with black beading she wore reminded Griffin of a hornet. She wrinkled her nose at him as he sank into the seat between her and Sybil. "That seat is for our brother."

Griffin poured a glass of wine and took a long sip before setting it down before him. "Malcolm is seated next to your father."

Cornwall came to stand behind Griffin. He crossed his arms and hummed, "Move."

Griffin reached over Esmera's plate to the cheese platter and took the largest slice he could find. "I like this seat." He dropped the cheese on the plate before him. "Lady Sybil, would you kindly get me some apple slices?"

Sybil shook her head at him, smirking, as she grabbed two large pieces.

"Jori, my brother shall sit beside me," Esmera griped.

"*My* brother already is." Jori waved at one of the servants standing against the wall. Another chair landed with a thud at the end of the table. "Sir Cornwall, that chair is for you," the prince exclaimed. "A fine chair, finer than even mine, for it has arms. Does that please you?"

Cornwall scowled at him and started to speak but was cut off by the high-pitched squeaks from Sybil pulling the new seat beside her out for him. "Sit, Cornwall. Tell me what it was like to stand in the arena today."

Griffin ate, then drank to soothe the ache in his face that flared as he chewed. Cornwall spoke little of the arena. Instead, he boasted about new armor his father had made for him for the tournament. "New hauberk, much thicker than my other. With a layer of thinner beneath. It's ingenious."

"Mail isn't useful against the draignochs," Griffin said. "Too heavy."

Cornwall pounded the table with his tiny fist. "The fangs carry venom and—"

"The claws too." Griffin held up his injured hand. "Felt the sting this morning, but if you think layers of mail, thinly linked or wide, would stop the pinprick point of a draignoch's claw or fang, let me tell you, you're very wrong. My advice, save your ingenious hauberk for battle. It'll only slow you down in the ring."

"Sir Griffin has a point, Cornwall," Sybil said.

"A sharp point of his own, and one wishing me defeated. I can think for myself, thank you very much." Cornwall got up, taking his cup with him, and padded to the other end of the hall, near Oak.

"He's . . . impertinent," Sybil quipped.

"If you say so." Griffin had other choice words to describe Cornwall, which he kept to himself. He broke off a piece of bread and held it out to Sybil.

She took it and picked at the crust.

She wore another matching dress to her sister's, yellow, without decoration, but she didn't need it. She was more like her brother Malcolm than her sister, with an earthy quality. She had a warmth, though, unexpected, considering the rest of her family.

"I was speaking with Esmera." Sybil nibbled on the bread. "Since her marriage to the prince is to take place so soon, and our families will be joined, I have been informed that I will be remaining in the Walled City."

Griffin was surprised by her crisp wording and disappointed tone. "That displeases you?"

She set the bread down and said so only he could hear, "The thought of being locked up with Esmera in a fortress for the rest of my life makes me want to vomit. At home, at least, I can escape on my horse, but here . . ."

"Understandable," Griffin said. "Yet here we are. About to share the same burden."

"Yes. Forced friends, I suppose." She smiled. "It would be nice to see more of the city, if you have time to show me."

Griffin's stomach tensed. King Umbert's words returned to him. Had he already told Sybil's father that Griffin should marry her? "I'll be busy with the tournament, I'm afraid. But I'm sure one of the guards could escort you."

The corners of her mouth curled into a secret smile. "You don't have to be afraid of me. I don't want to marry you, Sir Griffin."

Griffin swallowed hard.

"But I would like for us to be friends. I don't know anyone here other than my siblings, who are all busy with . . . their own pursuits." Sybil picked at a loose thread on her sleeve, her eyes glossing over, staring at the throngs stuffing themselves at the tables before them.

Griffin knew he was turning red. "Yes. Of course . . . I'm . . ." He couldn't formulate any way of coming out of this with his dignity intact. She had completely disarmed him. "Friends. I'd like that too."

"Good."

The lute and lyre plucking a lively tune faded. It was time for the great Xavier Ambrosius. Time for Griffin to unravel his routine . . . and win a peek at that new draignoch.

Griffin pushed his plate out of the way and moved his cup

too. He wanted to make sure he didn't miss a single move the supposed sorcerer made.

The entertainment entered. Xavier first, arms akimbo, his head turning here and there, bones clackety-clacking in his hair with each pass. His grin creeping wide, his eyes bulging, he looked every bit the part of the mad sorcerer.

In the West, as a small child, Griffin saw many magic-worshippers like Xavier. His parents' farm was near a dense forest. The woods were rumored to be haunted by demons. Some believed the draignochs came from there. Gypsies camped close to them, but never entered. They strung beads and tied bones in their hair. Threw stones to predict futures, telling all what they wanted to hear for the price of a coin.

Xavier's assistant, Maggie, followed him, walking at a steady pace with her hands fisted at her sides.

The guests fell into a familiar pattern of exchanging smirks and whispers as yet another supposed sorcerer made their way to the middle of the tables, where the props had been placed.

The assistant stepped behind the small screen. Her gaze fell on the royal table. Then she gave a hint of a smile.

Griffin returned it, flattered she'd seen fit to steal another glance at him. But then she gave a nod, and he realized that her smile wasn't meant for him. Her gaze was fixed on Jori. And his on hers. Griffin wasn't the only one who noticed. Esmera's lip curled. She cast her hand across the table, spilling her wine.

"Oh my!" She hopped up, but most of it spilled on Jori, soaking his white shirt in red.

Servants rushed to clean up the mess. Jori barely looked put out. He stood, wiped it off, and sat back down, all the while eyeing the assistant.

She, though, had turned around, her attention now on the audience, her face hidden from them.

"Who is that?" Sybil asked Griffin.

"Her name is Maggie," Jori answered for him. "Daughter of Xavier, the Ambrosius."

"You say his name as if it should mean something?" Malcolm asked, taking Cornwall's vacant seat.

"It will mean something," Jori enthused. "Just watch."

Maggie's focus shifted to the windows, passing by each as if looking for something. She stopped on the fourth and closed her eyes. She must've found what she was looking for, but Griffin could see nothing but the waxing moon.

Jori stood. The crowd silenced. "Guests of the Draignoch Tournament and Festival feast . . . I give you Xavier Ambrosius."

"Noble families! Good people of King Umbert's court," Xavier cried so loud it hurt Griffin's ears. "It is an extreme honor to be welcomed in the Walled City, and to be able to perform for you all, and our illustrious king." He bowed to King Umbert, who tilted his head in acknowledgment, then picked his teeth with a chicken bone.

Griffin laughed, catching Xavier off guard. This was too easy. Jori should've known better.

Xavier scowled at him. His lip twitched, then he spun, giving his painful grin to the room. Maggie was looking at Griffin too, a crease forming between her brows. There was a strange weight to her glare, like a boulder sitting on his chest.

Xavier started again. "To all those nonbelievers in the room, I will surely change your mind by the time I'm through, and prove to you once and for all that—"

"Oh, will you get on with it," Griffin groaned for all to hear.

"He's at it again," Oak called out from across the room.

Laughter spread like wildfire. Jori would normally join in with Griffin. But not this time. He coveted Griffin's dagger as much as Griffin wanted to see the draignoch.

"Yes, yes . . . let us get right to it . . ." Xavier bumped into the props table. The stacked-up bowls teetered on the edge, threatening to spill over, but landed back on the table. He took a long deep breath, color returning to his face. Perhaps he was finally ready to begin.

Griffin sat back as the magician did simple sleight-of-hand tricks. He made a coin disappear, then two coins, then ten. All the while the audience remained in a state of stoic, unimpressed silence.

After a bit involving color-changing sticks failed to rouse a single clap, Esmera gave a prolonged yawn. The audience went back to eating and drinking, loudly clanking their glasses down on the tables, gaveling the end of Xavier Ambrosius.

But the sorcerer plowed ahead. This time with upside-down cups and a vanishing rock.

Griffin hissed laughter. The lutes added insult with a playful tune that plunged octaves the very second Xavier showed off the empty cup.

"Come now, give him time," Egrid said. "He's quite fun."

"Laird Egrid, you speak of eternity. None of us are given that kind of time on this earth," Griffin answered.

"King Umbert, you should feed him to the draignochs for lack of originality," Silas yelled.

Maggie glared at Griffin as if it were he who'd said to feed her father to the beasts. Griffin frowned, pointing at Silas, then laughed, turning Maggie furiously red.

Esmera laughed along.

Sybil didn't. She leaned back in her chair, watching Xavier's every move.

Jori looked crestfallen as Xavier dropped a small crate and accidentally kicked the prop table. A crow flew out from underneath, soaring through the open door. "Oh dear . . ." He paled and fell backward on the table.

Bowls toppled.

Sand spilled.

He was a disaster.

The room erupted in laughter.

The king's uttered words were barely audible, so he raised

his voice. "I said enough! Guards, get him out of my sight."

Griffin's foot tapped in excitement. The prize was in his sights.

Prince Jori hopped up. "Father, wait." He held his hand out to Raleigh, who repeated the gesture to the armed guards stationed around the room.

Griffin couldn't fathom why Jori would speak up for this charlatan.

"All we've been doing is waiting," Malcolm bellowed.

"Nice of you to help the cause, Sir Malcolm," Griffin said, waggling his eyebrows at Jori.

Malcolm slapped him on the back, as if they were sudden friends.

Sybil elbowed her brother and Griffin in turn, trying to shush their laughing. "Bullies. Both of you."

"Your Majesty," Xavier said with a quivering voice. "I, um, I'm sorry. My assistant missed her entrance. Clean those things up, Maggie lass. The real magic is about to begin. I promise." He closed his eyes, whispering words Griffin couldn't understand, rubbing his thumbs over the stones on the backs of his hands.

With a look of serious determination, Maggie picked up the bowls and slammed them on the table, one after another, so loudly it silenced the laughter and snide comments. With the last bowl still on the floor, she scooped the sand into it and turned so that Griffin was in full view.

"I believe you've upset the assistant," Esmera sniggered.

"Look at her. Seething like a wild animal."

Xavier's fingers stretched over the top of the bowl, clasping it tightly. Another hand cupped the bottom. "Maggie, let go."

She did.

The bowl and its contents hit Griffin. Expecting sand, he gasped as cold water drenched him.

Esmera screamed and jumped out of her chair.

"Sister, be calm. It is only water," Sybil called.

Griffin couldn't hide his surprise. He shot up to examine the floor.

So did Malcolm. "Where did the sand go?"

"Where *did* the sand go?" Jori smiled at Griffin.

Griffin shook his head at the prince. "Into a hatch at the bottom of the bowl."

Xavier spun round to address the others, who were now, at Griffin's expense, paying much more attention. Even the king. "Yes, fair people of the Walled City, sand to water."

The rebecs and lutes wound together into a triumphant yet irritating series of chords that stretched until Xavier picked up a wooden box. The sorcerer's confidence might've returned, but so did his simple tricks, all ones Griffin had seen before. Using trapdoors and hidden compartments, making silver spoons vanish, and changing a raven to a bunny that hopped up on the table and nibbled on glazed carrots, to the audience's delight.

Griffin leaned over to whisper in Jori's ear. "Jori, I say we go to the Oughtnoch as soon as this is over."

Jori appeared unfazed. He arched a censoring brow. "It isn't over yet."

"Is this ever going to end?" King Umbert growled.

Xavier's face paled. He cleared his throat. "Yes, Your Majesty. We have saved the very best for last."

Maggie handed him his staff.

"Keep your eyes on the gem," Xavier said, touching the top of the staff. His eyes slammed shut. His hands trembled, shaking the staff as he mumbled an unintelligible enchantment.

Maggie placed her hands beneath his, gripping so hard her knuckles turned white. Xavier called out more incomprehensible words, while Maggie's eyes closed.

A moonbeam shot through the loop, striking a jewel in the top of the staff.

Gasps and screeches echoed off the high ceilings.

Blue light flashed, blinding Griffin.

Xavier squealed with delight.

When Griffin's vision cleared, a glistening white cheetah bared its long, sharp teeth at him. But unlike the stuffed creature outside the Great Hall, this one seemed very much alive. Or was it? It appeared to be drawn from moonlight.

"Are you seeing this?" the king cried.

"Is that real?" Sybil gasped.

The room filled with screams. Chairs clattered, falling as everyone jumped out of their seats and backed up. The animal leaped onto the head table, stalking toward Griffin, its paws brushing forks and knives, the mere contact sending them flying in all directions.

"That's not possible . . . ," Griffin uttered in horror as he stood. What was this thing?

The cat jumped off the table, nearly landing on top of Sybil. Malcolm grabbed her, pulling her out of the way just in time.

The cheetah paused only inches from Griffin, its head tilting, its eyes narrowing, ready to pounce. Griffin leaped over the table, but the animal followed.

He heard Jori cackling. "Run, Sir Griffin! Run!"

Griffin did. Out of the room, hoping the bloody thing would stop to eat someone else on the way out. What was he thinking? It wasn't real, was it? It was an illusion, made of light.

Then again . . . maybe it was . . .

In the hallway, Griffin pulled his knife on the fly. The cheetah's glow grew in brightness. It was right behind him, and closing in. He used a column to reverse course. Griffin's arm cocked, his knife's blade down, he stabbed the vicious animal right between the eyes so hard his hand plunged through its head.

It burned—so cold—like the weapon had been chiseled out of a frozen lake.

"Ah!" Griffin ripped his hand and weapon out of the shimmering creature.

The cheetah melted into thousands of glistening stars, which dimmed, then went out.

"Did you see? It was the moon and the stars!" a guard exclaimed.

Everyone in the Great Hall spilled out the door, having witnessed what Griffin had: Xavier performing an inexplicable, miraculous feat of magic.

There was applause, yes, but also whispers of shock and fear. In his heart, Griffin knew there had to be an explanation.

Griffin didn't notice Maggie or Xavier behind him until Maggie shouted, "Xavier, the divine Ambrosius!"

He slammed his staff into the stone floor and took a dramatic bow.

King Umbert rose from his seat. He pointed at Sir Raleigh, then at Xavier, bellowing, "Bring him to me."

Raleigh pushed through the throngs until he was at Xavier's side. Two guards trailing after, he led Xavier back into the Great Hall.

Prince Jori sauntered over to Griffin, wearing a cheeky grin. "I'll take that." He pointed to Griffin's dagger.

"Magic isn't real, Jori."

"How did he do it, then?" Jori's unending smirk grated on Griffin's last nerve. "Hmm? Come now. You make a bold statement like that, then you must have another explanation."

"I . . . I don't know. A powder of some kind."

"A powder?" Jori took the dagger then. Griffin didn't protest.

Attendees rushed to get a look at Xavier's props.

Jori sheathed Griffin's blade, then padded around Esmera,

who had rushed forward with Sybil, to get to Maggie.

"I was worried for a moment," Jori said to her as Griffin moved beside him. Esmera and Sybil completed the circle around her. "Griffin had him flustered."

"*Flustered,*" Maggie repeated, the word and its harsh tone aimed at Griffin. She crossed her arms over her chest. Her sleeve inched up enough for Griffin to see a strange scar on her forearm. It looked as if she had been branded. She caught Griffin staring and pulled the fabric down until it was covered.

"Jori, shall we return to the table?" Esmera hooked her arm through the prince's.

"Lady Esmera, this is Xavier's daughter, Maggie," Jori explained.

"Nice to meet you," Maggie said to Esmera. Yet her gaze traveled the room, never landing long in any one place. To Griffin, it seemed like she was looking for an escape.

"Are you hungry, Maggie?" Griffin asked.

"Yes, you must be after such a long trip here." Jori stepped between him and Maggie, waving at the Great Hall. "Come. Have something to eat."

"No, thank you, Jori."

"Jori?" Esmera snapped. "You mean, Prince Jori? Or Your Highness, or sire?"

"Whichever you prefer, Lady Esmera." Maggie turned her back to them. She faced the courtyard, frowning.

Was she frightened? The fortress gates were closed. Guards were placed every few feet. Nothing was getting in. "It's all right. You're safe here," Griffin explained.

She looked over her shoulder at Griffin with an expression that said he patently was wrong.

Sir Raleigh and three guards padded toward them. "Maggie, your room is ready."

"My room?" She sounded put out. "I'm staying here? In the castle?"

"Yes." Jori smiled. "As is Xavier, of course. Do you think I'd relegate you to a servant's quarters?"

"She *is* a servant," Esmera insisted.

"She doesn't have a title, but she's not a servant," Jori corrected her.

Esmera shook her head. "Titled or not, all daughters are to their fathers. Told what to do and when to do it." Her pensive gaze darted from Jori to Maggie. Griffin knew she could see what he had. Jori wanted Maggie close. "Enough. I'm hungry and this conversation is boring." She turned on her heel, linked arms with Sybil, and retreated into the Great Hall.

"Maggie, you're tired. Perhaps you should retire. Sir Raleigh will take good care of you. I'll have a plate sent to your room straight away. Please excuse me," Jori said, then hurried after Esmera.

Griffin snorted. "Sorry. Lady Esmera is—"

"Not wrong. The prince is a rake," Maggie blurted.

"I'm—"

"An ass? Oh, I know that quite well. Stay away from me if you know what's good for you."

Sir Raleigh chuckled as she walked away. "I would do as she says. Moldark nearly lost a foot to her knife. Deadly accurate strike. Maybe even better than you could've done under the circumstances." He and his guards followed, catching up to her on the stairs, leaving Griffin with a feeling that was pure hatred.

Stay away from me.

Stay away from me.

Griffin heard Maggie's refrain all the way back to his room, planning to do just that.

SEVEN

MAGGIE

I woke up bathed in delicious warm sunlight. It poured through a loophole above the biggest, most comfortable bed I'd ever slept in. My legs wrapped around a soft yellow blanket embroidered with blooming red roses. I had always assumed that the king's affinity for red came from the color of blood, not flowers. But the blossoms were everywhere. And so was the cloying fragrance.

I unraveled slowly. The effects of the long day before had settled deep in my muscles. They ached, protesting even the slightest move. Testing my legs first, I set my feet on the floor and stood slowly, trying to regain my wits.

I was here, in the Walled City, and so was the draignoch.

Posted guards refused to allow me out of my room last night. Sir Raleigh's excuse was that it was for my own safety. Someone had tried to poison the king in Raleigh's absence, and he was taking no chances.

Raleigh expected shock, I suppose, but all I could think to ask was, "Is this the first attempt? The king is so despised, I'd think a great many people had tried before."

At which point he had shoved me through the door and slammed it shut.

Exhausted and overwhelmed by the long day's events, I had fallen into bed, fully dressed. I didn't remember falling asleep. The haze of that kind of deep unconsciousness lingered, fogging my brain as I tried to take in my surroundings.

Coals smoldered in the fireplace. Before it were two chairs with a small table between. An oversized wardrobe and a wide changing screen with dresses draped over the top sat in the far corner of the room. Red, yellow, and blue. They weren't mine. All at once I wondered if I was somehow in someone else's room.

I stared at my fingers, the sensation the moonlight cast dulled since last night, but it was still there. More in the pit of my stomach, like a single drifting snowflake waiting for the blizzard to begin.

The door cracked open. Bony, familiar fingers curled over the door. Xavier poked his head in. "Good. You're awake."

"Whose clothes are these?" I asked, pointing to the dresses.

"Yours. Gifts from the prince." He was pleased.

The bones in Xavier's silver curls had quadrupled overnight, and where there had been one, there were now three red gems on the back of his visible hand.

"Those gifts from Jori as well?"

"Jori. Listen to you, already so informal." That pleased him too. "No. These are from the king." Xavier swept into the room wearing a red wool cloak with a black fur collar hung to the floor, dusting the back of smooth black leather trousers. He had no red shirts or cloaks among his things. His clothes must've been gifted as well.

With the gems and bones and expensive clothes, his costume made him look the perfect combination of regal and mystical. He was finally the sorcerer he'd always wanted to be. If only he really had magic.

I wanted to tell him the truth, that *I* was making these things happen. If I didn't, he could end up imprisoned for lying to the king. Or worse. But I couldn't forget what had happened in the wagon. If he found out, would he do to me what he did with all things he believed stirred the elements? Tie me up like the bones in his hair or drink my blood like the snake in the woods?

"Come in already," he fussed at someone in the hallway.

A flustered girl with wheat-colored hair weighed down by grease, wearing a dismal gray smock, entered the room carrying a tray. A basket of bread, manchet if my nose was to be trusted. As she set it down on the small table near the fireplace, water sloshed out of the pitcher, missing the tray, spilling on the floor.

Xavier snapped, "Clean that up. Can't have my assistant's room a slippery mess."

I wiped it with my sleeve.

"Stop that! Maggie, *we* are honored guests in King Umbert's castle. You must start acting like you understand that."

I knocked the pitcher over. Water spilled everywhere.

"Honored guests aren't locked in their rooms!"

"Ungrateful child! I have given you everything! Protected you. Sheltered you. Fed you!" Xavier yelled. "You will not ruin this for me." He tore the red dress off the screen and tossed it at me. I let it fall to the floor.

Fine linen. Beaded blue thread, but it was a color I would never wear. I examined the other two. The yellow with puffed sleeves and wide cuffs would be kindling as soon as Xavier left, but the last, the simple pale blue, wasn't horrible.

Xavier saw dissent on my face. He picked up the dress off the ground and hung it over the screen. "The red. Put it on. It pays homage to our host."

The girl shifted the screen, revealing a steaming wooden tub. She poured oil from a small red bottle into it.

"Did you come into my room while I was asleep?" I asked her.

She nodded and set the bottle down.

"We're to be at the tournament in precisely one hour. This one"—he tilted his head at the girl—"is here to help you look presentable. Her name is Petal. She doesn't speak."

"Why not?"

"I don't know. You can ask her when I leave. Oh! And the king has ordered a private performance. Tomorrow night. You will be assisting me."

Petal went about setting pristine white towels and a comb on a small chair beside the tub. She wasn't leaving anytime soon. I would have to wait to talk to Xavier.

"The second day of the tournament begins soon. I will walk with King Umbert, Prince Jori, Laird Egrid, and his family. Sir Raleigh will escort you when you're finished."

With everyone out at the tournament, many of the guards included, this would be my best chance to sneak out of the castle and find *her*. Along the way, I could attempt something else. All at once I remembered this magic belonged to Xavier, and him alone. I would have to be covert in any practice. But that could be fun too.

"I wasn't bred for all of this, Xavier. Why don't I stay here? That way, you won't worry about me embarrassing you," I said, peeking in the basket. It *was* manchet.

Xavier slapped at it, dumping the lovely breads on the floor. "I've had enough disobedience from you over the past two days to last a lifetime. You will be on the balcony, with the king and his son, and you will do everything you're told, or there will be consequences!" He spun on his polished black heel and stormed out without so much as a glance back.

I picked up the manchet, about to hurl it at the door, but it smelled heavenly. I shoved the whole thing in my mouth, letting crumbs dribble all over.

"Don' clea' dat up." The *p* spat bits all over the floor.

Petal shook her head, wiped the ground with a wet cloth, and grabbed my wrist.

"Hey . . ."

For a four-foot bag of bones, she had a deadly grip. She led me to the steaming tub.

"A bath? Why won't you just speak to me?"

Her mouth opened. There was no tongue.

"I, um, see. King Umbert's cruelty knows no bounds."

Petal's wide-eyed, weary gaze shifted to the door. She clapped her hands, sounding an alarm of sorts. Then she thrust her arms at the tub, gesturing to get in, stamping her little bare foot, pushing on my back. Truth was, I couldn't wait to sink into it. Spending most days and nights on the move, we bathed in whatever cold rivers and lakes we happened upon. Only on days when we performed did we have a roof over our heads, and never with a tub inside the room. This was a gift from the gods and I was more than happy to take it.

I dropped my clothes in a pile on the floor and dipped my toe in the bath. The temperature was perfect. Rose petals floating on the surface parted as I sank in. Hot water against the skin was something I'd only experienced once before when we found a hot spring in the West, on the edge of the craggy hills.

Petal pressed the top of my head, dunking me under. I shot out, thinking she was going to drown me, but her weapon of choice wasn't water. Initially, it was a bottle of astringents, followed by oils, all massaged into my hair and rinsed. Then came the blasted comb. She picked every section, working through knots, then lost patience and ripped heaps out.

"And they say draignochs are dangerous!"

When she grabbed a bar of soap and scratchy towel, I took them from her. "I can do this myself, thank you!"

By the time I was done, the bathwater had turned gray from all the dirt I'd brought back with me from the journey. Afterward, she wrapped me in a linen towel, and, through painful gesturing, told me to sit before the fireplace and not move. She braided my hair and picked over and under my nails.

I was then finally allowed to get dressed. She brought me a new shift. Linen so soft it felt like new skin. Then the blue dress. Xavier could protest all he wanted. I would never wear the king's colors.

Petal drew the laces tightly over my chest. She crossed the room to the wardrobe and returned with a brand-new pair of shiny black leather boots that fit perfectly.

"How did they know my size?"

She picked up my old pair of boots.

"You came into my room while I was asleep and did all of this?"

She nodded.

"How could I not hear you?" I glanced back at the bed and cursed. "Damn thing left me unconscious." I vowed to sleep on the floor tonight, if I was still here.

As I slid my dagger into the top of my boot, Petal pushed the screen aside. She pulled open the wardrobe. Mounted to the door was a mirror. I padded over slowly, staring at my reflection. Petal waited, fishing for a compliment. I didn't recognize the woman looking back at me. She was too pretty, too sophisticated, and much too clean.

A costume. I stood taller and stuck what little bosom I had

out, but I didn't look very convincing. "A lady, I am not, and honestly never wanted to be," I told Petal.

She let out an aggrieved breath, wrenching my shoulders back.

Someone rapped on the door. "Maggie. It's Sybil. Sister of the Lady Esmera. Um . . . may I come in?"

She entered uninvited. Her footsteps made no sound at all. In lavender that highlighted her pale skin and red hair, she stood in the middle of the room with her shoulders back, her clasped hands at her waist, the picture of nobility. "Goodness, you scrub up well. My sister will be most put out." She smirked in a way that made me think the thought of that appealed to her. "That blue is lovely on you too. It brings out your eyes."

Sybil looped her arm through mine as if I'd known her for years. "Sir Griffin thought you might like a friendly face to show you to the arena."

"Who?" The first word I'd spoken to a lady and I sounded like an owl.

"You don't know who Sir Griffin is?"

"Should I?"

"He won the tournament last year at sixteen. Youngest ever. Tall. Dark. Had a stitched fresh wound on his face. Do you not remember him . . . from last night?"

I knew exactly who he was . . . she was talking about the heckling fool. The one who tried to tell me I was safe within these walls. I'd thought him older than me, but we were the same age. "Figures that blathering blockhead would be King

Umbert's champion." I let go of her arm. "I recollect telling him to stay away from me."

Sybil wrinkled her freckled nose. "I don't blame you. He was a prick last night. My brothers are the same, Cornwall more than Malcolm. All men are blathering blockheads and unworthy of our time, if you ask me."

"Prick? Are ladies allowed to speak that way?"

"Ladies can do whatever they want, but you will find I'm not much of a lady when you get to know me."

"You two will get along swimmingly, then. Neither is she." Sir Raleigh appeared at the door, standing stiffly. He kept his hand on the pommel of the sword hanging from his belt, not in a menacing way but because it seemed his natural stance. Road dust clung to his black leather tunic and trousers. He either didn't care or didn't have time to clean up. I guessed the latter. He was always around. Always watching. Always seeing more than he should.

"This is becoming old, Sir Raleigh. Don't worry. I'm not going to burn the place down."

He arched a brow. "Not yet, but given time, I have a feeling that you will. And my instincts are never wrong. Time to go."

As I passed by, Raleigh stopped me at the door and knelt. He lifted the skirts of my dress.

"This is highly inappropriate, Sir Raleigh."

"You won't need this, Maggie." He pulled my knife out of my boot.

Sybil yanked one out of her boot, resting it on Raleigh's

bald head. "A woman needs protection. Give it back."

Raleigh glanced up at me, wearing a knowing smirk. "Moldark is assigned to you, Maggie. He may recognize it."

"What's he talking about?" Sybil asked.

"Long story." I groaned because Raleigh was right. I took the knife and tossed it into the fire. The wooden handle caught. "That's the end of that, then."

In the hallway, I saw Sir Raleigh give Petal a coin and a pat on the head.

"She nearly ripped out all of my hair," I called to him.

"Yeah, well, it was quite the task I put upon the little thing." He waved, giving Petal her leave.

"What task was that? Turn me into a lady?"

"That would be asking too much of anyone. Told her to make you smell less like a pile of dung. No need for everyone around you to be punished."

Along the corridor, soldiers joined us. One of them was the size of a tree with greasy black hair and missing teeth who walked with a pronounced limp. Moldark.

"My ladies." He bowed, but his eyes admired Lady Sybil in a way that made me uncomfortable.

Raleigh set a stiff hand on my shoulder. "Maggie, you will be followed everywhere you go."

"Is all this really necessary, Sir Raleigh?" Lady Sybil said.

"Yes. I'm hardly worthy of all this . . . attention." I tried to imitate her smile but had a feeling I looked less than sincere.

Raleigh leaned over me. "Prince's orders. He considers you

very worthy, Maggie. You would do well to show him your gratitude by holding that sharp tongue."

With Sir Raleigh in the lead to our destination and Moldark and the others lagging behind, there would be no escape, for now.

The old knight moved at a fevered pace out of the castle, down the steps into the courtyard, and through the fortress gates that separated the king from the Walled City. He never glanced over his shoulder to see if I was still behind him, but I got the feeling he didn't have to.

"It's a beautiful day," Sybil said as we fell in step with exuberant crowds.

The air was crisp, the skies a delicate blue. The sun was beaming, but it was the moon I felt, dancing on my shoulders, chilling my palms, leaving them tingling as if saying good morning. The feeling was strange but growing more familiar, and thrilling. I wanted desperately to try something else. I longed for the sanctuary of the caves on the beaches, or the deep woods where I would get lost when Xavier wanted rid of me for a day. I would be trying all sorts of things. Drawing a bird with moonlight. Making it take flight. Now, that would be something.

As I padded through the crowded streets, guarded like I mattered, there were too many eyes. I couldn't do anything with all of them seeing. Even still, it gave me a kind of confidence I'd never felt before, as if I had a secret weapon in my pocket. "It is a beautiful day."

Although we moved swiftly, it would take time to get to the arena. Time I could use to look for the draignoch's keep. Ten minutes into the walk, I recognized nothing from last night's trip into the city. Everything looked different in daylight.

So, I asked Sybil.

"I don't know where the keep is. Sorry. I know very little about this place. Until a couple of days ago, my home was in the North. I thought I would be returning there with my father and brothers after the wedding, but apparently, I'm to stay here with Esmera." She sounded dismayed.

"Wedding?"

"My sister, Lady Esmera, is betrothed to Prince Jori."

"Your father is Laird Egrid? Chieftain of the North?"

"You know the North?" Sybil smiled warmly. She was fond of home.

"Never been. Like to, though. Only heard bits about it on the road. What happens when your sister marries the prince?"

"My father will no longer be laird. The North becomes . . . encumbered." Sybil fingers gripped my arm harder.

Encumbered was the right word for it. "Why would your father do that? Hand your lands over to King Umbert? Did you not ride through the Hinterlands on your way here? You see how he treats his people."

Her eyes on the ground lifted to find mine. "He fears for our safety, I think. My father's not in good health. Our armies aren't as vast as they once were either."

"He brought you into a lion's den. One with no escape." I

nodded to the giant impenetrable wall.

"You sound like my brother Malcolm. And"—she glanced back at the soldiers, checking their distance, and whispered—"he's right. But my father trusts the king."

I huffed a laugh. "Probably get him killed."

Sybil's face fell, and she nodded. For the first time in a long time, I regretted my words. Strife among the ruling families frequently ended in bloodshed. And a father was a father, even if he was a laird. "I've gone one step too far. I have a knack for that, it seems. Sorry."

"Nothing to be sorry for," she said.

After that we walked in uncomfortable silence.

The oval-shaped monolithic stadium butted up against the wall surrounding the city. I paused to take it in. In all my travels, I had never seen anything with such impressive engineering. As the city descended the high mount, so did the exterior wall to the arena. The city and stadium were separated by fifty feet at the Top, decreasing in length as the hill expanded.

Raleigh explained that each section of the city had its own entrance, which became visible when we reached the end of the quartz-paved road in Top and stepped on a gilded bridge made of steel. The stone rail had many posts, all topped with carvings: a clawed foot, a wing, a serpent's tail, parts of the draignochs, a foreshadowing of the butchery we would witness. My stomach turned.

I looked down.

It was a long way between Top, Middle, and Bottom. But the divides were much greater than just the bridges taken.

Those around us, coming from the Top, were much fewer in number. There was ample space between families on the road, the way there was between their homes. The Toppers, as Sybil clarified for me, wore fine linens in colors I'd never seen before. Dark purples, burnt oranges, brilliant reds. With groomed ruddy and black fox furs, livery collars of silver and gold, and jewels galore, I had never seen so much wealth in one place. The steel bridge beneath us in the Middle had no decorations. It was crowded, but still many fewer than the droves taking the road from the Bottom. Middlefolk donned smoothed leather and pressed linens and wools, and carried baskets and waterskins as if they were attending a party.

The Bottom was so far away it was impossible to see anything except the crowns of their heads, of which there were so many the sea of people moved at a turtle's clip. Thousands stacked to pass through a single entrance like sheep waiting to be penned.

Halfway across the bridge, cheering broke the awed silence. Names I'd never heard of volleyed back and forth, growing in volume and frequency the closer we came to the arena. Sir Griffin's name heralded the loudest of all, echoing off the wall from the Top to the Bottom. The devotion was almost majestic. The people of the Walled City worshipped him. *Fools, the lot of them.*

Sir Raleigh corralled us to one side, moving away from the

Toppers and into a separate, well-guarded tunnel, at the end of which was a large wooden lift that I suspected was used to lower competitors to the arena floor. Five men stood against the wall. And yet, looking closer at them, only three of them could grow proper whiskers. The other two's cheeks still puffed with baby fat.

Griffin stood closest to the arena entrance. In a smoothed red tunic, he looked every bit the picture of one of Umbert's soldiers. Wealthy too, by the look of his clothing. And yet his face told another story. The fresh wound, but also a deep older scar across his forehead, and another from his ear that ran down his neck and disappeared beneath his tunic. Those kinds of scars were the marks of a survivor.

A boy handed him his spear, but his eyes were suddenly on me. He looked away, checking the spear's weight, then the sharpness.

I recognized another from the royal table last night too. In all black, he had red hair like Sybil.

"You missed the theatrics," he said, smirking.

"Theatrics?" I asked.

"A long arduous play commemorating how the king became king, as if the people didn't already know," a blond burly man said. "Sir Silas." He tilted his head in greeting.

"Hello." I smiled.

"Hello. I'm Oak," a plump boy with a ponytail perched on his crown said from the far end of the tunnel. He blushed three shades of red.

"Hello, Oak." I waved back. They all seemed friendly enough.

"Happens every day of the tournament this year. Thus, why we took our time," Sybil said with a wink. She turned back to a handsome red-haired man. "Malcolm, this is Maggie. Maggie, this is my eldest brother, Malcolm."

He tilted his head in greeting, then set his spear down and stretched his arms over his head.

"Maggie?" Griffin fumbled his spear, wincing.

I caught it before it hit the ground.

Griffin gripped the shaft beneath my fingers. It was the briefest of brushes, the pass-off. But I could still feel it lingering afterward.

"I thought you said Griffin was a champion, Lady Sybil. But it seems he can't even carry the weight of his own weapon."

Sybil took my arm. "I believe he's stupefied by your transformation, Maggie."

"It's simply . . ." He paused, trying to find words. I expected a snide comment, but instead he said, "I didn't recognize you."

"This is not my spear!" A fair-haired boy at the other end tossed his weapon on the ground as if it were worth nothing. I'd seen men kill each other for less steel than was in the tip.

Groaning, Sybil let go of my arm and padded to him. She picked up the spear, turned it over, and showed him the bottom. "This is our seal, Cornwall. And it's too short for Malcolm, so it must be yours."

Cornwall snatched it from her. "It's heavier than it should

be. Someone's tampered with it."

"Then maybe you should step out of the competition," Malcolm said.

"Oh, you'd like that, brother, wouldn't you?" Cornwall lifted the spear and aimed it, not at Malcolm but at Griffin. "I'm coming for you."

Griffin laughed at him, flexing the fingers on his gloved right hand. "Odds feel in my favor if you can't recognize your own weapon."

Cornwall took a menacing step toward him, but Sybil pushed him back, shaking her head.

Griffin turned away from him. I leaned over and caught another wince, more subtle this time as he clenched his fist. A bandage poked out the end of the glove. Cornwall was embarrassingly full of bluster, but there was a reason for his boast. The champion was worried. It must be his throwing hand. And Cornwall knew it.

Knock him off his dais, young Northman. Griffin deserved heaping buckets of humiliation after what he did to us last night.

"Maggie, shall we go up?" Sybil asked.

Raleigh yanked open a door I hadn't noticed before. Beyond it was a staircase leading up, every step saddled with a guard at attention.

Griffin set his spear down and met us on the first step. "I'm sorry to keep you. I just wanted to say—"

"What? After last night, what more can there be for you to say?" I asked.

"Sir Griffin! Time to lead!" a man called from the lift.

"I'll go." Cornwall made only a step before Griffin slammed him into the wall so hard Cornwall's eyes bulged from losing his breath.

"No. You won't." His arm still on Cornwall's chest, Griffin snatched his spear, then marched down the tunnel and onto the lift. As it lowered, Griffin's stern frown remained fixed on me.

The private staircase filled with the arena's blistering reverie, which rose to full heart-pounding volume when we reached the covered balcony, a constant chorus of one word: "Grif-fin! Grif-fin! Grif-fin!" I rolled my eyes, wanting to join in with a very unladylike addition to the chant, but refrained.

Over and above it, though, I suddenly heard *her*. The draignoch.

Her resonant whimper, repeating. It was coming from beyond the other side of the arena. Was that where they kept the draignochs? It would make sense. If draignochs were all as large as she was, they were far too big to be moved vast distances without worrying about the damage they would do to the city.

The others on the balcony paid no attention. No one else seemed to hear her. Not Xavier seated next to the king, waving like a fool at the competitors and attendees. He was already well into his cups. Not any of these others: Esmera, the prince, who ate and drank on the opposite end of the balcony. Not Sybil, who went to help an old man with crutches, her father I presumed, lower to his chair. And not the few gray-smocked servants who fussed refilling empty plates and glasses, or many guards posted.

Her voice traveled on a different plane. They couldn't hear it, because if they did, they too would want nothing but to find her. She was so close, but at the moment I found myself utterly surrounded. There was no way to get to her.

I moved to the balcony rail to try to pinpoint exactly where her voice was coming from. The scar on my arm burned. I winced, pressing down on it.

Sybil padded over. "Are you all right?" She reached for my arm, but I put it behind my back.

"Yes. Clumsy. Banged my arm on the banister. Another bruise," I prattled.

She pushed back her sleeve. There were several fading purple-and-black spots. "Sparring. A favorite pastime in the North. We use short staffs to keep from killing each other." She smiled and waved at Malcolm and Cornwall below.

"Esmera spars?" I couldn't hide my shock.

Sybil guffawed. "No. She stitches Father's treasure troves to her dresses these days. But my sister is of the North. We all know how to fight. It is our way."

"I really would like to visit someday," I mused.

"You asked about the draignochs." She pointed out a huge

metal gate. "They come out there, so I imagine the keep is connected to the tunnel."

"Yes." All I had to do was make my way through too many guards, through the tunnel, into the arena—while the door was open. The plan was both impractical and implausible. I would have to find another way.

Three servants sipped from a single tankard before passing it to the king. Tasters. King Umbert was ruthless, but poison was a coward's act. Hinterfolk would never stoop to such pathetic ways of killing him. After all he'd taken from them, they'd want to feel the blade enter his chest.

It was probably someone inside the city. Maybe even someone he knew. I glanced around the balcony, catching Prince Jori's stare. He smiled.

The prince and his betrothed, Lady Esmera, were seated together. He in a long red cloak matching his father's, and she in a lavender dress like her sister's, only hers was trimmed with blue teardrop-shaped gems. They looked the absolute picture of a future ruling family.

Sybil took the empty chair beside her sister, leaving only one left on the other side of the prince.

As I sat down, he said, "You look much more at ease than you did last night."

It was a strange thing to say. "Was that a compliment?" I wondered aloud.

He laughed, his dimples cratering, his eyes twinkling with mischief. "I meant it as such."

Esmera's legs were slanted to one side, her heels were crossed at her ankles, and her hands folded in her lap. I tried to mimic her, but it took too much work to keep my legs fashioned that way.

"Well, the bed was very comfortable. Too comfortable, if you ask me."

"Especially if you're used to sleeping in pigsties." Esmera wrinkled her nose.

I sniffed my arm and held it out to Esmera. "*I* smell like roses. Go on. Take a whiff."

She shoved my hand out of her face. Her expression so repulsed that Sybil and I laughed.

"Everything in this place smells like rose. Why is that?" Sybil asked Jori.

"My father has an affinity for them," the prince answered, sounding as if he didn't share his father's taste.

The king raised his hand.

Horns blew.

The throngs silenced.

"Finally. Here we go," Jori declared.

The five knights stretched across the back edge of the oval-shaped arena. The marshal marked a throw line ten feet in front of them, which gave them little space to run before release.

"Let the spear contest begin!" King Umbert bellowed.

Malcolm went first, wasting no time. Three sprinting steps

and he released. The spear sailed over a hundred yards.

The audience was impressed, applauding, whistling, and yelling, "Northman!"

Silas was next. He came closer but didn't beat Malcolm's throw. Oak, the youngest of them, barely made it half the distance. Cornwall was up next.

"He'll top Malcolm," Esmera said smugly. "Has all year, hasn't he, Sybil?"

"Malcolm is always full of surprises."

"No. He's not," Jori scoffed. "Predictable by nature, and why he'll never be champion. He'll never beat Griffin. Neither will Cornwall."

I didn't care. I only wanted to get this over with so I could find the draignoch's keep.

Cornwall tested the weight of his spear until the crowd grew impatient.

"Throw it already!"

"Nerves got you, boy?"

Laughter spread. Griping too.

"Get on with it!"

Cornwall drew back, ran toward the line, tripping, and had to start over at the last possible second.

"Like his mother was, that one. Takes a year to figure anything out," Laird Egrid croaked. "Just throw it, boy!"

Cornwall did. A good throw too. It stabbed the earth right beside Malcolm's. He bumped into Griffin, into his injured hand carrying the spear as he walked back to the line.

Gasps rang out.

"Knocked him on purpose!"

"Get away from our champion!" a boy yelled from far below.

"Cheater!" another called.

Griffin leaned the spear against his shoulder and pumped his injured fist. The crowd mumbled, several voicing concerns about his injury. Did their lives depend on Griffin's performance? They literally hung on his every move.

Griffin glanced around, looking at the people. He gripped the spear tightly in his injured hand and was rewarded with steady clapping for support. But then he tossed the spear to his other hand. He was going to use his left?

I could see his conceited grin all the way up on the balcony.

The crowd jumped, laughing, relishing this game. Heavy anticipation forced a silence. A short run, a serious heave, and the spear sailed in a low arc, striking the ground a yard beyond Malcolm's and Cornwall's.

The raucous cries caused my heart to skip a beat. The stadium shook. The cheering deafened. Prince Jori ran to the balcony rail to exchange a fisted salute with Griffin.

The people called out the prince's name along with Griffin's, sharing their accolades with him, although I didn't see him do anything to earn it.

Griffin dashed into the lift without gloating. The others

followed, as if it was always their place to walk behind the champion.

Minutes later, the cheering quieted as Griffin and the others exited the lift, disappearing into the tunnel. Breathless, Prince Jori sat back down. "I need a drink. Bradyn!"

A dark-haired boy padded toward him, carrying a tankard. Griffin burst through the balcony's door, knocking the mead out of Bradyn's hands and all over the prince.

"What's the rush, Griffin?" Jori yelled, wiping off.

Though he was calm on the outside, Griffin's eyes told another story. He looked spooked. Griffin pulled Bradyn to the door. "Go back to the castle. Your father needs you in the kitchens."

"I can't leave, Sir Griffin. The prince asked me for mead and you just spilled it all over him." Bradyn started away from Griffin, only to get dragged back. "What is it? Is my father hurt?"

All of us were watching Griffin now. He turned to Prince Jori, and then King Umbert, and said, "Buffont requires the boy in the kitchens."

The king gave a half-hearted wave.

"Good." Griffin pushed Bradyn through the door. "Go. Now. And don't come back today! Heed me, boy!"

Bradyn took off running.

Griffin shut the door.

Something bad was about to happen. I could feel it. And I

wasn't alone. Sybil got up and walked toward Griffin.

A guard passed him and went immediately to the king to deliver a message. It was easy to read his lips. He said, "They're ready."

King Umbert walked to the railing and raised his hand. "Traitors!" he cried.

The throngs silenced.

"Delay the fight, for another has come! Traitors!" He spat the last word.

The crowd hushed.

"Two nights ago, a pair of fools thought to kill your king." He lifted his mug, sloshing liquid over the edge. "But they failed. As all will who try to take me from my people."

Guards pushed two men onto the lift and descended into the arena. Once there, they ripped cloth off their covered heads.

Gasps spread like pox through the seating. Two men, not much older than I, or the prince for that matter. Hands bound behind their backs. Feet chained. Faces bruised. Eyes so swollen they had to be led into the middle of the ring.

A woman wailed. I found her in the middle of the rows, arms flailing, screaming, "My sons!" then, "No. Please!"

A man beside her grabbed her, shuttling her up the stairs to an exit, but the guards refused to let them go.

"No one may leave," King Umbert declared.

All were to witness King Umbert's brutality. Did they expect less from this monster?

"Wait. I've met them. Haven't I?" Esmera asked as if she was asking after a long-lost cousin.

"The first night we got here," Sybil explained.

Prince Jori nodded solemnly. "Halig and Capp. My father's chamber servants. They confessed. They were responsible for poisoning the mead that almost killed your brother."

Griffin frowned at Jori, looking less than convinced by the prince's explanation, but he said nothing to stop the proceedings.

King Umbert raised his cup again. "Yes. Traitors! In our midst. My hounds gave their lives to protect mine, and so their brothers and sisters will be allowed to take their revenge."

The king nodded and a trapdoor near Halig and Capp slid back. Greyhounds rushed from the pit, tethered by ropes that gave plenty of lead for the dogs to reach them.

Sybil and Esmera hid their faces. Even Griffin, champion beast slayer, master spear thrower, turned his eyes to the ground, unable to watch.

Not me. I'd seen punishment in the name of the king. It was a rite of passage in the Hinterlands—to bear witness. An old man told me right before they strung him up that he was being punished for eating an apple from his own orchard. An apple meant for the king's taxes.

And so, I watched. I watched that old man. I watched every time. Out of respect for those at the wrong end of the king's wrath.

It went on for a long time, too long, until finally the boys' screams ceased and they stopped writhing. All around me, the upper decks were littered with raised fists and claims of justice.

The king nibbled on a chicken leg as they dragged what was left of the bodies into the pits with the dogs, clearing the ring. He dropped the bone on his plate, wiped his hands on a towel, and stood up once more, waving, the signal to begin the tournament again.

The marshal appeared at the end of the tunnel, stepping onto the lift, using it as a balcony. "People of the Walled City, Sir Malcolm."

The lift descended with Sir Malcolm aboard. Sporadic applause was all the people could muster for the Northman.

"Is that why you asked the boy to leave?" I asked Griffin. "So that he didn't see that."

He couldn't or wouldn't look at me. "They were his cousins."

He shifted, his soft, mournful eyes finding mine. His look was haunted—as though this was not the first time he'd seen people he cared about die brutally.

"I'm sure that was upsetting, Maggie. Come, sit beside me," Prince Jori called.

It didn't sound like I had a choice.

Griffin stood off to the side, leaning on the railing, his focus never leaving Malcolm.

A spear in hand, a sword hanging from his belt, Malcolm waited near the metal gate that inched upward. He wore a steel chest plate, and gauntlets to cover his hands and fore-arms, but no helmet.

With each creaking pull, more of the draignoch became visible. I leaned over, trying to get a better glimpse of it, my stomach flipping at the thought it might be *her*. From the feet I knew it wasn't. She had black skin, and this creature was sparkling yellow. Halfway up, other differences were apparent too. In size and proportions. Both were reptilian, but she was elegant, lean and muscular, where this beast was . . . clunky.

Yet still fierce. One look at Malcolm, and it rammed its head into the gate until it could finally break free.

The throngs rose to their feet once again, yelling at Mal-colm, who rolled out of reach of snapping jaws and stabbing claws, finding a good position. His spear struck beneath its limb, in an armpit.

The animal reared.

Malcolm yanked the spear out and spun behind it, then stabbed again. The draignoch screamed. Huffing and panting, it backed away from Malcolm.

All I could think was, what if it had been *her*? "This is bar-baric."

"These animals destroyed our lands once upon a time," Prince Jori said.

"Well, that's not what's destroying it now!" I snapped at him, catching Griffin's curious stare.

I saw Malcolm drop his spear and pull his sword.

The creature returned for another pass, but Malcolm was

ready. With a running start, he jumped higher than I had ever seen anyone jump before, landing on the middle of its back, startling the crowd and me. The draignoch reared, trying to throw Malcolm off, but he held on, somehow even climbing. Then he stabbed the poor animal in the neck.

The sight sickened me. Unlike the men who'd tried to kill the king, this animal's only treachery was that it had been bred within the city's wall for public slaughter. Ice, frigid and blistering, drove through my veins. My hands were so cold, I clenched them into fists. Was this the effect of the moon or my anger? Or both? I wanted to look at my palms but was afraid the light might be there and someone, even with daylight, would see.

Jori set his hand on one of mine, then grimaced. "Poor thing. Your hands are freezing." He added his other hand to my other fist. "Don't fret. It's almost over."

I could feel Esmera glaring daggers at me and slid my hands out.

Sybil yelled for her brother, cheering him on.

Malcolm delivered another blow. This time to its side. The draignoch fell over. He stopped suddenly and padded to the other side of the arena, looking up at King Umbert.

The people jumped up, clapping and cheering Malcolm's name, calling for the draignoch's death.

King Umbert held out his fist and dropped his thumb.

"What?" Sybil gasped.

Laird Egrid pounded his crutch in anger. "Did you not see

that jump Malcolm made? Not even Griffin could have done it! And you insult him?"

"Are you questioning me?" King Umbert hissed. Guards padded toward him.

"No. Never," Laird Egrid sniveled. "I am ever your humble servant, and so are my children, Umbert. But this feels wrong."

"It's done. Get over it." King Umbert belched.

It was over, for the draignoch. The king stopped Malcolm from finishing it off, but there was no way it would survive. Not with those wounds.

The crowd groaned in disappointment. Malcolm was furious. He threw his sword on the ground beneath the dais and stormed out of the ring.

The gate rolled up. Chains pulled, and the draignoch was forced to crawl with what little strength it had left out of the arena.

Thankfully, the morning events were over. I took a deep breath, feeling my chilled blood warm—a little.

People started to file out.

I got up too. If I could get into the tunnel quickly, I could sneak through that gate before it shut.

But Sir Raleigh blocked the door. "We will leave after the crowd."

"I'd like to go for a walk."

"No." Raleigh took a menacing step forward.

I stepped backward, bumping into Prince Jori. "What's the matter?"

"I wanted to go for a walk, find where these majestic creatures are kept. Seems Sir Raleigh isn't keen on letting me leave."

"Leave for the Oughtnoch? I can't say I blame him, Maggie. It's far too dangerous." His endearing grin only added to the sting of him saying no. "Besides, if you leave before the rest of us, I will be denied the pleasure of your company. Which I greatly enjoy."

I glanced over at Esmera, who was watching us, as was Griffin, and Xavier, and everyone else on the balcony.

"That's nice of you to say, Prince Jori. But if you'll excuse me, my father wishes to speak to me," I lied. Anything to get these prying eyes off me.

I padded to the end of the balcony, smoothing my dress as I saw Esmera do when she stood up. Once beside Xavier, I hoped that would be the end of the prince's advances.

"Prince Jori is smitten," Xavier whispered. "That's good. That's very good." He patted my arm as if I'd done something right for the first time.

There was nothing good about the prince's advances. If he wouldn't let me go to this Oughtnoch place, which I surmised was the name of the pound where they kept the poor creatures, then what good was he to me? Smitten, he would only get in my way.

As the gate rolled down, cutting off my access, my heart sank. There had to be a way, and I needed to find it soon.

EIGHT

GRIFFIN

Griffin went straight for the practice field, hoping Bradyn would be there. He hadn't been in the kitchens or at his home. When he didn't find him, he stayed to spar with Mutter and Wilson, two of the boys who worked in the armory. After what had happened in the arena, even with his sore hand, it was much more appealing to practice than returning to the castle and being forced to make polite conversation about the tournament with Jori or the king.

Public executions weren't abnormal, especially when offenses were egregious. If Halig and Capp were responsible for the poison, then Griffin understood the reason for showing no mercy. But to do it that way—at the festival, in the arena with every family there, including the boys' own—was wrong.

Griffin thrust at Mutter's huge head. Mutter raised his shield, blocking it, leaving him blind. Griffin kicked, sending him crashing to the ground, then pivoted, catching Wilson's lunge with his crossbar. With a hard twist, Griffin disarmed him.

"Mutter, deflect with your shield."

"I was blocking, Sir Griffin."

"You were hiding behind it like it's a tree. Deflect and attack." Griffin hit Mutter's wooden sword with his own shield, knocking it out of his hand, then thrust, stopping a thumbnail before his throat.

He tossed Wilson his sword. "You walk like a fat old horse, giving away what direction you're coming from."

"I can't help that," Wilson whined.

"Sure you can. Get faster." Griffin raised the practice sword over his head and stabbed. Wilson rolled, squealing like a fool, as if the wooden weapon was made of steel.

Beside them, all training ceased. Sparring stopped. Silas, throwing knives, held his dagger, then drew up stiffly and fell into a bow. It could only mean one thing.

"Here he is," Jori called.

Griffin glanced over his shoulder, finding Jori, Malcolm, Cornwall, Esmera, Sybil, and Maggie all strolling toward him. Jori made quite the spectacle at the festival, fawning all over Maggie, when he should've been attentive to Esmera. Why was she invited with them again? Could he not go anywhere without her?

Three soldiers traveled with them, Raleigh included. Raleigh had only ever been seen before at the king's side. It was quite the entourage for the prince.

The others went back to work.

"Prince Jori was just giving us a tour," Sybil explained.

Griffin nodded, remembering she had asked him to do that. He walked to the prince to greet him, trying, all the while, to keep his eyes off Maggie, but failing miserably. She turned her back sharply, staring out over the city, searching for something.

Griffin approached cautiously. "Can I help?"

"Help with . . ." Maggie still hadn't turned to look at him, which he took as a bad sign.

"Finding whatever you're looking for?" Griffin asked.

Maggie didn't respond. She padded toward the end of the grass, where there was a good view of the north side of the city. Griffin wanted to apologize for how he'd treated her in the Great Hall, but she would never give him the chance. She wouldn't even look at him.

Raleigh inched closer to her. Two soldiers with him folded in around her as well. *What is this?* Why were they treating her like a prisoner when she was an invited guest?

"Sir Raleigh, no business in the Hinterlands this week? The king—"

"No, Griffin. I am posted here within the city for the present. I have new responsibilities," Raleigh said, bristling.

Responsibilities that included Maggie? The prince needed a soldier with Sir Raleigh's skill to keep track of a young woman from the Hinterlands?

Jori picked up a practice sword from the rack, swinging it

around, showing off, then padded into the center of the field.

The sparring stopped. The men waited for the prince's orders.

"Griffin! Come! Attack me!" He waved him over.

This again, Griffin thought. He held up his injured hand. "I'm afraid I cannot possibly take any more damage, sire."

Jori tossed the wooden sword to his other hand. "Wise man. Oak, how about you?"

Oak jogged over as if this was a privilege. Griffin supposed it was—for him. Poor Oak would be flying high right up until the moment the prince made a mistake. Which he would, because he always did. He had no instinct. No second sight. Hugo, the blacksmith, always spoke of it. Either a fighter had it or he didn't. It couldn't be taught. No amount of hunger or anger could bring it out.

The heartbeat of indecision would come. Oak could capitalize on it, humiliate the prince—and then the prince would make Oak pay.

Griffin knew the game far too well.

He padded over to Malcolm. "You had a brilliant match."

Malcolm shrugged the compliment off.

Cornwall slapped Malcolm on the back. "The king saw it differently."

"We can all see the king's motives," Malcolm said.

"Better not do that to me when I fight, or I'll—"

"You'll what, Cornwall?" Esmera hissed a small laugh.

"You'll blame your poor performance on the king like Malcolm?"

Maggie snorted. "Poor performance? Did you not see your brother leap on the back of the draignoch?"

"No. I didn't."

"At least he didn't have to kill the beautiful creature," Maggie added.

Griffin stared at her in disbelief. "Beautiful?"

Jori growled, begging for attention, ending the conversation. He advanced on Oak like an arrogant dog let off his leash. Oak parried his every move, then made the obvious mistake of attacking with a weak grip. A returned swat and Oak's sword flew out of his hand, fast and hard—and into Maggie's.

Esmera flinched as if it had hit her, because it should've. No one could've caught that sword, not even Griffin.

"How did she do that?" Cornwall asked Malcolm. "I didn't see it coming."

Malcolm shrugged, dumbfounded.

Sybil laughed. "Perhaps it should be Maggie in the arena rather than you, then."

Malcolm popped Cornwall on the back of the head. "Sybil has a point."

"Oh, you'll pay for that," Cornwall goaded. He walked backward, arms out, taunting Malcolm. "Come on then, brother, put me on my ass."

Malcolm grabbed the longest wooden sword and tossed it

at Cornwall, picking another for himself. It was the first time Griffin saw them act like brothers who liked each other.

"I've seen enough fighting for one afternoon," Esmera declared. With a last long look at Maggie, she left.

Sybil picked a practice sword from the rack. "Is this game for all?" She swung at Griffin.

He easily blocked it, but she kept coming.

"You're quite practiced at sword skills, Lady Sybil."

"I am, Sir Griffin." Sybil jabbed, forcing him back. Then thrust.

He blocked and locked their swords. With a hard spin, he whipped it out of her hand.

Sybil clapped. "Even one-handed, you're still a champion."

"Maggie, want a go? Or are you too fragile now that you've been made over as a lady?" Griffin teased. He kicked a weapon in her direction.

She picked it up. "I've never been fragile, Sir Griffin." Maggie swung, twirling her weapon as if it were part of her hand. "I've not played with wooden sticks in a long time, I think."

"I'll go easy on you." Griffin smiled.

He attacked. She blocked without hesitation. As he'd suspected, she knew exactly how to handle the sword. He advanced and attacked again. She ducked, and before he knew what was happening a sharp pain spread like fire in his injured hand. He clutched it to his chest.

"That was for last night," Maggie hissed.

"My turn," Sybil said, attacking.

When he'd disarmed her and looked back, Maggie was taking on Silas and Oak. Two at once, and she was *winning*— albeit with a few dirty tricks. She kicked as much as thrust, landing blows on Oak's shins and Silas's privates, leaving him bent over.

She caught Griffin staring and shrugged.

Griffin laughed. She was funny, if not a little scary. Her eyes darkened to an inky blue color, and she smiled. It was the second time he'd seen that smile. First in the tunnel, laughing at his clumsiness, and now when she was being admired for her ingenuity. His pulse raced at the sight of it. That smile was her most dangerous weapon.

"Where did you learn to fight like that?" Griffin asked.

Maggie's brow creased. "Out of necessity." She padded over and spoke in hushed tones. "Will you really help me?"

The question caught Griffin completely off guard. "Help you what?"

"See the new draignoch. She came in from the Hinterlands."

"She? Draignochs are neither male nor female. They're eggs born fertile."

"Oh, but this one is certainly female. I need to see her."

Griffin couldn't believe what he was hearing. She wanted to visit the Oughtnoch? He did too, of course, but for entirely different reasons. "They're not beautiful, Maggie. They're dangerous. Just look at the scars on my face. Damage done by their fangs and claws, and I've been trained to kill them."

"What are you two whispering about?" Jori called.

"Sir Griffin was saying he thought Xavier's magic truly false. It seems he still doesn't believe," Maggie lied. She smirked and whacked Griffin's chest with her wooden sword, harder than necessary.

"More likely attempting to argue back his dagger, which is now mine." Jori rested his hand on the pommel at his waist. "Xavier is a real sorcerer, Griffin. He is the one and only Ambrosius," he exclaimed loudly, as if he were preaching to the whole practice field. "But now, I'm bored. A new contest. The Northman against Sir Griffin and me." He jostled his wooden sword back and forth. "For all the bragging rights."

Griffin raised his wooden sword at Malcolm, leaving Cornwall to Jori. Maggie and Sybil walked to the end of the field, and the others circled, all wanting to see the two kingdoms go at it.

Griffin attacked first. Malcolm deflected and thrust. Griffin sidestepped, blocking, and swept his leg, knocking Malcolm off his feet.

Griffin reached to help him up. Malcolm latched on, laughing, and yanked, flipping Griffin over him. The two scrambled to their feet, ready for more.

Jori and Cornwall danced through them, parrying across as if neither had the courage to overtake the other—until the end of the green—at the edge, where the Top fell down to the Middle.

A fence protected any from falling, except in a spot where

a board had loosened during practice the day before. Griffin knew it because he was there when the horse reared, striking it. But Jori didn't know, and neither did Cornwall.

Cornwall pushed on, and on. Jori grabbed the loose board, his eyes widening as it fell out from beneath him, taking his balance with it. Jori's heel slid, and Cornwall lunged.

His heart pounding, Griffin barreled into Cornwall, sending him careening into the grass, while grabbing Jori's flailing arm. Palm to wrist, Griffin pulled him to steady feet.

"I've got you," Griffin said.

He never saw Malcolm coming.

Malcolm shouldered Griffin, crushing his injured hand. White-hot pain spread through his palm. He knew instantly the center bone had snapped. He fell on top of Cornwall, shoving his hand underneath his arm to protect any further damage. But it was too late. His hand was broken. With only a few days before he would have to fight another draignoch, his hand would never be healed.

Griffin rolled off Cornwall to laughing applause, Malcolm's chortle the loudest.

"Brother, whose side are you on?" Cornwall steamed. He got up and stormed off like the spoiled child he was.

As he padded with Jori back to Maggie and Sybil, Griffin did his best to hide the pain. *Never let them see you hurt.* Raleigh had told him that the first time he laid him flat on this very field. And it was true.

But by the looks in the women's eyes, they saw right through it.

"Do you want to see the physician?" Sybil asked.

"It's nothing." Griffin shifted his hands behind his back.

Maggie leaned over to get a better look, but he pivoted. He felt it swelling. He wasn't sure it would fit in his gauntlet.

Raleigh came up behind him. "Malcolm and Cornwall did that on purpose. You played right into their game."

"No. All in good fun. I'll be fine," Griffin said, bristling. But the old man was right. For the first time in his life he thought his next draignoch fight could be his last. Nerves choked Griffin.

"You should make them pay now, while you have the chance," Raleigh argued.

Griffin couldn't take the chance on damaging his hand more. He shook his head and looked away.

A soldier jogged down the hill, calling, "Prince Jori! Your father needs you in council."

"Duty calls. Let's all head back together," Jori said, and started walking.

"I'm going to stay. Work on my throws for tomorrow." Malcolm pulled a knife from the scabbard on his belt.

Jori arched an offended brow at him, then let it fall. "After losing to Griffin with spears, extra time on the practice green would be a suitable afternoon pursuit."

Barely drawing back, Malcolm threw the dagger at the

target, striking dead center in the bull's-eye. "I just like to throw knives."

"I'll stay too," Maggie added.

"No. You'll return to the castle, Maggie." Raleigh stepped toward her.

"I can escort her back," Griffin volunteered, surprising himself.

Jori shook his head. "I promised her father to see her safely back, and that I must do." He extended an elbow to Maggie.

She didn't take it. "Don't you trust him?" she asked Jori, nodding to Griffin.

"Of course." Jori didn't look happy, with good reason. A prince had offered his arm, and she'd dismissed it like it was nothing. Jori and rejection had never before met. He was lost at what to do. Griffin pressed his lips together, painfully so, to keep from laughing. "But that doesn't mean I'm going to go back on my word to Xavier," he added.

Jori's eyes crinkled the way they always did when he was lying. He wanted Maggie to leave with him no matter the circumstances of how it happened. The chase for him was a game he wanted to win.

As Griffin turned to go, he saw Maggie's expression dip into a deep frown. Her eyes fell on Raleigh, then the prince. She didn't like being watched every second, and she wanted to see the draignoch. He wanted to see it too.

Griffin hesitated at the stupidity of what he was about to

do. But the truth was, even if he told her where the draignochs were kept, she would never be able to get there. Not without his help.

"Wait, Maggie," Griffin blurted. "Can you please take a look at my hand?"

Jori looked put out. "We have a physician for that, Griffin."

"A quick glance . . . ," Maggie said to him, but didn't wait for permission.

Griffin put his back to the others, and slowly, carefully, pulled back a corner of the bandage. Maggie padded around him.

"Can't see much of anything unless you take that off." Maggie fingered the wrap.

"Just pretend to look." Griffin faked a wince at Jori. "You really want to go to the keep?"

Maggie scrutinized his fingers, nodding.

"Midnight. I'll get you from your room."

"But Raleigh—"

"I know." He watched, but Griffin had a way around that. He tucked the bandage. He held his hand up. "Better already."

Sybil hooked Maggie's arm with one hand, and Jori's with her other. "I do love walking in parties of three."

Griffin stared at where Maggie had stood long after she had gone. Getting her out of the castle was going to be difficult. Getting her into the Oughtnoch impossible. But he too wanted to see this new draignoch, because if she—as Maggie called the beast—could take down twenty men, then Griffin might as well slather himself in butter and lie down in the middle of the arena. He hoped he'd make a tasty meal.

NINE

MAGGIE

Late afternoon dullness swept the castle. A time between festivities. Xavier drank too much in the morning, so it wasn't
surprising he didn't go to lunch, and I didn't go to dinner. It
was strange, not seeing him for a full day. That hadn't ever
happened that I could remember.

I had been too nervous to leave my room. If I'd seen Sir
Griffin, I would not have been able to keep myself from asking
him how he planned to get me out. And then we would likely
have gotten caught by the prince.

When I told Sir Raleigh I wanted to eat in my chamber, that
I worried the prince would be hounded by Lady Esmera if I
sat with them at dinner, that I wanted to save the kind prince
from torment, he smiled with something like relief. Like I was
making his life easier and he appreciated it.

Petal brought me a tray of mouton and bread. She set it
before the fire and left me to eat alone. Afterward, it was
hard to keep my eyes open. The fire smoldered, casting a hazy
warmth. The chair was so soft, I sank into the cushions.

A stiff, annoying finger poked my shoulder. Then a strong

hand shook it. Dreaming the rabbit had gotten out of its cage, I reached to swat it, too late waking to the reality that rabbits didn't have hands. My slap was met with an unbunnylike hiss. When I opened my eyes, Griffin was bent over, his hand under his other arm, writhing in silent pain.

I jumped out of the chair. "Oh, I'm—"

He slapped a hand over my mouth and nodded to a sleeping form on a mat on the floor beside the changing screen.

Petal. Curled into a ball with her back to us. I vaguely remembered her coming in to take the tray of food, but it seemed she never left. Raleigh had her sleeping in my room. What exactly did the man think I was going to steal? A linen towel? A silver mirror? That torturous comb?

Griffin's hand lingered over my mouth longer than necessary. I nearly bit him in protest. He lifted it off a finger at a time, as if he didn't trust me to stay quiet. But I knew what was at stake.

He lowered his arm, his good hand then taking hold of mine, leading me toward the small space between the wall and the bed. Then he let go and fell on all fours, then to flat on the ground. Barefoot, he inched forward, slipping underneath the bed.

I did the same, seeing him disappear through a hole in the wall.

A secret exit. This was too good to be true. On the other side was a small tunnel. A lantern flickered at Griffin's feet. The space was only tall enough to sit. He reached around me and, very slowly to remain quiet, moved a piece of stone over the hole.

"Do these passages run all over the castle?" I asked in a whisper.

Griffin sat back on his heels, squinting at thin charcoal lines crisscrossing his hand.

"Is that a map?"

He raised a reproachful finger to his lips, then slipped on a pair of black boots he must've left to enter my room so silently. He waved, beckoning me to follow.

Stopping twice to refer to the map, a few minutes later, Griffin pushed open a grate barely big enough for his square shoulders to fit through. The exit left us in a dead-end hallway.

Griffin picked something up from the corner, hurling it to me. A long black cloak.

"Put it on. Pull up the hood. Cover your face," he whispered.

It was much too long for me. Anyone with a good eye would know it wasn't mine, but I did as he asked. "I won't let you get in trouble. If I'm recognized, run."

"As if the guards wouldn't recognize *me*?" He tucked my hair and assessed my appearance. "It'll do."

"I need to see the draignoch."

"You mentioned that. And so, I'm taking you." Griffin's fingers slipped through mine, sending an unexpected jolt through me. I told myself it was the thrill of the adventure rather than his hand itself causing my heart to skip a beat. I hated Sir Griffin, didn't I?

"Keep your head down and don't let go," he added.

With my eyes on the ground, all I saw were stone floors and steps until we reached fresh air. The moon shone, drawing a line through the courtyard and out the gates.

"Where you going, Sir Griffin?" a guard called in a haughty voice.

"Wherever this lass leads, sir. She is most insistent that I follow her."

Ah, so this was my way out. I was to be one of the women pining for a kiss from the big, brave champion. I thought of the women I'd seen in the Great Hall. Giggling fools who wielded shy glimpses like pitchforks. I laughed, but it came out more of a chortle. Griffin crushed two of my fingers together. His way of telling me to quiet, but it hurt. I fought the urge to kick him.

"Is that the redhead?" one of them called.

"Good night," Griffin yelled back, tossing them coins. They slid the bar, unlocking the gate, and pulled it ajar enough for us to get out.

As soon as the metal clanked behind us, I breathed a heavy sigh. Being champion had its privileges, it seemed.

We walked swiftly through empty streets with little light, other than the moon. I took stock, bathing in its cool glow, and in the freedom from Raleigh and his goons.

The feeling of victory didn't last. The draignoch's whimper

traveled through the night to brush my ear, raising the hair on the back of my neck.

It was several long minutes before I realized Griffin's hand was still tightly clasped on mine.

"Oh, sorry." He let go. His narrowed gaze shifted from dwelling to alley and back again.

He kept his injured hand tucked against his chest, his other hand on the pommel of his sword, the way Raleigh always did. I didn't get the feeling he was afraid of imminent attack but rather that he walked through life every day prepared for it. In that, I thought, we were alike.

The view was spectacular. The skies clear. Stars brilliant. The city lay out before us, in a descending display of tightly connected rooftops and thinning roads, but it all ended at the wall. Nothing beyond was visible. It was too high. A visual testament that freedom in the Walled City had its limits.

Griffin kept a quick pace. It was difficult to keep up with him without jogging. His legs were twice as long as mine. We passed several bigger estates, careened around a bend, then continued along another path, all the while heading downhill.

Around the next corner, I smelled horses. Padding down stone steps built into the hillside, we came to a paddock. A boy held on to the leads of two saddled horses.

"Nicely done." Griffin waved his hand with the map on it at him, smiling.

"Impressed you could follow it," the boy whispered, smirking.

Griffin mounted.

The boy offered a leg up to me, and I took it.

He looked up at Griffin. "Leave the saddles on the wooden horses. That's where I found them."

"Good man, Bradyn. Now go home quickly. Don't let anyone see you," Griffin told him. "After what happened today with Halig and Capp, I couldn't live with getting you in trouble with the guards."

"You're the boy who was on the dais? Is that right?" I asked. Bradyn nodded solemnly.

"I'm truly sorry for your loss, Bradyn."

He smiled half-heartedly. "Nice of you to say, my lady."

Griffin waited until the boy was out of sight to start moving.

"How long will it take to get there?" I asked.

"We will have to move slowly, so as not to raise suspicion. Could be as long as an hour. Maybe more. The Oughtnoch's entrance is all the way in the Bottom."

That sounded far. "Can't we walk through the arena somehow?"

"No. Arena's locked and heavily guarded. The gate to the chute that leads to the creature's pound is bolted from within." He brought his horse closer to mine. "We should ride side by side. And if we happen upon the guard patrols, smile. Act like you belong. And it wouldn't hurt if you could try and pretend as if you like me." He swallowed that last sentence.

I grinned and batted my eyes. "Like this?"

He laughed. "Maybe not quite that hard." He kicked his horse.

I followed suit, getting mine moving. "It shouldn't be too hard to pretend. I do like you. I think."

He laughed again.

I suppose it was a funny thing to say. "But I guess it depends which is the real you. The person who sent that boy, Bradyn, out of the arena to keep him from watching his cousins torn to shreds, the one I sparred with on the practice field today, or the bastard from last night?"

"I'm sorry. I was extreme. But if it makes you feel better, your stellar performance cost me a Phantombronze dagger."

My jaw dropped. "Phantombronze?"

"A gift from the king. I bet the prince that Xavier's magic wasn't real. All the sorcerers that he's brought to the castle to perform have been pathetic tricksters. Obvious in their lack of any real magic. Not that I believe what Xavier did was magic either, but when I couldn't explain the illusory cheetah, I was forced to relinquish the knife." He grinned at me. "Want to tell me how he did that so I can get it back from Jori? I *am* doing you a very big favor right now."

The horses' hooves clomped along the stone pavers, ticking off how long it was taking for me to answer him. His hopeful gaze fell by degrees into a disappointed frown.

He *was* doing something very dangerous for me. Defying the guards by sneaking me out, taking me to a place neither of us was supposed to go. If the king found out, it would be very, very bad for Griffin. The least I owed him was the truth. "You won't like my answer. I'm afraid the dagger will remain with the prince. It *was* magic, Griffin."

"There is no such thing." He kicked his horse to a trot. The hooves' clatter was so loud, speaking over it would require shouting. But what was there to say? I didn't care if Griffin believed in magic or not.

The Top was quiet. Peaceful. Crisp night air mixed with smoke from smoldering fires. After roads of spacious homes, a steep crag led to the Middle, where a fair few stumbled out of taverns, singing off-key, staggering for home. Griffin finally slowed as we passed a row of shops that included a blacksmith. He paused, his gaze passing through the shop as if he were looking for someone or something.

"Is someone there?" I asked, worrying.

"No. I'm betting they're all in the tavern this time of night," he said.

"Perhaps you should avoid making bets in the future."

He laughed. I liked making him laugh.

"Is this your family's shop?"

He smiled as we moved on. "I suppose they are my family, though not by blood. I haven't any of that variety left."

"I don't understand."

"My parents were killed by draignochs when I was small. Our family farm in the South devastated. I came to the city, looking for work."

"And the smith hired you? Were you an apprentice?"

"Not a very good one. Spent too much time practicing with the swords. Caught Sir Raleigh's attentions. Luck aligned. With a good deed for the prince, a wish granted by the king, and Raleigh took me on, training me for the armies I think, but I knew I wanted to enter the tournament. It was all I ever wanted. So last year, I did. Raleigh told me I was too young. That I wouldn't make it past the first draignoch. When I did, he didn't take it well."

Now that he was talking, I found I liked the sound of his voice. He had an easy way about him, calming. Helpful since I felt so lost in this labyrinth. "Why not? I would think him proud if he taught you."

"It was his title I took. A title he had held for a very long time. And when I won, the king's favor shifted from Raleigh to me. I was moved into the castle. He was moved out."

"Was he angry with you?"

"Anger I could take. He's been distant." A crease formed between his brows. "I'm not sure why I told you all of that."

"I won't repeat it."

"No. I don't think you would." He took a deep breath, letting it out slowly. "And you?"

I shrugged. "There's nothing to tell."

"What happened to your mother?"

"I don't know, actually. I don't know who she was."

Curiosity pursed his lips. "Xavier never told you?"

I shrugged. "Xavier doesn't know."

"Now you're just being contrary. Is this all some kind of secret?"

My eyes lifted to the moon, unsure of the answer to that question either.

"Xavier isn't your father." His face lit up as if he knew he was right. "You look nothing like him. Not a hint of relation. And if you're with him, and not your parents, I would guess they're either dead, and you're a foundling, as I am, or they sold you."

"No one sold me. Although Xavier threatened to on more than one occasion."

"They're dead, then?"

A strange knowing prickle tickled deep down inside. "I—I don't think so."

"You've lost me, Maggie." He sighed but smiled.

I'd lost me too. Whenever Xavier and I got to a new place, I would ask if anyone had lost a little girl. The answer was always the same. No. And every time, hearing that word, or seeing their heads shake, hurt just as much as it did the first time. I stopped asking and accepted the fact that I was on my own in this strange world.

I didn't know if it was because Griffin had done so much to free me tonight, or because I never really had a friend, and I wanted one. But I decided to trust him. I told him. Everything. About Xavier finding me. About not knowing who I was or where I came from. About the travels through the Hinterlands and Xavier's relentless search for magic.

Griffin asked a few questions here and there. What was the East like? Had I been to the North? He'd always wanted to see the North. "Like me," I told him.

I left out the recent bits, about seeing the draignoch, meeting Jori in the woods—about the strange connection with the moonlight, the magic, because it wasn't mine. As far as he knew, it was all Xavier.

"I wish I could remember something about my family, but I can't. Not a thing," I said.

"I have a hard time remembering my parents' faces anymore. I can't see the house we lived in or the lands we farmed. Only the day they died. Something I wish I could forget, honestly. And this draignoch? Why do you want to see it? Is it possible it killed your family?"

I gazed at Griffin. His moonlit eyes looked the same murky green color of a sea turtle's shell. His parents were killed by draignochs, and we were the same age, so it was a definite possibility. There were many orphans from that time. Parents who hid children in underground cellars and went out to fight the draignochs, never to return. It was a story I had heard from loads on the road. But I had no answer to that question either.

Griffin nodded as if he could read my unspoken thought. "So, you're just alone, like me?"

The softness in his tone gave me pause. It was a sadness I knew all too well.

"Yes." Only, riding beside Griffin, I was the least alone I had ever felt.

Another turn and the wind hit us. I shivered and pulled the cloak's hood lower, getting a whiff of a familiar scent. "Is this Sybil's?"

Griffin shifted forward in his saddle. "Yes. I told her you looked cold today and she said I should give that to you after dinner."

"Wouldn't have expected Sybil to be the way she is. Charitable and all. She's nothing like her sister." I couldn't keep my eyes from rolling.

Griffin reached into the pouch on the side of his saddle and came out with two apples. "Hungry?"

He tossed one to me before I could answer.

"I missed dinner," he added.

His injured hand rested on his lap, barely holding on to the reins, while he ate with the other. He was in pain. That's why he'd missed dinner. So no one would see the extent of his injury. A pull in my chest, like a taut bowstring, ached for release. The moonlight seemed to hum, vibrating through me, making it difficult to keep from touching his hand. It was the same instinct that hit me hard at the practice field when I saw the bandage. I wanted to heal him. To take his broken hand and mend it. I would too, if he would let me. But he didn't believe in magic.

"Sybil said you sent her to escort me this morning."

"I did ask her to check in on you."

"Not that I'm not appreciative. I like her. But why did you do that?"

He chewed over his next words carefully. "Because I couldn't."

You're safe, Maggie. That's what he said to me last night. Maybe it was his nature to be protective. I met many men on the road like that. For every one trying to pull up my skirt, there was another telling him to stop. Not that I needed their help. Most of the leeches ended up like Moldark, with a knife sticking out of their boot. But I appreciated the thought—the effort.

"Is that why you tell strangers you don't know that they're safe?"

He gave me a sort of secret smile. "My best mate, Thoma, said that actually, first day we met. The city feels big and scary, but there are good people here who watch out for each other."

"So, you wanted me to know you were watching out for me?"

"I guess I did."

Griffin stopped his horse outside a small tavern.

"We don't have time for ale, Sir Griffin."

He smirked. "This was my home until last year. We can leave the horses here."

Griffin dismounted. I did as well.

Lights flickered through the window. The place was crowded with revelers, drinking and singing along with the lute player's pluck. The sign on the door was a painting of a wilting red rose. I laughed. Perhaps not all in the city were happy with the king.

The door popped open.

"Look out!" Griffin pulled me out of the way as a bucket of piss landed on the street.

A boy our age with a mop of light hair leaned out. "Griffin?" He sounded confused. He hustled over, wiping his hands on his apron. "That really you?"

Griffin let go of my hand. "Thoma—"

"Didn't expect to see you slumming it down here," Thoma sniffed.

I suddenly felt like I'd walked into the middle of an argument. "This is your best mate?"

"Well, yeah," Griffin answered me, then frowned at Thoma. "Oh, is that how it is, then? That's hardly fair."

Thoma suddenly realized Griffin wasn't alone. His face broke into a huge grin. "I saw *you* on the king's balcony." He narrowed his gaze on Griffin. "You dating Topper ladies now?"

"I'm not a Topper, and not a lady," I exclaimed harsher than intended.

"Certainly look like one." Thoma smiled.

"Thoma, meet Maggie . . . of the Hinterlands. Maggie, meet Thoma, son of the owner of this fine establishment called the Wilted Rose."

Thoma softened at that. "Yes. My inheritance is secured with ale and a job by day at the blacksmith shop. All I need now is to find a good woman. I'm not discriminating. Hinterland girls are always welcome at my table, and other places," he said, and winked at me.

"That's enough," Griffin insisted.

Another boy walked out. Similar height and age to Thoma, he was dark haired, only his was cropped short. His eyebrows were so thick they looked like they could pop off, crawl away, and have a life of their own. He didn't look so happy to see Griffin either.

"Well . . . look who finally decided to grace us with his presence?"

"Dres, Griffin's with company," Thoma said.

"Company, is that what he's calling it now?" Dres laughed, staggering back into the building.

"Ignore him. He's drunk," Thoma explained.

"We should go anyway," Griffin said to me.

"Go? Because of Dres? Martha and Hugo are here too. All the gang from the shop. My father will open a fresh keg. Come on. Let us toast *our* champion." Thoma's proud gaze fell on me. "King takes credit when it's us who made him what he is."

Griffin sighed, as if this was a repeated refrain. "I wish I could, but we have something else to do right now. It's important. I need a favor."

"He's too good for us lot anymore, Thoma." Dres came out. He leaned on the side of the building to keep from falling over, his drink still in his hand. "Go back to the castle, Griffin. No one wants you here."

Thoma tore the glass from Dres's protesting hands, spilling it all over his trousers. "Get inside, Dres, before you fall down."

Dres made a rude hand gesture, then tripped down the steps into the tavern. He must've bumped into a table because suddenly his name was yelled out by many.

"He's a cheery fellow," I said.

"He's . . . well . . . Dres." Thoma shrugged. He cast a weary glance to Griffin. "You want to leave the horses? That the favor?"

Griffin nodded, looking relieved. "Thank you." He tied both sets of reins to the hitching post, then grabbed a torch tied to his pack and handed it to Thoma. "Can I get a light?"

Thoma went into the tavern and returned with the torch lit. He handed it to Griffin.

Griffin tossed him a coin.

Thoma held it up and gave them a cheeky grin. "I'm not too proud to take it. My someday wife is going to need pretty things." He winked at me, sliding back into the tavern, and shut the door.

Griffin and I started walking again.

All the doors in the Bottom were shut, but the windows were open and loud conversations spilled into the street.

"You lived there? In the Wilted Rose?" I asked. I liked the name.

Griffin nodded. "I stumbled down the stairs practically frozen in the middle of the night. Half dead from working in the ducts. The stench must have been pouring off me." Griffin cringed. "Thoma got his father to let me work for supper that night, stink and all. When it was done, Thoma hid me in the cellar with the casks. Gave me a bucket to wash myself and a cot. I lived down there for a week before his father noticed. Wolfbern's his name. Told me I could work there at night in exchange for the cot. First home I had here. They live above it."

Griffin pointed to the dark windows above the tavern.

I nodded. "And the Hugo he mentioned. Is he the blacksmith you worked for?"

A slow, shy smile spread over Griffin's face. "You were listening."

"I'm always listening."

Griffin glanced over his shoulder at the old tavern. "They don't like me much these days. My life feels so far away from them, and so different from theirs. Know what I mean?"

"Yes, and no. I don't have friends like that. Xavier and I, we move all the time."

"That hard?"

I shrugged. "It's all I've ever known."

It was all that I could remember. . . .

As we passed under a wooden arch, Griffin's demeanor changed. He handed me the torch without explanation. His shoulders lifted. He shook his sleeve. A dagger dropped into his palm, the blade's tip visible in his hand.

"What's wrong?"

We stepped beyond a gap between buildings. I heard scuffling.

"Muggers," he groaned.

Before I knew what was happening, a pudgy, sweaty arm grabbed me around the neck, pulling me against a soft belly. Another plump limb knocked the torch out of my hand and pressed a dagger against my chest. "Donna move." His breath smelled like ale.

Another stepped out of the shadows. A boy close to our age, he was short, light-haired, in a black cloak that was far too big on him, and as scarred as Griffin. Maybe more so. His scars started at the patch over his left eye, heading both north and south, with wide berths.

"Lookie lookie, Finn," he said, spitting at Griffin's feet. "If it isn't the reigning champion. Slumming, *Sir* Griffin? With this fine-lookin' lady too." He pulled a dagger. "If you don't want her cut like your ugly mug, hand over your pockets."

Griffin held his hands up, his expression turning cold. "My pockets are empty. Check for yourself if you don't believe me."

The blade inched upward to my cheek. "Careful, Nesbit, he's quick."

"Not so quick as we are," Nesbit said, inching toward him.

A second later, Nesbit was facedown on the ground, gasping for breath, Griffin's own dagger digging into his shoulder blade. Griffin managed all that one-handed. He turned on the larger man holding me. "Let her go." When he didn't, Griffin applied pressure.

"Gah! Let her go, Finn. Do it."

His grip loosened. I ducked out, kicking him in the shins on my way to retrieving the torch. Griffin yanked Nesbit up, shoving him at his partner. "Now run." He spun the grip, taunting them.

Our assailants fumbled over each other, racing into the shadows.

I laughed. "They can't be very successful if you could run them off so easily."

"Was that an insult to them or to me?" Griffin shook his head, feigning offense, then checked my cheek, his fingers lingering longer than necessary, but I didn't mind in the slightest.

"I'm fine." My cheeks burned, and not from the moon. I looked down, trying to hide my face.

Griffin and I walked on swiftly. He kept a firm grip on his dagger as we continued on, changing sides with me so he passed closer to any dim spots.

Not long after, we came to what I thought was a dead end, but it was actually the beginning of a long thin set of stairs, descending between the buildings. I couldn't see where it went. It was so dark I couldn't see anything beyond the first step. My palm tingled. I wondered if I could draw down a beam to light our way, not that I would. My magic was Xavier's, I told myself, although I was starting to hate the sound of that.

"Ten more of these and we'll come out beside the base of the arena."

"Lead the way, Sir Griffin."

About halfway down, I heard crowd noises coming from open windows. A girl not much older than me stumbled drunk out of a basement door. She stepped under the glow of a torch. I could see her dress was slit up the sides, the bodice cut low, revealing too much. As she turned her head, catching my stare, I saw bruises on her cheek and scratches on her neck. She quickly turned away, embarrassed or frightened. A soldier spilled out after her, adjusting his trousers. He sneered at Griffin, then started walking toward us, using the stone facade to prop himself up.

"Over here, my lady. Got a pretty coin, just inside." He patted his crotch.

"And I'm sure a rash as well."

Griffin wrapped his arm around my shoulders, pulling me down the stairs.

"As much as you seem to like to goad everyone you meet, please remember we're not supposed to be here!"

"Sorry." The draignoch's voice carried on the cold breeze, raising goose bumps on my arms. She was close. "We should hurry too. Let's move faster."

The stairs, going both west and south, descended into the lowest part of the Bottom, where the putrid odor from the ducts nearly knocked me off my feet. It permeated everything.

My legs ached as I stepped out into full moonlight. But my heart leaped. To the left was the base of the arena. The structure towered over us. The bridges from the Top and the Middle were visible far above our heads, showing how far we had traveled tonight. The Bottom was at the very bottom of everything in the Walled City. To the right an enormous square tower connected to a long wall, stretching some forty feet high. I couldn't see where it ended. A prison built to hold dangerous creatures.

The draignoch must have felt my arrival. Her calls rose to a fevered pitch.

"I'm coming!"

Griffin skidded to a stop, shushing me. "Who are you yelling at?"

"The draignoch."

"You *hear* her?" He sounded skeptical.

"You don't? Did you get hit in the ear in a match?"

"No . . ."

I cupped my ears, realizing all at once that it did nothing. Her clammers still banged *inside* my head. It was altogether incredible, yet irritating.

We crossed the grass to the wall and paced for at least fifty feet before finally finding a wooden door. The latch wouldn't budge.

"It's locked," I whispered.

"Of course it is." Griffin pulled a small knife from his boot and used it to lift the pins from the hinges. The door jerked open a foot.

"You really aren't the tosspot I thought you were."

"Probably the nicest thing you've to me said all night." Griffin dropped the torch, rolling it until the fire doused. He took the lead into the rectangular compound. It was huge, twice the size of the arena floor. We walked by penned cows, pigs, chickens, lambs.

"Food for the beasts," Griffin whispered.

Then by several empty cells. Then several with draignochs. All huddled pressed against the back walls, far from the reach of the bars. My heart ached at how many times guards must have stabbed spears through their cages, like Moldark had done to *her*, to instill such behavior. None came to greet us. People were feared.

For such large creatures, the draignochs were very quiet. She had gone quiet too.

Someone exited the tower, carrying a torch. Griffin and I hid behind a hay wagon. The light flickered closer. I held my breath and crawled under with Griffin. It felt like an eternity until the person left and we heard the tower door close and lock.

Griffin hurried out.

I heard her again, and caught his arm. "My turn to go first."

We passed another draignoch cell. The poor yellow beast Malcolm had fought moaned. Its neck and side still bloody, a sticky sap held the wounded flesh together. At the sight of me, it lifted its head and let out a strangled cry.

Worried the guards would come out to see what was wrong, I ran. Griffin followed and a minute later we stood in front of a very different kind of cell. Larger than the others, the top and sides had stone exteriors, but the front of the cell and the insides were lined with glistening bars.

"Phantombronze," Griffin whispered in awe. "I didn't know this much existed in all of the Walled City."

She scraped her claws in the dirt, and I knew she wanted me to come inside, but the cell was locked and the bars too close together for me to fit through. She lowered her head, straining against the chains digging into her neck. I could see her pale blue eyes glinting in the moonlight.

Griffin squinted, looking from her to me, seeing what I was, that our eyes matched in color and shape. He paced to the end of the cell and back again, trying to get a good look at her, but the space was too cramped and dim.

Griffin settled beside me and whispered, "It's enormous. And the wings are much larger, that much I can see."

"Her wings . . . ," I corrected.

She shifted, chains clanking, to show me her side was peppered with stab wounds from the soldiers' spears. "She needs me, Griffin."

"Needs you? For what?" he growled.

I stretched my arms as far as I could into the cell. If I could touch her, perhaps I could heal her wounds.

"Maggie, have you lost your senses?" He grabbed my waist, preventing me from reaching her. His face winced at the pain he must have felt in his injured hand by latching on to me, but it wasn't nearly as much pain as he was going to feel if he didn't let me go!

"She won't hurt me." I struggled, but his grip remained

clasped like irons. "Please . . ." I was begging. But it didn't matter. Nothing mattered except *her*.

"Maggie!" He yanked.

"I said let go!" I grabbed his hand, putting intense pressure on it, feeling the broken bone shift. He cursed.

His hold loosened enough for me to reach far enough inside. Her head brushed my hand. My palm flattened until I was well and truly touching her. Then, all at once, blinding light forced my eyes shut.

When I opened them, I was no longer in the draignoch's compound. No longer in the Bottom, or in the Walled City at all. Or even in the Hinterlands. I was someplace else. Flying above treetops, soaring through night beneath the blazing full moon, like a bird in flight.

A beam struck the earth. A loud crack deep in the heart of a dense forest caught my attention. The moon left a path from the heavens for me to follow.

Downward.

Descending through light, I found the tree. It was sliced clean and steaming from the frigid moon's carving. As the fog cleared, a baby cooed. I landed on the lip of the trunk, staring into blue eyes. My gaze jerked to the baby's arm, where it was marked with my scar. That was me in the tree. I was the babe I was seeing.

I glimpsed the wing flapping beside me. On the other side, another.

I wasn't me at all. This was the draignoch's doing. These were her memories of the first time we'd met.

A woman with long black hair appeared out of the darkness.

She was naked, as was the tiny boy whose hand she held. "As I foresaw, Armel. This babe will give you what you need. She only needs to reach her age of enlightenment."

I took to the skies, following after the woman and the baby. Or rather, the draignoch did.

Images flew by. Glimpses in time.

The draignoch looking back at the girl crawling after her. The woman catching her, slapping her for running off.

Wings cascading over a crying girl's bruised shoulders and back, giving a gentle hug.

"Get away from her! She belongs to me!" the woman screeched.

An arrow whizzing by, missing, barely.

"Yeah!" The boy hurled a rock.

The little girl ran, following the draignoch.

"Get back here! Worthless child!"

Through woods, across streams, into a cave too small for the woman to enter. We hid there, wrapped together. Girl and draignoch. No. Not draignoch.

Dragon.

Looking down on the girl, on me, older now, maybe five, staring at my reflection in a smooth pond. Wild sun-dusted raven hair. Blue eyes. Covered in mud.

The earthy scent of the woods after rain. The leaves green and plentiful with tiny burgeoning buds. It was spring.

A playful whine echoed from the dragon. The girl looked up and started running. The dragon took to the skies, sailing through fluffy white clouds, slicing them into different animal shapes as the girl called them out to her.

"A wolf!"

"A bear!"

"A fuzzy rabbit!"

"Rendicryss!" the girl called.

The dragon landed then, for that was the name I had given her. We were both still small. Rendicryss whinnied, wanting a pet, which my tiny hand gave her on the nose. In return she licked the mark on my arm.

A sudden forceful surge rocketed through me.

Moonlight struck palms, leaving a line from the heavens, leading directly to us. I wasn't scared, but rather dancing and laughing, winding a light web, a cocoon around us.

A rock pelted Rendicryss's side.

Armel's snivelly pug-nosed face peeked out from behind a tree. He hurled another rock.

I caught the rock in my moonlit web and hurled it back at him. Then chased him, for I was tired of running away from him and the woman we both called Mother.

He tried to run but there was no escape. He was hunched over, his eyes not level, which made him slower, off balance.

I threw another rock. "Stay away from us!"

It hit him, and he fell on all fours. His back trembling, not with fear but laughter.

"She's here, Mother!"

I hid behind a tree. Rendicryss perched on a branch, too big to be missed.

"Worthless!" she yelled. "You cannot run anymore."

An arrow sailed at Rendicryss. The jolt knocked her out of the tree.

I slapped a hand over her mouth, holding back her scream. Pulled the arrow out. A tiny hand over the web. Glistening white light. The hole knit together. The wing healing instantly.

"I'm going to chop up that creature and throw her in my cauldron!" She pinned another arrow, drawing the string taut. "And then you with her!"

The arrow hit the dragon's other wing.

"Fly!" I screamed. "Please!"

The dragon did, but always keeping me in her sights.

I ran hard. Feet pounding soft ground, tripping over rising roots.

At the edge of the woods, I skidded to a stop. It was too dangerous beyond the woods.

Mother chanting. She stepped out from behind the tree. An arrow struck Rendicryss's wing.

As the images spun, I saw myself start running again. I saw Mother throw a curse. Me, falling out of the woods.

Wounded, the young dragon attacked, chasing Mother away from the edge of the woods, away from me, giving me time to run.

Rendicryss returned to the edge of the woods, but I was gone. She roared and her cry broke my heart. The world spun through setting suns and rising moons—

"Hey! You there!"

Griffin grabbed me, lifting me off my feet, pulling my hand off Rendicryss. The images cut off. My dragon hissed at the guards. Her hind legs and neck chained, her wings tied down, she slammed her tail against the bars, drawing their attention.

Griffin put a clammy hand over my mouth as he set me on my feet and backed us into an empty cell. He pressed my head into his shoulder, trying to keep me quiet because I couldn't stop crying. My hands wouldn't stop shaking. For all these years, I had been lost to Rendicryss, and she to me. But not anymore. My dragon had found me. Her sting broke through the curse, giving me back what was rightfully mine. But she wasn't finished. She had more to show me! More I needed to see. The power of the moon flowed through me like a raging river, but I had no idea what to do with it. I balled my hands into fists.

Guards and a familiar stick figure appeared. Griffin pushed me down and covered me with hay. "Don't come out," he whispered.

"I should've known." I recognized Perig's sniveling voice. "Leave us," he shouted at the guards. Their footsteps softened until they were gone.

I heard Perig step into the cell. "Popped the hinges, did we, Sir Griffin? I'm going to have to bolt the gate now."

"I just wanted to see her," Griffin confessed. "*I* have to face *that* in the arena. Not you." He sounded angrier than I'd ever heard him before. "I understand if you feel the need to report me, but if it makes you feel any better, she is so bound, I learned nothing."

"Did you call it a she?" Perig asked.

"I meant *it*," Griffin corrected himself.

"All the others have tossed gold at me. I assumed *you'd* understand, and have your bribe at the ready," Perig laughed. Griffin blinked at him. "Yes, the others have all paid well to see it. Don't look so surprised. I carry a death sentence so long as I work here. This coin will ensure that I can eventually leave this job." He wiggled his three-fingered hand. "I've lost enough to these monsters. Twenty pieces is all I ask. My life is worth more than that, is it not?"

Griffin puffed a breath. "You take this secret with you to your grave or I will put you in it."

"Bring me payment tomorrow and you have my word." Perig scurried out of the cell. "Go now. The way you came. I will bring the guards inside the tower until you are gone so no one can say they bore witness to your entry or exit. I'll tell them it was another, a drunk man from the Bottom. They will enjoy trying to find out who it was."

Griffin returned a minute later. "He's gone. We have to go."

"I have to free Rendicryss," I said, trying and failing to brush the hay off my cloak.

"Are you mad? You cannot let that thing loose."

"Thing? That thing is my past!" I shoved him, struggling to get to her again, but he refused to get out of my way.

"Okay, let's say for the sake of insane arguments that I believe that you believe that this monster is somehow from your past. She's locked in Phantombronze. We have no key. You cannot free her."

He danced, keeping me from her. Why didn't Griffin understand this?

"Was this your plan all along?" he accused. "To let that monster out? Do you know the damage she would do to the city? To the people?"

Rage flooded through me. "She's not the monster! You are!"

"I am? I am the monster?" His cheeks flushed with anger. He checked the tower door, then dragged me into the shadows. "And when they discovered you gone, and a draignoch escaped, they'd interrogate the guards, who wouldn't want to get in trouble, so they'd tell the king they opened the gate for *me*."

Tears free-flowed. "Fine! Just let me touch her again!"

"We're out of time, Maggie! Please . . ."

The thought of leaving Rendicryss hurt me like nothing I had ever experienced before. "I don't know what to do."

"Yes, you do. We need to leave."

He was right.

There was no way to get her out tonight. No time for me to sit beside her and see what more she had to show me. But I would return. I would figure out how to free her, then we would both leave this place.

A lump lodged in my throat, making it impossible to speak, so I nodded. We sprinted across the compound, Rendicryss's sad mew crushing my heart with every step.

But we kept running—taking the stairs in the dark, making it halfway up until we both had to stop to catch our breath.

Griffin leaned his back against the wall, clutching his hand, writhing in pain. "Dammit."

His injury was worse. I could smell the beginnings of infection. I wanted to hate Griffin for what he'd said, but he'd helped me, and I owed him. "I always repay my debts. Give me your hand."

Griffin recoiled. "Why? You don't owe me anything."

"You brought me here. You're going to have to pay that whiny fool, Perig. I owe you." I held out my hand, palm up in expectation. "Give it to me. Now."

He placed his left hand in mine.

I smirked. "The other one."

"I'm not a complete idiot. It's already broken. You need not try and make it worse. If I met your best friend in the ring, I would be a tasty meal as it is."

"I wasn't intending to make it worse." His scowl was proof he didn't believe me. I wiggled my fingers, goading him. "That infection will leach into your bloodstream and kill you long before Rendicryss has a chance."

Griffin contemplated, biting his lip.

"What do you have to lose by letting me see it?"

He remained frozen as I slid my palm beneath his. He let me move his other arm out of the way so I could sandwich the broken one between mine. I slowly unraveled the bandage, growing ill at the sight of what lay beneath. Swollen and festering, blood and pus oozed from the gaping wound left by a draignoch's spike. The broken bone separated so far, his fingers pointed in unnatural directions. The worst part was the smell coming off it. It was all I could do not to vomit. I never liked the sight of blood, and this was so much worse.

His brow was sweaty; he was fevered. "How long has it been like this? Poisoned?" I asked.

"I'm not sure," he said, his gaze fixed on mine.

The moon wasn't visible any longer, but if I was right it shouldn't have to be. The moon simply *was*, visible or not. I felt it in the air around me, the push and pull—and I knew I could draw from it. A deep breath and I closed my eyes. A pin light in the darkness grew brighter. A surge rushed down my arms, into my hands. My palms collapsed on his, glowing brightly.

"Maggie! Your hands . . . your hands!"

All at once Griffin roared in pain. He tried to pull his hand out, but the force holding us together was too strong. My eyes still closed, I could see the cracked and separated bone in my mind. The fluid swelled like a growing tide with nowhere for it to go.

Griffin hissed.

I was making it worse.

My fingers stretched as far as possible. I blew out a long breath, the power jolting through my hands, and finally into his. The jagged shards moved until they were aligned, then knitted together, becoming one again. The infection from the wound took more effort. My whole body trembled, drawing out the toxins until the smell of rotting flesh was replaced with only Griffin.

Winded and weary beyond belief, I opened my eyes to his surprised smile.

"What . . . ? How . . . ?" he stuttered, flexing his fingers freely.

And then . . . he hugged me. The smell of rot gone, replaced by his own scent, which I liked more than I should.

I laughed to hide my embarrassment, but I didn't let go. "No one can know."

Griffin leaned back, his warm hands cradling my shoulders. "Are you insane? Why would you hide such a gift? Do you know the kind of influence you could wield at court?" He grew more excited by the question, then stopped. "*You* brought the moonlight into the Great Hall, didn't you? *You* made that cheetah chase me!"

I laughed at what sounded like fear in his voice. "Oh, come now. It was only moonlight. You can't be afraid of—"

"It wasn't just light. It burned me, Maggie."

"Burned?" I stared at my hands.

"Not with heat, but with cold."

"That is . . . unexpected!" I paced, unable to hold still. "In the memories—the ones I just saw—I used the light like a fisherman uses a net. I caught a rock thrown at her." I reached a hand up, willing moonlight to come to me, but nothing happened. "But alas, I don't know how I did it."

"Memories?"

I nodded. "Griffin, I saw her memories of *us*."

He pursed his lips, bemused.

"Not you and me. Me and Rendicryss!"

He leaned against the wall, his face a mask of skepticism. "What did you see?"

"How we came to be separated. My mother cursed me. And she had a son, Armel. Wicked boy. Jealous." Griffin looked as confused as I felt. "Yes. Unbelievable, I know. But it was real. I know what I saw was real." I traced the mark on my arm. "I don't know what that curse did to me, but when I found Rendicryss a few days ago, it broke some part of it. Because that very night, I healed a squirrel."

"A squirrel?" he chided.

"Don't mock me."

"Never." He raised his hands, surrendering.

"Then, I helped a boy on the road. And now you!" I squeezed his hand.

He smiled. "But . . . how does it work?"

I looked at my palms, then at Griffin, shrugging. "I have no idea. Rendicryss knows. I know she does. I have to . . ." The look on Griffin's face stopped me. There was no going back. Not tonight.

"Well, it's miraculous, Maggie. However you do it." Griffin flexed his mended fingers, grinning. "But what of Xavier?"

I shook my head. "His tricks have always been that.

Nothing more. I daresay if he knew what I was capable of, what I knew, my life with him would've been very different." Xavier was both a father figure and crazed with the pursuit of magic. When the two aspects were pitted against one another, the truth would win. He wasn't my father. Not really. And even if he were, he would care most about the magic. "No one can know, Griffin. The king believes it is Xavier, and Xavier believes it is Xavier, and I don't want them to know it's me—at least, not until I'm gone."

We started climbing the stairs.

"But why leave? Think of the wealth and status the king would grant you, Maggie. You would want for nothing."

"Riches? I don't want riches, especially from the king! You saw what he did to those two men today? His men do the same *every* day in the Hinterlands. Starving men strung up for not being able to afford ridiculous, high taxes. Soldiers raping women as payment for outstanding sums. Or worse. Kidnapping them for brothels here in the Walled City." I clutched the train of the blue dress I had on beneath the cloak. "I could never have worn a dress on the road. It was too dangerous. The king's men are the danger."

Griffin didn't argue, and his expression was more than enough for me to know he knew some of what I said was true.

"You idolize an evil man, Griffin."

"I don't idolize anyone. I'm a survivor, like you." He sounded hurt and a little angry. "All I have is because of what the king and Jori have given me."

"A room? Food? Weapons and clothes? Please. I saw how the people cheered for you, from Top to Bottom. You're more to them than a sword. So much so that when you stand beside the prince, the people cheer for him too. You've earned everything the king has given you and more."

He wrestled with that while we continued up the steep stairs. My legs ached. My heels felt raw with blisters. I was looking forward to the tavern, and my horse.

"All of this must be our secret. You cannot tell the prince or the king!" I poked him the chest. "Promise!"

"I promise. It's the least I can do. You saved my life." He held his hands up. "Now I'll be more than ready for my next turn in the ring."

It occurred to me that I was missing a vital piece of information. "Why did you bring me here?"

"What do you mean? You asked me to," he blurted, but I could tell by the look in his eyes he knew exactly what I meant.

"You wanted to see her. To get a leg up on battling her, didn't you?"

Griffin stared, mouth hanging open. I was right. "Maggie, you said it yourself. I earn my place with the king and Jori with my sword. If I don't win in the arena, if I lose favor with the people, then I have no value to them. I could lose everything."

"And if you kill her, I lose everything." My legs cramping, I pressed on, hurrying as quickly as I could up the stairs, refusing to look at him.

His footsteps were constant, never waning, but the silence spoke volumes.

Night was almost over. It would be morning in a few short hours. Thankfully, the horses stood where we'd left them at the tavern. Riding uphill would be hard on them, but my legs would go no farther.

Griffin made sure I was tucked into the cloak before knocking on the fortress gate. The guard chuckled, shaking his head, and opened it just enough for us to slip through.

We entered the castle through an alley door this time. The delicious aroma of baking bread met us in the kitchens, as well a heavyset balding man covered in flour and smelling of a long night of ale.

"Griffin?" His eyes fell on me. "Bradyn thought you already back. Moldark's just come for her tray. He's on his way to her room now."

Griffin grabbed my hand and ran. Up a spiral staircase, through a door that entered the Great Hall, which was unnervingly silent. Through three more stretches of hallways until we reached the one with the grate.

Griffin went first.

Crawling quickly bruised my knees and palms. He rolled the stone to the secret entrance into my room as quietly as possible. The only noise was a slight tap when he leaned it against the wall.

The room was still dark. Griffin tugged the edge of the cloak, reminding me I wasn't wearing it when I left. I pulled it over my head and gave it back to him. His hand brushed mine and squeezed. There was no time to ask him why he did it, or what it meant. No time to understand why it made my heartbeat quicken. I wasn't sure I liked him any more than I did when the day started, especially if he was planning to try to kill Rendicryss.

I scooted around him and slid out the hole beneath the bed. Someone knocked.

Petal's feet emerged from behind the screen. I could see her bare heels. Her back to me, I exited on the far side and threw the covers back as if the knock had woken us both.

"Who is it, Petal?"

Holding a tray, she glanced over her shoulder, first at the chair where I had fallen asleep earlier, then at the bed. The door cracked, and I could see Moldark's toothless scowl leering in.

"Good morning, sunshine."

Xavier shuffled around him and slammed the door shut. His eyes sunken and bruised, he took one look at Petal and opened the door again.

"Get out!" he yelled at her. "Now, before I box your ears!"

Petal set the tray on the table by the fireplace and ran out the door.

Once alone, he paced. "Maggie, we're in trouble. I've been trying all night. All night! And nothing . . ." He held his bony long-fingered hands up, showing them empty. "There is no magic. The king is angry. I saw it in his eyes." He was near tears.

"I don't understand. What happened?" I sat down in the chair before my legs gave out.

"After dinner, the king bade me to perform, and I did. Everything the same. Gems. Bones. Staff. I called to the moonlight, and it wouldn't bless me! I tried to heal our squirrel, but he died on the table between the roasted pheasant and baked apples."

"What did I say about hurting the animals, Xavier?"

"It would've been a real crowd-pleaser, lass, if I had been able to save the little bugger! That evil northern boy Cornwall, and Lady Esmera, they laughed—at *me*! I went back to my old tricks, which displeased King Umbert. He called me all manner of names and threw me out of the Great Hall!" He dropped his head into his hands. "Why? Why is this happening?" His neck craned, his eyes on the ceiling. "One day, I'm blessed by the gods, and the next they take it all away!"

He burst into tears that mixed with the thick layer of black kohl, turning his deep wrinkles into muddy rivers. "Prince Jori spoke on my behalf. Said that I was tired, and without my assistant. That I deserved another chance." He sighed, regaining slight control. "And so tonight I perform in the king's chambers. And you . . . you *must* be by my side. Understand?"

The king was cruel but nowhere near as stupid as Xavier. If I went with him, in what I expected would be a small private room, and helped him, King Umbert would know—he would deduce the magic was in me.

After all my snapping at Griffin, I couldn't help thinking

that perhaps he was right. Perhaps I should tell King Umbert the truth. Maybe the king *would* give me everything I asked for, including Rendicryss. . . .

I would've laughed at myself if Xavier wasn't in the room. King Umbert never did anything for anyone without it benefiting him. He would try to use me and Rendicryss one way or another. Whatever the outcome of this performance, nothing good would come of it.

I poured Xavier a cup of water from the pitcher on the table near the fireplace and handed it to him. "I understand, Xavier. I understand everything."

TEN

GRIFFIN

Griffin delighted in his ability to use both hands to crawl out of the passage. He had no way of knowing what lay on the other side of the wall for Maggie, but her room was dark and silent. A good sign their secret outing would remain a secret— once he paid off Perig.

Twenty pieces of gold coin. His entire life's savings. He stretched his fingers, feeling no pain. It was more than worth it.

Maggie's touch lingered in his healed hand as he padded softly through the dimly lit hallways. Dread swept through him at the thought of her anger when it came to her draignoch's death. *But wait.* Not a draignoch. She called Rendicryss a *dragon.*

It was impossible to see much in the darkness of the cell, but one thing was for certain: Rendicryss was a different kind of a beast. Bigger wings. Longer, thinner body. She would be a fierce match for any knight in the tournament.

Maggie would never forgive him if he killed Rendicryss, but she didn't understand what Griffin did. His mother's screams as draignochs dragged her into the woods. His father calling out for help as they tore him limb from limb. Griffin was alone in the world because of these kinds of monsters. And if it came to a choice between his own life in the arena or the dragon's, Griffin would choose himself every time.

Maggie had to understand that, didn't she? No. Of course not. She only thought of herself and what was right for her. He'd risked everything for her tonight, and was she even grateful? She accused him of going to the Oughtnoch for himself! And while that was partially true, he never would've gone if she hadn't asked him to help her. What was wrong with him? Why did he go to such great expense for her? But he knew. Deep down. Because as much as he wanted to yell at her, he, to the same extent, wanted to kiss her.

He groaned.

The castle wakened. Hustling boots scraped against the stone-cold floors. Servants raced to bring food and clean clothing to the many visitors for the tournament. Patrolling guards nodded to Griffin as he jogged the rest of the way, exhausted, confused, starving, and in desperate need of a change of clothes.

Griffin found Bradyn waiting for him in his room.

"I was so worried." Bradyn set Griffin's breakfast on the table beneath the window. "Father said you only just returned. Did the horses get back?"

"The horses are near the stables. I didn't have time to take their saddles off."

Bradyn cursed. "You didn't unsaddle them? What took you so long?" He threw up his hands. "Gah! I'll take care of it. I'll go now and meet you in the tunnel with your axe before the melee."

Bradyn started to leave but Griffin called him back. "Wait. Have another bring me my axe. I need you to do a different favor for me."

Griffin pulled out his money box from the wardrobe and handed it to Bradyn. The boy's knees buckled at the weight. "Hide this in something and take it to Perig at the keep."

"All the way to the Bottom? I'll miss the melee," he griped, shuffling toward the full laundry basket.

"You said it yourself yesterday. You have no chance of winning. And I really need you to do this for me. I wouldn't ask if it wasn't very important. Life-or-death important."

Bradyn groaned, dropping the box on the dirty shirts. "Is this about last night?"

Bradyn asked too many questions. "Never mind what it's about. It's better if you can honestly answer that you don't know."

Bradyn buried the box beneath the clothes. "You go for a walk with a beautiful woman that the prince swoons for, and come back with secrets?" He was too close to the truth. "Let me guess. Perig caught you two. Were you kissing?" He hugged himself and kissed the air with closed eyes, making irritating mewing sounds.

Griffin popped him on the back of the head. "Get a move on!"

Bradyn heaved the basket up. "All right. But that's sure a long way to go to kiss."

Griffin shoved him toward the door.

Bradyn's sarcastic laugh was irritating. "She's very pretty. Probably worth the prince's anger."

"Yes, well . . ." It was wrong to mislead Bradyn, but a romantic stroll was the excuse that got them out of the fortress. If Bradyn was questioned, the answers would align. "The prince swoons for every pretty face."

Unable to stand any longer, Griffin sat down on the edge of his bed.

"I dunno. I heard he sent dresses to her room. Fancy ones . . . before she even arrived."

Griffin's stomach twisted into an irritating knot. "I'm sure Prince Jori has sent dresses to many women."

"Maybe, but this morning I heard he went to the treasure room . . . for jewels." Bradyn hefted the basket higher, waggling his eyebrows.

Griffin yanked off his boots. "Jewels for Esmera, Bradyn."

Bradyn wrestled with opening the door, nearly dropping the heavy laundry basket. "I guess we'll see soon enough."

Griffin hurled the boots at him, chasing him out.

The morning went by in a mechanical blur: food, washing, dressing, all in an exhausted fog from lack of sleep. Worst of all, Griffin lost track of time. He was forced to sprint the road from the Top to the arena, almost missing the turnoff for the tunnel because of his sour mood.

The jewels were for Esmera. But what if they weren't? It wasn't as if Jori's intentions were to make Maggie, a common-born woman, his queen. But his consort? Perhaps. What kind of life would that be? Griffin wondered. One like his, where he performed at the prince's whim.

Only for Maggie it would be a very different kind of performance. . . .

The thought made him boil. Maggie would reject the prince if he made an advance, wouldn't she? But if she did, what would happen then?

What was worse, Griffin couldn't figure out why he cared. Maggie was stubborn, and angry at everything he said or did. He had to coax a compliment from her, and even that was coupled with criticism. *She would choose that dragon over me!*

So then, why was he still thinking about her? It was infuriating!

By the time Griffin arrived at the tunnel, the melee was long since over. Griffin didn't know who'd won, and honestly it didn't matter—not like it did yesterday. A spark of sadness ran through him as he stared at the back of his hand, seeing the bones move in perfect unity. For better or worse, Maggie's touch had . . . changed him.

The other knights stood ready with axes in hand. Oak wore a red tunic, while Cornwall and Malcolm were in brown today. Silas, in his armor branded with a *U* for the king, prepared to take his turn against a draignoch afterward.

"Sir Griffin . . ." A twitchy boy Griffin didn't recognize held out his axe to him with hands trembling.

Griffin took it with his left hand. He would throw with his right, but wanted to play a surprise on the people, show off how he had miraculously healed. Prove he was set apart from the other knights—because with Maggie's help, he was.

"You new to the armory?" Griffin asked the boy.

"I, uh—" He shook his head and ran off.

"He is starstruck, Sir Griffin," Jori said, entering the tunnel with Maggie on his arm.

Swallowing did nothing to alleviate the bitter taste in Griffin's mouth from seeing them together. "As he should be," he jested, giving a slight bow. "Maggie, you look well this morning."

She wore another new dress, red this time, and a necklace of shimmering rubies. Griffin's breath caught. Jori may as well have draped her in his family's sigil.

"Well? She looks well. Is that all you can say, man? She looks beautiful," Jori boasted. He kissed her hand, surprising Griffin and, by the look on her face, Maggie too.

Maggie still hadn't said a word. Her regard ventured past him. She craned her neck, trying to see beyond Griffin, beyond the other competitors, beyond the tunnel. She was looking for Rendicryss, worrying it was her turn in the arena, but there was no way to know until the gate rolled up.

Malcolm and his brother stared at Jori, their expressions dimming by the second.

"Where's my sister?" Cornwall barked.

"My dear brother. She's on the dais. As is Lady Sybil," Jori responded with extreme politeness that turned Cornwall beet red. The prince turned to Griffin. "Come up when you're finished so we can toast another win." He extended an elbow to Maggie. "Shall we?"

"Good luck, Sir Griffin," Maggie said, meeting his gaze. From her tone, she could've been cursing at him.

After they were gone, Griffin tested the weight of his axe. He tossed it from one hand to the other but was plagued by the image of Jori kissing Maggie's hand. He fumbled the handle, and the axe rattled to the floor. He scrambled to pick it up, mortified.

"She makes you nervous," Silas said, chuckling. He tucked his long blond mane into the back of his tunic.

"I understand, Griffin. She is . . . disarming," Malcolm admitted.

"You're a fool, Malcolm," Cornwall growled at his brother. "She's a trollop. Her father's probably put a spell on Jori, all so she can swive a prince and bring a bastard into the world. A claimant for the throne."

Griffin heard enough. He threw Cornwall up against the wall. "Maggie is no trollop. And her father wouldn't know a spell if his life depended on it."

He let go but glared at Cornwall as he slid down the wall and slunk away, rubbing his arm.

"You defended her, rather than your prince," Malcolm said, coming away from the exchange knowing more than Griffin should have allowed.

The skies were blanket gray, with darker, more threatening clouds rolling beneath. What's more, Griffin's knee ached along the cap. It was going to rain, and soon. The arena's roof only sheltered the spectators. The center was open to the elements. When it rained, the dirt turned to slippery mud, giving draignochs an advantage because of their weight. Griffin was glad he wasn't fighting today.

A horn declared the axe competition, and Marshal Duncan called the knights. Sleep deprived, on the ride down into the ring on the lift, Griffin's body felt like it was at the end of a very long day rather than the beginning. Not even the people chanting his name energized him.

A drizzling rain started. He lifted the axe with his healed hand, wincing. Then he shook his hand out, grimacing. He set the axe down between his feet and cracked his knuckles.

"Is he all right?" he heard someone call from the stands.

Griffin picked up the axe, tossed it in the air, caught it, and was rewarded with whistles and cheers. He lifted it above his head.

"He is! Sir Griffin's hand is healed!"

They hooted, clapping their hands.

The king raised a glass at him, calling, "The champion is ready."

As Griffin lowered his arm, he felt a strange jerk in the handle of the axe that sent his pulse racing.

While Silas threw first, Griffin examined the wood, finding a split that would leave his throw unbalanced.

"What's wrong?" Malcolm asked.

Griffin ground his teeth. "Handle's split."

"The champion, Sir Griffin, didn't check his weapon?" Cornwall sniggered.

"Shut up, Cornwall." Malcolm shoved his brother. "Go change it out, Griffin."

"There'll be none of that," Duncan declared. "Rules are rules. You'll have to throw with it."

"That's ridiculous, and dangerous," Malcolm exclaimed. "When I beat him, it will be fairly."

"But that's exactly the point, Sir Malcolm—fairness. Sir Griffin does not get to alter the rules. He will have to throw with this axe, or bow out," Duncan spat.

Bowing out, he could never do. Griffin was afraid to test the axe much more in fear of making it worse.

A cheer went up from the crowd. After two perfect rotations, Silas's axe struck the far left of the target.

"Next, Sir Griffin," Duncan called. He took several steps back, giving Griffin a wide berth.

Griffin raised a finger. The wind had shifted with the drizzling rain. The ground had become slick, the top layer a muddy stew that stuck to Griffin's boots as he stepped to the throwing line.

King Umbert and the prince both stood at the balcony railing, waiting for Griffin to raise a fist in their honor.

Time slowed.

His stomach churned like he'd eaten broken glass. Griffin held his breath, his chest warming with fear. He stepped forward, swinging downward, then raised the axe over his head and threw, releasing as his arm paralleled the ground.

Griffin heard the crack when it left his hand. He watched in horror as the head came off with so much momentum carrying upward, it spiraled out of control toward the stands filled with people. Shocked screams sailed with it, turning to shrieks when the blade struck a boy in the first row of the stands. In the Bottom's rows. His shirt was instantly soaked in blood.

Griffin blinked. *Did that really happen?*

The horn blew, halting the event.

Griffin's knees wanted to buckle, but he refused to let them. He didn't care about the boos that followed him as he sprinted across the arena. He deserved them all. Stupid. Careless. Irresponsible. How could he let this happen?

He slipped twice in the mud, skidding the last five feet, and looked up the twenty-foot smooth wall that was impossible to climb. His father cradled the boy as he wailed and gasped in turn while another man coaxed the axe out of his shoulder. Tiny, he couldn't have been more than three.

"Got it!"

The axe head fell over the wall, nearly hitting Griffin on the head.

Thoma had somehow worked his way over to help. He stood beside them, leaning over the rail.

"He's bleeding bad, Griff."

From the concern in Thoma's voice, Griffin worried he didn't have long. There were only two physicians in the Walled City, none of them accessible to people in the Bottom. No one would help him, unless . . .

Maggie!

The wall was too high, but if he could get the boy to the lift, and ride him up to the Top section . . .

"Can you lower him to me?" Griffin asked, gesturing frantically. "Use your cloaks! Hurry!"

His father gaped as Thoma took him from his arms. "Are you mad?"

"I know someone who can help!" Griffin insisted. "Please! Let me try!"

Within seconds, Thoma lowered the boy in a makeshift cradle into Griffin's waiting arms. The boy had gone quiet. He was still breathing, but barely.

"What the hell is he doing, Jori?" King Umbert's furious bellow echoed in the ring.

Griffin didn't care about the king's anger either. He had the boy, and now all he needed was Maggie. Racing back, he passed his gawking competition, only adding to his anxiety. He lunged into the lift. The other competitors joined him; why? He didn't know, but their weight would make it impossible to move quickly.

"Get out!" he barked.

All did except Silas. "I've already thrown."

"Your fight is next!" Griffin yelled in a rush.

"They won't start without me, that's for damn sure. Let me put pressure on the wound. Might give him a few more minutes!"

Shocked the old chieftain's arrogant son would care whether a Bottom boy lived or died, Griffin nodded, grateful.

Silas stomped to get the damn lift moving.

"Hurry up!" Griffin yelled at the men on the pulley ropes.

"Put your backs into it!" Silas added. "The boy's life depends on it!"

Silas ripped his shirt beneath his tunic, balling the fabric. He sucked in a sharp breath at the sight of the wound, but pressed the fabric, then pushed the boy's arm across his chest, holding it there. "Surprised his arm is still hanging on."

His heart in his throat, Griffin couldn't speak. He only wanted to get to Maggie. She would be there, waiting for him in the tunnel. Even if she hated him, she would help if she could.

When the lift jerked to a stop at the top, Maggie wasn't

in the tunnel. This could expose her gifts, something Griffin knew she was against. But he was only a tiny boy!

He moaned against Griffin's chest, the vibrations stabbing his heart. He tried and failed to open his eyes.

"Fine." If Maggie wasn't coming to him, if she was too much of a coward, Griffin would take the boy to her. Once she saw him, how could she refuse him help?

A single guard blocked the door to the stairwell leading to the balcony. Griffin recognized him from the king's chambers the other night. The rest of the guards had taken up positions on the bridge.

"Wait here," Griffin said to Silas.

Griffin nodded to the guard, who didn't hesitate. He pulled open the door to the stairwell. But Griffin only made it three steps when clanking and banging stopped him in his tracks.

Daylight burst in from the top.

"I don't give a rat's bottom about what the prince wants!" Maggie growled, racing down the steps.

"Maggie!" Griffin was overwhelmed with emotion.

"Made quite the mess of things, Griffin of the Bottom." She yanked the boy from his arms. The little thing's eyes parted; his mouth dropped. He gasped for breath.

"Get back here, lass, or I'll lock you in irons!" Raleigh threatened. He barreled down the stairs.

"Don't let him follow me!" Maggie kicked the door open and darted out.

Griffin rushed up the stairs, arms extended, leaving no

room for Raleigh to get by. Raleigh shouldered him, knocking him into the wall so hard his breath caught. He snaked around Griffin, but Griffin pivoted, landing a stiff kick in Raleigh's back, sending him careening down the stairs.

Griffin leaped over his disoriented mentor, making it into the tunnel before he could recover. Griffin slammed the door shut, put his back to it, and dug his heels in.

"Maggie left, with the boy?" Griffin asked the guard.

He nodded, pointing a finger toward the bridge. "Went that way."

"Excellent." Hope bloomed as the door jerked, smacking him in the back.

"Um, Sir Griffin, what're you doing?" the guard asked.

"Giving her a head start, obviously." Griffin winced as the door jolted again, harder this time. "She's taking the boy to the physician. She is very gifted in the medicinal arts. Raleigh was put out. Didn't want her to leave."

Silas added his weight to the door. "Why?"

Griffin groaned at the burning in his thighs. "It's a mystery to me. Perhaps he too thinks her a rare beauty and didn't want her to get her hands dirty."

"She is that." Silas strained. "How much longer do we need to give her?"

Griffin ticked off a few more seconds in his head. "That should be good." The two simultaneously stepped away from the door.

Raleigh and Moldark fell out.

"Ah, Moldark," Griffin cried. "That's why we were having trouble, Silas."

"What's that mean?" Moldark growled.

"Shut up, fool," Raleigh griped at Moldark. "Where is she?" he barked at Griffin.

"That way." The guard pointed again.

Raleigh went after Maggie, with a cursing Moldark drudging behind him.

The rain picked up.

The crowd grew restless, stamping their feet, calling for the marshal to do his job. Guards flooded the tunnel from the balcony. The largest settled beside Griffin, standing arms crossed, like an immovable mountain. "King demands the event to start back. Says you're to have another go. That axe was tampered with."

"It's true!" Bradyn called, jogging into the tunnel. He was out of breath, his cloak sopping wet. He carried another axe with him. "This is your new one that Hugo brought you the other day, Sir Griffin! They brought you the wrong one!"

"Then it wasn't tampered with," Griffin said.

"Maybe it was, maybe it wasn't. All I know is that this is your axe." Bradyn thrust the handle at Griffin.

He hesitated. His mind told him to do as he was told. No one in the Walled City, especially not the king, ever gave second chances. But *he* had thrown the broken axe. He could have yielded his turn, but he did not. It was *his* mistake. And as much as his head begged him to do it, swallow his pride and take this gift from the king, his heart refused. His hands red with the boy's blood, he didn't deserve another throw.

"I can't."

Bradyn nodded, but not with disappointment. Even at his age, he understood.

Griffin elbowed Silas. "Get down there."

Silas patted Griffin on the shoulder. "Yes. Don't want to leave Northmen waiting in the rain too much longer." He winked and paced slowly to the lift at the end of the tunnel.

Maggie was taking too long. She'd healed his hand in seconds. What if Raleigh found her before she could help? What if the boy was lying in the streets, dying?

Griffin tried to walk past the guards, hoping to be of some use to her, but they refused to let him out. "Sorry, Sir Griffin. King's orders. You're to be taken up to the balcony as soon as this event is over."

There was only one reason a knight was called to the balcony: praise or punishment. There was nothing to praise today. King Umbert preferred public punishment to demean those who let him down. A sign the king had lost faith in him and was perhaps seeking a new champion.

And here he thought if anyone would've caused him to be disgraced before the king, it would've been Maggie over their excursion last night. Instead, this mess was of Griffin's own making. He didn't check his weapon before the event. He lost focus, and it cost him. It cost that poor boy. If Maggie couldn't save him, Griffin would never forgive himself.

He leaned on the wall, scraping the dirt with the heel of his boot, trying not to vomit as competition started. He padded to the end of the tunnel to watch. The rain was light but steady; all threw at a fast clip. Malcolm's throw hit beside Silas's.

Oak's release was slow. The axe lumbered, barely making a complete rotation before it hit and stuck in the far outer ring.

Cornwall strutted to the line, taking his time, raising his arms to the crowd as if he had fans. As Griffin watched him, anger blossomed. The younger Northman waited to go last on purpose. It was probably he who damaged the other axe and paid the boy to bring it to Griffin. With Griffin humiliated, last was as coveted as first because it was infinitely more memorable than somewhere in the middle, so long as Cornwall bettered the others. A plan extremely well executed if he hit dead center.

A tie would be a dull ending, but a boy, even younger than Griffin when he won last year, a true underdog, if he could win, they would recount the tale tonight in the pubs and over the supper table. They would ask his name and remember it, watching for him especially when he fought his first draignoch.

The people stood up and quieted.

Smooth lift. Confident release. Cornwall's form was perfect, and so was his throw.

The axe struck dead center with a definitive thwack.

A bull's-eye.

Rocking fists, surprised laughter, and unbridled cheering erupted. Cornwall jogged the rim of the arena, milking out every last bit of applause, soaking up every bit of fame he could muster.

After, the knights entered the lift. Griffin paced, worrying about Maggie and the boy. Where was she?

The lift returned with the other competitors. Cornwall made the mistake of sauntering up to Griffin, beaming with pride. "Fickle bunch, aren't they? Fair-weather fans. No real respect for their champion at all."

Griffin backed him up to the wall, pressing his forearm against his neck, feeling the pissant's fragile pulse beat beneath his wrist. "You've won nothing. It was you, wasn't it? You split the wood on the handle of that axe? You paid to have it brought to me? You arrogant bastard! That boy is likely dead because of what you did!"

"What are you saying?" Malcolm tried to pull Griffin off, to no avail.

Cornwall gagged. He beat Griffin's arm, trying to get free, but didn't stand a chance. His eyes bulged past normal. With a hard jerk, Griffin could snap his scrawny neck as easy as a chicken's.

"Griffin, stop!" Malcolm insisted.

"He's a liar!" he spat at Malcolm. "Nothing but a no-good cheat!" Griffin snarled in Cornwall's ear.

Cornwall coughed, trying to shake his head.

Malcolm yanked on Griffin's wrist, giving Cornwall a small measure of relief. "He was with me all night last night, and this morning. Believe me! He didn't tamper with your axe."

"Then who did?" Griffin eased off.

Cornwall slipped far enough away to pull his sword. He aimed it in Griffin's direction.

"Go on then! Let's finish this if that's what you want!"

Silas laughed at him. "Put that away before Griffin kills you, worthless, and then we have to kill your less-than-worthless brother for defending you."

"Glad to know I'm less than worthless," Malcolm added.

Scrambling footsteps behind them stole their attentions. Griffin heard her before he saw her.

"Get your filthy hands off me!" Maggie yelled.

Twisting and turning, she grappled with Raleigh and Moldark, the two struggling to lift her by the arms. Her dark curls had fallen out of the elegant braided bun. The hem of her red dress whipped, tossing muck from the damp road. But it was her hands that drew Griffin's attention. They were covered in blood.

Blood.

Griffin pulled his sword. "What did you do?" He shoved Moldark off Maggie.

Moldark bounced off the wall, stumbling over his own foot, crashing onto his back, barely missing Griffin's stretched blade.

"Stop!" Maggie exclaimed. "It's not mine. It was the boy's." She gave a sad, resigned sigh. "Alas, I was right about you, Sir Griffin. You're a terrible shot. Beneath all that fabric was a scrape."

"A scrape?" Silas asked incredulously.

"The boy's arm was nearly severed, wasn't it?" Oak said.

"Where is he?" Griffin asked Maggie.

"I ran into your friend. The one with the eyebrows so thick they deserve names of their own."

"Dres."

"That's the one. He promised to return him to his father. He knows the way to the Bottom," Maggie explained.

"Because Dres belongs in the Bottom, and has no business sitting with the Top," Raleigh said for Griffin's benefit.

"Why not? All the seats look the same to me." Maggie smiled.

Griffin could kiss her. That was, if either of them wanted anything like that.

One of the guards whispered in Raleigh's ear.

Raleigh, still holding on to Maggie's arm, spat on the ground in front of Griffin. "The king wants a word."

"Yes, I was informed." Griffin plastered a smile on his face, trying to cover the stabbing daggers in his stomach. "If the king wants a word, then he shall of course have it." He held an arm out to Maggie. "The stairs are steep."

Raleigh arched a brow at Griffin but let go of Maggie.

She held on to Griffin, gracing him with a tired grin. "This has been a never-ending day, hasn't it?"

And it wasn't over.

In the darkness of the stairwell, Griffin laid his hand over Maggie's resting on his elbow. Ahead of them, Raleigh's footsteps moved much faster than theirs.

"The king wanted you to throw another axe," Maggie whispered.

"I didn't deserve another chance."

"Will he be angry?"

Griffin squeezed her hand in answer.

"Are you scared?"

"A little," Griffin admitted so quietly he wasn't sure she heard.

"Me too. For you."

"Don't worry about me. Worry about the prince."

"The prince?"

"You're all muddy. The dress he gave you ruined." Griffin sounded bitter even to his own ears.

"Are you jealous?" Maggie asked, sounding amused.

Griffin refused to answer that but squeezed her hand so hard she yelped.

The end of the stairs loomed.

Maggie let go of his arm. She rubbed her finger through soft mud flaking off her sleeve, then wiped a streak down the back of Griffin's neck, sending chills down his spine. Her touch was unlike anything he'd ever felt before. "For luck," she whispered.

Griffin took a ragged breath.

As they took the last three steps, the space between them felt much more than the mere inches it was, the air increasingly magnetic. Griffin wanted to say something brilliant, but her sweet almond scent overwhelmed him. He looked down at her, not seeing much of her in the dimness, hoping something would come to him.

But then she kissed him.

Soft and quick on his lips.

Too quick, because Raleigh yanked the door open and daylight poured in.

Maggie went first.

Griffin let out the breath he was holding before following. As soon as his foot stepped over the threshold, the rain lightened to barely a drizzle.

The revered balcony.

From this place, the king loomed over events like a god watching his creations, deciding who to bless. To be asked to join them was the greatest reward a knight could hope for. After the first match in last year's tournament, when Griffin had killed a draignoch in a record five precise moves, King Umbert had invited him to the balcony. On that day his arrival was met with pats on the back as throngs cheered his name from every part of the arena.

This time, things were very different.

With the delay in the tournament, the crowd focused on the king. Fingers pointed. Mumbling grew until it sounded like swarming by flies. Everyone on the balcony turned to look at Griffin, and immediately stopped talking. Or eating. Or drinking. Or serving.

Esmera laughed at Maggie. "Most people don't go to the privy and come back looking like they were chased by wild boars. Did you fall in?"

Sybil stifled a laugh, but then sobered when she saw Maggie's hands covered in blood. "Are you hurt?"

"Maggie! What happened?" Jori, who had been in deep conversation with Esmera, turned so fast he knocked over a full water pitcher on the small, intricately carved table between them. The water cascaded into Esmera's lap. She hopped up, screeching.

"Jori!"

He ignored her. Servants rushed over to help.

"Did you cut yourself?" Jori flipped Maggie's hands over and back again, not finding the source.

"I'm fine. I slipped in the mud is all."

"What's this?" Xavier roared. He set his staff down, vacating his seat beside the king to check on his supposed daughter. His face was stained pink on the cheekbones and eyelids; the bones in his hair clapped like wind chimes in a storm as he rushed to see what the fuss with Maggie was about. His face fell at first, then transformed into a beaming smile at the sight of Jori holding Maggie's hands.

Maggie took her hands back. "It's not my blood."

A crease formed between Jori's brow. "Whose is it?"

Maggie rolled her eyes at him. "I'm sure Sir Raleigh will fill you in."

Jori's lips pressed into a thin line. "Maggie, the protection is for your own good. The Walled City can be dangerous."

"You've mentioned that, and yet the only danger I've seen so far has been from your soldiers, guards, and your . . . competitors in this disgusting arena," Maggie snapped, catching the attention of the king.

Jori shrank from her.

Griffin bit his lip to keep from laughing as Maggie's honesty drove Jori all the way to the chair beside Esmera. His betrothed whispered something in his ear that eased the ticking muscle along the prince's jawline.

Malcolm and Cornwall came through the door. Esmera and Sybil took turns hugging Cornwall, congratulating him while Malcolm went to attend his father.

Griffin had procrastinated as long as he could. Maggie gave him a worried glance as he walked by on his way to the king.

"You wish to see me, sire?" Griffin bowed.

King Umbert drank from his tankard and belched. A sound that echoed, drawing attention to Griffin's humiliation. The crowd's mumblings dissolved, all wanting to hear what was being said.

"That's what I thought of that performance, Sir Griffin."

"Pathetic sight, if you ask me." Laird Egrid slurped his cup. His cracked tongue lapped wine dribbling down the fur collar on his cloak.

"It was an accident," Prince Jori offered, coming to stand behind his father.

"It was no accident," Malcolm interjected.

"Any fool could see the shaft was cracked on purpose," Cornwall added, surprising Griffin.

"And this fool should've seen it too!" the king bellowed. "I give you a chance for redemption and you throw it in my face. Who do you think you are, Griffin of Nowhere?"

Mumbling gossip spread like wildfire through the stands.

"I'm sorry, sire" was all Griffin could think to say.

"You are sorry. You sit in for Prince Jori one time, and suddenly you're as incompetent as he is."

"Father!" Jori exclaimed.

"Shut up!" he yelled at the prince, then returned to spitting all over Griffin. "You have a single task, and from what I've seen, you're going to fail!" King Umbert smacked the high table next to Griffin, sending a dirty plate toppling to the ground. Pheasant carcass flew in all directions.

Servants rushed to help. Maggie too.

"No!" the king snarled at them, his fists and belly shaking with anger.

Lady Sybil took Maggie's hand, pulling her aside.

King Umbert snatched another bird leg from Xavier's plate.

He ate the meat off in three bites and threw the bone at Griffin's bowed head. "Griffin will pick it up. All of it. He'll need another job when he loses his title. A Bottom feeder who will return to the Bottom, and to cleaning the ducts."

Griffin could never forget those days—sitting in the refuse up to his eyeballs with a rake and scrub brush, breaking up clogs, which happened on a daily basis. Griffin had spent his first year in the ducts. Came down with fever three times. His stomach soured at the memory. He would rather die in the arena than ever step foot inside those ducts again.

King Umbert rose out of his chair, signaling the marshal that it was time for the main event.

Maggie remained a worried fixture in his sight all the while he cleaned. By the time he finished and could move away from the king, Xavier had Maggie sitting by his side. She tried to rise, but he pinned her in place with a glare.

As Duncan announced Silas's match, Griffin thought of how he may have misjudged him this past year. The two hardly spoke when they saw one another in the palace for meals or on the practice greens. Griffin saw him as Zac's older, arrogant brother. Where Zac was warm and gracious, Silas was cold and brooding. Griffin believed Silas proud, a true Topper, the first son of a rich honored chieftain, but for all Jori's claims of friendship to Griffin, he wasn't the one in the tunnel putting pressure on the boy's wound, and he could have been.

Jori would've seen Griffin bring the boy up the lift. He would have known Griffin needed an ally. Even if there was no way to save the boy, a true friend would have been there to meet him. He glanced at the prince, who stood behind Esmera with a hand on her shoulder and eyes on Maggie. The prince only cared about one thing: himself.

Silas carried a spear with him as he took a knee before the king. His helmet had a face mask with thinly shaved eyes, and a long hooked nose that came to a sharp point. Seemed rather comical, and completely useless, but perhaps it would ward off a draignoch like it would the plague.

"Does he intend to peck the draignoch to death?" Cornwall asked, laughing.

"He wants to give the audience a good show," Griffin answered, then padded to the other end of the balcony, as far away from the king as possible.

On the other side of the balcony, King Umbert raised a fist to Silas. He bellowed to the stands, "This man deserves your utmost respect! The eldest son of Sir Ragnas."

Griffin felt Maggie's gaze on him. Her expression was understanding; his fear of losing the king's favor was happening right before her eyes.

Griffin looked beyond the dais. Silas's family, his younger brother, Zac, along with their esteemed father, Ragnas, and mother, Aofrea, claimed the most prestigious seats beside the king's balcony. Ragnas was fit for an old man. His long gray hair was braided at the temples, the rest smoothed and tied off at the base of his neck. He wore a red tunic with gold stitching, a nod to Umbert, but a reminder of his own wealth.

Aofrea's hair was still fair. She wore sapphire combs in the sides of her hair. The lines on her face were the only clues to her age. Her dress was also red. Zac too had dressed up for his brother's match. His red tunic was even branded with a *U* to show his loyalty, and destiny. He was to join the king's armies in the Hinterlands come spring for his first tour of duty.

The king lifted his glass, toasting the match and the former laird of the East. "A noble by birth. A former soldier in my armies. A guard on your watches, and a true and valiant knight."

The entire Top row rang bells and stamped feet, chanting, "Silas. Silas. Silas." The Middlers joined in too, but for the Bottom's attendants, the wind shifted. Unlike in the past, when they would follow the others' leads, they stayed quiet, showing their disapproval. For all the harm Griffin had inflicted on one of his own, the Bottom was still with him. He choked on gratitude.

Griffin stepped forward, lifted his arm, placing it on his chest, his fist over his heart, and bowed to them.

"Careful," Jori said to him.

Griffin set a hand on his shoulder, showing his loyalty for the prince. "That's exactly what I'm being, sire."

Mostly drizzle and mist now, the ground looked like a pigsty. Silas stomped in a circle, his boots leaving a trail of punctures. He had strapped cleats to the soles. The throngs cheered their approval.

Malcolm came to stand with Griffin and Jori. His red hair was so wet from the rain it looked brown. He crossed his arms, leaning on the balcony railing, closely watching the gate. "Think it's the new one he'll face?" he asked Griffin.

"Don't know." Griffin looked at Maggie, who was also fixated on the gate.

It finally rolled up.

Griffin was relieved for Maggie, for it most definitely wasn't Rendicryss, although he wasn't sure Silas would fare much better with this bastard.

The purple draignoch had nearly taken Griffin's head off last year. The creature still bore the scars from the match on its abdomen and was missing the top of its wing.

Taller than most, and fiercely fast, it sprinted from the keep, snarling and frothing, and was on Silas in seconds.

Silas spun but wasn't fast enough to get out from underneath its lowering jaw. A fang cut across the top of his helmet, then stabbed, ripping it off, taking it with it as it circled the arena, stretching as far as the massive leg irons would allow, banging into the walls, shaking the stands. The audience enjoyed the show the beast was putting on for them. Squealing with delight as it passed, jumping startled with every jolt it gave.

Unlike Griffin, they hadn't yet seen the blood dripping down the side of Silas's face. He shuddered. The pain from the venom left behind was likely driving Silas mad.

The knight stumbled.

The crowd gasped in unison.

The draignoch sprinted toward Silas. He yanked out a white cloth from inside his tunic, pressed it over the tip of the spear, and threw it. The draignoch's attention followed the white flag, as it always did.

"See that?" Cornwall said to Malcolm. "That's what I was telling you about. They're attracted to white."

Silas pulled his sword and staggered after the monster, trying to sneak up on it from its hindquarters. The draignoch's tail swung, hitting Silas in the chest, knocking him off his feet. He landed hard on his back. His sword flew across the arena, far out of reach.

The bottom fell out of Griffin's stomach. He gripped the banister with both hands.

"You planning on leaping down there to help him?" Jori asked. His subsequent laughter stung.

Before Silas could get up, the draignoch pivoted. Its claws stabbed the *U* in the center of Silas's chest plate. The crack of punctured metal echoing in the stunned silence was broken by Aofrea's screams.

Griffin's breath caught. Cornwall backed away in shock. Malcolm let out a long deep sigh, knowing as Griffin did that this match was long since over.

Griffin cast a wary eye on Silas's family. Ragnas wrestled with Zac, likely trying to keep him from running down into the ring. Silas's mother bent over, reaching for her son, screaming his name.

Maggie wrestled away from Xavier. She stormed at the prince. "Why doesn't the king stop this?"

"Maggie, deaths are upsetting," Jori said with a placating tone, "but you don't understand—"

"Oh, I understand all right." She glared at the king, then hurried to the railing in time to see the draignoch pull its claws out and stab again.

"Griffin . . . ," Maggie gasped. She was shaking with distress, with ire.

He laid a hand on hers on the banister. "Do you still believe they're not dangerous?"

She tore her hand away from him. "I understand. They killed many." Her jaw set defiantly. "But the draignoch didn't ask to be tossed into the arena. You can't blame it for defending itself."

As a knight, he too had been thrown into the ring for price and sport. "No. I suppose I can't."

Their eyes met as she looked away from the horror.

Boos. Hisses. Cursing. All manner of hate poured down on Silas as he took his last breath. The Bottom, out of loyalty to Griffin, was the loudest. They started chanting his name—"Griffin! Griffin!"—over and over.

They wanted him to exact revenge. Against the draignoch, against the king, against every aspect of the wretched lives that had been forced upon them. They needed him to.

Maggie stepped away from the rail. His heart sank, worrying she didn't want to be seen with him. That her kiss meant nothing. That it was simply a kind gesture. Compassion. But that she preferred the company of the prince. Less scarred by life, coffers filled with riches he hung around her neck. It was an obvious choice. But then, he knew Maggie well enough to know she was a great many things, but obvious was not one of them.

King Umbert sucked air through his teeth so loudly Griffin could hear it. He stood up and threw his glass of wine into the ring.

"Worthless. Leave his body. Let the beast feast on it," the king shouted.

"What?" Griffin blurted. "Sire, Silas is from a noble family!"

"He has dishonored that family in defeat!" the king bellowed. "Now he will pay the price."

"No!" Ragnas called.

"It is for your sake that I command this, Ragnas, so that your family may be free of this stain! As I say, so shall it be!"

Jori looked as if he'd eaten something sour.

Malcolm hissed a dark laugh. "You expected less?"

Silas's family rushed for the exit. Others in the Top followed, refusing to watch. Griffin wished he could go with them, but he had already insulted the king today.

The king sat down and sighed. "Lucky day for you, Sir Griffin. Silas was one of your chief competitors. Now he is lunch."

"Yes, sire," Griffin answered back, feeling anything but lucky.

Exhausted from his all-night outing with Maggie to the Bottom, his brain fogged. For the first time in his life, he started to question himself. Why was he fighting? Who was he fighting for?

His parents had been avenged many times over. He had achieved the highest honors, but what had it truly gotten him? A room in the castle? A place beside the prince at the dinner table? Where he used to only count on his own wits and hard work to survive, he now was forced to worry over every word he spoke and every action he took, all for the love of a king who would see him massacred on a whim. Defiled for his own amusement.

The revelation left him looking for Maggie, but she wasn't there. Neither was Xavier.

Griffin leaned on the rail. The draignoch's chains chinked as it was allowed to gorge on Silas's corpse. The sounds of ripping flesh and crunching bones were more than Griffin could take. He turned away.

"I . . . don't want to be eaten," Cornwall said.

Griffin met his worried stare. "Neither do I."

ELEVEN

MAGGIE

"Let us go rehearse," Xavier ordered.

I could nearly read his thoughts as we tore our eyes from the bloody spectacle below. Silas's family were members of the court. We were nobody. If we performed poorly—that would be our fate, too.

The return to the castle took us over the gilded bridge and through the Top. All the while, we passed by grieving nobles. Frightened and confused by the king's wrath.

I laughed at the hypocrisy. The entire kingdom had suffered under his reign. It was high time they felt the sting of his cruelty. As I climbed another hill, it occurred to me that living on their divine perch, far away from the filth and stench of the Bottom, nothing dirty touched their cared-for existence. If Xavier wouldn't have told Raleigh to muzzle me, I would've yelled, "Allow me to introduce you to the turd you call king. The man who hangs an old man from an apple tree for eating from his own orchards. A man who burned down an entire village for two pieces of silver. A man whose men are told to take and take, pillaging the poorest in his kingdom to feed and clothe you and yours!"

The sitting room Raleigh found for us to rehearse was above the kitchens and unbearably hot. My stomach growled at the constant smell of roasting meat and baking bread, furious I hadn't eaten since this morning. High arched ceilings did nothing to alleviate the heat. Neither did the burning candles, which were necessary because there were no windows and Xavier wanted the doors closed. He didn't want any witnesses.

The tables and chairs were stacked in the corner. The only thing left was a cow-skin rug. Healing was as much a part of my body as my heart, the act as innate as breathing. But it wasn't what Xavier or the king wanted. They wanted to see the illusory rabbit I'd produced in the woods, and the cheetah in the Great Hall. But how I'd done that escaped me.

Although I believed I had done it easily as a small child, the ability to use the moon's aura at will had vanished from my memory. Without Rendicryss to advise me, I would have to figure it out all over again.

I went over the other two times that had worked in my mind. Step by step. Both times I was angry—once with Xavier, and the other at Griffin. Both times I touched the animals near the instant it happened.

At the start of the practice, I brought out the rabbit and the turtle.

After which, as always, I held on to the staff with Xavier, conjuring images of the animals in my mind, including the cow we stood on, but no matter how I focused, the moonlight never surfaced. It remained locked in a Phantombronze box in the pit of my stomach.

All the while, Xavier knelt and twirled. Lunged and hopped. He mumbled, sang, chanted and yelled spells, growing more and more agitated, falling into a sobbing, petrified mess in the middle of the rug with every failure.

I pressed on regardless, suggesting we try again, but even I knew it was pointless. The afternoon was a complete disaster. I couldn't do it on command, and it would be the death of us.

We were all trapped here—me, Xavier, even Griffin.

Griffin . . .

Like a recurring dream, he kept returning to my thoughts. But why? He was a playmate for the prince, a puppet for the king. He was everything I despised.

"Maggie, what's wrong with you?"

I lowered my hand. "Nothing."

I staggered across the room, resting my back against the wall to keep from falling over. Running on no sleep and only a small scarfed-down breakfast, I thought I was going to pass out. I had sweated through my last remaining dress, the yellow with puffed sleeves. Not that I minded ruining such a hideous drapery.

I was desperate to get outside.

I inhaled deeply, over and over again, but it was never enough. "Can't breathe . . ." This room was literally sucking the life out of me.

I stumbled to the door and banged on it with all the energy I had left. Raleigh was waiting, as always, on the other side. But also, Prince Jori.

My knees gave out.

"Maggie!" The prince caught me. "You're burning up."

"Outside. Please . . ."

Jori didn't hesitate. He scooped me up in his arms. I wrapped my arms around his neck as he carried me down two hallways and climbed an unending spiral staircase. How he managed, I didn't know. I was slight, but still. The prince was much stronger than he looked.

I heard Xavier calling my name, straining to keep up. I wasn't sure where we were going, but at the end of the stairs, there was another hallway, and then the air cooled. Almost instantly, I could breathe again.

Jori stopped. My sweat chilled, leaving me a shivering mess. He held me close. "She's freezing. Get a blanket, Raleigh."

Raleigh snapped his fingers at someone I couldn't see.

"I'm all right. Please, set me down."

Jori did but didn't let go. His arms were still around me. I was grateful for the warmth. It took a second to realize we were on a wooden bridge that connected the castle to a looming tower.

Gray skies were gone, replaced by hints of blue and white fluffy clouds that reflected the setting sun, giving everything a brilliant orange glow. The moon wasn't visible, but nevertheless I could feel it feeding me.

Petal came from the tower. She held out a gray wool blanket to me that smelled musty, like it had been in a trunk for too long. Jori leaned me forward. He wrapped the blanket around my shoulders.

"Shall I send Raleigh for the physician?"

"No. It was just very hot in that room."

"She should eat too, sire," Xavier added. "I've had her locked up since the festivities this morning."

It hardly seemed fitting to call the morning's display festivities. There was nothing festive about them, at least not to me.

I turned in Jori's arms to speak with him, and suddenly our faces were inches apart. I could feel his rapid breath. His lips parted. I squirmed from his grasp, afraid he was going to kiss me.

"Let's get you back to your room." Jori's hand rested on the small of my back as we started into the castle. "Raleigh, have the girl bring food and drink, and draw a bath."

We passed by the Great Hall on the way to my room. It was less full, but still crowded with well-dressed families stuffing their faces.

I was grateful when we were in my room. I fell backward on the bed, never wanting to get up. The doors closed. Prince Jori began untying my boots.

"I can do that." I sat up, trying to take my foot back, but he refused to let go.

"No. Please. Let me. I never get to take care of anyone."

His expression looked innocent enough, so I let him.

As he yanked one boot off and moved to the other, I looked at him. Prince Jori was handsome. His small chin and thin lips were like his father's. But that was where the resemblance ended. His dimples cratered and brown eyes narrowed when he smiled, which he did a lot. What didn't he have to smile about?

His shirt red, the collar and seams stitched with golden blooming roses, he was dressed for dinner.

"Shouldn't you be downstairs?"

"Yes. But I wanted to tell you something." Jori picked up both boots and set them down beside my wardrobe, then returned.

His smile fell into a deep frown as he sat next to me on the bed. "Xavier had difficulty last night. My father was furious. He spent the better part of two hours berating me over it and threatening to have him imprisoned . . . or worse."

"He'll do better tonight, Your Highness. He's been working so hard—"

He pressed his fingers to my lips, silencing me. If he weren't the prince, I would've bitten him.

"I care about your father. I do. But if he doesn't prove to my father that his magic is real, it could mean a death sentence."

I pushed his hand off me and got up. "Do something, then!"

"I am. I-I did," Jori stuttered as if I'd made him nervous. He took my hand. "I spoke to my father. He knows that you have nothing to do with this deception. You will be safe."

"Deception?"

"You cannot lie, falsely claim to be the Ambrosius before the king, not without consequences. If he deceived me . . . deceived the king . . ." Jori didn't finish that sentence. "I'm very much hoping I'm wrong."

"This is outrageous. Do you hear what you are saying, Jori?" I tore my hand back and crossed my arms over my body in protection. "We did not ask to come here. We did not seek the king's favor. Now, simply because you came across us in a tavern in the middle of nowhere, our *lives* are in jeopardy?"

"Listen to me." He latched on to my shoulders. "If Xavier fails tonight, it will not be held against *you*. I don't want you to be afraid. I would never let anything happen to you." He squeezed my shoulders, probably trying to be reassuring, but it felt patronizing. "You are special, Maggie. I know you've heard I am betrothed to Esmera, but I don't want that. She doesn't want it either."

"I'm sorry" was all I could think to say.

He stared at the floor, his face a mask of confusion. This conversation wasn't going the way he'd planned. When he looked up, his hand moved behind my head and he pulled me to him, hugging me. "I'm trying to tell you that I want *you*, Maggie."

I laughed, pushing him away from me. "You don't even know me. You shower me with presents I don't want. Dresses aren't important to me." I gestured to the puffed sleeve. "Jewels are only worth what I can sell them for." I unlatched the ruby necklace, placing it in his hand.

"What is it you *do* cherish, Maggie? I can get it for you. Anything you want. All you have to do is tell me." Jori looked lost.

"Freedom. I want my dragon released from that horrible place you have her locked in, and I want to leave the Walled City."

"Your *dragon?*" Jori asked.

"I meant draignoch. That one doesn't belong here. It belongs in the wild."

"I don't understand. You're telling me you want me to release a dangerous creature upon the Hinterlands, and you wish to go with it rather than living here—in safety and luxury?" Jori stood taller. "Draignochs cannot roam free, and neither can you. It is—"

"Too dangerous. You say that a lot."

Jori held my hand. "You are the most beautiful creature I've ever seen. I'm telling you I want you to stay with me and all you can think of doing is leaving."

"You don't. Even. Know me."

"But I want to." He dropped his forehead on mine. "Doesn't that mean something?"

"Not in the way it should, sire." I took a step back from him, the implication causing his expression to fall into a scowl.

He ran his fingers through his hair and rubbed his face. When he looked at me again, his demeanor changed. He was trying for indifference. He clicked his heels formally, and then he left. And I could finally breathe.

I slept like the dead.

Petal woke me by waving a bowl of baked apples under my nose. After I ate every bite of it, I started in on a plate of roasted meat and buttered potatoes like a wild animal, using my hands until she hit me with a wooden spoon on the back on my head.

My bath was warm, not hot. She had probably drawn it a while ago. It was dark out, but the waxing moon cast a beautiful glow through the window. When I got out of the bath, Petal held up two new dresses as high as she could, leaving two feet of linen dragging on the floor. One was pale blue, like the last, but with thick cuffs of silver threading and white crystal beading. The other was the color of the setting sun, a hazy burnt orange, with maple-shaped leaves across the chest, stitched out of spun gold. They were the most beautiful dresses I had ever seen.

"From the prince?"

Petal nodded, grinning.

So. He was undeterred.

She held them up to me one at a time, then settled on the orange dress.

A short time later, Raleigh led Xavier and me across the bridge and into the tower we had seen earlier. The king's private chambers were on the very top. Four guards posted; two pulled the double doors open, allowing us entry without breaking pace.

An enormous window gave a fantastic view of the Walled City. There were no curtains or tapestries, nothing to obstruct the king's ability to see anything and everything around him. An ornate chair with a high back and long arms sat facing the window.

King Umbert's throne. He probably spent every available minute spying on his own people.

The fire burning in the fireplace snapped and hissed, bathing the room with comfortable warmth. Carved rose vines decorated the mantel. A rose-scented oil pot was given the unfortunate task of masking the pungent odor of stale ale and wet dog. The combination of the three left me nauseated.

Xavier went immediately to a table where several pieces of Phantombronze armor sat, dust covered as if they'd been there a long, long time.

I picked up the gimlet and slid my hand inside the glove. Much too large, the fingers still moved easily because it was so light. "Xavier, have you ever heard of anything that can break Phantombronze? Or cut it? Or maybe melt it?"

"I don't, lass. I've never seen it in true form before. All found in the Hinterlands turned out to be false. Pyrite mixed with copper."

"Phantombronze cannot be melted or cut. It runs hot through the mountain beneath this fortress, in underground rivers. Thousands died to extract or smith what you're wearing right now," Raleigh explained, removing the gimlet from my hand. "Don't touch anything."

The door next to the fireplace swung. Greyhounds, like the ones who mauled those men in the arena, growled and barked, their leashes straining against a post as the king and prince entered the room. Jori gave me a reassuring smile while closing the doors, dampening the dogs' relentless fury.

I could guess what they'd served at dinner tonight from the bread crumbs and crusted stew on the front of the king's red robes. His gold crown had been removed, but there was a ghost band on his forehead as if it was still there. The air stiffened with his mere presence. My stomach tightened as he approached. This man had no regard for life. Unless I could wield the moonlight, impress the king with a magical act, Xavier would be put to death.

Xavier bowed for the king in grand fashion. I gave a slight curtsy, hoping not to fall over. Bradyn entered, bringing a tray with a single glass and a pitcher of ale. He set it down on the table and turned to leave, but the king called him back.

"Taste that ale. Remain here too in case I need more. Curse your cousins' spirits for your added work."

Bradyn poured a full cup, raising it as if toasting their graves, then drank half of it down before using his sleeve to catch the overspill. "I feel fine, Your Majesty."

"Good. Sir Raleigh, you should go," the king added, waving a dismissive hand.

"I'm ensuring security for Xavier and Maggie, sire."

"Ensure it outside the door," the king growled.

Raleigh's eyes shifted to the prince.

"You look to my son?" King Umbert roared. "Leave before I sic the dogs on you, you old useless cur!"

The way the king treated him, I would've felt sorry for Raleigh, only I wanted to leave too.

Jori nodded, and Raleigh left.

My stomach twisted into a knot. I knew this was going to be a private affair, but the room was too small, and the audience was too close. They would see way too much. My heart hammered, and my palms started sweating.

For too long, no one spoke.

Jori's warm brown eyes remained on me with unwavering intensity while King Umbert poured a glass of ale. He drank the whole thing in three loud gulps, then slammed the glass on the tray so hard I thought it would break.

"Xavier, you have been a bitter disappointment. A single flame, a glimpse of the spectacular, put out by what feels like utter ineptitude."

"Ineptitude, sire?" Xavier's knees gave an inch. He leaned on the staff for support, his hands sliding up and down in a nervous volley for position.

King Umbert poured another glass. Bradyn shifted the throne to face the room before the king plunked down, spilling his drink.

Strange how distance distorts reality. Up close, King Umbert looked even fatter, older, and more tired than I'd previously thought. He walked as if his days on earth were numbered. He stared at Xavier like a man trying to stake his claim in immortality. As if a sorcerer could save him from time.

"Other than my son, no one has ever heard this tale I'm about to tell you and lived to retell it." He pinned Bradyn with a stern glare.

Bradyn bowed his head, retreating to the shadows in the corner behind the throne.

Xavier sucked in a mountain of air, sputtering it out in short bursts. "Maggie lass, perhaps you should leave."

"Yes," Prince Jori agreed.

King Umbert raised a hand, stopping him. "No. Xavier needs incentive." The king's throne creaked as he leaned forward. "Maggie will stay. If he fails, they both suffer the same consequences."

Jori's eyes bulged. "Father, we discussed—"

"Shut up, Jori. No one cares what you think and won't until I'm dead." King Umbert leaned back.

Jori's narrowed glare was ignored by his father. I got the impression this wasn't the first time, or even the hundredth, that King Umbert had said that to him.

The king cleared his throat. "Once, I had an older brother. A tormentor type. Called me all manner of names. Hit me whenever my mother wasn't looking. Took what little food I was given and fed it to his tiny rat dog." King Umbert drank from his glass as if these were hard memories, as if we should feel sorry for him. *So the bullied became the bully* almost came out of my mouth. For once, I held my tongue.

He shifted the empty glass. Bradyn rushed with the pitcher and refilled it, then retreated from view again.

"And then one day, my mother sent us together to fetch water from the nearby river. She wanted two full buckets from each of us. Anything less, and we'd get the strap. On our way back, he kicked me from behind. Both buckets spilled, and I had to return to the river. He left his there and followed me back, the whole way telling me he would never let me get home with full buckets."

King Umbert hefted his large form out of the throne, and paced. "At the river, he did as he promised. He kicked over every bucket. I was so small, and he so much bigger, I knew there was only one way this feud would end. Either he would die, or I would. It was his fault, you see. He knew I carried a dagger, and yet he looked so surprised when I used it. He pulled it out, though, and gave me a nasty cut."

Umbert pulled back his sleeve, revealing a scar that went from wrist to elbow.

"Then, I slit his throat. As I washed his blood off my hands in the river"—the king pantomimed, and glanced over his shoulder, at his view of the Walled City, his eyes lowering to the arena—"I met my first draignoch. It chased me deep into the forest. By the time I was able to escape its sights, I was lost. I'd lost so much blood I could barely stand. Then I heard it." He cupped his ear. "A woman calling my name. Delirious, I thought it was my mother. I followed her voice farther into the woods. I found her sitting on a rock, barely clothed, staring into the blue flames of a fire. It most definitely wasn't my mother."

He laughed in a way that gave me gooseflesh.

"She invited me to sit and get warm. Said she had been waiting for me to deliver a message." He drank from his cup before continuing.

"She said that I would one day form a fierce army, and with a single great deed would unite the kingdoms and grow to be their king. That I would build a great city within an impenetrable wall. The greatest city these lands had ever seen. But that one day the wall would come down, and I would lose my throne unless true magic stood by my side. For magic was coming, she said, and I was either friend or foe. My kingdom would not survive if magic was not with me." His hooded gaze fell on Xavier. "I fell asleep beside her fire. When I woke up, the fire was out, and she was gone." His gaze drifted to the corner of the room. "I thought it was a dream, only everything she said has come to pass."

"*That's* why you brought Xavier here?" I asked Jori in a sharper tone than I should have, judging by his creased brow.

The prince looked panic-stricken. "Your father has shown real magic, Maggie. You know this better than any of us," he insisted.

I didn't know who the bigger fool was: Jori for believing Xavier could be anything more than an entertainer, or me for helping to put Xavier in this position. If I had known . . . We needed to leave this place.

Tonight.

"Are you saying Xavier is a fraud?" King Umbert asked me.

"Of course not, but you're putting too much pressure on him. His magic cannot flow under these conditions. He needs time to—to allow the stress to ease so that his powers are not restricted."

Umbert shook his fat head. "No. The deed is done. No one leaves this room until Xavier shows me something spectacular or lies dead at my feet. With you beside him." He smiled then, and I saw his yellow cracked teeth for the first time.

Even under the stern glare from his father, Jori took a step closer to me. Maybe he wasn't as bad as I thought.

Xavier slammed the staff down dramatically. "Very well, then you shall see something spectacular, sire. For I know in my heart that I am the one you have sought all these years."

"Wait."

King Umbert glared at me. He swatted the glass off the throne's arm, spilling ale all over Xavier. "Wait? What for?"

"Maggie!" Xavier barked. "Keep to yourself, child!"

"No. If the king is to see your power, your real power, what do you get in return?" I clasped my trembling hands behind my back.

"Real power?" King Umbert asked. "Are you saying that your father has been holding back?"

I laughed. "Wouldn't you? A garnet. A ruby. You get what you pay for."

The king sat down in his throne. His laughter started slowly, then rose, filling the room. "She's good, Xavier. I can see why you haven't sold her or married her off. My son could take a few lessons from her."

Jori laughed nervously.

"What is it you want, Xavier?" the king asked.

"Time and freedom." I answered for him because that was what I needed. Time and space to move so I could figure out how to get Rendicryss free and us out of this place. "The constant threat of death, and the guards traipsing after, would be more than anyone could take if asked to do the impossible." I turned to Xavier. "Isn't that right, Father?"

He stared at me, bemused, but then he seemed to understand. "Yes."

The king frowned, so I was surprised when he agreed. "Time and freedom. Done. Now, what miracle will I be witnessing?"

Xavier licked his lips. "Better not to tell you but show you. If I could ask you, sire, to step away from the dais. I would like to use that space."

The king moved to the other side of the room. Bradyn inched out of the shadows, curiosity getting the better of him.

Now came the hard part. Earlier, in that windowless room, my energy drained like a bladder with a slow leak. But if anything, since walking into the king's chambers, I had only grown stronger. The moon was three-quarters full, and so close I could see visible peaks and valleys mixed in with the brightness.

You can do this, I thought, taking long breaths. My heart

pounded. Pulse raced. My nerves heartily disagreed.

I stood behind Xavier. Confidence rising, I grasped the staff, sliding my hands until they bumped Xavier's.

Xavier chanted, lifting the staff and lowering it, over and over, his call to whatever god or goddess he prayed to growing louder and louder. . . . Maybe the words meant something. But within this small room, with only three in audience, the language sounded fake. Made up.

Meaningless.

In the past, I'd thought it was charming, how he put this whole show together, but standing here, with our lives on the line, it made me angry.

I thought to get this over with quickly. A rabbit or a cheetah, the sense memories of their soft and stiff fur coming to mind easily. Shielded by Xavier from the prince's and king's prying eyes, I opened my palm, feeling the intensity of the light through the window. So close, but so far too. Silently summoning, I was ignored.

I tried drawing the animals with fingers, but the room remained empty of moonlight. Closing my eyes did nothing either.

Those other times I had touched the animals immediately prior. That was what was missing. If I could get to the greyhounds, it could work, but that was impossible. The magic needed to happen *now*.

I growled, frustrated, garnering the king's attention.

"What?" Xavier mouthed, then sang an ominous tune,

raising the staff, aiming the sapphire at the moon.

Before I knew what I was doing, I lifted the staff higher, and slammed it down on the dais.

Bright light shot down from the moon, striking the glass window, burning a perfectly round hole. A high-pitched shriek came with it, whining until it found my hand. The energy thrummed. The humming radiated. My teeth rattled. I clamped down hard and turned my palm up. Like striking a mirror, the light changed direction, traveling up the staff, hitting my target. The sapphire. The moonbeam struck a facet with so much intensity, it shot as if it was an arrow taking flight from a released bowstring.

Bradyn screamed.

King Umbert squealed with delight.

Panicked, I closed my fist and my eyes, willing the moon to let go of me. The humming ceased. My hand cooled. I did my best to hide my excitement.

But when I opened my eyes, Xavier's jaw dropped. His expression turned cold. He had seen. He knew it was me.

"You did it!" I hugged him, making a show for the king.

Bradyn slumped on the ground.

"Bradyn?" I gasped. *Oh, no. What have I done?*

I ran to him and picked up his head, feeling warm wetness. Blood. Sick over what I had done, bile rose in the back of my throat, making my mouth taste like vomit. "He's bleeding." I swallowed repeatedly. I needed to heal him, but I couldn't do it here. Not with them watching.

King Umbert had the nerve to clap, and then he laughed. "You *are* the magic, Xavier. You are the Ambrosius! You have your time and freedom. I want more of this! Much more." I could hear the lust in his voice. More of *this*?

"Bradyn needs help! We need to get him out of here!" I called to Jori.

Bradyn was more than half my weight, and I struggled to pick him up. Jori helped at first.

"Where are you going?" King Umbert snapped.

"The boy's badly hurt, sire. I'm taking him to the physician."

"What? No. Leave him there." King Umbert fingered the sapphire in Xavier's staff. "We have important things to discuss, Jori."

Jori's hands fell away. He didn't have the courage to disobey. "He'll be all right."

"No. He won't!"

The door opened. A big servant carrying a tray of ale pitchers took one look at me struggling with Bradyn and went to set the tray down. He nodded in the king's direction and let out a fright-filled whimper as he lifted an unconscious Bradyn into his arms. He left in a hurry.

"Maggie, get back here!" Xavier called.

But I was already gone.

"Time and freedom!" I called. And they began tonight.

TWELVE

GRIFFIN

Cold wind swept the bridge between the castle and the king's tower as Griffin paced. He shouldn't be here, but he found it impossible to stay away. Dinner in the Great Hall had been an abysmal affair. Silas's death weighed heavy, smothering conversation and appetite. Ragnas's table was empty for said reasons. The same likely happened last year as competition died in the arena, only if it did, Griffin had been too thrilled by his advancement to notice.

He hardly knew the competitors then. They were all from families in the Top, where people could afford to spend hours on a practice green. If it hadn't been for Thoma's father, Wolfbern, giving him lodging in exchange for work, and Hugo giving him paid hours off at the smithy to spend with Raleigh, Griffin could never have afforded training. But after living a year in the palace, Griffin knew them all. After what Silas had done to help the boy hit by Griffin's axe, he couldn't sit there, listening to Jori regale them with the story of Rendicryss's capture, which he'd told many times before.

Maggie wasn't there. She was smart enough to nap through it, Griffin suspected.

As he rose to leave dinner, intending to go to Ragnas's house to pay his respects, Jori had stopped him.

"Where are you going?"

"I thought to pay a visit to Laird Ragnas and Lady Aofrea."

"I shall go with you," Malcolm said, rising. "Cornwall, you should as well. Brother?"

Cornwall had then stood, but Jori was having none of it.

"No. Silas's death is his own fault. His match was over before it started. A true embarrassment. His father and mother couldn't even show their faces here. I doubt we'll ever see them again within these walls."

Griffin was shocked at the prince's venom. Cold. Callous. He sounded very much like his father when he spoke to Jori.

The prince's gaze shifted to his father then. "Sit down. All of you."

Malcolm threw his napkin on the table and walked out. Cornwall's eyes shifted from Jori to Malcolm, then he pushed his chair back and went after his brother.

"Malcolm! Cornwall?" Esmera stamped her foot.

Sybil drained her ale and jogged after her brothers.

"Sybil, get back here!" Esmera called, but Sybil walked out the door without looking back.

Jori clung to Griffin's wrist. "After your performance today, Griffin, you need every possible second with my father."

King Umbert heard Jori, stopping his fork from reaching his mouth. He looked in their direction, a curious brow arching. His face flushed. His anger was palpable from ten feet away. He had barely spoken.

"He's in a frightful mood," Jori added.

Griffin had had no choice but to sit back down.

"Don't look so put out. This will all be over soon enough. Xavier has a performance in the king's chambers tonight. If you feel a sense of purpose in visiting Ragnas, go then. No one will miss you."

But he hadn't gone to see Ragnas, as he told the prince. He had gone to Maggie's room, finding it empty. And he knew Xavier had taken her with him. The king's mood sour, if Xavier failed to perform, if Maggie failed, Griffin foresaw a grim end with Xavier in the arena fed to a draignoch, and Maggie's tongue publicly lopped off for lying to the king.

Raleigh stormed out of the tower. His back to Griffin, he punched the metal door closed.

"It has been that kind of a day, has it not?" Griffin said.

"You backstabbing fool!" Raleigh grabbed Griffin, throwing him up against the metal door so hard he bounced off, sharp cobblestones digging into his back.

Griffin groaned, the air racing from his lungs. "Have you gone mad?"

Raleigh snared Griffin's shirt, tugging him up, then punched him in the stomach. Griffin took it in stride, responding with a right cross that sent Raleigh careening into the railing.

Moldark and a soldier Griffin didn't recognize came across the bridge.

They tackled Griffin, wrenching his arms behind his back. "What's the matter with all of you?"

Raleigh's lip split and bleeding, he spat at Griffin's feet. "I'd tell them to break your arm, but what would be the point? The lass upstairs would only mend it, as she did your hand."

Griffin couldn't hide his shock.

"That's right. I know. I also know the two of you went to see the draignoch—or should I say *dragon* . . ."

"What's a dragon?" Griffin asked, trying to hide his shock, and failing miserably judging by Raleigh's dark laughter.

"I suppose you haven't seen all of it. You will soon enough." He wiped the blood off his lip with his thumb, then patted Griffin's cheek with the same hand. "You would be wise to heed a last piece of advice from me, whelp. Focus on the tournament. Play the part you've been lotted. Stay away from the girl." He glared over Griffin's shoulder at Moldark. "Men ready?"

"Yes. What do you want us to do with him?"

"Let him go, of course. The people need their champion."

Indecision hung over him like a dagger on an unraveling string. If Raleigh knew what Maggie was capable of, who else did? The king? The prince?

Likely both.

It all made sense to him now why Jori was heaping riches

at her. They wouldn't kill her tonight. They wouldn't kill her ever, would they? She was too valuable to them.

So why was Griffin still here?

Griffin had never believed in magic before—but there was no refuting its existence now. He held up his hand, tracing the healed bones. Unknowns frightened Griffin. The draig-nochs were mysterious, coming out of nowhere in the middle of the night, taking everything from him. Without that great unknown, his life would've been set.

Working in the fields with his father, food every night on the table from his mother, a river nearby to bathe in. A fire beside his bed to keep him warm, rather than freezing to death in the tavern's basement. A step up from sleeping on the frozen streets the first year he arrived in the Walled City.

But they had come.

And all he'd worked for these past years could so easily be taken away. There was a mysterious dragon in the Oughtnoch, an unknown to be unleashed on him in the ring, and then there was Maggie.

What was a dragon? What was Maggie? Worst of all, why did he care so much about her?

The door flew open. A servant, the same who'd brought the ale in moments ago, stormed out of the tower with an unconscious Bradyn in his arms.

"Bradyn? Is he all right?"

"Obviously not!"

As the servant slowed, Maggie flew out the door, her orange

dress streaked red. She grabbed Bradyn's limp wrist. "Put him down! I can help him!"

"Get off." He tore Bradyn from her, hefting him higher, and then started walking at a brisk pace. "Sir Griffin, I'm taking him to his father!"

"I don't understand. Was this the king's doing?"

He didn't respond to Griffin's questions or Maggie's pleas for him to stop. She wanted to heal him, but if she did that in front of the servant, it would expose her magic and Griffin's awareness of it.

"Stop! Please!" Maggie yelled. But he kept going.

"What happened to him, Maggie?"

Tears brimming, she shook her head, then hurried after the servant. Griffin kept pace, his chest tightening with each passing second.

"Is he badly injured? Maggie. Maggie!"

She either couldn't or wouldn't tell him.

The servant's heavy footsteps bounced off the walls as they descended the stairs that ended in the hot kitchens.

The place buzzed with help cleaning up from the banquet. Dishwashing, mopping, wiping; there were staff everywhere, but Buffont wasn't among them.

"Buffont!" the servant called, spinning in circles. "Where the bloody hell are you?"

A frail man in a greasy gray smock frowned with worry when he saw Bradyn. His hands beckoned for them to follow. He led them around the ovens, which were forever spinning meats, and then through the butchery, which had yet to be cleaned.

Plucked feathers stirred from the piles on the tables, sticking to Bradyn's blood on Maggie's hands. She wiped it off on the dress.

Two steps down, into a brimming pantry. In his year of living in the palace, Griffin had never been in here. No windows to keep it cool, the room was stocked with enough sacks of flour to feed the Bottom for years. Buffont was there, his bald head sweaty, his apron covered in flour, holding a stick to the bags, counting.

"Bradyn?" Buffont dropped the stick at the same time his wife, Molly, hurried to them from a room beyond. Perhaps another pantry. Her chestnut hair braided down her back, she rushed in, wiping her hands on her apron.

"Bradyn?" She grabbed his hand and pulled, taking them back through the kitchen to a small cove with a cot that was occupied by another boy. Bent over, the boy's cheeks black from soot, a bucket between his knees—he was recovering from turning the spit. When he saw Bradyn, he got up to make room for him.

Molly touched the back of his head and screamed. She held her palm up for all to see it was covered in blood. "Sander!" Molly shrieked. "The physician! He's upstairs. In the hall."

"What's the matter with him?" Buffont asked.

"Stay with him!" Molly called as she left.

The servant laid him down. "I heard a loud crash in the

king's chambers. When I got in with the ale, I found him like this on the floor with her trying to pick him up."

"Griffin, help me. Get them out of here," Maggie whispered to him.

"I'm not sure it matters anymore," Griffin said.

Maggie gaped at him.

Bradyn seized. He gasped, trying to catch air into his lungs, then went into a stiff trembling, bounding off the cot like a fish out of water.

"Molly!" Buffont called helplessly.

"Move!" Maggie yelled, shoving the big servant out of her way.

Griffin pulled Buffont so Maggie could get around him too. She clasped her hands, threading her fingers, then cradled Bradyn's head, covering the wound, but he was moving so much it was impossible.

"Griffin! Hold him down!"

"What she's doing?" Buffont asked.

"Saving his life." Griffin sat on Bradyn. He grabbed his hands and held them by his sides.

Buffont leaned on Griffin, trying to push him off. "You're hurting him more!"

A guttural growl exploded from Maggie, shutting him up.

His head in her hands, Maggie took a deep breath of cool air from the open window above the cot.

"Look at her eyes," said Buffont with awe.

The deep blue glowed in the dim cove. Once again, Griffin

found himself asking the same question. *What is she?* She gasped, her eyes slamming shut, then she let go. "It's done," she said, breathless.

Bradyn remained unconscious.

"Bradyn . . . ," she coaxed, tears brimming. "Please wake up."

Griffin shook his legs. "Bradyn. Wake up!"

Bradyn gasped as if freshly born.

His father knelt beside him, hugging him, crying harder than Griffin had ever seen a man cry before. "I thought we'd lost you for sure, lad." Buffont smiled through his tears at Maggie. His hand patted hers, which was coated in a fine layer of his son's drying blood. "You did that? You healed him?" Buffont opened his mouth. Nothing came out. He squeezed Bradyn to him.

"You're crushing me, Da."

"I cannot believe you're alive," Buffont exclaimed. "Thank you," he said to Maggie.

"I don't deserve your thanks."

"She nearly killed me," Bradyn said, without malice. From the looks of his wide eyes and big grin at Maggie, he didn't mind in the least. "It was brilliant." He smacked his father in the arm. "It was like—boom! Knocked me clean across the room with a brilliant blast of light!"

Buffont frowned at Maggie.

Griffin's mouth fell open. If Maggie could do that . . .

"He hit his head. He doesn't know what he's saying," Maggie

said, laughing. "It was Xavier, remember, Bradyn?"

"We're here!" Molly burst into the kitchen through the alley door. Sander wasn't in the hall. Molly had roused him from bed. He was in a yellow sleeping gown. His silver hair was pointing in every direction, and he was barefoot.

When Molly saw Bradyn standing, she scolded him. "Were you playing a trick on me? What is wrong with you, boy? I thought you were dead!" She reached for his head to check it.

"I'm fine, Ma." Bradyn swatted her hands, trying to ward her off, but she kept coming. She twisted and turned his head. "Gah! Woman, can you *not* do that."

"No. You were lying there. Your hair is still matted with blood. Let the physician have a look at you."

"Listen to your mother," Sander said, shaking his head. "Had her so worried, she wouldn't let me get my shoes on."

Bradyn opened this mouth, about to give Maggie away, but stopped when he saw her sternly shaking her head. He gulped.

Buffont exchanged a confused stare with Griffin, pushing Bradyn at Molly. "Not in the kitchen. Take him home, Molly."

"I don't need to go home," Bradyn griped.

"Move . . . ," his mother insisted.

Once they were gone, Buffont brought Maggie a bucket and rag so she could wash the blood off her hands. She sat down on the cot, dipping and scrubbing. Griffin sat down beside her, close enough that he could feel his leg against hers. The proximity set off a jolt that was both comforting and disquieting at the same time. He scooted farther away.

"Please don't tell anyone what happened here," Maggie asked Buffont.

He chuckled. "I'm not sure anyone would believe me."

"Walk me back to my room?" she asked Griffin with a look of determination.

She wanted an explanation. "Of course."

They walked through torchlit hallways in silence, the only sound coming from their visible breath. Temperatures plummeted, skating through fall, plunging into winter with a vengeance.

Griffin glanced over his shoulder several times.

"What's wrong?"

"Checking to see if we're being followed," he whispered.

"And?"

Griffin shook his head but was still grateful when he turned down a familiar corridor. Not a single guard was posted in the passageway leading to her door.

Maggie closed the door behind them and locked it. Then she checked behind the screen. "No Petal either."

They were alone, for now.

"Strange to find no soldiers," Griffin mused. "Raleigh has barely left your side since you arrived. He knows the truth, Maggie."

She frowned slightly. "I may have tipped my hand on accident in the Hinterlands with him, the same way I did with Buffont just now, only I wasn't entirely sure he saw."

"You never said."

"What would that have changed?"

She was right. Griffin bit his lip, contemplating. "If Raleigh knows, then so do the prince and the king."

She shook her head. "Not the king. He called Raleigh an old cur. He threw him out of his chambers in the tower, refusing to let him stay for the performance."

"That explains why Raleigh punched the door. Then struck me."

"Why?" Maggie tried to look at Griffin's cheek, but he moved her hand away.

"It was coming for a long while." Griffin stepped away from her. "But he knows we went to see Rendicryss."

"What? How?" She sounded accusatory.

"I certainly didn't confess to it! Could be Perig got caught taking bribes or Raleigh had you followed. Or Jori. He's certainly obsessed with you."

The fire snapped, putting an end to the argument, but not the tension. Minty-sweet eucalyptus burned, killing the cloying rose oil scent. A short reprieve, but appreciated. If Griffin never smelled another rose, it would be too soon.

Maggie shoved a chair closer to the heat and sat down. She picked at the blood marring her orange dress. "You should go. I'll only bring you more trouble. Especially after what happened tonight."

Griffin had no doubt Maggie could take care of herself. His gaze lifted to the door, but he couldn't bring himself to do it. No matter how much his head told him to run, his heart refused.

Griffin poured wine, handing Maggie a glass, and took the other seat. He greedily drank it down. The numbness it brought was welcome.

She leaned forward, cradling her glass. "Explain this to me, then. Who is Raleigh?"

"When I met him, he was the king's most trusted adviser. Had been since the city was built. A soldier who fought with King Umbert and the old lairds against the draignochs. That's how he came to have so much experience with killing the beasts. The tournaments were his idea, according to him. He was highly respected by the king. But after I won his title from him last year, the king sent him into the Hinterlands, put him in charge of collecting taxes."

"Like an old horse put out to pasture."

Griffin nodded.

"But then, why is he remaining in the city? Shouldn't he be out pillaging?" Maggie stood up, intrigued by the mystery. "And since he's not, then one must ask oneself, if the king has no use for Raleigh, who does?"

"You speak of the plot to kill the king. He wouldn't have any part of that. He's worked too hard to put these lands together. He's a constant at Jori's side these days. Raleigh is still loyal to the crown." Griffin took another sip of wine, trying to wash away the seeds of doubt.

"Then why not tell the king about me?"

Griffin was asking himself the same question. "I don't know."

"I do. Because he told the prince. I don't trust him."

"He's the heir. What would he have to gain by killing his father? The title falls to him."

"Maybe it's not falling fast enough for his liking. He's pretty awful to Jori, from what I saw." She sat down again, abruptly asking, "Why were you on the bridge?"

"I was waiting . . . for you," he admitted.

That earned him a smile.

"Oh, I have something for you." He had completely forgotten the delivery from Dres. He pulled out a folded bit of parchment from his tunic and handed it to her. "It's from the boy I injured at the arena. The one you helped. His father gave this to Dres and asked that it be given to you. The boy drew it, as a thank-you I suppose."

Tiny sooty fingerprints were pressed into the fabric as if it had been folded in a hurry. Her breath caught at what she saw inside. Griffin's had too. He had drawn the scar on her arm—three lines—three dots—in rough coal.

"Perhaps you should burn it."

She surprised him by tucking the fabric inside her sleeve.

"Is that yet another new dress from Jori?" Griffin set his wine down, trying to hide his irritation. "You look beautiful in it."

"Thank you." She flushed, unable to meet his eyes. "I told

him to stop, but he's persistent. I keep ruining them anyway. I suppose he thinks I should try to look presentable." She played with the folds of the skirt.

"Not an easy task." Griffin smirked.

"So rude." She smiled. "What do you think of the prince?"

"You clearly don't trust him."

"I don't trust anyone in this place," she admitted.

Griffin's mood plummeted. "He's been a good friend."

"Not to you. He tried to stop me from leaving the balcony and helping that boy. Helping you. If Raleigh knew that I could heal, then why did the prince order him to stop me from leaving?"

"The king—"

"Wants rid of me all the time. He would not have noticed me gone."

Griffin's stomach soured. "I can only imagine he doesn't know the truth, then."

"You're lying to yourself, Sir Griffin."

"Perhaps, but I'm not willing to concede the point. For all we know it's Malcolm Raleigh serves now. He could've easily gone North during the last year and no one would know."

Maggie cradled her glass. Maybe she didn't really want Griffin to leave. "You trust Jori that much?"

Griffin chose his words carefully. "No trust can be blind. The foundling hordes taught me that. After nights with them in the Bottom, I fell asleep and woke up alone with my only pair of shoes gone."

"Teaching you to sleep with your shoes on. That's what I do . . . did . . . in the Hinterlands."

Griffin smiled. "Thanks to Jori and the king, I have more than one pair."

"But you worry they'll take them away from you. Take all of this . . ." She gestured around the grand room.

Griffin felt naked, exposed. She made him question everything, and he wasn't sure he liked it. "After this day, the thought of returning to my old room in the Wilted Rose and sleeping with my shoes on isn't altogether displeasing." He drank down his glass of wine.

"You miss it? Your life with Thoma and Dres? You're much more at ease around them. Thoma especially. You hardly speak around Jori. Probably afraid of saying the wrong thing."

"Unlike you, who always says whatever pops into your mind. And to your point, I miss many things. But then I'm not sure I would be welcomed back in the same way. You saw how Dres acted. Everything has changed. I have changed. And then I would be letting them down too. I would be letting down everyone who has supported me. The people of the Bottom; what would they think? Even after my axe struck one of their own, our own, they still cheered for me. I in no way deserved it."

"Of course you deserved it. You cared nothing for yourself or your position when it happened. You ran straightaway to help him. Their loyalty to you is beyond reproach because you give it back in equal measure. I think they would understand completely wanting to leave a dreadful place like this, where you never know who your friends are. A place where you can't be yourself but have to put on a show . . . all the time."

Griffin deftly changed the subject. "What about you? You must have friends all over the Hinterlands. Suitors . . ."

Her brow furrowed, her stare floating to the ceiling. "Not really. A night here. Day there. Many days alone, waiting for Xavier to return from scouting. It takes time to travel with the wagon. We never stay anywhere long enough for me to make real friends." Her blue gaze glossed over. "The memories I saw with Rendicryss were remarkable. The connection so real between her and me." She hissed a laugh. "The only real friend I have in this world is a monster locked in a cage, who I can't even remember."

"You have me." It was out of his mouth before he could stop it.

"I'm not looking for pity, Sir Griffin." She patted his hand that was nervously clasped to his knee.

Griffin caught it, keeping her from escaping. His thumb skating over her palm. The memory of her soft lips touching his in the stairwell returned. Her delicate scent surrounded him. He never wanted to kiss someone so much in his entire life. "No. I don't expect you ever would."

When her deep blue eyes met Griffin's, her lips parted slightly. Did she want to kiss him too? He swallowed the urge, forcing himself up to pour another glass of wine, although he wasn't thirsty. "Will you tell me what happened in the king's chambers?"

"The king told us a story." She set her glass down and launched into it without hesitation—from a strange beginning to an unbelievable end. The young king murdering his brother in anger, being chased by the draignoch into the enchanted woods, finding a seer woman who spoke of prophecies, of the birth of magic in these lands, and how his rule depended on finding it.

"That's why the king and Jori have searched for magic all these years? Because she told him he would be king?"

"It's all come to pass, Griffin."

He couldn't deny that was true. "She was speaking of you, then."

"The king firmly believes it was Xavier she spoke of because he proved himself tonight. Or I did, nearly killing poor Bradyn."

"How exactly did you do that?"

She shrugged. "Don't know. I've never done it before. Not even in Rendicryss's memories that I saw. It happened so fast." She thrust her arm out, palm up. "Then . . . boom."

"Do it again."

She stood up, intrigued. "Here? What if someone sees or hears? Bradyn was blasted across the room. It was all very . . . loud."

"Really?" Griffin jogged to the door, peeking out, and returned unable to hold back his grin. "Come on. There's no one in the hallway. Besides, if it draws attention, we'll come up with a good explanation." He waggled his eyebrows. "Take advantage now. Show me. . . ."

"I don't know if I can." She held her hand out, aiming it at him.

"I have enough scars." Griffin scooted out of the way. He pressed her elbow, shifting her outstretched hand to face the changing screen. "You won't miss that."

Maggie narrowed her eyes on the target. A crease formed between her brows, as if she were concentrating hard, trying to will it to happen. Seconds later, she was still standing in the same position, as was the screen. "It's not working."

"You should close your eyes." The room was stuffy. Griffin paced to the loop, opening the window, allowing fresh air in.

She glanced back, taking a deep breath, and Griffin swore he saw the moon pulse like a star.

Griffin moved behind her. He turned her hips, straddling her stance. "For balance." He picked up her other arm. "Open your hand. Can you feel the moon outside the window?"

She closed her eyes. "Yes."

He drew upon his own training. What he was taught when he first began. Understand the weapon's particulars first. "Let's think of it this way. The energy is the arrow, and you are the bow. Draw back, taking it with you, then let it travel through you, out your other hand."

Her eyes flew open. "I don't think that's how it works."

He leaned on her, whispering in her ear, "You'll never know unless you try."

She reached back, pressing her fingers on his face, pushing him away. Her fingers were bitter cold, as if dipped in a brook in winter. It hurt. "I have a better idea," she proclaimed, stretching farther. She made a mad scooping grab, and suddenly light emanated through the cracks of her clenched fist.

"Maggie . . . look . . ."

She opened her eyes, squealed, and threw it at the screen. But the shock-white light had another target in mind. It arced at an angle, instead hitting a table, sending it crashing into the door.

Maggie cringed. "Oops."

"It was brilliant! You did it!" Griffin could only imagine what it would be like to have that kind of power at your beck and call.

"Pathetically. I cannot aim it."

Griffin padded to the other side of the room, beside the head of the bed, and held two fingers up. "How many fingers am I holding up?"

"Two." She scooped the light, pitching it at him. He flinched, but the light bent, smashing into the changing screen. "I can see perfectly well, Griffin."

He laughed. "And you can shoot moonlight." He picked up

a smoking shard from the broken table, regretting the decision. His fingers burned before he could drop it. "It's frigid." He shook them out.

"The moon looks like it would be very cold, doesn't it?" Maggie clapped. "What if this . . . this power could break Rendicryss's chains?" Her eyes went wide with excitement. She went to the wardrobe, retrieving Sybil's cloak, as if she were leaving to find out right now.

"You can't do that."

"How will I know unless I try?"

"What will you do if it works? You'll just let her loose on the city?" Terrifying images flashed through his mind. That dragon crashing through the city's buildings, stampeding the many, many people who called this place home.

She brought the wool over her shoulders, closing the clasp at her neck. She was really going.

Griffin blocked the door. "I won't help you free a creature that will hurt innocent people!"

She stamped her foot. "How do you know she'll hurt anyone?"

"How do you know she won't?" He unclasped the cloak. It fell on the floor behind her.

"What are you, a child?" She picked up the cloak. "You're being ridiculous!"

"And you're being impetuous! I know you think that creature is linked to you—"

"Think? I know she is, Griffin. But you don't believe me, do you?" She stepped back, crossing her arms.

The door rattled. Someone knocked hard. It was locked but Griffin leaned on it anyway. Whoever was on the other side pounded impatiently.

"Maggie? Are you in there?"

It was Jori. He would stop her.

Griffin yanked the door open. "Sire."

Jori's hands slipped formally behind his back but he didn't enter the room. "Griffin. What are you—"

"He helped me with Bradyn after you refused," Maggie said bitterly.

Jori looked completely flummoxed. "I didn't refuse, Maggie. My father—"

"Yes, well, doesn't matter now." She waved, literally dismissing the prince.

Petal walked past the prince and around Griffin, bringing fresh linens. She eyed them both as if they had the plague.

Maggie waved them out the door.

"It's late and I have to be up very early in the morning. Good night, Sir Griffin. Prince Jori. I will see you both at the tournament." She closed the door, throwing the bolt.

"Was that her way of asking us to leave?" the prince asked.

"I believe it was."

"Women."

Prince Jori hardly spoke on the return to their side of the castle until they reached Griffin's door. He was about to say good night when the prince asked, "Why does she have to be up early?"

Griffin's heart lodged in his throat. Why hadn't he picked up on that? "To rehearse with Xavier before the tournament." One day soon, these lies on her behalf were going to catch up with him.

"I see. Well, good night, Griffin. And good luck tomorrow."

As Jori walked away, Griffin was tempted to go back to Maggie's room and seal up the hidden passageway he'd taken her through, but what was the point. She was going to try to free Rendicryss and there was nothing he could do to stop her.

THIRTEEN

MAGGIE

I woke before dawn, dressing in the dark, hoping not to wake Petal. I intended to use the secret passageway Griffin had showed me to sneak out of my room and leave the castle for the Oughtnoch. Risky, yes, but it was necessary for two vital reasons. One, to see if Rendicryss could show me any memories that might help me wield the moonlight. And two, to see if said power could break her Phantombronze bonds. But I never made it out of my room.

As I reached for my cloak, there was a knock at the door. Petal came around the screen, yawning, her eyes bulging when she saw I was dressed. I had chosen the blue, which had returned from the laundry looking better than new. I couldn't decide if she stared that way because I was already dressed or because I had put the dress on myself. Voluntarily.

"Good morning," Prince Jori sang, sweeping into the room uninvited. With his fair hair pulled back, dressed in all red—tunic, trousers, and boots—he was a triumphant tribute to his father. His hand rested on the pommel of a dagger's jeweled grip. I suspected it was Griffin's Phantombronze knife he'd lost betting against me.

Serves him right.

Petal retreated behind the screen.

Holding a small wooden box seated in his armpit, he skated toward me. His warm brown stare floated from my loosely braided hair to my laced boots. "I'm most glad I caught you. Griffin said you were rehearsing this morning with Xavier. It utterly escaped my mind that you didn't know."

I would have to remember to thank Griffin for the excuse. How could I have so stupidly revealed my plan? "Know what precisely?"

"Xavier's lodgings were moved into the king's tower."

That sounded ominous. "Why? I thought the bargain was—"

"Ah yes, the bargain was for you and Xavier to have no guards and be free to rehearse without constant supervision. A relief that has been afforded to you. But my father worries that word has spread already. I questioned Buffont myself on my way here and it seems Bradyn told his father that Xavier threw him across the room with magic. A story repeated to Bradyn's mother, as well as Sander, the court physician, and, well, I'm sure by midday, all of the melee participants will know."

With that, I needed to sit. I claimed the chair near the smoldering fire. Jori claimed the other. "What does all that mean?"

"For Xavier? It means he will be heavily guarded. But

you will have space. No guards. You're free to move about the palace grounds. Beyond that, I would ask that you let me accompany you or someone I trust on any excursions in the city."

"What about our rehearsals?"

"No. Xavier will need to fend for himself, at least for now." Jori smiled.

I cringed with worry. Xavier would not last long under the king's scrutiny. "May I see Xavier?"

"You will. On the dais." Jori lifted the box out from his armpit. "Blue is utter perfection on you."

Why did it turn my stomach when he complimented me, yet not when Griffin did? It felt unfair, but there was no denying the difference. Still, I thanked him. If nothing else, I was hoping it would get him out of my room.

"I have a gift for you. I know you said you don't like jewels, but . . ." He opened the box. Inside was a stunning cabochon sapphire pendant and matching ring. "They were my mother's."

"They're beautiful. But Jori, I can't accept—"

"I know she would be happy to have you wear them in her stead."

"What about Esmera?"

"These are much too small for her. She'll take no notice."

I laughed, but my resolve waned. These gems could be useful.

"I cannot forgive myself for letting Raleigh nearly cut off

your beautiful hand." He lifted my fingers to his lips, kissing the back of my hand. "I knew you were a woman, and yet I hesitated."

"Your father's men are vicious. I hope when you are king that you will stop them from pillaging the Hinterlands," I offered as a parting piece of advice.

"I will be a very different kind of king, Maggie," he promised. "If I may?" He held up the necklace.

I stood and gave him my back, allowing him to fasten it around my neck. When I turned, he touched the pendant, straightening the gold chain, letting his fingers linger too long on my chest.

I stepped back. "Was this a gift, or are you expecting something in return?" I reached back to undo the clasp. "If that's why—"

"No!" Momentary anger flickered across his face, but he recovered quickly. "It is a gift. Please. Keep it. Blue is definitely your color."

Another knock at the door brought a large breakfast.

"Since we're both up early, I thought we could have breakfast here? Get to know each other better. Then we don't have to worry about Esmera."

It felt wrong to refuse. And for once, he was asking rather than ordering, so I said yes.

We ate at the small table. An intimate affair, with Petal serving freshly baked bread, poached eggs, honeyed ham, and spiced warm water. Petal tossed worried glares at me throughout. She didn't like the prince, especially him being in my room, that much was clear.

Prince Jori talked, mostly of growing up in the palace in the Walled City, at the Top of his father's kingdom.

"My father sent me on missions from an early age. I would take riding and sword skills lessons with the old lairds' children, but during those times I was tasked with asking a great many questions."

"About what?" I sipped the spiced water.

"Their old lands. Their old homes. What their houses were like. Did they leave anything important behind when they moved into the Walled City."

"Anything important? Like what?"

"Weapons, wealth, a son who might challenge the throne. It is my father's greatest fear, that someone will take it all."

"Did you ever learn anything?"

Jori nodded, smiling whimsically. "That I was a terrible spy."

I laughed. "I could see that."

He visibly relaxed. His shoulders slumped; he extended his legs, crossing them at the ankles. For the first time, it seemed the prince was content to set aside his invisible bravado armor. I could see how he could be charming. "He could too, I'm afraid. It was the beginning of the end of his respect for me."

"I'm sorry."

He shrugged as if it didn't bother him, but I could tell it did. "Made it very difficult to keep friends. No one trusted me, until Griffin, that is. He was the most honest, true person I ever met, until you."

I smiled at the compliment.

"My father admired Griffin. Saw in him a young Raleigh. A scrapper. Taking what he wanted rather than waiting for it to be handed to him. He let him into our lives with no questions asked."

I didn't want to talk about Griffin. "It couldn't have been easy, when you were small."

"I had my mother, until I was nine. Then my father took her from me." Jori picked at his manchet, his eyes glossing over, his brows furrowing. His expression turning cold.

"Took her how?"

"Told me she fell to her death crossing the bridge to their shared tower, but I knew better."

"Your father killed her?"

"I snuck in the tower every day to sleep by her side. I never liked to sleep alone. I would hide in her wardrobe when my father would enter. I heard the fights. Mostly they would argue about me. Over his treatment of me. He was difficult, especially when he didn't get his way."

"I'm sorry."

Crinkles formed around his eyes with his knowing grin. "Enough of my pathetic whining. So, tell me of your mother?"

The woman in Rendicryss's memory I called Mother was evil. She beat me. She tried to kill Rendicryss. She said she was going to kill me, and when I ran, she cursed me. She took my power from me. I hated her. She was nothing like Jori's. If anything, she was like his father. Waiting to take away what I had and give it to that tormenting Armel. Perhaps I should feel grateful my memories of them were wiped clean. "I don't remember her."

"Xavier told me she died when you were born."

I nodded. "Yes. That is what he told me too."

He blinked repeatedly at my answer. "I suppose we have that in common, then."

"I think a life of knowing a mother and having her taken away would be harder than never knowing one at all. I have nothing to miss. No shared laughs. No warm hugs. You, on the other hand . . ." My finger lifted to the smooth sapphire. ". . . lost something special."

If he wished me to see him as the sad broken prince, it worked. His loneliness was palpable, but his desperation was too.

He broke a piece of bread off and fed it to me like I was a child.

"I can feed myself."

"I've seen. But I like taking care of you, Maggie. Is it so hard to let down your formidable guard and accept my hand as genuine? Let me take care of you a little? You don't have to go it alone."

It wasn't an order, and I supposed I could let him—a little. But I wasn't altogether confident there wasn't hidden meaning in what he was asking. I clarified. "It isn't so hard, sire." I half smiled. "But it would be helpful if you would allow me to ask for things, rather than have them foisted upon me. My formidable guard typically acts on instinct. I wouldn't want you to get hurt—by accident."

He laughed heartily.

After breakfast, it was time to go to the arena. The prince strapped on my cloak, and I let him, only rolling my eyes after he turned to open the door. The wool was a welcome layer against the cold in the hallway. As the corridor sloped and we started down the stairs, I asked about which draignoch would be fighting today.

"Will it be the one you caught when we met?"

"A magnificent monster. So much larger than the others. I know you have a strange affinity for it. Don't worry. Although that kind of power must never go free, it hasn't been harmed, if that's why you frown. It will be able to defend itself."

"Will it fight today?"

"Against Oak?" He shook his head. "No. That would be a waste. That creature is being saved for a particular challenger, but I can say no more." He winked.

In the pit of my stomach, I knew he spoke of Griffin.

Sybil and Esmera waited outside the Great Hall at the top of the large stone steps. Both in brown dresses collared with chestnut-colored fur. The lapels were embroidered with flowers made of silver thread. Teardrop-shaped milky-white stones dangled from the center of Esmera's flowers.

Clouds hung low in the skies. The air was chilled and thick, hinting at rain.

"Brisk today," Esmera said as we approached.

"It is," I said, trying for politeness.

"Is that my cloak?" Sybil scowled. "I was missing that."

I thought Griffin had borrowed it, not stolen it. Mortified, I started to unclip it, but she stopped me. "It's fine. Don't freeze today on my account. It looks good on you."

"That's a beautiful necklace," Esmera chimed. "Did you steal that too?"

"No. A gift from my father to hers." Jori's lie was spoken sternly, closing the line of questioning. He extended an arm to Esmera, which she took as they started down the stairs.

"I am not looking forward to another day of this." Sybil groaned, attempting to take my arm, but that would have made my fall impossible. With her strength, she would've caught me, and I had no intentions of going to the tournament today. Xavier would have to wait. I let my heel catch on the first step, purposely tripping, and fell, rolling down the rest of the stairs, crashing into the courtyard.

"Oh!"

"Maggie!" Sybil and Jori yelled.

"Ow!" My dress wet, I felt a fine layer of dirt on my backside as I shifted. I fell back down, grabbing my ankle.

"Are you all right?" Jori asked.

He and Sybil helped me stand.

I limped, cringing, shaking my head. "My ankle feels turned. It needs tending. I think I should return to my room."

Jori looked put out. He sighed but nodded. "Yes. We cannot be late." He waved a guard over. "Can you please escort Maggie to her room?" He looked at me. "Do you need the physician?"

"Yes, sire. Would be good to have him check it."

"Then get the physician. Sander may be at the arena by now," he told the guard.

"Of course, sire."

They left, Sybil smirking over her shoulder at me, probably wondering why she hadn't done the same thing.

As the guard set me down outside my room, I made light of the physician.

"On second thought, Petal is here. She can wrap my ankle. No need to rush the physician over. If it's worse by afternoon, I'll send her to get him."

I waited until he was gone to wind my way to the kitchens, hoping to find Bradyn. A place that never seemed to rest, it smelled heavenly, of baking bread, but was so hot I sweated beneath my cloak. The fires burned, gaunt men turning mutton spits. Others chopped fruits and vegetables on the butcher's block, everyone dressed in the same gray smocks. None spoke to me or to each other. There was a strange melancholy over the palace, a curse of its own. Perhaps the happiness died with Jori's mother, or perhaps it was never within the walls at all.

I rounded the corner, padding toward the pantry, running

into Bradyn's mother, Molly, covered in flour, kneading dough.

"Bradyn is at the arena. Did you need something?"

"A horse. I'd like to go to the market in the Middle."

Her frown dipped contemplatively. "Buffont!"

The heavyset cooker poked his head out of the back pantry. He wore a floor-length red wool vest in a failed attempt to hide his greasy linens. He was going out. "Stop your fussing. I'm leaving already!"

Light flooded the room he was in. He was leaving by way of another door.

Molly whacked the rolling pin on the block, calling him back. "Lady Maggie will ride with you in the wagon to the market is what I was going to say." She shook her head.

"Will she now?" He chuckled. "Anything Lady Maggie wishes is granted! Let's go, lass!"

A small wagon hitched to two sturdy horses sat waiting in the alley outside the kitchen door. The rear was filled with oversized baskets brimming with grains, potatoes, and apples. Part of the king's loot from the soldier's raids on the South. The king wasn't a king at all. He was an artful fence, filling his coffers selling his pillaged bounty.

Worried the guard in the courtyard would stop me, I asked Buffont if he minded very much if I rode *inside* one of the baskets.

He understood without explanation, squeezing another in the middle. He covered the top with a burlap cloth. As the wagon jockeyed out the gates, I held my breath. The guards stopped another wagon on the way in, but paid Buffont no notice.

Jostling through the Top, I saw a heart-stopping sea of red through the slits in the weave. Soldiers posted every few feet. Troops dragged a man, woman, and boy not much younger than me through the gates of their home, shoving them. Buffont stopped the wagon. After they crossed the road, I recognized Silas's father, mother, and brother.

"No one gets a pass. To the arena now," the soldier barked.

Several followed them in escort, while others proceeded to the next house. The past few times I'd walked through the streets of the Top, I never saw soldiers. Something had changed. If so many were here, I hoped the Middle and Bottom would be less encumbered.

The melee must have started. An hour at most from now, the arrow competition would follow. Then after that, Oak would battle his first draignoch. By my calculations, I had three hours until anyone found me missing. Three hours should be plenty to reach the market, buy the change of clothes I required, and enter the Oughtnoch to release Rendicryss.

My dragon.

The word raised the hair on the back of my neck. If I could break her chains, she could fly out of the Walled City. I would have to find a way to sneak out. The ducts were an option, although I wasn't entirely sure if they were grated. If so, I could think of no more horrible a death than drowning in the Walled City's piss and crap.

To my dismay, the Middle was worse than the Top. Red patches expanding, troops banging on every door, entering houses. I saw soldiers carrying away weapons. Most of the dwellings were empty because of the mandatory attendance at the festivities; soldiers pushed anyone found in the houses into the street. Buffont kept his head down, plotting a jarring course to avoid running them over. Shaking fists and cries of thievery earned Middlers cracks to the head and punches to the stomach. A few were put in irons.

I didn't need to ask anyone to know what was happening here. The king's laws restricting weapons in the Hinterlands had moved inside the great wall. I could've pondered why now, what had changed, but I was too busy worrying about how to avoid being arrested. In a blue dress with Jori's mother's jewelry on, I would stand out like a bonfire in the Middle's market.

Not long after, we rolled up to the square. Buffont parked the wagon behind a long line of others, next to a waist-high set of posts, demarcations for the beginnings of the market. I crawled out of the basket, peeking over the vat of potatoes, taking a good look.

Vendors readied their stalls for business after the tournament festivities. The carts were set up in a large square, leaving the center open for patrons to move about easily. Besides the fruits and vegetables, there were carts selling baked breads and cheeses, crated live pheasants, even an apothecary with healing oils and herbs. But I found what I was looking for tucked at the end of the western side, a stall selling clothing and blankets. Directly opposite, two soldiers were busy ransacking the cutlery cart.

Buffont helped me climb down. "Thank you for the lift. I'll find my own way back, Buffont."

"Be careful. There's an ill wind about. So many soldiers."

"You be careful too."

He nodded.

I had but one idea, to walk with purpose, as if I was allowed to be here, and if soldiers appeared, run. I slid the sapphire ring off, clutching it in my fist, and padded across the market square. My stomach tensed with guilt. This was Jori's mother's ring. A queen of these lands, deceased mother to the only prince, and I was going to trade it for trousers and a tunic.

I crossed to the tanner's stall and rifled through a stack of leather trousers. A tired-looking woman in a wool dress with an empire waist cinched above her very pregnant belly rose to greet me.

"Market's not open yet." Her eyes darted to the soldiers, then back again. "I've seen you on the dais in the arena." She seized my wrist above my clenched fist, stretching my arm beyond the edge of my cloak, exposing my mark. "It is you. You healed that boy Griffin hit with his axe!"

Her loud exclamation drew the attention of the soldiers. Heads flipped. Knives clinked in crates as one dropped what he was doing and started moving in our direction.

"Hey. You! Lass, get over here. You should not be here!"

The first pair of trousers would have to do. I took them, receiving a furious glower from the woman that eased when I tossed her the sapphire ring. I grabbed a tunic on the end of the table, a red cloak hanging from a hook, and sprinted down an alleyway.

Several twists and turns later, their footsteps were almost on me. I dove into a stairwell, which led into a dank cellar that smelled of moldy cheese. I ducked, hearing them pass by.

I left the pretty blue dress and Sybil's cloak as a gift for whoever lived in the house, and tied my hair at the base of my neck with a useful piece of rope found in Buffont's wagon. Tucking the sapphire pendant beneath the tunic, I put on the last part of the costume, the red cloak, solidifying my transition to an adolescent boy serving in the king's army. I raised the hood and stepped out of the cellar.

A few minutes later, I was well and truly lost. The good news was that if I continued downhill, I would eventually find the Bottom. The bad news was that if I circled too far east or too far west, I could end up far from the Oughtnoch. The best course of action was to find the Wilted Rose. I knew my way from there.

Four streets later, I smelled the blacksmith shop, and was lost no more. Charcoal smoke fumed, giving me direction. A narrow alley dumped me outside the building. The double doors open, no one worked. Cabinets were locked. Hammers stowed neatly beside the anvil. All would be in the arena, including the blacksmith, Hugo, that Griffin mentioned, and his friends, Thoma and Dres.

I borrowed a hammer, tucking it beneath my cloak, and continued on.

Rain started, making the steep cobblestone road slippery. I slipped three times before finding the Wilted Rose. Troop numbers thinned the farther down I traveled. From what I could tell, they were working their way from Top to Bottom, but were still trapped in the vast Middle.

Passageways narrowed, dumping into the steep descent through the Bottom. The brothels closed. The muggers sleeping with daylight. I made it to the Oughtnoch without incident.

But as I took the last step, Rendicryss was quiet. Dead quiet. The last time I was this close, she'd let me know how to find her. What if Jori had lied? What if she was in the ring?

There was no time to waste.

My heart racing, I had two choices. Hammer the metal door, which would be loud, and garner too much attention. Or try to wield the moon, which could potentially take less time, and would be silent . . . until it wasn't.

I decided to go with the second choice.

Adrenaline coursed through me as I set the hammer down. The power chilled the back of my neck, running down my spine. The moon wasn't visible. But it was there, behind the clouds. Waiting.

I reached up, taking what I could, drawing the moon's

energy to me, then heaved it at the door.

The explosion blew me across the road into a pile of dung.

"Ow." Everything hurt.

Sucking down a deep breath, I forced air into my reluctant lungs, regretting the decision, nearly vomiting from the putrid stench.

A long crack in the wall steamed. I missed badly. It was a good twenty feet away, but the metal gate opened. Red cloaks poured out.

"What the hell was that? Search the entire Bottom! Go! I want whoever did this found and now!" a soldier called.

He returned to the Oughtnoch, paying no attention to me, a similarly dressed, much shorter, thinner version of himself, following after, scooping my hammer along the way. With soldiers searching the Bottom, and the others dealing with the draignoch in the tournament, the pound was empty except for the two of us, for the moment. He spun, arms stretched, probably to lock the gate. His sight above my head, he failed to see my hammer until it hit him in the stomach. He crumpled to his knees, bent over, gasping, but unable to speak. He reached for me. I whacked him over the head with the butt.

He dropped, still breathing.

The rope in my hair was long enough to bind his wrists. Days of rain left the ground soft enough for me to drag him into an open empty cell. I tried to pick up the chains used for the draignochs on the ground to wrap around his legs, but they were much too heavy. Twelve of me couldn't lift them.

I stuffed the drawing of my mark the boy made for me into his mouth to dampen his cries if he woke. "Let Sir Raleigh find that."

I searched him but couldn't find a set of keys on him. Not that I expected it to be that easy.

Cell after cell housed draignochs. With daylight, I could see their extravagant colors. Lavender, amber, azure, emerald green, and a dark shade of red. They were smaller than Rendicryss. Their wings would never give them flight. For them to be free, the wall would have to come down.

As I passed their prisons, my heart ached for them. Their strong hind legs chained together so they couldn't move. Their necks anchored to the ground so they couldn't stand tall. They crouched against the very back of the cells, as far from their human jailers as possible. What kind of monster did this? Where was the challenge in killing beasts tortured this way? I would choose death over a life like this. I had to imagine these draignochs would too. How could Griffin not see that?

Cheering exploded out of the arena. I was running out of time.

She cooed.

The relief was palpable. Explanation of why this creature meant so much to me escaped me, a creature I couldn't even remember, but she did. She was everything.

"Rendicryss . . . I'm here!"

Arms wrapped around me, hoisting me off the ground. "Let go of me!" I struggled, my heel striking calf bone, eliciting a familiar growl.

Griffin.

"You smell terrible."

"Put me down, then!"

"Have you lost your mind? We have to get out of here."

"No! If you carry me out, I'll come back tonight. I blasted that wall. Another go or two and it would come down!"

"You missed the gate badly and you nearly killed yourself in the process. I saw the whole thing!" He set me down, and I ran. His footsteps were steadfast behind me.

Her gilded cell was where it had been, on the end. This time I could see inside. Anger choked me. The Phantom-bronze chains binding her neck and ankles to the bars left raised bloody welts. Her red eyes were hooded. She was muzzled. That was why I couldn't hear her.

Griffin grabbed my waist, but I got hold of the bars.

"You cannot free her. She is a wild beast, Maggie! She will kill—"

"No. No!" I strained against his hold. Rendicryss's tail slipped through the bars, wrapping around us both.

My ears buzzed. My hands heated.

"Maggie, what's happening to me?"

Wind howled.

Then, *we* were flying.

FOURTEEN

GRIFFIN

Griffin fell through hot wind, dark clouds, then carved through sheets of rain. Lightning cracked. Thunder roared. He no longer felt. The only logical explanation: Rendicryss had killed him. And yet he didn't feel dead, at least not entirely, more fighting to wake from a nightmare. Trapped in a downward spiral, a diving bird, only much, much faster. Griffin tried to scream but whimpered instead.

His vision clouded from pain that wasn't his. A hill far below grew in size and scope until it was a mountain. Wings spread right and left, not much larger than draignochs', yet more than long enough and wide enough to carry the small body they were attached to. Too many arrows stuck in webbed flesh, making it impossible to stay aloft. Shaking hind legs stretched, landing first, scratching to a stop on a rocky barren spot. Griffin wasn't here at all. This was the dragon's doing, like she'd done with Maggie the last time they entered the Oughtnoch. Rendicryss wished him to see something, he hoped. Death would be so disappointing.

Rendicryss tried to tuck her wings but stopped, mewing in

great agony. She couldn't pull the arrows out. Griffin would've helped her, if he could, wouldn't he? All at once, Griffin's chest tightened. No. This was a monster. She would kill him, and probably had already.

The rain poured down. With it came a comforting light carried on wind, the kind that Maggie captured with her hands in her room last night, as if the moon were riding an ocean wave. It bathed the dragon's head in a warm glow.

Let them burn. The voice, feminine, was entirely unfamiliar to Griffin, but not to Rendicryss.

Fire ignited inside the dragon's veins. The heavy rain was no match for it. The arrows lit, melting to ash in seconds. But the holes in her wings remained, and there were many.

Rendicryss whined. It sounded as if she was crying.

It was not your doing she left the forest too soon. The banshee and her son will pay for what they did to my daughter. Their story has already been written.

As has yours. She will need you. She cannot be a light in darkness for the world if she's blind to her existence. The curse the shrew threw at her holds. You are the only one who can break it.

Rendicryss strained, trying to flap her wings, but she could not fly.

You are unfinished, little one. You must wait until you are strong enough. You must heal and grow, as must she. For now, her heart beats for us all in the world of humankind. The first of us in their lands, the bearer of great gifts that will rain down on them in the form of hope or destruction. That part is up to them. As was told to the man who would be king, only with magic by his side can he keep his kingdom.

Rendicryss craned her neck, mewing at the bloody holes in her wings, arrows shot by humankind. Her clutched jaw opened wide. She let out a rattling howl, a wolf summoning its pack.

They're gone. The draignochs left the forest some time ago. Much too soon, unevolved, and sadly are now too far away for that to change, I fear. Perhaps one day, you, Rendicryss can help them too.

The light on the wind darted skyward, slicing through dark clouds.

Find my daughter and break the bonds of the curse so that she can use all that I have given her to fulfill her destiny.

Griffin woke with a start, crushed against Maggie, snared by the dragon's tail. Maggie gasped in his arms. Rain poured from the skies in sheets, washing away everything except the stench coming from Maggie's cloak.

Griffin wasn't dead. Not yet. He hugged Maggie. "That was . . ."

"You saw?" she whispered against his chest.

"Yes."

Rendicryss's tail slid off, curling around their feet protectively.

"I have to free her, Griffin." Maggie drew a tiny drop of moonlight out of thin air, making her palm glow, then slammed her hand down on the Phantombronze bars. The light grew brighter, then snuffed out. "Why won't it work?" But the bar was left changed. The orange darkened to rust, losing integrity. Eventually, Maggie would be able to free her.

Griffin's stomach wrenched into a tight knot. He couldn't believe what he was about to say. "Because you're not ready. You have to grow your power. You saw Rendicryss and heard the voice. Your mother's voice."

She looked at Griffin, startled and confused. "You heard her too?" She sounded relieved, then her expression soured. "First I thought the woman in the other memories Rendicryss showed me, the banshee who cursed me, was my mother, and now this woman calls me daughter? She couldn't even show her face!"

"Maggie—"

She beat the bars. "I suppose it shouldn't matter who my mother is. She abandoned me!" she said, way too loudly. "Whoever she was, she left me in the middle of the woods! Gleefully, no less! What kind of a person does that? And for what? Destiny? Prophecy? Conquest? So more can come? If they're anything like she is, who wants them here?"

Rendicryss whined, likely in agreement.

Maggie looked at Griffin as if he had answers . . . and maybe he did. "Rendicryss saw your mother, as you did, and I did. Maggie, she was and simply is the moon."

Griffin looked up, blinking through raindrops. Maggie too.

When he stared into her eyes again, he saw confusion melt to comprehension. He nodded. Griffin cupped Maggie's cheeks, wiping the mixture of rain and tears spilling down them. "She gave you a great power. A weapon that can free Rendicryss."

"A weapon I don't know how to use!" She looked at Rendicryss, and her face crumpled. "We have to get her out of here!"

The ground shook. Chains on pulley wheels creaked. The gate in the arena was going up. The match was over.

"We have to go!" Griffin said, but Maggie didn't move. "Perig and all the guards are about to descend upon us. Maggie, please!" Griffin started to walk away. He wouldn't force her. Not this time. She needed to decide if she was willing to trust him. He looked back and saw Rendicryss shaking her head and scraping her hind legs, moving away from Maggie's reach. When she didn't leave, the dragon swung her head, banging the bars.

"I can't believe I'm saying this, but she knows I'm right, Maggie. She wants us to go."

Maggie gave the tiniest of nods, and they ran.

As they sprinted out the open gate, Griffin heard Perig yelling. Twenty soldiers posted outside of the Oughtnoch's wall paid little attention to two dressed similarly to themselves, running away from the crazed gamekeeper. They probably wanted to do the like.

Griffin's mind raced as they climbed the stairs, taking two and three at a time. Rendicryss wasn't a monster. She was intelligent, and she loved Maggie, and was distraught at not being able to find her. "Your mother said those draignochs would've been like Rendicryss if they'd stayed in their forest. What do you think would happen if they returned?"

"You're changing your mind about them?"

Griffin's sword weighed heavier on his belt with every new step he took. "They killed my parents. They killed many."

"So have you."

Maggie scooted into an alcove, catching her breath. Griffin slid beside her.

"Killing them didn't bring your parents back, Griffin. I don't think they'd want you spending your life avenging them in this forsaken place. That's not living, is it?"

He shook his head. He could barely speak past the lump in his throat. He took her hand and pulled her out of the alcove, back into the rain, and started climbing again. "Let's go to the tavern and dispose of these clothes."

"I rather prefer these clothes to the flamboyant costumes Jori puts in my room," she huffed, keeping pace with him.

"You smell, Maggie. Badly."

She sniffed. "Really? I'm not sure I can smell it any longer."

"How nice for you. . . ."

Thoma was unlocking the tavern door when they arrived. His gray cloak soaked and dripping. He shook his wheat hair, glued to his head like a wet dog, in greeting.

"Oof, you two are more of a mess than I am. Come." As soon as Thoma got a fire going in the hearth in the middle of the room, Griffin unclasped Maggie's dung-drenched cloak and threw it on the flames.

He knew Thoma had no time for them. He had work to do. Stools were still stacked on tables. Kegs needed tapping. Thirsty crowds would descend soon, and he was likely due at Hugo's shop shortly. Thoma draped his cloak on a hearthstone and started on the stools. Griffin helped him.

"Where's your father?" Griffin asked. It was unlike Thoma to return alone.

"At the market," Thoma explained. "How did you get here so fast from the arena and why are you dressed like that?"

"It's a long story." Griffin removed the red cloak. "Did you have other clothing? This outfit might give you away," he said to Maggie.

"I lost my dress. I don't suppose you have an old flame's downstairs?" Maggie asked, cocking an eyebrow in expectation of an answer.

Thoma laughed at him, giving away that the possibility existed. Griffin glared at him.

"No. Griffin would never," Thoma clarified. "I know of something that might do. Follow me."

He led them upstairs, to Thoma's father's room. Griffin had never been in here before. His father was a very private man. It looked like Thoma's, bare mostly, with only necessities. A bed, wardrobe, and washing table. Thoma lifted the lid on a wooden trunk beneath the only window.

"My mother's clothes are in here."

The musty smell of wool stacked away too long filled the room.

"Take what you need."

"Are you sure?" Maggie asked him.

He smiled warmly. "Been seventeen years since this has been opened. Da won't mind."

Griffin wasn't sure that was true. Thoma's mother had died when he was born. His father never remarried. Never talked about women. Never looked at a single one in the tavern. "You find one worth dying for, and she feels the same," he told Griffin one night when he'd had too much to drink. "That kind of love is enough to carry you even when you're not together, because no matter what, in this life or the next, you know you'll find each other."

Griffin had never believed in love. He'd never believed in magic either.

Maggie lifted the first one, a simple wool dress dyed dark blue. "This is perfect."

Griffin waited for her downstairs, helping Thoma finish the stools and carry up enough kegs to be grateful he didn't have to do this anymore.

As they set the last one behind the bar, Griffin remembered the tournament. "How did Oak do?" he asked Thoma.

Thoma shifted filled mug trays from the drying rack to the bar. "You left the tournament and time with your precious king and prince to go to the Oughtnoch with her? I know she can, you know"—he leaned in even though the room was empty—"heal things. Dres told me. And Da, and most of the tavern that night." He plunked another tray down. "She's quite the celebrity round the Bottom for healing that boy . . . but she must be something really special for you to do all that, risk being caught, for her."

Griffin hammered the tap into a keg harder than necessary. "I went because she's headstrong and foolish and was going to do something that would've likely ended with her dead."

Thoma laughed at him. "Keep telling yourself that."

"What?" Maggie asked, coming down the stairs. Her hair loose, her curls hung almost to her waist. The simple dress fit her perfectly. She had never looked so beautiful. Her gaze shifted, catching him staring. Griffin dropped the hammer on his foot.

He winced while Jori laughed, enjoying Griffin's mortification.

"Oh, well, Griffin bet me Oak would last ten minutes with the draignoch. He only made it sixty seconds. Slower than a turtle, that one. A good swat of the tail sent him flying halfway back to the lift. He ran the rest of the way, holding his ribs. It was the yellow one, big, fast. Almost had him. Oak curled into a ball and they hauled him out." Thoma shook his head, holding his hand out.

Griffin picked the hammer up and slapped it into his palm, drawing a satisfying seized breath from Thoma. "I'll have to owe you."

Maggie tossed the tunic and trousers into the fire. "No

evidence, although I doubt we'll make it back before the prince has checked on my injured ankle. I suppose we should go."

Griffin smiled at the disappointment in her voice. He felt it too. Here, in this tavern, they were among friends, and prying eyes were off. Griffin could let his guard down, be more himself. Maggie had been right about that.

"Thoma, can I borrow the horse? I'll have Bradyn get it back before sunrise tomorrow."

Thoma didn't look happy. "You better. If I have to carry the kegs on my back from the far cellars, you'll be paying me twice what you lost in the bet."

The door opened. Several men from the tanner entered. At the sight of Griffin, they extended hands in greeting, offering congratulations.

"What for?" Maggie asked.

"I won the arrow competition today."

"Ah! He's left the best part out. He split that ruddy North-man's arrow. The big one," one of them said.

"Malcolm must be unhappy," Maggie laughed.

"The king was pleased; especially after yesterday, that's really all that mattered," Griffin explained. "I was in a hurry to leave. There was no time for humiliation on the dais."

Maggie smirked, her brow twitching. "I suppose then I should do headstrong and foolish things for the rest of the tournament."

A few minutes later, Maggie rode holding on to Griffin's waist, making it difficult to think. He managed to break the workhorse into a canter for a good portion of the ride through the Middle. Neither spoke much. Griffin relived every moment of what he'd seen, stumbling headfirst into the realization that Rendicryss could fly.

By the time they reached the stables, it was midafternoon. The place was empty at this time, horses out for exercise or work. Griffin pulled into a stall. He dismounted and helped Maggie down, then removed the saddle, setting it on the ground in the corner. Bradyn would have to ride him back down after the feast. His list of favors owed to him had grown tenfold in recent days because of Maggie.

"We should return to the castle separately," she said.

"Can you find a good lie?"

"No, but I can come up with one that will leave Jori guessing. My ankle needed tending. I slipped on wet stone. Dress tore. Someone loaned me a new one."

It wasn't horrible. "Maggie, what I saw, where was that? And how did the dragon show me?"

"I'm not entirely sure on either account. How can I do what I do? My mother said she gave me my gifts to bring me out of the forest. So returning there is not my destiny." She crossed her arms. "But then she spoke of bringing hope or destruction. Tall orders and vast extremes. Not that I could accomplish either anyway. I don't know how to control my abilities. You were right. I meant to break open the gate. I barely cracked the wall, twenty feet away." Her steely gaze lifted to Griffin's. "Rendicryss decided to trust you. I want you to know I trust you too, Griffin." She took his hands in hers, threading her tiny fingers through his. His heart skipped several beats. "I don't know anything about destinies, but what I do know is that I have to free Rendicryss before she's hurt or worse in that horrible arena. And I can't do that, not without help."

He swallowed the terror attempting to choke him and nodded. "And then you'll try and leave with her."

It wasn't a question because he knew the answer.

She nodded all the same.

He refused to say he wanted to go with her, because it was a ridiculous notion, wasn't it? Would Maggie even want him? She hated him, didn't she? Her fingers closed around his said otherwise. And Thoma saw through him with ease. Griffin liked Maggie. Could he maybe even love her? One thing was for sure, he knew he wanted to help her however he could.

"What you were doing to the Phantombronze affected it, but it wasn't enough. The one thing I've learned after training to use all sorts of weapons is that all of them took time and practice."

"You'll help me?"

"If you'll let me, I'd be honored to." Griffin conjured a plan. "I'll come to your room tonight, after dinner. Bolt the door and get rid of Petal. In the reverse order . . ." He laughed nervously.

Maggie inched closer, neck craned, so close he could feel her warm breath tickling his chin.

"Maggie," he said, his voice straining. "I really . . ."

She smiled. "Okay."

"Good . . ." And then he kissed her.

Softly at first, a feather dusting, then harder.

Hungrier.

He could tell she wasn't completely innocent to kisses. He wasn't either. Those same girls in the Middle and Bottom who winced at the sight of his scarred face sought him out night after night in the tavern after he won his title. None stuck out as special.

Not like this.

He cradled her head, slowly pressing his hand against the small of her back until she was flush against him. Griffin didn't want to stop, but time had long since run out.

He pulled back, regretting it. "We have to get to the palace, Maggie."

"I know." She kissed him again. "But I truly wish we didn't."

A last embrace, and Griffin was forced to let her go. They parted, both breathless, both grinning like idiots.

He let her leave first. He would wait several minutes, then enter through the kitchens.

As Griffin walked out, he looked up—for the moon. He couldn't believe what had transpired. Or how much he had changed in the short time since Maggie came through the gates of the city.

Hope or destruction. Two extremes. With both healing and explosive powers, Maggie was capable of either. He was putting all his faith in her, with hope that he made the right decision. Because whether he intended to or not, he had made himself the only thing standing between the king and Jori— and the thing they wanted most of all.

Magic.

FIFTEEN

MAGGIE

Footsteps trailed behind me as soon as I left the stables. Shushing though the paddock of tall grasses. Skating on pebbles dumped on the muddy road. But no matter how many times I turned around, whoever it was hid. If they wanted to try to hurt me, capture, confront me, they had ample opportunity. I was in no mood for whatever game he or she or it was playing. My lie firmly in my pocket, I limped as fast as I could, hoping it was the correct ankle. Griffin's kisses had left me wanting more.

I felt guilty not thinking of Xavier since yesterday. I would ask after him the next time I saw Jori. With his newfound friendship, perhaps he would find a way for me to speak to Xavier. Like the rest, his time was running out.

At the palace gates, the guards stopped me on the way in.

"What's your business?"

They didn't recognize me.

"Lady Maggie lives here, fool." Jori walked swiftly up the road, taking my arm. His hair was matted, his red tunic turned maroon, streaked with raindrops. My heart riveted with worry his footsteps were the ones I'd heard since the barn.

"Get out of her way. Can you not see she's injured?" He touched my leg.

I tried not to stiffen.

The guard slid out of the way, letting us pass. He led us straight through the courtyard busy with post-tournament guests without stopping to speak to any of the nobles calling his name. The prince's grip tightened with each anxious limping step I took. The doors to the Great Hall were open; servants hustled with plates, glasses, linens, and candles, preparing for the nightly feast.

"How was the tournament?" I asked, trying for small talk.

Jori shook his head, dismissively. "How is your ankle?" he asked, sounding as if he already knew the answer.

We started up the stairs.

"A little better. I sought the physician but couldn't find him. I should've let the guard fetch him for me. I fell. A nice woman loaned me this dress. Mine was soaked."

The corners of his mouth lifted, a tiny hiss escaping with an even smaller laugh. He didn't believe me.

When we reached the top, his fingers dug into my arm.

"I can find my room by myself, Jori."

"Best if I escort you. Wouldn't want you to slip and fall for a third time today."

We took the hallway to my room in uncomfortable silence. Petal opened the door. I was glad she was here. I could tell by her set jaw she didn't like seeing Jori enter my room again. She wanted him to leave, and so did I.

I limped into the room, sitting down on the edge of the bed, regretting the decision. The prince sat down beside me.

Petal started to help me take off my boots, but the prince shooed her away. He lifted my left leg to his lap. I used the post to pull up, sliding away from him, and smoothed my skirts down.

"Sire, if it's all the same to you, and Petal, I can remove my own boots."

He stood up, his lips pressing into a thin bitter line. "I thought we were on better ground."

"We are."

He stepped closer. "Then why won't you let me touch you?" He lifted my hand to his lips, kissing my knuckles.

I took my hand back. "Because I don't feel that way about you."

"But you do about Griffin? I saw you in the barn, with him," he said with malice. "When he left the arena in a hurry, I worried there was trouble. Eventually I was able to extricate myself from the festivities, and what did I see while rushing back to the castle? You on the back of a horse he was riding. And then . . . you in his arms." His whole body tensed. "You slip and send word for help from Griffin? You let him take care of you, but not me? You want him, is that it? You want to marry Griffin?"

"Marry?" I laughed. "I don't want to marry anyone."

"Then why would you be kissing him?"

Jori's question took me by surprise. Wasn't it apparent? "Because I wanted to."

His expression turned grim, and suddenly I feared for Griffin's place beside him. "It was nothing. Jori. Only a kiss." A lie, but a necessary one for the prince and myself. Griffin's kisses meant more than nothing, but I wasn't staying.

"I don't understand."

"I want to leave the Walled City. I don't belong here, sire."

"And respectfully, I disagree," he said in a hushed tone. He placed his hands behind his back, a gesture I took as acquiescence, at last. "Xavier asked after you today."

"Can I see him?"

"He is performing and has asked for you to assist him. Can you manage that with your ankle?"

"Yes. I can't let him down."

He padded to the door, opening it. I moved with him to bid him goodbye and lock the door after his departure.

"May I?" He extended his palm. He wanted to kiss my hand farewell. It wasn't an abnormal move for the prince. He'd done it with others, and I could hardly refuse after I dismissed his affections so blatantly. I wasn't completely heartless. I set my hand in his.

He moved to kiss it, but frowned instead. "Where is my mother's ring?"

"Oh, it's here somewhere. I took it off before I left. Easy to hide the necklace. But I didn't want to lose the ring to muggers."

He pushed the door wider, glaring at Petal. "Have you seen it?"

Her eyes flew wide. She trembled, shaking her head, creeping behind the screen.

"She's a thief," Jori accused.

"Jori, stop this! How could you accuse her when you have no proof at all?"

"She's convicted. Why do you think she's serving you? Lied when caught red-handed stealing food from the kitchen pantry."

"Which was stolen from the Hinterlands!"

"You can defend her all you like, Maggie, but it changes—"

"It was me." I took a menacing step forward. "I sold the ring."

He blinked. "For what? What did you purchase?"

I had nothing to show, except . . . "I lied. I bought this dress. It wasn't given to me."

"That ugly smock for a sapphire ring?" Jori laughed. "I don't believe you. You're covering for her."

"Believe what you want, but it's the truth. Petal didn't take anything."

"Yes, and when it appears on your night table, I expect a full apology." His glare returned to Petal once more. "And she will be severely punished." He shrank from the door and bowed his head formally. Then was gone.

I slammed the door shut, bolting it, then pressed my back against it—just in case.

Petal cried. She had good reason. The prince had made his intentions clear. Even if I were to get the ring back, he wouldn't be satisfied with the truth. Fear rippled through me, chilling my bones. He planned to punish me by punishing Petal.

I hugged her to me. "Petal, you need to leave the castle, and never, ever return. Can you go? Now? Unseen?"

She cried, shrugging, biting her lip, turning this way and that.

All at once I understood. I saw it in her eyes. "You have nowhere to go."

She nodded.

"Yes. You do." I laid one of the red bath linens on the table and used a stray piece of burnt wood from the fireplace to draw my mark on it. I tucked it inside the sleeve of her smock. On another, I drew a picture of a wilted rose. My artistry was pathetic but with a little scrutiny, Bradyn would puzzle it out. "Go now. Hide until the prince and all are in the feast. I don't want to risk him coming back looking for you in here. Then make your way to the stables. There is a large fat mare in the fourth stall, a weathered saddle in the corner on the ground. Bradyn should be there after his duties are done." I handed her the picture of the sad flower. "Give him this. He'll understand you need a lift to the same place he's going. When you get to the Wilted Rose tavern, find Dres. Dark hair. Bushy eyebrows. An ugly scowl all the time. Give him the other parchment. He'll understand I sent you. You can trust him, and Thoma. His father owns the place."

She wiped her eyes, nodding, then hugged me. I patted her back, racking my brain to think if I missed anything. "Thoma has hair like yours. Fair. If they don't understand my clues, cry. He's a sap and likes to take in strays."

She smiled at that.

"You need a cloak." I used the smallest blanket on a chair near the fireplace, and tore a hole in the middle, then yanked it over her head. "Not my best work, but you won't freeze."

She squeezed me again.

"This is my fault, Petal. I'm so sorry to have brought this on you, but you'll be safe there. Now go."

The hallway empty, I watched as she jogged in the shadowed corners at first, then slipped behind a tapestry I hadn't noticed before. Perhaps she too knew the ways through the secret passages.

I closed and locked the door.

Pacing, I went over my entire conversation with the prince, all the simple clues I'd left him. He could trace my explanation of the sale to the market. With a little interrogation of the vendors, he would find the pregnant woman, and his mother's ring. Petal should be safe then. But if I was in the Middle, he would wonder why.

He would think I was going to the Oughtnoch to see the draignoch he captured because I had foolishly told him I wanted her released. There he would learn there had been a struggle. When interrogated, my opponent would describe what we looked like. And that would lead them back to me, but also, to Griffin. The prince would know there was more between us than a kiss. My stomach knotted until I wanted to vomit.

I was coming between Griffin and the crown.

I would be his undoing.

Music and conversation drifted out of the Great Hall as I came down the stairs in another new dress from the prince. Green this time. Xavier waited for me outside the Great Hall, beside the cheetah, draped in red robes. His gems and bones in place. He reeked of so much rose oil I held my nose as I approached him.

"Maggie." He sounded so relieved it broke my heart. "You're here. When I didn't see you on the balcony, I worried that . . ." He let out a long sad breath, shaking his head dismissively. "Well, at least you don't plan on leaving me to the king's hounds."

"What do you mean?"

His lips pressed into a thin line. His glare floated, searching for guards and their distance from them. It was sufficient.

"Do you want to do the same show as last time?" I pressed, running my fingers up and over the rough fur on the back of the poor stuffed animal. "Shall there be a cheetah chasing after Sir Griffin, or perhaps the king? I'm told it hurts."

"No. Not the king. Never!" Xavier's head cocked like a curious owl. "Tell me, Maggie, why is it I can do nothing on my own, and yet with you beside me, there is something?" His face dipped into a deep angry frown. "Has this been the truth of you all these years? Are you a snake beneath a rock, waiting for a time to strike?"

"You killed the snake and drank its blood. I don't want to strike at anyone. I only want to leave and—"

"No!" He slapped me then, hard. He grabbed my arms by the wrists, pinning them at my sides, speaking in hush tones. "I could have left you to die, but I didn't. I stayed by your side. You will stay by mine. You will never leave. You will make this magic look as though it comes from me tonight, and every night. And you will do all that the king asks. You will manifest a cheetah and send it after Sir Cornwall of the North. That is what the king has asked and that is what will be done."

I twisted my wrists, trying to break his grip.

"Xavier, stop!"

Prince Jori stepped out of the Great Hall. "Xavier, Maggie, what's taking so long? The guests are waiting."

Sir Raleigh trailed after him, a sardonic smile curling his lips at my reddening cheek.

Xavier let go and my hands went to cover the pain. "I'm not feeling well. I . . . I think I should go back to my room."

"But Xavier needs you, Maggie," the prince said in a sickeningly sweet tone. "Come. Perform and I'll make sure your meal is brought to your room after."

"No."

Jori walked behind me and leaned over my shoulder. "This is what I want, Maggie. Can you please do this, for me? You want Griffin, you want your dragon. You want. You want. I want you go into that hall and help put on a magnificent show—for Xavier's benefit."

Did he know? Did he know for certain now that I was the source of Xavier's magic? I supposed I shouldn't have been surprised. Word was spreading throughout the Middle. The prince didn't threaten Griffin or Rendicryss in words, but the implication was there, nonetheless. It changed nothing. I wanted my dragon. I didn't want Griffin hurt because of me. I would have to figure another way out of all of this.

Perhaps using the moon's gift.

I nodded.

"Good. You see, Xavier? She *can* do as she's told."

When I returned, dinner was in my room as promised, but I wasn't hungry. I vacillated between telling Griffin about the incident with the prince, or guarding that information. The only way I was getting out of this place was by using my power. I didn't necessarily need Griffin for that, but I cared for him, more than I wanted to let on to him. He was becoming . . . important to me. For those reasons, I decided to keep the incident from him. If he turned on the crown completely, it would likely be the end of him.

I shifted the bed to better glimpse the moon, then stared at it until my eyes glossed over. Step one was for it to be there when I called. I held my hand up. With little thought, the moon reached out to greet me.

I smiled greedily. "That was easy." It was as if we were two halves of a whole. Bathed in the cool white beam, I felt its power coursing through my veins.

A large hand grabbed my ankle. I yelped, startled, and whipped my hand down. A beam cut across the legs of the bedside table. It collapsed. A bowl of floating rose petals toppled all over Griffin's head.

"Ow."

"I'm so sorry!" Concentration fled through the window with the fleeting moonlight.

He climbed the rest of the way out from beneath the bed, and immediately examined the table's cut legs. "How did you do this?"

Griffin was wearing the same thing he had at dinner: a red linen shirt, a fur-lined brown leather vest, and similar-colored trousers.

"I don't know."

"That, Maggie of the Hinterlands, will not be good enough anymore." His expression serious and brooding, he showed me the wood, the edges steaming, the cold of my moon touch fighting a losing battle against the warmth in the room. "From now on you have to dissect every motion you make, every sensation you feel, and every action the moonlight takes in response. I have been thinking about this since we left the Oughtnoch."

"Clearly." My resolve waned. I had to tell Griffin at least part of what I knew. "Griffin, Jori saw us in the barn."

His fallen expression told me all I needed to know.

"You should go. I'm putting you in danger."

He laughed much harder than necessary.

"How is that funny?"

He picked up my hand and ran my fingers across the scars on his face. "I put me in danger all the time. You let me worry about me. We have two days. Tomorrow, Cornwall fights. And then I'm in the arena with Rendicryss. I'm sure of it. That is when you will free her."

"In the arena? Are you mad?"

"Entirely. But all that will be holding her are three Phantombronze chains. If I can get you into the ring, you can cut them, and she can fly away."

"Fly? Over the wall?" It sounded ridiculous.

"Crazy, I know. But there is no other way out of the city."

"What about you?" Fear lodged in my throat, making it difficult to breathe. "The king's anger would be extreme." I was afraid to whisper what was in my heart. And yet, I felt compelled to. "Would you come with me?"

"I would." He didn't hesitate. Not in the slightest.

"Just like that. You would leave all of this behind . . . for me."

He pondered that for a minute. "Not just for you. I don't think I'll ever look on a draignoch the same way again after what Rendicryss showed me. I cannot fight for the prince and king. I cannot slaughter these creatures anymore."

"And all the people you've been fighting for—"

"Would understand if I wanted to leave a place full of pomp, where I am always balanced on a razor's edge." He rubbed my cheek with his hand. "It's red and a little purple here."

I blinked back tears of relief. It was a good answer. A right answer. "I'm fine. It's nothing." Two days wasn't much time. "What do I do first?"

He lifted my hand, placing it on the broken chair leg in his other hand. "Step one, technique. Step two, grow the powers. You must use your weapon like an extension of your arm. The same way I use my sword. Show me how you capture the moonlight."

I thrust out my arm, opening my palm. The moon fell, greeting me.

Griffin smiled, chuckling. His fingers clasped my elbow. The light dimmed. "Concentrate."

I closed my eyes, pushing away the intense draw of Griffin's touch for the moon's.

"Better. Hold it. Don't let it go." He shifted my arm, turning my palm up. "Take hold of it, Maggie. Like gripping a sword."

I did, and opened my eyes. The beam had straightened.

"Astounding," he said. "Pull it toward you."

I drew it downward, bringing it to me.

"How does it feel? Move it back and forth. Feel the weight." He moved my arm by the elbow, swinging it. The beam danced along, whipping ever so slightly beyond.

On the next pass, momentum carried it too far. The beam struck his forearm.

Griffin yelped.

I lost concentration, and connection. The moonlight retreated.

"I'm so sorry!"

A spot on his forearm was now sleeveless and blistering red. I reached out, wanting to heal it, but he caught my hand. "No. Leave it. Tell me what you learned."

"I . . . um . . . its weight is lighter than I expected."

"Good. What else?"

His thumb brushed the back of my hand, making it very difficult to think about moonlight. "It's drawn to me. As I am to it."

"What does it feel like in here?" He tapped my palm.

"It wakes up every nerve, every hair stands on end. Thrumming."

"Like a heartbeat." He stepped closer.

I shook my head. "Like a running water. A stream in a drought when I'm so far out of its sight, and a raging river when I'm beneath it."

He smiled down at me with infectious excitement. He released my hand, the aftermath of which left me much more confused than when the moon let go.

"Very good. Work with that. Have another go, only change up your motion. Grow accustomed to the light's range of movement." Griffin moved the chair into the middle of the room. "And when you're ready, attempt to strike the chair."

I nodded, already raising my hand. The grip happened faster, the moon encircling my hand in a glowing ribbon. With a hard snap, it struck the floor. Stone cracked, steaming cold, leaving a straight scar.

Griffin leaned on the chair. "The chair is over here, Maggie."

"Why don't you sit in it and I'll try that again?" I smirked at him.

He settled in, wearing his own ridiculous smirk. "You'll never hit me."

"Want to bet?"

"Aha . . . what's your wager?"

What did I want from Griffin? Not monies. He'd lost too much for me already. "Another kiss."

"That's unfortunate." He sighed, my heart breaking ever so slightly. He winced. "That would've been my wager too. How about we cannot share another kiss until you hit the target?"

My cheeks burned. "You better get up, then."

I spent the next few hours trying, adjusting stances, holds, finger positions. Black lines scarred the floor in a repeating pattern. The temperature in the room fell to frigid, a wintry tundra, making our breath visible. Griffin had wrapped a blanket from the bed over his shoulders at some point.

"Again," he ordered, his teeth chattering.

My arm ached. Another try and it would fall off, but I wasn't giving up. The last missed by less than a knuckle's width.

And I had another idea.

I gripped the moon, then pulled, whipping it from the side rather than over my shoulders. The beam sliced through the wooden back like a freshly sharpened knife on brisket.

"I did it!"

Griffin moved across the room, sweeping me off my feet. Then we were kissing. Like in the barn, but less hurried. I could think of nothing, except never wanting to stop.

Except . . . "I should do that again."

"Until your arm falls off."

By the time the dark skies faded to purple, and Griffin left through the passageway under the bed, I had cut the chair to kindling. One move. A sideway whip. With one more day to rehearse this performance, I prayed it would be enough.

Griffin's scent lingered as I went about stacking broken furniture bits beside the fireplace. I climbed into bed, thinking of Petal and how I missed knowing she was behind the screen. I turned on my side to gaze out the window at the moon, taking comfort that perhaps, just maybe, another was watching over me.

SIXTEEN

GRIFFIN

The next day came too quickly. Griffin walked with Malcolm to the tunnel, listening to him worry over his brother having to fight a draignoch for the first time.

"I know you don't like him, Griffin. Hell, I think he's little better than a runny-nosed brat. But he's my brother," Malcolm mused. "It's my job to protect him. I need him to drop out, and I need you to help."

When Griffin said nothing, Malcolm played his last card.

"Family is everything," he said.

"I wouldn't know," Griffin answered, because he had none.

"I know. And I know how they died," Malcolm said, nodding an apology. "I've tried speaking with him. But I might as well be talking sense into a pile of rocks. He doesn't act like it, but he respects you, Griffin. More than most. If you tell him—"

"Tell him what? That he won't be disgraced in dropping out? He will be. I would be lying."

Malcolm turned as crimson as his hair. "What matter is that? At least he would be alive."

Griffin sighed. "Would you drop out, Malcolm? After so

much boast. It would take more courage to endure that than facing the beast."

Malcolm's jaw worked as he wrestled with Griffin's words all the way to the tunnel's entrance. "He won't live through the match."

"More likely, he will. And we'll have to hear about it for years to come." Griffin smiled, trying to lighten the mood, but Malcolm didn't rise to the occasion. He nodded as if accepting this was out of his control, because it was, and no amount of conversation with Cornwall would change a thing.

There was no melee today. Zac exited after his brother Silas's death. Others followed in support of the noble family. Wallison and Bradyn were the only two who showed up this morning. The event was cut altogether. All that was left was the opening dramatics. Dressed in bright colors, acrobats flipped, jumped, and bent, entertaining the restless crowd.

As soon as it was over, Duncan called for the challenge event. In the tunnel and on the lift down into the ring, Griffin examined his staff with great care, as he had every weapon since the accident. The spectators quieted as two rectangles were drawn. The goal was to knock your opponent out of the space, eliminating, until the last man stood in the center.

With three left in the competition, Malcolm and Cornwall fought each other first. The winner moved on to battle Griffin. Being champion had its privileges after all.

The two stepped inside the first rectangle, Malcolm wearing black, and Cornwall in brown, both paying tribute to the

North with blue-and-green tartan sashes. That would surely anger the king.

For the first minute Malcolm toyed with Cornwall. Faking jabs, goading his younger brother.

"What's wrong?" Malcolm taunted. "Afraid of what comes next?"

"Excited." Cornwall raised his staff above his head and swung down, hitting Malcolm's hand.

"Ow!" Malcolm backstepped. "Full of surprises, aren't you?"

"Will you shut up already and hit him! Pathetic! I could do so much better. They should let me in the tournament," Sybil cried, howling with laughter from the balcony. Three days ago, Griffin had seen Sybil on the practice fields. He was glad she wasn't a competitor. She was as accomplished as Malcolm—and wilier.

Malcolm rained down heavy strokes, jabbing between, all of which Cornwall blocked. Cornwall knocked Malcolm back with a hard cross-body lunge. Malcolm countered, and the two stood in a grunting stalemate, until Malcolm used his chest, throwing his weight on the staff in a sharp jerk. Cornwall stumbled sideways, cursing, stepping out of bounds.

The crowd gave a round of applause but held back; there was another match before the delivery of the final victor.

Malcolm helped his brother up. "Go get ready for what comes next. I expect to be toasting your victory tonight, little brother."

Cornwall seemed surprised by Malcolm's words. He half smiled, slapping Malcolm on the chest, then jogged into the side, slower than he usually moved.

Griffin rubbed dirt on his staff and stepped into the center rectangle. He rolled his neck, cracking it, trying to wake up. He was in Maggie's room far too late, but it had been worth it.

Malcolm held his staff in both hands, across the length of his body, but his stare was on his brother.

Marshal Duncan walked the perimeter with his hand in the air, and the crowd's full attention—then dropped it, starting the match.

Malcolm jabbed, a hard cross-body check Griffin blocked, pushing him back and almost out of bounds.

"Stop worrying over your brother and fight me," Griffin said.

Malcolm swung an overhead drop, nearly banging Griffin's staff out of his hands. Griffin jabbed, hitting Malcolm in the gut, bending him over, then struck him again on the back.

Malcolm staggered backward, staying inbounds, recovering fast enough to block Griffin's next jab, then advanced, rowing the staff, thwacking Griffin's, backing him up until he teetered on his heels on the edge of the line. Griffin landed a sharp uppercut to Malcolm's jaw. He fell forward—out of bounds.

The crowd cheered. He could hear Jori from the balcony, calling, "Sir Griffin!" Griffin should acknowledge him. Pay homage to his prince, but he couldn't. Not anymore. Griffin reached a hand down to Malcolm, helping him up.

The people chanted Griffin's name into a chorus. Griffin took a quick bow, then walked straight to Cornwall, who stood off to the side of the ring, strapping on bulky leg guards. Between his heavy chain mail over the thick leather padding and his metal body armor, Cornwall would move slower than Oak on his fastest day.

Maggie waited on the balcony, and Griffin was in a hurry to see her, but after passing off his staff to an assistant, he walked back. He had to say something to the cocky whelp before his first fight.

"Do you wish to see sixteen, Cornwall?"

"I don't want to hear from you, Griffin. I know what I'm doing." Cornwall lowered his helmet's face mask down.

"You'll move too slow with all this on. Ask your brother."

"*This* is the most advanced defensive equipment the kingdoms have ever seen." Cornwall checked the sharpening on his sword. "The sun is out. The ground dry. I will move just fine. I don't need my brother, or you, to tell me anything."

Griffin threw up his hands in surrender, leaving, but then stopped. "Last piece of advice, and then I'm gone. If you lose your footing or get injured in any way, head for the lift as fast as you can. The draignoch's chains won't allow the beast to reach that far."

Cornwall sheathed his sword. "I'll be the butt of the king's jokes."

"At least you'll be alive to hear them." Griffin set a heavy hand on his shoulder. "Don't you understand? Surviving is the ultimate win."

Cornwall stared at his feet, nodding, giving Griffin hope that something he said broke through that heavy helmet.

As soon as Griffin came out on the balcony, Jori handed him a chalice. "Well done." The prince raised his own glass, first to the people, and then to Griffin.

"Thank you." Griffin searched for Maggie, letting his gaze linger longer than he should when he found her. Stunning in a yellow dress, she was being held hostage by Xavier at the other end of the balcony, beside King Umbert.

An arm fell over his shoulders. "Come," Jori said, demanding Griffin's attention. "You won't want to miss a second of this." He led Griffin to the other end of the balcony.

Esmera and Sybil got up to give a standing ovation to Cornwall as he exited the tunnel. His sword in one hand and a shield in the other, he dropped to one knee when he reached the center of the ring.

The throngs silenced.

King Umbert stood, leaning on the railing so hard it creaked under Griffin's hands. "Well, second son, let's see if you can redeem the brothers from the North."

Egrid wrestled with his crutch, nearly falling over. Maggie hurried to his side to help.

"Where's Malcolm?" Esmera asked.

"In the tunnel, I suspect," Sybil answered.

A bell gonged. The drums began their slow beat, pacing

with the rise of the gate. A sharp pounding inside began, quaking the stands. People mumbled with worry.

Maggie closed her eyes briefly. When they opened, she tried to run, likely out the door, but Xavier was holding on to her wrist. He yanked her, holding on to her but not for long. She kicked him and he let go, cursing her. She headed for the door, but the guards prevented her from leaving. She found Griffin. Her mouth parted, her chest rising and falling in fear.

"It's Rendicryss."

The gate had barely parked when she raced into the arena, roaring with unbridled fury. Taller and thicker than she appeared in the bestiary, her skin shone black as night, but as the sun hit her back, the light broke into a rainbow of colors. Her eyes too had changed color to fiery red. Her wings unfurled, and Griffin gasped, seeing they spanned a quarter of the ring, ridged bones aligned throughout.

There was no doubt in Griffin's mind that what he saw was real. With those, she *could* fly.

Maggie looked at him, helpless. She was too far away to even attempt cutting those chains. Rendicryss canvassed the ring, swinging her head back and forth, pausing at the balcony, at Maggie. Maggie gripped the railing, her stare locked on her dragon.

Jori moved between them, his hand falling over hers. "Don't worry, Maggie. I'm here. And I'm sure the draignoch will be fine."

"Are you mad? Cornwall is untested!" Griffin yelled at Jori.

"This is for you, Griffin. For your benefit. *You said you wanted to see it before your match,*" Jori said.

"Stop this," Griffin cried. "For the love of the crown, don't do this."

"Griffin," Jori said in a placating tone, "Cornwall has been told a thousand times to step out of the competition. He refused. I cannot stop it. Look at his father."

Griffin found Egrid leaning forward, a smile of anticipation on his lips. Did he actually believe his son could win against the creature that faced him?

Rendicryss let out a high-pitched scream that had all covering their ears.

The audience chanted, "Corn-wall. Corn-wall. Corn-wall."

Cornwall scooped his spear, jogging across the ring from her, as far away as he could get.

Rendicryss lowered her snout, bared her teeth, all chiseled fangs, and sprinted at Cornwall, her chains giving plenty of lead.

"What *is* that? That's not a draignoch. Is it?" Esmera asked for all to hear. "Jori! Stop the fight! Stop it now!"

"Sit down, Esmera. No one needs to hear your whining, particularly not me," Laird Egrid snapped.

Cornwall raised his shield. The dragon swiped, raking a claw, the toes catching the edge, flicking it out of his hands. It flew into the lowest row, hitting a man in the head with such force he was knocked into the row behind him. Blood ran down his face.

Cornwall threw his spear—his best weapon. The tip hit its mark, but didn't penetrate Rendicryss's hide. It bounced harmlessly to the ground.

The crowd gasped.

"Did you see that?" Sybil said, sounding panicked.

"Cornwall! The lift! Run!" Esmera cried. But her brother didn't listen.

Zigzagging to avoid Rendicryss's snapping jaws, Cornwall pulled his sword. He thrust at her side, but Rendicryss anticipated every move he made. The dragon whipped her wings, lifting off the ground the few feet the chains allowed, twisting out of the blade's range.

The crowd reacted, ducking and shouting.

Cornwall jabbed, cutting across the dragon's hip. A move that would've been enough on a draignoch, but it was only a nuisance to Rendicryss. The dragon jumped, landing on Cornwall's legs. His bones snapped like twigs. He howled in terror and pain.

"Stop this! Stop this now!" Sybil yelled. "Cornwall!" Her cry echoed every part of the arena.

"Please . . . no," Esmera whimpered softly, dropping her face into her hands, refusing to look at all.

Egrid sat stiff as a board, barely breathing.

"Cornwall!" Malcolm yelled, his voice coming out of the tunnel. The lift still at the bottom, he grabbed hold of the pulley rope, intending to slide down, but guards grabbed him. It took three to hold him back.

Unable to move his legs, Cornwall did the only thing he could. He slashed his sword wildly, trying to keep Rendicryss's lowering fangs from taking his head off. The blade nicked the dragon's snout. She recoiled, blood streaming over ridges, falling like boiling rain around Cornwall. Every drop that hit Cornwall melted through his armor, through his chain mail, until it found skin. Cornwall screamed. He thrust his blade at the same time Rendicryss's hind leg whipped forward. The sword stabbed, but not nearly hard enough. Her claws dug into Cornwall's chest—into his heart—killing him instantly.

"No . . ." Maggie clutched her chest.

Griffin wasn't sure if her pain was for Rendicryss or Cornwall. He suspected, like his, it was for both.

"Cornwall!" Sybil wailed.

Griffin pulled her to him. "Don't look. Keep your head down."

Sybil shoved him away. She ran through the door. The guards were so transfixed on the dragon, she pushed them aside and left. Esmera went with her.

Maggie slid over, her hands cupping the railing, finding Griffin's.

"Look at what they've done to her . . ."

"I'm so sorry, Maggie."

The people quieted. Stunned into horrified, mouth-covering silence. Not even a whisper floated on the breeze.

Whimpering, Egrid leaned forward, using the railing to pull himself to standing. King Umbert got out of his chair, taking his chalice with him, and peered down at Cornwall's lifeless body still stuck on Rendicryss's claws.

Xavier peeked over the edge. "Poor boy. Least it was quick. All we can ask for. A quick death."

Griffin wanted to throw that idiot over the railing.

Rendicryss's head shifted until she found the king. Her red eyes narrowed. Nostrils flaring, she reeled back. Cornwall's body flew through the air, heading straight for the balcony.

Xavier somehow yanked the king out of the way. But Egrid wasn't so lucky. Cornwall's body hit the old laird so hard he barreled through a table, plowing into the wall behind it.

Shocked silence followed. For several long seconds no one moved.

Malcolm, Sybil, and Esmera burst through the door, onto the balcony. The Northman gently lifted Cornwall off Egrid. "Fath . . ." He never finished. He saw what Griffin did. The old man was dead. His eyes fixed beyond, to whatever came next.

The people looked on, their faces a mixture of horror, compassion, and disgust.

Griffin helped lift Egrid into Malcolm's arms, unable to take his eyes off the insanity he saw in the king. With a sharp turn, Malcolm carried away his father's body, while Umbert leaned on the railing, a low wicked laugh escaping for only the balconies' ears. He looked back at Sybil cradling Cornwell's head in her lap, sweeping his hair out of the blood on his face. His nostrils flaring, he stamped his foot, jerking his head, indicating for the few remaining guards to get on with removing the body. They made for a messy pulpit.

But the guards hesitated. Sybil was crying, mumbling, "Time to go home. It's time to go home."

Esmera knelt beside Sybil, pulling her off Cornwall so the guard could more easily get to him.

As he lifted Cornwall's body, Esmera took Sybil's hands off, hugging her sister from behind. They got up together, leaving with their brother's body.

Rendicryss lunged forward for King Umbert, screaming an ungodly sound from deep in her throat. But the chains held fast. Umbert raised his fist at Rendicryss, taunting her, then turned to address his people. "I foresaw this! This monster is what comes next from the forest. Do you see? An omen stands before you! The wall, my soldiers, and my magic will protect you! Your king will protect you!"

A few clapped for their king, but most stared at Rendicryss, mouths hanging open, clutching their heaving chests or holding their children against them.

The dragon's throat rumbled a growl. She lunged once more but the Phantombronze chains would not yield an inch. Umbert laughed, shaking his head at her as if to say, *You will never win.* By the look in her eye, Rendicryss took that as a challenge. The gauntlet thrown. And Griffin would never bet against that dragon.

She chuffed.

"A mocking lizard for sure," King Umbert yelled, stepping away from the spectators' view.

King Umbert yanked Jori beside him. He nodded for Xavier to stand by his other side. Jori gestured for Griffin, but Griffin refused. He remained with Maggie.

Rendicryss reached back, biting down on Cornwall's blade still stuck in her hindquarters. Without flinching, she ripped it out, hurling it at her enemy. The sword should've hit the king, but a guard jumped in front of him, blocking it with his shield, sending it spiraling downward on the Bottom's rows.

Rendicryss roared.

"This is madness!" a woman wailed. "Let us out of this place!"

"Silence her. Throw her to the beast," King Umbert ordered.

Griffin couldn't believe his ears.

The woman sprinted up the aisle toward the exit, only to be captured by the king's soldiers. Three from the Bottom's rows came to her aid, trying to fight them off, only to be seized by other guards, dragged to the edge, and thrown over with her.

It was only then Griffin realized that one of the brawlers was Thoma.

"This can't be happening. . . . Get out of my way!" Griffin ordered the guards at the door, but the king shook his head, and they refused to let him leave.

"Do you wish to save them, Sir Griffin?" King Umbert bellowed. He held his hand over the rail. "Go on, then. I grant you permission to jump."

"What?" Griffin would die from the fall.

"If those Bottom feeders mean more to you than your king,

go ahead. Jump to save them, and I'll let the draignoch feed on you as well."

Thoma helped the woman to stand, yelling, "Run!"

The four sprinted toward the lift, but the dragon beat them easily. Rendicryss swung her head, crashing into their only way out. The lift flew into the air a few feet off the ground. The dragon's hind leg caught it midair, slamming down, crushing it. She roared then, thrashing her head from side to side.

A tear fell down Maggie's cheek. "She's in pain, Griffin. The chains are burning her."

"Maggie . . . please . . ." He said her name in prayer.

She looked down at the four. Thoma stood with his back to the other three, trying to protect them. As she had so many times the night before, Maggie closed her eyes, stretching her hand ever to the sky. From a point Griffin couldn't see, the moon answered her call. A light beam as long as a sword was all that was visible.

"By the gods!" someone called.

"Look!" another yelled.

And they all did.

"Is *she* doing that?" King Umbert cried.

"No, sire." Xavier remembered his staff beside him and held it aloft.

His stare fixed on Maggie, the king pushed Xavier out of his way and started for her, but made it only three steps before slipping in a pool of Cornwall's blood.

"Father!" Jori gasped, looking for help. "Get my father out of here!" he yelled at the guards left. Three guards rolled the king to standing and rushed him off the balcony. The prince headed for Maggie. Griffin put his back to her, arms stretched, refusing to let the prince near her.

"Griffin, you're making a mist—"

Griffin kicked him. He fell into the guards behind him. The prince recovered, returning, turning red with fury.

"Take him," Jori ordered.

The guards advanced. Griffin heard the snap of Maggie's power coming closer. He ducked.

She whipped her arm back, striking the guards. Their bodies went rigid, as if struck by lightning. They crashed to the floor, and never got up. Maggie threw her arm out, the beam expanding. She drew more power than Griffin had ever seen her do before. Like Phantombronze in daylight and tilted on edge, the moonlight was rendered invisible, but Griffin could feel the cold power emanating off her. It was most definitely still there.

Frothing at the mouth, her fiery red eyes sparking with sun, the dragon tossed her head back and forth, working into a frenzy.

"Rendicryss!" Maggie swung overhand. A thunderous snap shattered the crowd's awed and terrified screams. Moonlight struck the ground beside the dragon. If she was trying to hit the chains, she missed, badly.

The dragon stopped roaring. Jori, Xavier, every single person in the arena stopped too. Rendicryss craned her neck to look at Maggie.

Maggie shook her head. She held out her hand, her palm up. Rendicryss lowered her head so it was on the ground. Her eyes closed. When they opened again, they were no longer red, but blue, like Maggie's.

"Raise the keep's gate!" Griffin called. "Get them out of there!"

The throngs joined in, transforming Griffin's orders into a riotous demand. Before the prince could say yea or nay, the marshal's voice yelled, "Raise it! Raise it now!"

Pulleys creaked. The heavy metal rolled up.

Thoma's wide-eyed gaze flipped from the opening to Maggie.

"What are you waiting for?" she shouted at him.

The woman pushed the others, crying, "Hurry!"

They sprinted across the ring, skating around Rendicryss and through the gate. All the while, the dragon stood still, as if waiting for Maggie's next command.

Rendicryss lowered her wings, tucking them to her back. She opened wide, squeaking, then her three sharp claws stabbed the dirt. Then again, scraping. She stepped closer to the keep, so all could see. A symbol. She'd drawn it in the dirt. Xavier's gasp was so loud, Griffin heard it from the other side of the balcony.

The symbol. It was Maggie's.

SEVENTEEN

MAGGIE

Soldiers flooded the balcony, Raleigh leading the charge. I glanced at Griffin. His jaw clenched. He spun to attack at the same time I stretched, reaching for a blessing from the moon. Two men grabbed my arms, pinning them behind my back.

Four more wrestled Griffin to the ground as they yanked me away from the railing.

Rendicryss screamed, running across the ring until her chains would allow no more. She reared, thrashing her head from side to side, flailing her front legs, claws extended.

Soldiers manning the exits refused to let panicked attendees leave. The fleeing masses stacked up, climbing over each other, the small and unfortunate falling underneath, trampled.

"Get her out of here!" Jori ordered.

They dragged me into the dark stairwell. Two sets of iron cuffs locked my arms behind my back at elbow and wrist.

"Griffin!" I screamed.

"Shut up!" Moldark shouted. He threw me over his shoulder, carrying me down the stairs.

"Put me down!" I squirmed and rolled. He bumped into

the wall, but he was too big for it to be anything more than a slight irritation.

We exited the stairwell, Moldark stumping into the tunnel where he tossed me into the back of a waiting wagon. I kicked, scooting as far away from him as possible. He got one ankle, then the other, holding my legs together while another soldier added leg irons to the mix. A third gagged me and covered me with a thick gray blanket. Weight shifted with soldiers getting in, sitting on the blanket. I wasn't going anywhere.

"Hup!" Moldark called.

The wagon jerked, moving forward, the driver whipping the horses, whistling for them to go faster. The light shifted from dim to daylight. The wagon tilted, starting uphill. Rendicryss's heartbreaking bellows carried out of the arena until the sound cut off abruptly. She must have been pulled into the keep. Tears poured down my face. I'd failed her. I'd failed Griffin.

The wagon continued the steep incline. I could only guess we were returning to the castle.

Griffin would never make it out alive from the balcony.

This was all the prince's doing all along, with Raleigh's help, but to what end?

The blanket covering my head, Moldark carried me over his shoulder through what smelled like the kitchens. He lunged upstairs, padded through long echoing hallways, bending right and left, wending a familiar way, heading to where this day had started.

My room.

Inside, he dropped me on the bed and left, closing and locking the door. I rolled back and forth until the blanket fell off my face. On my stomach, facedown, all I could do was wait, hoping, praying, Griffin would come through the hidden grate behind the bed.

But he never did.

I fell asleep. When I opened my eyes, a man stood over me, shaking my shoulder. It took me several blinks to connect the face to the voice. Clean shaven, dressed in a formal black cloak, rather than his usual dirty tunic, Raleigh looked like a completely different person. He wasn't alone. Six more soldiers I recognized as palace guards were there, standing near the door, in similar tidy cloaks. All beardless like Raleigh, their hair was uniformly cropped short. They stared at me, hands on the pommels of their swords, but didn't come any farther into the room.

My gaze fell on the moon outside the window. Night had fallen. I took deep breaths, drinking it in, taking comfort that her power was there for me. As soon as my hands were free, I would wield it.

Raleigh gave a half-hearted grin, hauling me off the bed. He placed me on my feet, then removed the gag. "I would remove the irons, but your powers have grown to where I consider them too great a threat."

My mouth was dry; my jaw ached. "Where is Griffin?"

"Griffin? Alive. In his rooms. Where else would he be? He has a big match tomorrow. He and Malcolm. The finals, you see, against your favorite draignoch, followed by a celebration of the prince's wedding." Raleigh smiled. "We will all be there, you included, so long as you do as you're told."

Griffin was alive, and tomorrow Rendicryss would be in the arena. I needed to be there as well, unshackled. How? What would I have to give up? "What do you want?"

"Right now? For you to follow me."

The leg irons made it difficult to do more than shuffle, especially down steps. His men in front and behind, Raleigh walked beside me the whole time, a hand on my shoulder.

"Do you think I'm going to run?" I asked at one point.

His sardonic laugh was expected but irritating. "Your days of running are over. You cannot hide anymore, lass. What you can do is be smart. Take what rightfully belongs to you when it's offered."

"I don't understand. Did you stage a coup?"

He laughed again. "No."

As we passed the Great Hall, there was no music. No sounds of mingling guests or smells of scrumptuous platters of food.

"I suppose there was little to celebrate after what happened in the arena today." I thought of Cornwall and Egrid, and how Malcolm, Esmera, and Sybil were planning two funerals. The three of them rallied around, took care of each other, like the prince told me once he wanted to do for me. Only their love and kind gestures came with no cost. I thought Xavier's care came from his heart too, but in the end I wondered if I wasn't simply like one of the bones in his hair, collected because one day I might serve a useful purpose.

Perhaps that was what it meant to have family. People who did things for you without expecting anything in return. Griffin popped into my mind unbidden. He never asked me for anything in return for his aid. Like Thoma had done for him when he was young. Friends. True friends, I supposed, could be like family. With time, would Griffin and I have that? I hoped so. But we would have to survive what came next.

Raleigh grew quiet, contemplative, nervous even, which only added to my anxiety. "There is much to celebrate," he finally said.

We walked to the end of the hallway, climbed several flights of stairs, exiting where the short bridge led to the king's tower. I shivered, not because of the cold night air, but at the gruesome scene before me.

In the middle of the bridge, King Umbert sat on his throne. Arms and legs bound to the chair. Mouth gagged. His nose bent and covered in dry, caked blood, like it had been hit many, many times. One eye was swollen shut, turning yellowish purple. He looked barely conscious.

Xavier was beside him in the same place he had stood for the past week, only his hands were tied to the back of the throne, and his mouth was gagged. His staff sat in two pieces at his feet. The sapphire missing.

All horrible, but it was what I saw on the other side of the bridge that caused my heart to skip several long beats.

Bradyn and Buffont. Bound, gagged, and on their knees. Twenty soldiers in their new black cloaks stood beyond them, filling in the rest of the bridge to the king's tower.

I tried to walk to Bradyn, but Raleigh's firm hand on my shoulder held me in my place.

The line of soldiers parted. The prince walked down the center, his eyes fixed on me. His cloak was also now black rather than red. A new crown on his head. Not a simple band of gold like his father's, but ornate, with peaks and valleys, decorated with obsidian stones. He was carrying a smaller version in his hand, the obsidian replaced with sapphires.

The prince held the crown up as he came to stand before me. "Blue looks lovely on you." He tried to put the crown on my head. I retreated, bumping into Raleigh. "Did you think I only wanted to bed you?" Jori grinned as he did after the first time Xavier and I performed in the Great Hall, when he'd won a bet with Griffin, taking his Phantombronze dagger. He was gloating over his father's conquest, and mine. "I thought you would want them on their knees. Paying homage to the real Ambrosius, and my queen."

I opened my mouth to speak. He patted my chin sharply, closing it. "I'm speaking. You are listening." Jori placed his palms on my cheeks, forcing me to look at him. "What you did today in the arena. That was a thing of beauty. A single day of training with Griffin and you're on your way to using your gift. He has turned you into a weapon, as I asked him to."

"You never asked him that!"

Jori's lips curled into a mocking grin. "His wooing. Breaking into the Oughtnoch—twice. His late-night visits through the secret passageway underneath your bed. Why do you think I put you in *that room*? Do you really think my best friend would turn on me for a girl he met seven days ago? Beautiful or not, he's not that stupid."

Griffin couldn't have . . . wouldn't have . . . seeds of doubt spread like hot iron, leaving a wake of blistering anger.

"Oh, I can tell what you're thinking. But don't be so hard on him. He only did as I commanded."

I spat, hitting Jori in the eye.

Raleigh grabbed my elbows behind my back, yanking hard, nearly taking my arms from their sockets. "She's like a rabid dog, Your Grace. You really want to wed her?"

"I do." Jori wiped it off, his smile still frozen in mocking perfection. "But there's wedded bliss and then there's marriage. We all have choices to make. That's what pivotal moments are all about. My father taught me that." He sighed. "Maggie, I don't want to keep you in chains, but I will. I will cage you just as I have done your Rendicryss."

I was stunned into silence by the use of her name. I'd never told him that. Only Griffin knew her name. He'd lied to me. He'd told Jori everything. He'd used me. This castle was a tomb filled with twisted souls grasping for power. With hallways and secret passages, a maze to use for lies and deceit, and I'd fallen for it all.

I needed my dragon. I needed to leave. I stopped struggling, feigning surrender, hoping Raleigh would let go of my arms, but he didn't. If anything, he held on tighter.

Jori padded to the other side of the king, finding a wooden handle. He shifted it and a large square section of the bridge in front of his father dropped. "Do you know what this is, Maggie?"

Jori untied Xavier. He led him by the rope binding his hands until he stood beside the hole. A fall of more than a hundred feet stretched before him, ending on hard ground. A fall he wouldn't survive.

"It's called a murder hole."

"Murder? You intend to kill all these people?"

"That all depends on you, my lady."

"Don't call me that."

"You're right. You're not a lady." He laughed at my unease. "But you will be a queen." His penetrating stare searched for reaction, but I gave him none. "First things first. This will be a new start for you and for me. A beginning together, so we must rid ourselves of traitors in our midst and start our journey together with truth. Xavier's betrayal began the day we met. After your performance, healing that squirrel, I came to see you that night, but first, I spoke with Xavier. I told him what I suspected happened and made a bargain with him. Keep his mouth shut. Bring you safely into the city, and he would be well rewarded."

I suppose I should have been shocked. Xavier knew

everything from the first, and led me like a lamb to the slaughter. But I wasn't surprised. A thought that registered on Jori's face.

He half smiled. "He fed and clothed you. Kept you alive in the Hinterlands before the curse was lifted, when you were nothing but a helpless child. He could have so easily sold you. So you trusted him."

I took a step back, bumping into Raleigh again. "How do you know about the curse?"

Jori laughed at me in response, pulling Xavier against him. "Fresh start, Maggie. Is he worthy of standing beside you? I think not."

Jori wrenched Xavier forward, then drew him back before he could fall. Xavier's eyes were impossibly wide. His body shook, his face wet with a river of tears. He tried to speak with the gag but only mumbled. If I had to guess, it sounded like an apology.

I hated him for what he had done, but I didn't want him dead. "Don't! Please." I kicked Raleigh in the shin with my heel. He sucked in a sharp breath but held fast to my arms.

"I do this for you."

Xavier coughed and gagged around the fabric that refused him his last words. Wind swept the bridge. His bones clacked, this time serving a purpose, foretelling his end. Xavier plummeted through the hole. Even after his screams stopped, I could still hear them. A sound that would haunt my dreams, turning them to nightmares forever more.

Jori stepped back, giving me a resigned pitiful stare.

"You're no better than your father," I whispered.

Jori's expression turned to one of disbelief. "A man obsessed with something he could never have. A cruel master. And yet you fight, for him? I offer you a crown. I offer you a place beside me, to rule over these lands, and conquer more."

"Tell Raleigh to remove the shackles from my wrist and I'll show you what you'll get if you place me beside you on the throne."

Jori stamped his foot.

Raleigh yanked my arms, forcing me to my knees.

"You're a coward," I growled.

"And you're stupid. But I can live with that in a wife, especially one as lovely and as powerful as you."

"So long as I'm chained like my Rendicryss."

Jori padded behind me and took my cuffs from Raleigh. He forced me up and shoved me forward, beside the murder hole.

"Look at him."

I refused, training my eyes on Bradyn's fidgeting knees. I didn't want to see Xavier like that. It would be all I would remember if I did. Wind howled over the bridge again. I couldn't stop shaking.

Jori removed his cloak, placing it on me. It was still warm from his body heat. His curling breath fell over my shoulder. "He's nothing. You, you are everything. Don't you see that?" He pulled me back, shifting to stand in front of me. He grasped my chin, tilting it up, forcing me to look at him. "It doesn't have to be this way." He tried to kiss me. I turned away, my stomach heaving. He pushed me into Raleigh, disgusted.

A beat later, his demeanor changed. His expression returning to arrogant prince. "Would you like to know how I know about your curse?" His big brown eyes twinkled with unspoken secrets. "I can tell you do. You're quiet, and you're never quiet."

He stepped back and flicked two fingers at the soldiers standing closest to the tower entrance. It took three men to carry whatever was beneath the red cloth out the door.

They set it down with great care. Jori ripped the tarp off. My hair stood on end. I had seen that before. A true memory returned. Me, with my back bare, holding on to that stone while the banshee beat me with a switch. That came from her cave.

"The part my father left out of his story was that he went back to find the prophetic woman. It was long after the draignochs were defeated. After he'd been declared king and built the Walled City. He still hadn't found the magic she spoke of and went seeking more guidance. He never found her, but did find a cave where another woman lived with her deformed son. My father tortured her, eventually killing her when she produced no useful information."

Jori gestured at the four-foot-tall standing stone. "Except, he overlooked this."

It was a pillar common to the people of my childhood. Carvings on it told of each cave dweller's story. This one declared me a lost child of the forest and my dragon as the magic that got away. The script was carved into the edges, not in images but in our ancient language. The banshee and her son, Armel, had kept a record of me.

"He took this even though he didn't have the faintest idea of what it was. Kept it in the corner of his chambers. I would sneak up, trying to decipher it, but could never figure out what it said." Jori walked over to his father. He leaned over and whispered in his ear. "But it was the biggest clue of all."

His father woke then, struggling against the ropes binding him to the chair, but he wasn't going anywhere. The prince laid a firm, condescending hand on the back of King Umbert's bulbous neck. "After it was translated, of course."

"You can read it?" I asked in disbelief.

"No. But I found someone who could. The woman's son. Deformed. Smashed nose. Hunched over. Eyes not on the same plane."

"Armel."

"Yes. He had come to the Walled City looking for revenge. I recognized him from my father's description of him, and his thirst for revenge. He wanted to kill my father. I told him I too wanted my father dead, offered to let him into the heavily guarded tower, escort him personally to my father's chambers, in exchange for one small thing."

The bridge was filled with people, and yet all were silent. It felt like Jori and I were alone.

"It was on this bridge that I asked him to read this stone for me." Jori's fingers traveled from the bottom left of the stone. "It begins with a dragon called Rendicryss"—his fingers continued upward along the edge—"bringing a baby down from the night's sky, a baby whose blue eyes would glow with gifts bestowed upon her by the moon."

"What happened to Armel?"

Jori looked down the hole. "He fell. But not before telling me all kinds of things about you. My favorite was how his mother used to punish you. How as a baby when you would whine and cry, she would lock you in the back of the cave, sealing you in a tomb of rock, blocking you from the moon. How you would grow so weak you could barely move, but you would never die, as he wished you would."

And just like that, events from the past four weeks made perfect sense. "The practice room you gave Xavier."

"Yes. It was a good test. A punishment I will use again and again to my advantage. Keep that in mind." He patted my cheek. "Armel wanted to kill you too. He would have if he found you. You had no memory of who you were or where you came from. Lost in the Hinterlands."

"He could never have killed me whether I could remember how to wield my powers or not."

"You may be right. He was weak, and I have seen you fight. But to end my story, not long after Armel told me what to look for, I found the dragon. And then that same afternoon, I found you. It was divine intervention."

"Dumb luck," I mumbled.

"Fate. Destiny. I found you and Rendicryss. It was me who was meant to rule these lands, not my father. *Me*. With magic by *my* side. With you by my side." He picked up a pitcher beside the throne, pouring over his father's head, coating his bald head in rose oil. King Umbert screeched and snarled. Jori reached in his pocket and pulled out three crushed wild roses. Jori shifted his father's gag, shoving the flowers into his mouth. The king coughed, heaving breaths. "I believe my fiancée and I have heard enough, haven't we, Maggie?"

I had nothing to say.

"Wild roses were my mother's favorite. After her death, he had them pressed into oils, dripped in my baths. He had them stitched into my clothing, all as a way of reminding me of the power he had over me, the power to take her from me. But no longer. I have all the power now, isn't that right, Maggie? And all that remains for us to be free is for you to kill my father."

"If you want your father dead, why not throw him down the hole yourself. Like he did your mother?"

He laughed with mirth. "I want you to kill him because I'm telling you to."

The prince wanted to turn me into an assassin, a murderer. A monster like him. "No."

Jori scowled. "You don't get to tell me no. When you do, another will pay for your impudence." Jori's malicious glare fell on Bradyn and Buffont. "Which one shall it be?" He scooped Bradyn over his shoulder, moving beside the hole. Buffont cried and stamped his feet, trying to get the prince's attention. But the prince paid him no heed.

"What are you doing? Put him down!" I struggled against the cuffs, against Raleigh's hold, to no avail.

"Do as I ask."

Buffont inched toward the prince, his pleading sounds muzzled by his gag. A soldier latched on to his shoulder, holding him back. His frantic gaze on me, the cooker threw his weight, barreling into the king's throne, tipping it forward.

Several things happened at once. Soldiers reached for the falling chair, but the king's mass was too great. He went over, plummeting through the hole. Raleigh tossed me aside. He strode forward and without hesitation threw Buffont headfirst through the hole.

"No!" I screamed. "No . . . how could you? How could you?"

Jori was so baffled by what happened that when Bradyn started shrieking and wrestling in his arms, the prince nearly fell himself. Soldiers grabbed him, pulling him back.

"Well, that was unexpected," Jori said. He called a soldier over. "As soon as we're done here, bring Sir Griffin to my chambers. I will send our champion out to let the people know of the king's demise. The traitor was within the castle all along. Buffont poisoned the ale. And when all that failed, he took matters into his own hands."

Raleigh said what I was thinking. "And the witness?" He jerked his head at Bradyn.

"I'm afraid he will also have to disappear, forever."

"No. Please." I swallowed my pride, and it tasted like piss. "He won't tell a soul. I swear it. And I'll do as you ask. Just— you must spare him."

Jori took two long steps, grabbed my face, and kissed me, hard. I held as still as possible, suppressing the urge to bite his lip. He pulled back, still holding my face with a satisfied grin. "Good. Very good."

"You'll let him go?"

"After we're wed. After you've proven to me that you are being honest with me. After a while. For now, he will be locked away."

"Not good enough."

"I could take his tongue right now so he could never tell what he witnessed. Would you prefer that?"

I drove my forehead into his nose, delighting in his gasping screams. He stumbled away from me, craning this neck, covering his face. Blood seeped through the cracks between his fingers.

"Sire, we have things to deal with. I think a little cooling-off time is in order." Raleigh yanked my arms up, straining my shoulders. It hurt but I refused to show it.

Still trying to stop his nose from bleeding, Jori waved his permission.

Raleigh hoisted me onto his shoulder. "Bring the boy."

As he swung me around, I saw the other soldiers force Bradyn to his feet. Raleigh wanted my burden to remain in my sight. His way of telling me that Bradyn would die if I didn't do as he asked.

"You should let me go, Raleigh. If I marry the prince, I could kill him whenever I wanted to. His very days would be numbered."

Raleigh set me down in the hallway. He grabbed my throat, pressing me against the wall but not choking me. "Why can you not see what is right before your eyes? He offers you a crown. He offers you a home. He is a good person."

"Who asked me to kill his father! I suspect our definition of a good person differs in extremes!"

"A few hours from now, your definition of a good person will be vastly changed."

Raleigh scooped me up like a helpless child and started down a spiral staircase that had no visible bottom.

Minutes later we were swallowed by darkness. The dungeon. I could already feel the thick walls pressing in. The moon's energy draining from me—our connection thinning.

A soldier lit a torch to guide us the rest of the way. I heard Bradyn's chains clanking on the steps behind us.

"Think about this while you're down here," Raleigh said. "Good planning evaluates all possible outcomes. There is a plan for the best-case scenario, and the worst. Best case, you do as you're told. Have a life with him. Play nice. He's handsome. You could do worse. Give him heirs. Turn all that venom raging inside you on those who would seek to tear down all that has been built here. But if you can't, the other outcome will have you blamed for *his* death." He jerked his head at Bradyn. "And we'll add a few others to the mix. Lady Sybil, maybe? Griffin's pals, Thoma and Dres? All acts laid at your feet. Gossip will spread of your madness. And the prince will end your life and your dragon's. Either way, he comes out king. The only question in all of this is whether you will be on the throne beside him, or in a grave."

EIGHTEEN

GRIFFIN

Griffin lost track of time. After Maggie was dragged from the balcony, the guards finally let him go, but escorted him to the palace, directly to his room, where they locked his door—from the outside. His wardrobe and trunks ransacked, his sword table emptied, not a weapon remained. They even took the cheese knife, leaving the bloody stinking blue cheese. How long was Jori going to leave him like this?

"Let me out of here!" He hurled the board at the door.

The king had seen Maggie using her power and controlling Rendicryss. With little interrogation, he would find out Xavier was false. He wanted magic. He searched for it all this time. He would never, ever hurt her. Neither would Jori. He was infatuated on top of everything else. That gave Griffin hope.

The lock clicked. The door opened, and Lady Esmera swept into the room. There was blood on her dress and her hands. Cornwall's blood.

"Griffin . . ."

Griffin slid his boot in the door before it could close.

He tugged it open, finding a hallway filled with soldiers, all dressed in black cloaks.

"Return to your room, Sir Griffin. The prince will see you shortly." The guard slammed the door shut.

"What is going on here?" Griffin asked her.

Esmera threw her hands in the air. "Everyone is missing. Jori isn't in his rooms. Malcolm and Sybil have vanished. They went with my brother and father, to settle their bodies and have them taken to our soldiers outside the city, and never returned. The guards have every turn of every hallway blocked off. They won't let me pass." Tears brimmed. "I can't lose Sybil and Malcolm too."

"I'm sorry," Griffin said. "I really wish Cornwall had listened to Malcolm."

She sniffed, pressing a finger beneath her eyes to stop her tears from falling. "I wish he had too. He's so stubborn. Was . . ." She sighed, swallowing hard. She wrinkled her nose. "Don't you find it odd that the guards have all changed colors? Black, no less. I suppose I should take it as a compliment, a nod to my North." Esmera ran a finger over a black cloak hung over the chair. "You have one too?"

Griffin stared at it, the knot in his stomach twisting tighter. Weapons gone and a new cloak. Griffin opened the door again, finding a soldier about to knock. Esmera moved to stand in the entrance beside Griffin.

"Prince wishes to see you. Change," the soldier ordered.

"Get out of that red. It's not a safe color anymore."

"What does that mean?" Esmera asked.

The soldier looked surprised to see her. "You should return to your room, Lady Esmera."

"I don't take orders from you. I'll go with Griffin to see my fiancé." She tossed the cloak at Griffin.

"No. You're to remain—"

"No one asked you," she countered.

"Excuse us for a moment, please." Griffin closed the door. "Esmera, do you have any weapons in your room? A sword? Anything. Even a small, dainty knife with a pretty grip?"

"No. Sybil had an arsenal under her bed, but it's all gone. Griffin, what is going on here?"

"I don't know, but I believe we're about to find out."

Griffin removed the red tunic, replacing it with the cloak. He smoothed his hair down.

Esmera padded toward him with a wet towel. "Wait. You have dirt." She turned his cheek, wiping it off for him.

He flinched at her touch, which registered on her face. "I thought my scars offended you, Lady Esmera."

She pursed her lips, ruminating. "I'm sorry for that. I, well, your scars remind me of my mother's. Of what the draignochs did to her. That's all." She threw the towel on the bed.

Griffin was surprised by her honesty. "Then I'm sorry for that."

"It's hardly your problem."

The soldier knocked on Jori's door, announcing Griffin's arrival.

Positioned on the corner of the castle, Jori's suite had two rooms with no wall between them, only a deep bend. Griffin was led into the sitting area. Jori hopped up from the chair, rushing to the table, and poured wine for two. When he saw Esmera, he brought out another glass.

"I wasn't expecting both of you, but saves me time in hindsight. Come. Take a glass of wine. I have important news."

Griffin passed one to Esmera before taking one for himself. Jori frowned as he announced, "My father is dead."

"What?" Esmera blurted.

Griffin set the glass down. "How?"

"Buffont."

"That's . . . not possible."

"He did it, Griffin. He dropped my father through the murder hole on the bridge. I was there. I witnessed the entire horrifying event." Jori took a long sip of his wine, then turned to Esmera. "This changes everything."

Esmera set her glass down on the table so hard it was a wonder it didn't break. "What does that mean?"

"I will not marry you."

"Then you will not have the North. My brother Malcolm—"

"Is locked in the dungeon with your sister. If you behave yourself, I will have them released, Esmera, but to their rooms only. They will still be under heavy guard."

Esmera launched her glass at him. Jori made no move to avoid it hitting him. He let the red wine drip off his cloak onto the floor. "There is no reason to get emotional, Esmera. It is simply a matter of politics. I must marry—"

"Maggie," Griffin sighed.

Jori's grin didn't quite reach his eyes. "Yes."

"You marry a . . . a nobody?" Esmera countered.

Jori sighed at her. "Maggie isn't a nobody. She is the true Ambrosius. Xavier was a fraud."

"What are you talking about?" Esmera growled. Jori's answering snicker sent her to Griffin. "What's he talking about?"

Griffin stared at Jori. He had been playing a game all this time. All his maneuvers carefully planned. Griffin hadn't thought the prince had it in him. "How long have you known?"

"Much longer than you." Jori drained his glass and poured another. "And I want to thank you for training her in the short time you had together. Today was an impressive beginning. Her powers will only grow, and then . . ." He hummed.

Griffin wanted to punch him as realization dawned. "You let me take her to Oughtnoch, knowing full well I would want to see Rendicryss. You used me."

Jori smirked, his thin blond eyebrows lifting. "And I will reward you for it."

"Did it ever occur to you that your plan would backfire?" Griffin asked. "That I might have real feelings for her? And she for me?"

Jori set a hand on the pommel of the Phantombronze dagger, Griffin's dagger. There was a sword on his other hip. "Maggie has agreed to marry me, Griffin. It's done. But I haven't forsaken you or Esmera." He looked at Esmera, who was eyeing the sword on Jori's hip, glaring as if she wanted nothing more than to slit his throat with it. "You will marry Griffin, and we will all be one big happy family."

"No," Esmera said flatly. "Our treaty is broken. I will return home with my siblings to our people. We will not combine our lands with yours."

"Afraid I cannot allow that either. My forces are already heading for the northern border." Jori sat down, letting out an exasperated breath as if annoyed by the ignorance of his audience. "Our kingdoms will be joined, and I shall not have to marry you to accomplish it. We will seize control of the North as peacefully as the Northmen will allow. I will keep you here as . . . as a tribute to them. The North will still have representation at court."

"As a hostage," Esmera shot back. "As collateral against—"

"If you resist in any way"—Jori raised his voice over hers, silencing her outburst—"I will send word to attack, and order no able-bodied fighters left alive. The North may have difficult terrain, but Raleigh knows it well, and we have numbers on our side . . . and magic."

Esmera threw the door open. Several black cloaks prevented her exit.

Jori shook his head. "We're not done, Lady Esmera."

She turned around, her eyes narrowing to slits.

"Sybil will remain here as well, safe, but under my watch. Malcolm will be in the finals. He will face the new beast—"

"—who killed Cornwall?" Esmera shook her head. "No! You can't do this!"

Jori shrugged. "It is what my father wanted. He will likely die, but that is what happens in the arena. Malcolm knew well the dangers involved in the tournament. Griffin too will have to face the dragon." Jori winked at Griffin. "But Maggie would never let her hurt you, would she?"

Griffin couldn't believe Maggie would agree to any of this. "I should speak to her."

"Why?" Jori grimaced.

"To be sure she understands what's expected."

Jori hissed the smallest of laughs. "She understands. And she will do as I tell her to do."

Anger stiffened Griffin's back. His chest gave away his frustration. He took a long deep breath, letting it out slowly, methodically, changing his demeanor to play the part of the loyal best friend, until he figured a way out of this trap. "Why would she comply? For Xavier?"

"No. My father had him executed for lying before he died." The prince sipped the wine, his eyes looking beyond Griffin. Nothing Jori said was whole truths, but at least there was something to learn from him.

"Xavier is dead?" Esmera asked.

"Didn't I just say that? Gods, you really are stupid, Esmera."

Jori waved at the guards. "The Lady Esmera will return to her room and remain there until tomorrow morning."

Esmera looked at Jori as if he'd slapped her.

"I'll escort you," Griffin said, wanting to get out of this room as quickly as possible.

"Yes, you should do that, Griffin. The guards will shadow you both. I'm taking no chances. Tomorrow must go as planned. The people will see me and Maggie, side by side on the balcony, and we will watch our heroes take on the dragon.

"That is what they will witness. Me with true magic at my command, and my champion slaying the fiercest beast to ever walk into the arena."

Seven guards followed Griffin and Esmera as they returned to her room. Six posted outside, while one took up a position inside, beside the door.

Esmera plucked two long thin combs staking her hair in a bun, letting it fall, then spun. The sharp point of one pressed into the underneath of the guard's chin but not enough to break skin, yet. The other she fisted, resting the tip against his chest, over his heart. "Get out!"

Griffin opened the door, letting him scoot out, then slammed it shut, throwing the bolt. "That was impressive."

"Just because I know how to embroider doesn't mean I haven't trained in other arts." She slid the combs into her blonde mane.

Her room was cold. The fire out. Griffin set to building a new one for her.

"Stop that. We have more important things to do. Do you honestly think I didn't see this coming?"

Griffin turned, finding Esmera lifting a piece of the floor up. She waved him over. "Sybil's idea." Between two floorboards were three swords, several daggers, and a quiver of arrows. There was also a small bowl of crushed dark berries. "Belladonna. Concentrated. There's enough there to put several guards to sleep. We just need to mix it with wine. They'll never notice."

Griffin let a smile creep up. "You are my new favorite person, Esmera."

She glared at him.

"I am surprised as you are. Where's the bow?"

"Tacked behind the bed." She retrieved it, passing it off to him. "What do we do now?"

Griffin handed it back. "Keep it. I'll take only a dagger and the belladonna. You and Sybil arm yourselves."

"Why? We can't fight hundreds of soldiers."

"You won't have to. I have a plan, but it all revolves around Jori believing we're going along with him."

"What is it?" Esmera asked.

"I can't tell you. Honestly, it is better that you have no knowledge in any case. That way, Jori can't leverage it out of you, and if it fails, only I'm to blame. Don't trust anyone. Not even those with as much to lose. I have to find Maggie. And right now, after what Jori likely told her, I'm pretty sure she would like to see her dragon eat my liver."

Esmera unsheathed a dagger, checking the blade, then handed it to Griffin. "Then I wish your liver good health and godspeed."

Griffin opened his door, handing one of the guards his untouched meal and full carafe of belladonna-infused wine.

"You have the finals tomorrow, Sir Griffin. You haven't touched your food."

"I can't eat. Help yourselves. There's wine too. Sadly, the king's favorite."

He closed the door. An hour later, he heard them laughing, then the sound of heavy thuds. When he opened the door, a guard fell backward into his room. He used his pillows to make it look as if he was in the bed sleeping, propped the guard beside his door, and made sure the others were sleeping before he entered the secret passage behind the tapestry.

He exited in the Great Hall, which sat dark for the first time since he'd moved into the castle. He snuck past several guards, tiptoed up the stairs, finding Maggie's hallway empty. Not a single guard was posted at her door. Which meant she wasn't there.

Next stop was the kitchens, where he hoped to find Bradyn, but he wasn't there either. Apparently, he'd been missing since lunch. His mother, Molly, was escorted out of the castle. Her husband declared a traitor. The baker, a skeletal old man with spindly fingers called Osperth, told him everyone assumed Bradyn was with Molly.

"Is that tray ready?" Raleigh called from the kitchen galley.

Griffin lifted a finger and dove into the pantry.

Osperth waited until Griffin was out of sight to answer him. "Yes, sir. A basket of bread and water only, as you requested. Who should it be delivered to?" Griffin heard him say.

"I'll take it."

Griffin heard Raleigh's footsteps clack on the tile floors, moving away from him. He followed him. It wasn't easy. Raleigh stopped every few feet, checking behind him. When his old mentor started down a particular set of stairs, Griffin knew he was heading for the dungeons. Maggie hadn't consented to anything, so the prince had locked her up in the one place the moon couldn't reach her.

Seven flights down. Three long tunnels. Only the light from torches led the way. Griffin gave Raleigh plenty of space. He glanced into the cells that were full of sleeping servants, those who worked in the castle.

Griffin heard a latch clank, and knew Raleigh was at Maggie's cell. His heart pounding, Griffin needed to act fast. He lifted the dagger Esmera gave him out.

"Griffin, you cannot think to sneak up on the man who taught you to fight," Raleigh called.

Griffin cursed. He hid the knife and turned the corner, padding down a ramp, descending into the deepest part of the dungeon. The walls felt like they were closing in. He walked with purpose. In the glow of the torchlight, he could see Raleigh and two other guards near the last two cells before the tunnel ended.

As he got closer, he saw both cells were occupied. On his right, Maggie was barely visible, curled up in a ball against the back wall. On his left, Bradyn. Both looked like they were breathing, but it was difficult to tell. His mind raced. Did Jori mean to do away with them too? "What the hell is going on here?" he yelled at Raleigh.

Bradyn crawled to the bars. "He killed my father, Griffin. He threw him down the hole after the king."

"How'd he get that gag off?" one of the guards asked. He moved to open the cell door, but Griffin kept him from getting to it.

"The prince wanted Maggie to kill the king and when she wouldn't, he said he would kill me. He was going to drop me." Bradyn's voice cracked. He started crying. "My father did it for me. He . . . he did it for me. And then . . . and then . . . Raleigh killed him."

Griffin shoved one guard into the other, then punched Raleigh as hard as he could. His mentor stumbled into the two guards.

"Let them out!" Griffin demanded.

Raleigh rubbed his swelling jaw. He pulled his sword. "You have a match tomorrow. You really want to do this?" He lunged.

Griffin spun out, bouncing off the wall, reaching for his knife, but Raleigh shouldered him, throwing him up against the bars of Bradyn's cell. Griffin felt the knife lift from the back of his trousers. Griffin ducked Raleigh's strike, shoving him into the bars, and Bradyn's outstretched hand. The knife punctured Raleigh's side, a fatal blow to the kidney.

Raleigh dropped to his knees, using the bar for support. Bradyn ripped the dagger out. The knife struck Raleigh's throat next.

It was over.

Bradyn's hands trembled. "He killed my father. He killed my father." He repeated that over and over again.

The guards looked back, hesitating at first. Griffin seized one in a headlock at the same time he found the guard's knife in his belt, getting it against his chest. That guard dropped his sword. The other wasn't as bright.

He thrust.

Griffin used the guard in his arms as a shield. The blade cut into the man's chest. Griffin threw the dying guard at his killer, then made use of the knife. His throw never wavered, striking the guard between the eyes.

It was over in less than a minute.

Raleigh's empty gaze was upturned, staring at the ceiling. Griffin's boots waded through blood from the dead guards. Like Bradyn's, his hands wouldn't stop shaking. He had killed many draignochs, but not people. Not ones who had once cared for him. Not like this.

"Sir Griffin?" Bradyn whined, breaking Griffin out of his trance.

Griffin searched Raleigh, finding the keys, opening Bradyn's cell first.

"Bradyn, you need to get out of the castle, and to your mother. Use the passageways but move slowly. Jori knows we've been using them."

Griffin handed the knife to Bradyn.

"What about you and Maggie?" he asked.

"Go . . . ," Maggie uttered.

Griffin pushed him. "I've got her."

Griffin didn't watch him leave. He pulled the guards' and Raleigh's lifeless bodies into the far corner of the empty cell, and locked it. Then he opened Maggie's cell. He padded over to her slowly, kneeling beside her.

"Maggie?"

She rolled over. He started at the gaunt look in her eyes. The blue in her irises faded to near white. Her skin graying, her mouth cracked and dry.

She tried to speak, but when she couldn't, she put that strength into her arm. Griffin caught her wrist before the rock in her hand hit him in the head.

He could tell the lies Jori told her racked her with anger, but he didn't care. He was so happy to see her. He kissed her forehead. Then her eyes. Her cheeks. He lifted her up, cradling her in his arms. "You'll have a much better chance of pummeling me after you see your moon."

Maggie stirred as soon as they reached the top of the spiral staircase. He set her down beneath the first window he came to, pushing it open. The moon didn't hesitate. Strands of finely spun silk shot down. Her eyes flew open. Blistering cold, his outstretched arms numbing, Griffin stumbled away from her. Her normally blue eyes gone. They were solidly white, and glowing. She gasped, her mouth falling open. With every inhale, the light faded, but Griffin never saw it leave her.

She stirred, trying to stand. He tentatively touched her. Her skin cool, but much more temperate, he settled an arm around her back, holding her up. "Can you walk?"

She tested her legs. "I think so." Then she started to walk away.

Griffin pulled her back. "Where are you going?"

"Away from you! Before I kill you where you stand."

She turned to leave but he grabbed her hand. "Maggie, let me explain."

"Explain how you tricked me! Training me to become some kind of weapon for the prince? Or should I say wife!" She drew a glistening beam of light as long as a sword, dropping it until it was only an inch from his neck.

"I did none of those things." Griffin let her go and raised his hands. The light so bright, his vision spotted.

"How am I supposed to believe you, Griffin? You take me to see Rendicryss. You help me grow my powers. You give me everything I ask for, except my freedom."

"Because the only one who can give you freedom is you."

He paused, letting that sink in. "We're all trapped. Rendicryss is your only hope. She will have to fly you out of the city. You will have to free her in the arena as we planned. It is the only way. It has always been the only way."

She stared at Griffin, incredulous. The internal argument played out in sneers, head shakes, and grimaces.

"I love you, Maggie. Jori knows that. It made it easy for him. I was too busy paying attention to you to notice that he betrayed me too."

The light faded. Darkness fell. "He wants you by his side, Griffin. You're not tempted?"

Griffin stared at the blood on his hands. "No . . ." For the first time since his parents had died, he wanted to cry. "I never thought he was capable of this. I'm not sure I really know who he is, or who his father was. I only saw the prize. Being prized. But I don't want it anymore."

Maggie threaded her fingers through his. "What do we do now?"

NINETEEN

MAGGIE

My sleep was restless, filled with nightmares. In one I remembered well, Rendicryss couldn't fly. Her wings broken, hanging at odd angles, she ran around the ring, moving slower than a turtle. Jori took great pleasure ordering Griffin to cut them off. The sun burst through the windows in the queen's quarters, waking me before I heard Griffin's answer. I wanted to trust him, but some part of me still doubted his allegiance.

I was surprised yet relieved to see Petal come into the room. She had a fresh smock and a scarf around her neck. From the strong musky perfume, I could tell it was a gift from Esmera. From her gesturing, I gathered that she'd snuck back into the castle. I tried to make her leave but it did no good. A finger pointed at her heart, then dragged across her neck, and then aimed at me.

"I don't want anyone to die for me, Petal."

She had brought Esmera's lavender dress with her, new boots, and a knife, all a part of Griffin's plan. He should be at Jori's door, telling him that Raleigh arranged for him to speak to me, and that he convinced me to have a change of heart.

That I was moved to his mother's quarters to sleep in, heavily guarded of course, and that at this moment I was being washed and clothed to look perfect for my wedding, which was to take place after the final match.

And that Griffin's wedding to Esmera would happen directly after. Neither nuptials would take place so long as I could break the chains binding Rendicryss.

I wished to hear her all night, but she was quiet. Not even a whimper carried on the wind.

The queen's rooms in the tower were dusty, the last of Umbert's wives having died years ago. I didn't light a fire. It would've drawn too much attention. I slept curled up in a ball between the bed and the wall, wrapped in musty blankets. When morning broke, I saw the room was draped in red. From the curtains to the linens, the rugs and tapestries, all embroidered with creeping roses. It felt empty, void of not only life but memories. There was nothing, not even a dress in the wardrobe to say that someone once lived here.

Thirty minutes later, Petal was weaving small purple flowers into the curls in my hair when his stern knock was heard, and he walked in uninvited. Five guards were with him.

I shoved Petal behind the screen and stood to greet him, smoothing down the lavender pleats.

"Maggie." Jori said my name as if it were an order. His fair hair was slicked back. His normally soft brown eyes were harder, taking prominence on his face, making him look like an angry owl. He wore all leather, with swords crossed on his back. He looked like a warrior. A calculated move so that he appeared strong enough to lead when he revealed to the people later today that their king was dead.

I approached him with caution, the snake in the grass Xavier accused me of being. "Sire." I curtsied.

Jori nodded. Guards rushed me, throwing me down, binding my hands behind my back at elbow and wrist, as Moldark had done yesterday. When they were finished, they left me on my knees.

The guard handed him the key to my cuffs.

"I don't understand. I thought—"

Jori laughed at me. "Suddenly you're ready to take on your destiny? Do I look like a fool? Griffin may be so bewitched by you that he believes every word you say, but I am not. You can be a slave to me as easily as a wife." He bent over, dangling the key in front of my face, then put it in the pocket of his tunic. He nodded again, and I was hoisted to my feet.

"Today, you will make sure your dragon kills Malcolm," he continued.

"How can I do that with my hands tied behind my back?"

"You don't require your hands to speak to her. Armel told me."

"Armel was wrong." My heart pounded so hard I worried he would hear. Our plan would never work if my hands were bound this way.

He stared at me longer than necessary, then waved his hand. A guard brought him a long black cloak. He wrapped it around my shoulders, clasping it at my neckline, letting his fingers linger. He lifted my chin, forcing me to look at him.

"This will hide your chains. We will ride now to the arena in a carriage, for our safety, of course. On the balcony, I will announce my father's death. The last match will go on, during which Malcolm will die. Afterward, Maggie of Nowhere, you will swear your loyalty to me, and then we shall be wed for all to see. Am I clear?"

"Yes."

He patted my cheek harder than necessary. "Yes, what?"

"Yes, sire."

Esmera and Sybil were in the carriage when the guards carried me in. Both draped in black as well, they looked like they'd slept better than I had. Beneath they wore simple yellow frocks. Esmera's blonde locks were woven into tight braids, pulling the hair off her face. Sybil's red mane was tied in a ponytail at the base of her neck. Retrained hair, loose-fitting clothes—they were armed and, by the looks of it, prepared to fight.

"Why are you hunched over like that?" Sybil asked me.

She lifted my cloak and saw my hands were bound behind my back. She paled with worry, letting go of the wool as Jori climbed in beside me.

Esmera and Sybil exchanged nervous glances with each other, and then with me. The plan was for me to cut

Rendicryss's chains by wielding moonlight, which I couldn't do with my hands cuffed behind my back.

We would have to find another way to set her free. My only hope was that we would see Griffin in the tunnel before the match. If I couldn't get word to him, then hopefully Esmera or Sybil could.

Jori set a hand on my knee. "Is there something wrong, Maggie? Why do you stare at Sybil and Esmera so?"

"I thought we'd be riding alone." My glare shifted from Esmera to Sybil. "I do not wish to look at her, not on my wedding day."

I tried to shift away from Jori, force his hand to fall off my knee, but his fingers tightened.

Esmera glowered. "The ride will be over soon enough, and then I will have your champion to myself."

"And I your prince."

Sybil cleared her throat, her stare flipping between us as if we had lost our minds.

Jori ignored us, his mind and his attentions straight ahead, on the arena.

The carriage stopped and the door opened. I started to climb down but Jori pushed me aside to go first. Then he shut the door.

I leaned forward to whisper in Sybil's ear. "Griffin and Malcolm need to find another way to set Rendicryss free. Can you get word?"

"And how exactly will I be able to do that?" Sybil asked.

Sunshine broke through the clouds as the door cracked again.

"Let's go." Jori grabbed the fabric of the cloak at my shoulder, yanking me out. The bridge at the Top was empty. With the volume of noise coming out of the arena, it sounded like the people were already seated, and had been for some time.

Esmera and Sybil flanked me as we padded across. Jori walked ahead with several guards. In the tunnel, Griffin and Malcolm waited to enter the ring. Neither wore much armor, and neither was armed. I kept my eyes trained on Jori, too afraid to even glance at Griffin, for fear I might crack. How were we in this place—two nobodies from nowhere, both under the thumb of the power-hungry prince—both of our lives hanging in the balance?

The guards ushered me into the stairwell before the others. I heard Esmera and Sybil ask to speak with their brother, wishing him luck. Jori spoke to Griffin, but I couldn't hear what he said. The guards prodded me to start climbing. I tried to catch Griffin's glance, but he never looked up before the door to the stairwell shut.

At the top of the stairs, I was told to wait for Jori. I stopped and closed my eyes, praying to the moon that my dragon would be freed and we would live to see nightfall, and her in all her glory. I never believed in prayer, but with all else stripped away, it was all that was left. That, and a present Petal had left in my boot.

TWENTY

GRIFFIN

Last night, Griffin had returned to the dungeons and moved Raleigh's and the guards' bodies to a cold storage room, hiding them behind enormous ale barrels. The cold would hide the smell long enough, he hoped.

He went back to the old queen's room, where he put Maggie, finding her on the floor, tucked behind the bed, in the throes of a nightmare. He stayed with her, holding her, worried it would be the last time he would ever get to touch her. His plan was reckless. Outlandish. Impossible—but it was all he could think of.

Griffin went to Jori before dawn, telling him that Raleigh was in the Middle, dealing with unrest at the marketplace, but that Maggie was well guarded in the queen's rooms. Jori seemed to believe in Griffin's fealty, yet went to see her with his own eyes. "Just to be sure."

Jori had the guards remove Esmera and Sybil from the tunnel before speaking to him. He waved at a soldier who brought Griffin's and Malcolm's swords. The soldier passed Malcolm his weapon, then, at the prince's request, gave Griffin's to

Jori. He held it up, checking the sharpness and balance as if *he* was about to enter the arena. "Maggie was where you said she would be." Jori winced a smile, handing the weapon to him. "I hope you take no offense at my . . . confirmation."

Griffin did his own testing of the blade, hoping Jori would leave, but he didn't. He stretched an arm, leaning on the wall. "Griffin, where did you sleep last night?"

"What? What are you accusing me of?"

Jori walked around him. "I was told you left the queen's room before dawn this morning."

"You were told wrong." Griffin chuckled. "You're growing as paranoid as your father, Jori. You have the throne. You have Maggie."

"I do. And she cannot escape. Not this time."

Griffin smirked. "She's a wily creature. And powerful, as you well know. What makes you so sure?"

"She's shackled."

"Why?" Griffin asked more vehemently than he should have.

"Her power," Jori confessed, "is stronger than anything either of us has seen. I've bound her for the same reason we bind the creature you are about to face. To avoid becoming lunch."

Griffin gasped.

The dagger pierced his skin below his ribs. The blade was so light and sharp, the blow so hard, it cut through him like a butcher's first strike on a pig, deep and with purpose. Griffin couldn't breathe. He kept his back against the wall to keep from falling over.

Jori twisted the grip, then let his hand fall. "Your dagger. I return it to you. You won the bet after all."

Griffin looked down at the jeweled hilt protruding from his gut. The seeping blood was barely noticeable on his new black tunic.

"Now go out there and put on a good show."

"Griffin?" Malcolm caught his arm. "Griffin, what the hell? Jori!"

He slid his sword back into his scabbard. "Maggie! We have to get Maggie!"

Guards blocked the stairwell. More filed in from outside the arena, filling the tunnel.

"I have an announcement," Jori said to the guards. "As soon as it's over, Sir Malcolm and Sir Griffin will enter the arena. Tell Perig to bring Rendicryss."

Jori vanished into the stairwell. Malcolm propped Griffin against the wall beside the lift and waved, yelling for Maggie. Fruitless. Even if she heard, she would never be able to get down the stairs. There were too many guards. And her hands were bound. Griffin looked down. The Phantombronze dagger. *His* dagger, which the king had gifted him. He threw his head back, laughing. The message was unmistakable. Jori had been plotting for this day from the first moment his father favored Griffin.

All along he had acted, pretended, waited for the opening

he needed. Well, his moment had certainly come.

The pain in Griffin's abdomen was unlike anything he ever felt before. Cold more than hot, like the blade was forged with the same kind of magic that lived in Maggie.

"That's it. . . ." The answer to freeing Rendicryss hit him like a bolt of lightning. Bracing his back against the wall, Griffin pulled the Phantombronze dagger out. He fell to his knees, but managed to slide it into his belt before the guards hefted him to standing.

Jori's voice echoed through the arena. Griffin heard him tell everyone of his father's death at a traitor's hands. The people's reactions were swift and filled with disbelief and fear.

Jori told the crowd of the duplicity of Xavier the Ambrosius and revealed that Maggie was the true sorceress. "I will ensure your safety and guarantee the superiority of our kingdom in one fell stroke, by taking control of this sorceress and her immense power." Then he ushered her to the front of the balcony, in chains. "Before the sun sets on this day, she shall be my wife."

Outrage. He could feel it radiating off every man and woman seated in the arena.

The stands broke into a unified stamping. Griffin glimpsed flags waving in the Bottom section. Maggie's scar sketched on them. Above the noise, Griffin could just make out Jori saying Maggie's name and *fiancée* in the same sentence. There were boos and jeers and angry voices. The frustration in Jori's voice as he tried to silence them kept Griffin's heart beating, kept him alive and present much longer than he should have been.

Griffin never heard Duncan call for them to enter the ring. He didn't remember being lowered by the lift, but suddenly, Griffin was there. The throngs chanting his name while gasping as he stumbled here and there. His sword in his hand was somehow too heavy to hold. It clanked uselessly on the ground. Not that he would use it. Griffin had only one goal before he died: to save Maggie. For that, he hoped he had all he needed.

Rendicryss's chains rustled from deep inside the shaft of the tunnel in the keep. Malcolm drew an axe.

Griffin reached for Malcolm's shoulder, but missed and fell over. The crowd went wild with panic, demanding he get up. Malcolm knelt, his eyes fixed on the keep's dark tunnel.

Griffin grabbed his knee. "The pulleys; we have to break the wheels."

"Are you mad? That dragon will have enough lead to kill people in the stands. To reach my sisters!"

"Have faith, Malcolm."

"A dying man's last words are always of faith. Why is that, Griffin?"

"Because a dying man's last deeds are righteous." He rolled forward, yanking the dagger out, turning it over to Malcolm. "Phantombronze. I can't fight off the guards to get to the pulleys. You can."

"But the dragon?"

"She will be sufficiently distracted. Help me up."

Malcolm lifted him, then sprinted into the gloom of the keep.

Griffin held on to his bleeding stomach with one hand and reached for his sword with the other. The cold burn spread through his abdomen until he couldn't feel the wound anymore. He couldn't feel much of anything at all.

He heard Maggie call his name, but was afraid to look up. Cries of dissent echoed from the people. The stadium shook. The air vibrated with Maggie's name. Griffin's name. Malcolm's name. When Jori tried to calm them, the chant changed.

"Let us out."

"Open the gate!"

"No more wall!"

Rendicryss's ear-piercing cry halted the rioting. All stopped to see the dragon that had so easily slaughtered Cornwall. She was majestic in the way she walked. Not barreling or lurching like a draignoch. So light-footed and delicate, Griffin never felt her coming. Never anticipated a crafted and calculated tail swipe that sent him hurling across the ring.

Rendicryss ran to finish him off. But her long fangs stopped short. Her head jerked.

Maggie.

She was speaking to Rendicryss.

Griffin should've run, but he couldn't move.

The chain around Rendicryss's neck loosened. She used a long claw to pluck it off. But there were still other bindings, and a shackle on every foot.

Malcolm emerged, his axe's handle covered in blood. He lifted it. Griffin saw Sybil reach a hand into Maggie's boot. Jori was blind to Sybil sneaking up on him, but a guard wasn't. He grabbed Sybil around the waist, hoisting her up. Sybil let the dagger fall, into Esmera's hands. As Jori turned to see what the commotion was, Esmera drove the dagger into the prince's chest.

He staggered backward, falling over the railing, into the ring.

Rendicryss brought down her foot with a great thud, her claws ending whatever life was left in him.

The prince, the only heir to King Umbert's line, was dead.

The world swam before Griffin's eyes. Then all was dark. The last thing he heard was Maggie telling him to hold on. He couldn't. He couldn't feel anything anymore, except an intangible, inexplicable, impossible warmth and peace.

If he had to put a name to it, it felt like love.

TWENTY-ONE

MAGGIE

I called for Rendicryss, but the guards didn't need encouragement from a dragon to run. Esmera and Sybil helped me get down the stairs and into the lift without stumbling on the long cloak. The shackles cut into my wrists and elbows. The key to them had fallen with the prince into the ring.

Tears poured as the lift lowered. I didn't know when they'd started, but they weren't stopping anytime soon. Griffin was dying. Or he was already dead.

"We have not time for tears, Maggie. You are a healer, are you not?" Esmera insisted. "You must heal him."

"But I am bound!" I wailed.

"Not for long." Esmera turned to Sybil. "In his tunic's pocket!"

I leaped out as soon as the lift neared the ground and ran to Griffin.

I felt Rendicryss's cry run through me and understood her. *Healer*, I heard. *That is what the moon made you.*

Rendicryss was watching. She was giving me hope.

Sybil returned with the key. Her hands shaking, it took her

two attempts before I felt the metal slide off. I lost track of the other things happening around me, but they were happening.

Later I would find out that the people stayed. Afraid of my dragon, they didn't venture into the ring. They chanted Griffin's name and my name, weaving them together. As if that would save him.

Griffin's lips were blue, his green gaze fixed on me. His chest heaved with painful gasps, clinging to life. The wound crusted with ice from the Phantombronze. Its power was akin to mine. Like a frozen poison, its magic spread from the wound, freezing his insides.

"What do I do?"

Rendicryss slid her foot over Griffin's fallen sword, cutting it. But she did not cry out. She had done it on purpose. Her blood pooled and tiny flames leaped from the place where it lay.

Fire. While Griffin was ice.

Could I use Rendicryss's blood to heal him?

I gathered some in my palm and poured it into Griffin's wound.

His body jerked and he let out a wail of pain. I worried I was making it worse, until the blue faded from Griffin's lips. I picked up his hand, threading my fingers through his, feeling warmth return. His breathing eased. He squeezed.

I looked up at Esmera and Sybil. "It's working!"

Rendicryss roared, shaking the whole of the arena. Spectators ran for cover, though I wasn't sure why.

"Help her," Griffin whispered.

I reluctantly let go of his hand, and ran around Rendicryss, into the gate where the three chains stretched taut. With a high grab, I drew down the moon's power, whipping it at an angle, slicing through the Phantombronze.

"Remove the chains!" I called to Sybil, Esmera, and Malcolm, who did what they could to unravel them from her body.

A hard shake from the dragon finished the job. With a hair-raising shriek, Rendicryss's wings spread to their full and greatest height.

The spectators quieted with wonder.

Perig came beside me, staring in awe at Rendicryss. He bowed to her. She lowered her head and he used his keys to quickly remove the shackles around her feet. The angry burns on her skin from the Phantombronze would leave permanent scars. As it fell, she flapped her wings three times and spirited into the air.

Malcolm took his sisters' hands and led them up to the balcony. He stepped to the front and beckoned his sisters to stand with him.

Then he spoke.

"There is a whole world outside the wall of this city. This wall wasn't just built to keep draignochs out, but to keep you in. Do you want to live in a cage, or do you want to be free?"

He called on every section of the arena. If there were any votes for remaining in cages, they were thoroughly drowned out.

The people joined in Malcolm's chant of "Take it down. Take it down!"

Griffin sat up slowly. "Do it, Maggie."

And so, I did.

I reached for the moon, catching a beam, and hurled it at the wall. It left a mark, a target for Rendicryss. She made for the wall.

Her tail hit like an axe on a tree trunk, carving away at the stone wall until the wall weakened and fell in a heap of boulders and dust. The sun broke through the gray clouds, rays touching her back as the moon would touch mine. She returned, and lowered her head, allowing me to climb upon it.

She took flight.

We were two pieces of the same universe. Sun and moon. And we would always be a part of the same sky.

As Griffin and I left the city on the hill, we weren't sure which way to go. Malcolm and his sisters were returning to the North but agreed to stay on for a time to help guide those who remained in the city.

Malcolm asked if there was anything I needed from him. He was surprised when I asked for the draignochs to be freed so they could return to the forest. It was Rendicryss's request. She vowed they would remain there until they were fully formed dragons with the knowledge to tell right from wrong.

Perig opened the cages in the Oughtnoch. The draignochs

paraded in a long colorful line, following Rendicryss, who would lead them home, ensuring there was no damage done to people along the way. My dragon would find me when her job was done. Of that, I was sure.

Griffin and I slept under the stars, under the light of the full moon. I danced in her glory, taking with me long glistening strands. Arms extending, then drawn in, like my younger self in the forest, dancing for Rendicryss. This time, I was dancing for me.

Griffin sat, staring at me with a look in his eye that warmed my soul—a look of friendship, and maybe love.

Others came from the Walled City after us. People who wanted to see more than they had ever been permitted to—ever thought to wonder about before—and meet their new neighbors in the Hinterlands. They camped along the roads I had been so afraid to travel. Lit bonfires in celebration. They sang songs about the dragon, the moon child, and the champion.

With every retelling, a layer of wishful thinking was added, growing the tale from story to legend.

For me and for Griffin, this was just the beginning of our adventures together. I was no longer Maggie of Nowhere. He was no long Griffin of the Walled City.

And although our names would change over time, the name of our grandson would live on as the greatest Ambrosius to ever walk the Earth, Aurelius, sometimes known as Merlin.

ACKNOWLEDGMENTS

This book has been a fantastic journey filled with moonlight and dragons. From the first creative meetings with Pete Harris and Marty Bowen at Temple Hill, to the brainstorming editorial calls that really opened up the world with Kristen Pettit at HarperCollins. We could not have written Maggie and Griffin's adventure without you all.

A special thanks to the entire Harper Teen and HarperCollins family. To the editorial team, marketing, public relations, sales, the art department, and everyone who has worked so hard to make this book not only happen but look so beautiful!

And lastly, a very special thanks to Paul Lucas at Janklow & Nesbit for putting this together.